THE SIEGE OF X-41

Vic stopped at another staircase, longer than the last, descending into darkness. A muted clanking echoed from below. He stopped. It was louder than any of the noises they'd heard so far, but also muffled, like it had come from behind a closed hatch. The tempo of Vic's pulse kicked up a measure. Nature Girl halted too.

"I'm sure it's nothing," she said.

"Could you not tempt fate aloud?" Vic asked.

"This isn't a horror movie, Anole."

Clang. Slightly different, shorter and sharper this time. Vic's stomach lurched. He tried to convince himself he hadn't heard it, but he couldn't do it.

"You sure about that?" he asked.

Neither of them moved. Nature Girl had a kind of nervous smile – the kind that said she didn't believe what they were both thinking, but still couldn't stop thinking it.

"Let's split up, gang," Nature Girl said. "What could possibly go wrong?"

ALSO AVAILABLE

MARVEL SCHOOL OF X

THE SIEGE OF
X-41

TRISTAN PALMGREN

ACONYTE

FOR MARVEL PUBLISHING

VP Production & Special Projects: Jeff Youngquist
Associate Editors, Special Projects: Caitlin O'Connell and Sarah Singer
Manager, Licensed Publishing: Jeremy West
VP, Licensed Publishing: Sven Larsen
SVP Print, Sales & Marketing: David Gabriel
Editor in Chief: C B Cebulski

Special Thanks to Jordan D. White

First published by Aconyte Books in 2022

ISBN 978 1 83908 128 6

Ebook ISBN 978 1 83908 129 3

Cover art by Christina Myrvold

Distributed in North America by Simon & Schuster Inc, New York, USA
Printed in the United States of America
9 8 7 6 5 4 3 2 1

ACONYTE BOOKS

An imprint of Asmodee Entertainment Ltd

Mercury House, Shipstones Business Centre

North Gate, Nottingham NG7 7FN, UK

aconytebooks.com // twitter.com/aconytebooks

For those who keep us going.

CHAPTER ONE
Elixir

Josh Foley meant to confess what he had done. He'd promised Outlaw, his only friend, that he would. He'd promised *himself* he would. It would have been the first step toward some sort of recompense. It was supposed to have been the second thing he said to introduce himself in front of Dani Moonstar's class, right after his name.

He didn't even get his name in. The sight of so many mutants' eyes – feline, or bright red, or solid black, and more – caught him off balance. He'd arrived at the New Charles Xavier School two days ago, and was nowhere close to being inured to strangeness.

"He's a bigot," said one of the three identical blonde girls at the front of the class. The Stepford Cuckoos, he would find out later. Telepaths.

"He was part of a pack that hunted mutants," the girl seated right next to the first said, as if picking up her thought.

Josh was so caught off guard that he didn't have time to say,

"That's not true!" before the third girl spoke: "He cheered when speakers at the Reavers' rallies said that all of us should die."

Josh closed his open mouth. He couldn't say *that* wasn't true, because it was.

He had cheered. Everyone around him had been cheering. It had been normal. The kind of thing everyone did.

"But he did more than cheer," the second girl said.

"He put on his armor and strapped on his weapons," the first girl added.

"Along with all the other Reavers," the third finished.

That had been the part that, even when he'd promised that he would confess, he wasn't sure he could say. The Reavers were an anti-mutant militia, only a little less prominent than the Purifiers. And all the students seated in front of him certainly recognized the name.

That was how Josh ended up being escorted from class, heart pounding, five minutes into his first day, and without having said a word.

He spent the rest of that class period in Headmaster Summers's office, in shock. He was later told that a small riot broke out in the class he'd left. He stayed there even after Headmaster Summers told him he could leave and to take the rest of the day off from classes. Josh's teachers would deliver his first day's homework to him. After everything else he'd been through just getting here, he'd thought he was beyond being mortified, but he was wrong.

Josh sat in the tiny reception room, staring at the walls, until he couldn't hear any more footsteps out in the hall.

It was easy to tell when the hallways were empty. Everything in the New Charles Xavier Institute echoed. For safety and secrecy, it had been built out of a frozen old missile base in Alberta. Everything was made of concrete; everything felt too large and too empty. Footsteps echoed like a percussion symphony. Their teachers had made a valiant attempt to dress the place up – adding lights and colorful streamers over the hallways – but it was a little like putting frosting on a brick and calling it a cake.

There was another mutant school, the Jean Grey School, in New York. Josh would have vastly preferred living in New York, even if it had to be just as isolated as this place, but he hadn't been offered a choice.

The circumstances surrounding Josh's being sent here hadn't been much happier than he was right now. He hadn't spent all that long in jail before coming here, but sometimes he woke up and still saw bars etched across his vision.

The truth hadn't been as bad as the Stepford Cuckoos had made it out to be. But it was close enough that the nuances wouldn't have saved him. Everything they'd said *had* happened. Just long enough ago that it felt like a different lifetime.

In absolute terms, Josh supposed, it hadn't been that long ago. Less than a year.

His dorm room was in one of the base's far corners, where at least he could hear anyone walking up on him. He had no roommate. He *did* have a desk, a lamp, and a bed with too-thin sheets. He lay on the bed, stared at the too-high ceiling, and listened for footsteps to come his way. None ever did.

Most of him was glad for that. If anyone had come around, it wouldn't have been for anything good.

The old, extroverted Josh Foley, though, would have been incredibly lonely.

It was a good thing that that voice of his old self kept getting smaller and smaller.

Josh couldn't sleep. Insomnia was a new experience. Before he'd heard of the Reavers, and everything that had happened afterward, he could sleep like a two-day-old puppy. In high school, he could arrive five minutes early to class, nap, and be done before the bell rang.

Not that this place was conducive to sleep. The ventilation rattled. For all the hard, noisy work the fans put in, the air still smelled musty. When he'd found his room and seen the thin bedsheet, he figured he'd spend the night freezing. But his body heat warmed up the place fast. He lay above the covers and was still too hot.

There wasn't much to do besides stew and dwell. He never used to do that much either. That was one of the many things that had changed about him since the Reavers, though.

The Stepford Cuckoos had plucked his history from his mind. He'd figured that out a moment after they'd started speaking. But it had taken him a little while longer to figure out just how hard they'd twisted the knife they'd sunk into his belly.

Outlaw had suggested that he "might want to keep that little thing about the Reavers to himself for a while". But he'd known there were telepaths at the New Charles Xavier Institute. Not just among the teachers, but the students. He'd thought he was prepared for them. It would only have been a matter of time until he was found out. They had factored into his decision to come clean about his past.

If, somehow, the telepaths *didn't* read his past off the top of his memory, then a dark figure from his past would come back, or somebody would open the wrong file at the most inconvenient moment... things like that always happened around the X-Men.

No, he'd just confess. It would be better not to hide it. He had to be honest about it, or he would never move past it. But then the Stepford Cuckoos had done it first.

They hadn't just read his history. What took him too long to realize was that they'd read his plan to confess, too. Then they'd taken that from him.

He'd figured that the mutants here would hate him. And he knew that they'd be right to hate him. He hadn't figured that they'd hate him *that* much, though.

Josh had thought he'd prepared himself for it. That he'd made himself numb. He was astonished by how much it still stung.

He didn't get to come back into a classroom for another five days. When he did, it was into Emma Frost's. It didn't take him long to realize that she was so intimidating that none of the other students would dare act out in her presence.

Ms Frost strode and spoke in a manner that made her seem a foot taller than she was – and she was already close to six feet, even without taking the heels into account. When she told the other students that they would break themselves up into pairs for psionics lab, she didn't say it like it was a command but like it was a fact. Her class jumped to make it happen.

And it did happen. Exactly like she said. The student to Josh's right, a "normal"-looking late teen with an out-of-place suit and tie, took a glance ahead and behind. All his other neighbors were already coalescing into other groups. Josh's neighbor turned back to him, a skeptical eyebrow raised, and said, "All right. I suppose it's you and me for now."

Josh tried not to show his gratitude. From the way his hands were shaking, he knew he wasn't succeeding. He hid them under his desk. "I'm Josh."

"Triage," his partner said, as though just saying it made him tired.

"Is that your last name? Code name?" Everybody here had callsigns. Josh had one of his own: Elixir. "Do you have any others?"

Triage folded his arms. "For you? No."

Josh didn't press. He was too afraid to ask what a "psionics lab" was. Everyone else already seemed to know. The other students were shoving their seats closer to the walls. He and Triage remained where they were. Spacing seemed to be important.

Emma Frost's teaching assistant – a bald, gray-skinned student with flat, white eyes – handed a face-down playing card to each group. Josh picked theirs up. A two of spades. Just the kind of card he'd draw.

"We'll pick up from last week," Ms Frost said. "With your partner, you will attempt to withhold what you know about your card from light psionic probing. Remember, the best way to defeat an untrained telepath is to keep calm, keep cool, and avoid thinking about your secret. You will each be responsible for keeping your partner distracted as well as yourself."

She stopped by Josh's desk and, as if taking pity on him, said, "Just do your best for now, Josh. You have a lot of catching up to do."

It sounded like she'd just told him not to think of a pink elephant – and if he thought of a pink elephant, he'd fail. Great.

The other students had all started among themselves. Triage

kept quiet. Josh took a deep breath and worked himself up to breaking the silence. Talking was a distraction, and they were supposed to stay distracted.

"What's your deal?" he asked.

Triage's eyebrow went right back up. "Which deal?"

"You know, your..." Josh twirled a finger in a circle on his desk, trying to figure out another way to say this. "Your superpower. Your mutant ability."

"First things first. Some of us really don't like to talk about what we can do unless *we* bring it up. It's an invasion of our privacy."

Josh frowned. "I thought mutants came here because they're looking for a place where they can be out and proud about what they are."

"That's the ideal," Triage sighed. Josh got the distinct impression Triage was embarrassed by Josh's naiveté, though there was no one close enough to hear them. "A lot of students here *are* forward about their powers. But a lot of us have all kinds of traumas wrapped up in our powers and abilities. Traumas inflicted on us by the outside world, and by groups like the one you used to belong to."

Josh didn't answer. If that was the way this conversation was going to go, nothing he could say would make it better.

He just didn't *have* an answer.

Triage sighed. "The second thing is, I'm not one of those who mind saying so. I'm a healer."

"Really? So am I."

Snapback to a cold and grimy parking garage, the electric tang of ozone burning in his nostrils. Blood hot under his tongue, and the skin around his left eye tender and swollen. His friend Duncan, the kid who'd encouraged Josh to join the Reavers, lying on the asphalt, his armor pierced and broken, blood leaking through his fingers as he held his gut closed.

A search for a pair of mutant murderers on the run. One of them had whorled razor-sharp shrapnel around herself like a cyclone. Josh's hands brushed over Duncan's wound. The blood stopped. The wound closed – zipped shut like it had never happened.

Josh hadn't meant to do anything. He didn't even know he could. In the rush of adrenaline, it had just happened. Duncan looked at Josh wide-eyed, mouth hanging open, and said nothing. Until the other Reavers came running.

"That's too bad," Triage said. "You're probably not going to get many people to help you test your powers. Nobody's going to trust you enough to let you touch them."

"If I were them, I wouldn't trust me either," Josh said.

Triage didn't seem to know what to say to that.

"Two of spades," Emma Frost said from behind Josh, so suddenly that he jumped. "Keep a tighter leash on your emotions, Mr Foley."

"Sorry," Josh muttered, as she swept by.

He paid close attention to the rest of the class. He needed a defense against telepathy. When he stayed after and asked Ms Frost if anything she taught would help him against the Stepford Cuckoos, she smiled mirthlessly. "The sisters are my personal students," she said. "Your best defense against them is to be on their good side."

Too late for that. And the Stepford Cuckoos hadn't even mentioned his worst secret.

He wasted no time in transferring out of the classes he shared with them. Or that even went near them. If they hadn't already learned the other things he wanted to keep to himself, then he had no intention of giving them the opportunity.

His final schedule for the semester had him in "Decolonizing the History of Mutantkind" with Dani Moonstar, "An Overview of the Afterlives" with Ilyana Rasputin, "An Introduction to Quantum Chromodynamics" with something called Beast, and mixed martial arts with the ominously named Colossus. And, of course, "Psionic Defense for Non-Telepaths" with Emma Frost. Finally, healing lessons at the infirmary with the X-Man Angel. Angel was a healer.

The only one of those that was not an elective was the self-defense course. He just signed up for whatever would keep him out of the Cuckoos' way. He was more of a science and numbers guy than someone who would have wanted to take "Mutant Art and Literature Through the 20th Century" with Karma, even if the Cuckoos hadn't been in the classroom next door. Besides... he didn't know Karma, but he'd heard she was another telepath.

He had no plan for his education. It didn't take him long to learn that most of the other students wanted to be X-Men. Not him. He just wanted to get through. Unlike most of them, he didn't have a choice about being here.

He wasn't totally alone in wanting to stay out of the X-Men. Plenty of the other students just wanted to learn how to survive. How to cope with their powers, or at least be able to defend themselves when someone inevitably came hunting mutants. Or they just wanted to go to school with other mutants and be in a place where their powers didn't make them targets.

That was easy to understand. Josh used to live to fit in. In his last life, he had managed it. Here it was an odd day if he said more than ten words that weren't about schoolwork.

The days when he did were invariably worse than those when he kept quiet.

The Friday of the week after he started classes for real, he was late to the locker room to change out of his karate uniform. He was about to reach into his locker to grab his sneakers when a gnarled green arm slammed the locker door shut. The arm was the size and texture of a tree trunk, but tree trunks didn't have so much muscle corded underneath them.

Josh tried not to flinch. Very slowly, so as to not provoke whoever was doing this to him, he turned. At first, he looked two feet too high.

The mutant standing in front of him was a complete mismatch with the enormous arm pinning his locker door shut. The other student wasn't *tiny*, exactly, though he was on the short side. His *left* arm was proportionate to his body. And so were his legs.

It was just his right arm that looked like a piece of the Hulk had been grafted onto him.

He was also green. And a lizard. With bony ridges running along his cranium where hair would have been. But, next to that arm, those details hardly registered.

"Did you figure on ever telling anyone why you're really here?" the lizard asked.

His mutation made his age hard to determine at a glance, but he sounded about Josh's age: between eighteen and twenty years old. Perfectly unremarkable Midwestern accent. Somehow that made him a little less startling. Josh racked his brain for a name, and only came up with a callsign: Anole.

Dread prickled the back of Josh's head. "Yeah, right after I was gonna get those shoes on."

Anole's gnarled hand didn't budge. "You're going to go on pretending to be just another student?"

"The Stepford Cuckoos already made sure everybody knows where I came from, and what I did," Josh said, then muttered, "I was going to confess anyway."

"Confess the reason you're actually here?"

"Yeah? What do you think that is?"

"You're not a student. You're serving out a prison term."

Damn it. Josh had been given Headmaster Summers's word that wouldn't get out. Coming to the Institute was part of the plea deal Outlaw had arranged to spring him out of jail.

That wasn't Josh's biggest secret, but, if Anole knew that, he might have known the rest too. Casually, Josh tested the waters: "Did the Stepford Cuckoos tell you that too?"

"The records are right in Cyclops's office."

"So – what? You broke into the headmaster's office."

Anole's eyes flicked above Josh's head. For a moment, Josh thought he was looking at something. More mutants come to ambush him, maybe. But when Josh glanced behind him, there was nobody there.

When Josh turned back, Anole's eyes were blazing.

"Doesn't matter," Anole said. "I just wanted to make sure you knew that nobody's going to believe the poor-me-trying-to-be-better act. You're here because you were forced to be."

"Please, do me a favor. Don't tell me why I came here. While you're at it, give me another: don't pretend you know me."

"I don't need to pretend," Anole said. "I also wanted to let you know that when you get out of here, if you go back to the Reavers – or anything or anyone like them – or just plain anyone who ever sneezed on a mutant… we'll find you."

To hell with it. If this mutant was going to beat the hell out of him regardless of what he did, Josh figured he might as well deserve it. "How do you stay balanced?" he asked. "I bet I'd knock you down if I *did* sneeze."

That big arm tensed. The muscles flexed. Josh braced himself. But all the lizard mutant did was pull his arm away from the locker.

He hadn't even struck the locker, but his fist had still left a two-inch-deep dent in the metal. The door flopped open, its latch bent out of place.

Anole's fingers – not on his oversized hand, but his normal-sized one – had bunched up into a little fist, and they were trembling. He was on the edge of doing *something*. Josh didn't think even Anole knew what.

Josh waited.

Anole spun on his sneaker heels and stalked to the exit.

Josh turned back to his locker and tried and failed to close it. The dented door just bounced off its latch. His hand was trembling too. He remembered, far too clearly, the last time he'd felt this alone.

Snapback to the clink of chains against handcuffs. His old "friends", Duncan included, shoving him along. They'd kept him in a cage while they tested his DNA to be sure he was a mutant. The fact that he'd healed Duncan never came up.

He was being sold, manacles included, to a band of outlaws. Once the Reavers had found out what he was, they'd planned to kill him… but in swept this gang, led by a murderer named Wolfram. Wolfram offered to buy Josh off them, just like a slave.

All Josh knew was that they were going to put him to work. And that he felt cold whenever Wolfram smiled.

•••

Over the next week, Josh kept to himself as much as he could. That wasn't easy. The missile bunker was far larger than it needed to be to host the school, sure. But everybody was kettled in here. They couldn't exactly pop out to the corner convenience store whenever they wanted a snack or to get away. They could hardly even step outside. The place was half-buried in snow. He'd never felt anything so brutally cold as an Albertan winter.

Things were just enough like his old high school to lull Josh into a false sense of familiarity. There were bells to mark each class period, cafeteria lunches (and breakfasts, and dinners), school laptops, and everybody complained about the homework even when they didn't have anything better to do. But then there was the rest of it.

Other schools took their students on field trips to museums. So did the Institute. Triage told Josh a story about how, when he and another student had gone to the Grace Museum of Natural History in Chicago, they'd ended up running through the halls pursued by dinosaurs and Neanderthal remains brought to life by infernal magic, chasing after Sabretooth.

Things only got worse from there. The X-Men had *spacecraft*. They'd traveled the stars. At the end of the semester, they were going to choose a team to take into orbit. This week, they were collecting volunteers for a "team-building" trip to an undersea station. Josh had seen posters for it in the hallways.

Against his will, he started learning the names of the students in his classes. The Stepford Cuckoos weren't the only students he had to worry about.

Some of them didn't have to navigate the hallway crowds. They flew *above*. Like Pixie. Veiny, translucent dragonfly wings sprouted from her shoulders. She flew everywhere she could, and sometimes didn't even set down for classes. She perched owlishly atop a ventilation duct. None of their instructors ever mentioned it. They called on her the same as they did everybody else. Sometimes pens and pencils rained down on Josh's head, but he could never prove it was her.

Another student, Wind Dancer, created blasts of wind that lifted her right off her feet. She seldom traveled the halls that way, as the other students did not take kindly to their folders and papers being ripped out of their hands, but she was not above abusing it in martial arts practice. The only time Josh sparred with her, she'd blasted into the air, and then crashed her heel into the back of his head.

Some of the students had what others called "passing privilege". They could blend in among humans if nobody looked too closely. Even Emma Frost and Headmaster Summers (so long as he wore his visor or shades) could. Josh was one of the latter. His time with Wolfram's gang would have left him looking a lot worse, with a broken nose and a limp, if he hadn't been a healer. His most remarkable feature was his too-blond hair. He wondered if students like Pixie or Glob Herman held that against him, but it wasn't like they needed an excuse.

He shared two classes with a student who always wore a cloth wrapped around her eyes. In both classes, she had taken pains to sit as far from him as possible.

"That's Blindfold," Triage said when Josh asked. Triage wasn't exactly kind to Josh, but he was one of the only students who would answer his questions when he asked. "She was born without eyes, but she can see plenty of other things. Precog."

"Precog?"

"Precognition. It means she sees some of the future."

Josh was still new to the superpowered world. He didn't know the lingo. But it made sense that these people would have shorthand for powers. He didn't want to think too much about what it meant if she kept rearranging seats to be away from him. Hopefully just that she hated him the same way the others did. He didn't ask Triage. Triage was nice enough, but he always started to look uncomfortable if Josh talked with him for too long.

Not all of the other students shunned Josh. Ms Frost's teaching assistant, the gray-skinned student with the white eyes, was called Graymalkin. He was as polite with Josh as he was with everybody else, and didn't seem to mind working with him on catching up to where the other students were. Graymalkin had a British accent, but not a type Josh had ever heard before, and he pronounced some words in completely unexpected ways.

It was a while before Josh worked up the nerve to ask him about it. "It was standard enough in the New York Province some two hundred fifty years ago," Graymalkin said.

"Oh. So why…?"

"Do I speak it?" Graymalkin finished. He smiled sadly. "Because I am two hundred and fifty years old."

Something in that smile set off clanging alarm bells in the back of Josh's head – alarm bells with the voice of Triage warning him against prying into other students' traumas. He left it alone.

Just about every student had a callsign but also a given name. As always, there were exceptions – like Emma Frost or Graymalkin, who used only his last name – but for the most part people answered to two names. Some students went by their callsign most of the time. Others clung to their given names like they were their only lifeline to their pasts. Josh couldn't imagine wanting to go through day-to-day life being called Elixir.

One thing he'd learned quickly was to never call anyone by their first name unless he was absolutely sure that was how they wanted to be addressed. According to their class attendance sheet, Triage's given name was Christopher Muse. Josh called Triage "Chris" once, and hadn't even finished the next word before Triage snapped not to call him that.

One of the few students who used their given names on every occasion was Laurie Collins. She'd chosen the callsign Wallflower, but went as "Laurie" everywhere else. She was one of the mutants here who didn't look any different than a baseline human. He'd overheard whispers that she had some kind of mind control powers.

They were assigned to spar together during martial arts training. Her kicks and jabs were hesitant at first, but the first real blow she landed left him with a nasty bruise. She'd yelped when she'd seen it, her hands over her mouth.

He healed it right in front of her. The bruise faded into his skin. She was still shaking after that, but never again threw a weak punch. It was the first time he'd been comfortable showing another student what he could do. He'd healed enough minor injuries under Warren's tutelage that he could do so without thinking much about it, but usually he wanted to pretend it was something he couldn't do. Laurie made it different.

Later that same class, they were told to swap partners. Josh ended up with Blindfold. He would have felt apprehensive about being paired with the only student there who couldn't see if he hadn't already watched her predict Wind Dancer's punches and dart out of the way a second before they'd landed.

He never got a chance to try to defend himself. The instant Colossus turned away from them, Blindfold grabbed his uniform by the collar. She yanked him off balance.

"Refuse to partner with Laurie again," she hissed.

If she hadn't caught his shoulder, he would have fallen. "W-what?"

"I've seen what happens to her in other futures," Blindfold said. "It will *not* happen this time. She deserves better. I'll make sure that she gets better than you."

"Look, just because you don't like me, that doesn't mean Laurie needs you to swoop in to–"

"*You don't understand,*" she interrupted. He got the intensely uncomfortable feeling of being sized up by eyes he couldn't look back into. She hissed, "Stay away from Laurie Collins. She won't die this time if you just stay away."

When he looked at the clefts at the front of her blindfold, he felt something electrifying, like ants between his eyes. Like he'd looked into the face of someone who'd lived a thousand years. Graymalkin might have said he was over two hundred years old, but he had never given Josh that feeling. "OK. OK!"

She let him go.

He did as she asked and stayed away.

Snapback to a bloody gunfight. The sledgehammer blow of a bullet breaking his ribs. Trying desperately to heal himself. But seeing Wolfram bloody and dying a few feet away almost made the pain worth it. Her gunshots still rang in his ears.

Outlaw, aka Inez Temple, had tracked Wolfram's gang through Texas badlands on a personal vendetta. She'd killed them all. She was a mutant straight out of the best Western Josh had ever seen.

She wasn't an X-Man herself, but she was on fair terms with them.

She'd "saved" him… and then helped send him here. But he figured he could forgive her for that. She'd done what she thought was best, and he hadn't left her many options. He'd been facing some serious jail time. His old "friends" had pinned evidence from him on some of the Reavers' crime scenes. He'd told her he used to be a Reaver. He hadn't left her many good options. It was lucky that they'd found a juvenile court judge sympathetic to mutants.

The only people here he felt comfortable around were the teachers. Exactly the opposite of the way things had been at his last school. He found himself staying after classes. In his last life, not in a million years would he have done that. The breaks between classes were the only times he could chat with his friends during the school day.

Now he needed to strategically plan his life around them, and avoid the crush of people out in the halls. The school's concrete corridors were huge, but so were some of the students. There were only so many times Josh could stand being shoved into Glob Herman's gelatinous belly (he'd never forget the feeling of touching a living kidney).

If he timed things right, he could dart out of Ms Frost's classroom with two minutes to spare, and still make it to Quantum Chromodynamics with Beast. The halls were definitely emptier, and less fraught, by then. And that gave him more space to dodge the people still there. And if Josh was a minute or two late, what was Beast going to do, anyway? Give him detention? He was already in jail.

At first, his pretext for staying was picking up some of the mess, the loose papers and pencils and wrappers the other students had left behind. Ms Frost tolerated this for two days. On the third, before he could grab anything, he suddenly felt compelled to stop moving. He leaned hard on the nearest desk and slid into the seat.

"I had a chance to speak with Warren about your healing course," Ms Frost said. "He says you're quite promising. More than you've been comfortable showing him."

By "Warren", Ms Frost meant Angel: the X-Man who was giving Josh and Triage private lessons. Josh had to take a moment to catch his breath from whatever Ms Frost had done to compel him to stop moving. "Like he would know," he said.

Angel gave "practical" lessons. Real patients, real injuries. Students came to the infirmary all the time. That was just life in a place like this. The ones without serious injuries sometimes volunteered to let Angel's students diagnose and heal them.

"Warren has more experience with mutants than you could ever believe," Ms Frost said. "When he tells you something about yourself, listen. Josh, have you been taught what the words 'Omega-level' mean?"

Josh bit back his second snarky reply. He couldn't afford to get on Emma Frost's bad side. "Not yet."

"When we say 'Omega-level'," Emma Frost told him, "it sounds too much like it's been mapped out and categorized, scientifically analyzed. What 'Omega-level' really means is 'uncharted'. That no limit to that mutant's power has yet been discovered. Or, possibly, exists. It means a power that has an upper boundary we haven't found yet.

"Warren believes you have Omega-level biokinesis powers. He tells me that when you're closing up a cut or bruise, you hardly need any guidance. As though this is all basic for you."

Snapback to Wolfram holding Josh's arm out straight – then driving the heel of his palm into Josh's elbow hard enough to break the bone.

He'd forced Josh to set it while he watched. At first, Josh hadn't been able to do it right. Wolfram had broken his arm over and over again. He'd "taught" Josh how breaking his bones and healing himself afterward could make him a more dangerous and unpredictable fighter, or allow him to squeeze through tight spaces. That was why Wolfram's gang had bought Josh. And that was why, every day, Josh endured the same torture over and over.

Josh shrugged, feigning indifference.

Just by remembering Wolfram, though, he'd probably given it away. But for once Ms Frost didn't seem to be reading his mind. "If you've healed more people in the past and don't wish to talk about it, you don't have to," she said. "But Warren remains convinced that you have more potential than you want to admit. I believe him."

"Whether he's right or not, it doesn't really matter," Josh said.

"Have you given much thought to what you'll do when you're released?" she asked. "You're only compelled to stay here for eighteen months. But you can train with us for longer. If you would like to."

None of the other instructors or X-Men spoke so plainly about his sentence, or otherwise acknowledged that he was a prisoner. He appreciated that Ms Frost was more forthright. "I don't think I could ever be an X-Man," he said. "I'd rather just get back to my life. Thanks."

"And which life is that?"

Josh opened his mouth, expecting the answer to come quickly. It didn't.

His friends had all been in Duncan's orbit. Some of them had even signed up for the Reavers, too. Colleges famously found any excuses they could to expel or otherwise not have to deal with mutant students.

He hadn't spoken to his parents since his arrest. Shortly before the court transferred him to Outlaw's custody, he received a curt legal notice saying that his family had signed over his legal guardianship to the New Charles Xavier Institute.

Sure, his father was distant, and his mother could be cold ... and both of their politics leaned more toward groups like the Reavers than mutant rights ... but he'd never imagined they'd do that. Not until it happened. Then it made too much sense.

On the trip north, he'd harbored a fantasy that they'd only disowned him because of the shock over what he'd done, not who he *was*. That dream had withered after weeks of their not responding to his letters.

He'd been about to tell Ms Frost that he'd go back home.

Frustration boiled up inside him. Easier to be frustrated than to grieve.

"You *know* everyone here hates me," he said. "Your own prize pupils ... pupil? ... mentally pantsed me on my first day here. And you know what? I don't blame them. They've got good reason to hate me. Everybody knows I don't belong here."

"If you think they hate you, how do you imagine they feel about me?"

"They definitely respect you."

"They're terrified of me. And, like you said ... they have good reason."

"Yeah, well, you *are* a hard grader."

The air around her suddenly seemed much colder. Josh didn't remember anyone mentioning that thermal manipulation was one of her powers.

It must have all been in her expression. Josh had been watching her the entire time, and hadn't seen her lips so much as twitch. Her eyes were an impossible electric blue. Josh couldn't look away.

"I was the White Queen of the Hellfire Club," she said, her voice brittle as diamonds. "I've tortured members of the X-Men. There were times that I would have razed this school to cinders, wiped the memories of all the students here, and brought them over to *my* academy."

Then the sharpness of the color faded, and so did the chill around her. Josh breathed out. He hadn't realized he'd been holding his breath.

"I was hated," she said, "and sometimes am still hated, for good reason. But I didn't join the X-Men to be liked. I came here because I needed to be here. Just as Magneto needed to be here. The same goes for a dozen others, all of whom have done far worse things than you."

"Great," Josh said. "I'm happy for you. But I *don't* need to be here. I can't imagine a single person who thinks I do."

"Then you don't have much of an imagination."

When Josh had been very young, "imaginative" and "creative" had been on every report card his teachers sent home. But it had been a long time since anyone had accused him of being either of those things.

Snapback to a barren prison cell underneath a police station in El Paso. A sink that ran with cloudy water that tasted like rust. His leg shaking. Folding and unfolding the letter in his hands. His time as a Reaver forgiven. The crimes he'd committed in Wolfram's gang, erased. A free ride out of here. If.

If.

"I guess not," he said. "I've spent a lot of effort just trying to survive."

"A person convinced they don't belong anywhere usually finds ways to make it true," Ms Frost said.

"You don't know what you're talking about," Josh said, gathering up his notebook and pencils. He was going to be late to his next class. And now he wasn't sure he wanted to come back to this one tomorrow.

He didn't want to belong here. He wanted to go home. Home wouldn't have him back. Now he had no idea what the rest of his life would be like, or even if it would be worth living.

"I'm speaking from experience," Ms Frost said to his back. "Not that you would believe me."

She was right. He didn't.

CHAPTER TWO
Anole

Vic pretended not to hear Karma when she asked him to stay after class. His eyes remained resolutely fixed on the whiteboard and the sentence diagram Karma had written there in thick, black marker. The slimmest cover of plausible deniability might let him slip out at the end of class anyway.

Besides, he already knew what Karma wanted to say. They could both take it as read that he'd already heard it.

Karma wasn't of the same mind. She snapped her fingers in front of his face. He startled.

He didn't know when he'd stop being Victor Borkowski, Indiana kid.

Snickering rippled through the class. Vic's cheeks felt hot, although blood rushing to his cheeks couldn't achieve this. But he lived among the warm-blooded. It was a learned reaction, a sensory ghost. The kind of thing other people said he ought to be feeling.

Karma didn't ask if he'd heard her. She knew he had. She was making a point.

Xi'an Coy Manh went by her callsign, Karma, most of the time. Karma told her students that she was used to it being her "public" name, and that she'd even started thinking of herself as it. Vic wasn't on that level yet. His callsign, Anole, still didn't feel like him.

When the class bell finally rang, Vic waited while the other students filed out. Karma placed a stapled packet of papers on his desk. It was Vic's report on depictions of mutants in premodern literature.

For weeks after he'd received the assignment, he'd stared at a blank screen. He couldn't summon the will. The night before, while his roommate slept, he had just set his hands to the keyboard and started typing the inanest drivel he'd ever written.

Karma waited. She wasn't intimidating in the same way that some of the other teachers could be. Emma Frost was scary, like an icicle hanging precariously overhead was scary. If he had to put a word to the kind of fear that Karma inspired in him, it would have been "dread".

Fear and dread were her mutant powers. She was a telepath with a very focused talent. She could grab hold of a person's fears and nightmares, pluck them out of their heads, and then make them seem real. Vic had never seen Karma do it to anyone. But it made sense that, with powers based on fear, some element of them would leak into her day-to-day personality... even if she never meant for it to.

Vic didn't know her well enough to say if she meant to or not.

"I don't know what you expect me to do with this," she said. "You've already shown me how much better you can be."

Vic had been hoping to just get a quiet D and move on. "Can we just assume I get it?"

"It would have been one thing if you were like this from the beginning of the quarter," she said. "I can work with students who start off on a low note. But it's like you've flipped a switch. These sentences don't make any sense. They just go on. It's like reading somebody rambling. You weren't even looking at the page."

"I *get it*," he said again.

"At the start of the quarter, you at least tried."

With anyone else, he would have pulled the "new arm" card. His big, hulking new right arm had finished regenerating out of the stump of his old one scarcely three months ago. Like a lizard, he could regenerate lost appendages.

It wasn't as ungainly as it looked. That didn't mean it felt good. Or that he wanted it.

"I just had a hard time caring," Vic said, without thinking.

Silence.

Vic sat quiet, soaking in the dread. Karma could keep it up longer than he could take it.

"Sorry," he said, at last.

"You don't think this is important," Karma said.

He shook his head. "No, I know it's important that we understand how the world sees us. I can't go a day without thinking about that."

"Neither can any of us," Karma said. "But everyone else still wrote a coherent lit paper."

"Then I guess I'm not as good as them."

Karma looked taken aback, like he'd insulted her, though he'd actually aimed at himself. The words surprised him a little, too.

He'd been thinking them for a while, but this was the first time he'd said them aloud.

Not all that long ago, he hadn't been the best student, but he'd been a good one. Both in his high school and here. He found it hard to imagine that he used to care that much.

"This has been happening since your trip home," she said.

That was the last thing he wanted to think about, but his thoughts kept circling back into it, like water spiraling into a drain. "Trip" was not how he would have described it.

He couldn't shake the icy shock of the Purifier's blade striking bone. The phantom pain of fingers he'd no longer had. And the empty weeks of hiding afterward as the arm regenerated: a benefit of his mutant identity that, until then, he hadn't known he'd had.

"We've all been where you are," Karma said. "If you need some time off, you need to talk to someone, just say so. But we need to know."

"I don't need any of those things," Vic said.

"You clearly need something, because this work you're turning—"

The frustration still boiling inside him turned cold. Like there was a block of ice at the bottom of his throat. "I already understand how the rest of the world thinks of mutants," he said.

He met her eyes. His hands were tense and shaking.

"You might think you understand, but you don't," Karma told him. "Things are a lot more complicated than they seem in the heat of battle."

"Then why do I still feel so clear-headed?" he asked.

"You're making excuses," she said. "It'd be one thing if this was happening in just my class. You're slipping in all your classes, not just mine."

Vic fell silent. He dropped his eyes and resolutely stared at the wall.

"I didn't think you had an answer," she said. "I can give you an extension on the paper. If you need someone to help or read it over, some of the older students are running a writing lab–"

"I'm not going to turn it in again," Vic said.

Karma stopped. Her expression went neutral, other than a raised eyebrow.

"I've written everything I want to write," he said. "I'm not going to do it again. I don't think I'm going to do any more, either."

She turned and stepped away from him, arms folded.

"If that's what you're going to put into this class," she said. "Then get out of it."

He did as she asked. He gathered up his things and left. And he didn't look back.

Vic always knew when Santo was coming to visit. Everyone in his hallway did. Heck, probably everyone in the whole school.

Vic dropped his game controller. The *thump, thump, thump* of Santo Vaccarro's footsteps wasn't like anyone else's, not even any of the other megasized mutants at the school. Colossus's footsteps were more considered, more level. Glob Herman squished wherever he walked. But Santo had a relaxed, uneven gait… and the sound of stone grinding on stone.

Santo didn't mince his steps like some of the other Hulk-sized mutants around here. They were always afraid of breaking something. Santo was used to himself. Vic could never decide if he'd trained himself to recognize exactly how much punishment the things around him could take without breaking, or if he just didn't mind if they broke.

Most likely, it was the first disguised as the second. Santo was a lot cleverer than he let anyone catch on. He had to be clever, to survive what he had. And to become an X-Man.

Santo's callsign was Rockslide, and he used it more and more these days. Not with Vic, though. With Vic, he was always Santo. He was a real-deal X-Man now. He'd been an upperclassman when Vic had just been starting out. They'd found themselves in the same tight circle of friends ever since.

Santo was over six feet tall, but he looked squat because the rest of him was so big. He was made out of stone. It didn't always have to be the same rock type, either. He preferred a nice, solid granite, but Vic had seen him in obsidian. One time, he'd even made his body from half-molten sulfuric rock stolen from the depths of limbo.

Santo's knock was surprisingly gentle. Quieter than his footsteps. Vic threw open the door and wrapped his arms – partly – around him. He wasn't on the ground for long. Santo yanked him off his feet, hugging so tight it hurt. Vic couldn't hug him back anywhere near as hard, though he tried.

"Lizard boy!" Santo said. "Been too long."

"Just two months!" Vic protested. "What brings you out to the frozen armpit of the X-organization?"

Santo didn't answer. His attention was fixed on the TV. "Hey, that game finally came out? I thought it's been delayed for years."

Vic and Santo had been waiting for this game since before Santo had graduated. It had finally come out while Santo was out on assignment. Vic hadn't been thrilled with it. Too much grinding, too much microtransaction nonsense. It was dark, grungy fantasy, full of swords and blood, and, frankly, the visuals were gorgeous. But Vic had been playing it for so long now that he'd stopped seeing anything but numbers in front of a wireframe. He'd been playing as some kind of witch-lady and getting nowhere, but he'd sunk too much money into costumes to switch to somebody else now. The game had been something to quietly dislike for hours as he sat and tried to avoid thinking about other things.

Maybe that had just been his sour mood shading everything the same color of rotten. The moment he and Santo grabbed opposite controllers, things started to lighten. Games like this were best played together. The moment Santo got the hang of his character – a big, Hulk-sized swordswoman – a whole subset of his own powers *clicked* and started making sense. For the next hour, the game was all they talked about.

"Damn," Vic said, after Santo crushed their third straight boss and insisted on going on. "Don't they give you video games out in the field?"

"Nah," Santo said. "Too busy. They had my team hunting a rogue Sentinel across Antarctica for three weeks straight."

"Sounds awful," Vic said.

"Kinda was," Santo grinned. "We took down our first Sentinel at the end of it, though."

Vic looked at him. "Nice!"

Santo jostled Vic with his shoulder, trying to get him to turn without taking his hands off the controller. "Eyes on the boss!"

They lost that battle because of Vic. Santo pushed them right back in. A sudden paranoia about Santo prickled Vic's throat. "You traveled from pole to pole just to get back here?"

"I've got friends here I haven't seen in months. Like you, dude."

"Like who else?" A sudden deadly anger, so quick and cold it was just like being back in Karma's class, squeezed his chest. "If Karma or Headmaster Summers asked you to talk to me, I'll find out—"

"Whoa, Vic." Santo actually dropped the controller, and held up his hands. "Nobody asked me to do anything."

The lump of anger diminished, though it didn't get away. "Good."

"Why would Cyclops or Karma be asking around for that?"

"They think I need somebody to talk to," Vic said, recognizing the corner he was painting himself in even as he said it.

"Yeah?" Santo asked. "How's that?"

Somehow, Vic had always known it would come down to talking it out again.

Santo had been with him on his "trip" back home.

The last time he'd seen Santo, the two of them had been fighting for their lives in a collapsing church, fire and stinging smoke and gunfire all around them. Rage and fear and the heat of the fires had twisted into a knot inside Vic's head. He couldn't tell any longer how much of the fire he remembered had been real, and how much was the red behind his eyes.

Santo hadn't been bothered by the smoke, but he'd had plenty else to worry about. Like the roof collapsing on him. Or being blasted half apart, or having been shot a dozen times by the kind of weapons that could hurt even him.

There'd been all that, and there'd been worse. The Purifiers, one of a seemingly endless number of anti-mutant fanatics, had taken Vic's father hostage, to try to lure Vic and his friends in.

Emma Frost's teaching assistant, Graymalkin, had fought with them too. So had their stealth expert, Cipher. He'd only seen Cipher once in the weeks since then. For her, though, that was normal.

He couldn't remember any other time in his life when he'd felt the same kind of anger he'd felt when he was talking to Karma. Cold, icy rage, deep in his throat. His arms and legs tensing – not like he'd been about to attack Karma, but like he was going to start running. Except for that last fight, with Santo there.

Somehow he'd managed to avoid running both times.

"Yeah. It's been rough," Santo said. Coming from him, that was a big admission.

"Yeah," Vic said, which was about as profound as he felt emotionally capable of being.

"How's your arm?" Santo asked.

"Bugs me sometimes, but it's been all right." He took his regenerated hand off the control long enough to waggle his oversized fingers. "Plenty of manual dexterity. But I don't know how to sleep anymore. I used to lie down on that side."

"Now I bet it's like cuddling up to a log," Santo said.

"Fffft, yeah." He paused. "That's when it still doesn't feel like it's me."

"I'm lucky to be me," Santo said. "When you're all rock, everything else feels nice and soft."

"Never looked at it that way," Vic said. During the next loading screen, he asked, "You doing all right?"

"Doing better," Santo said, which was the closest he would come to admitting that for a while, he hadn't been. "Sleeping longer. I gotta admit, it was real nice traveling to the South Pole, and getting to tromp around in the open for a change."

"Maybe that's what I need," Vic said. "I'm crammed in here with all these people."

"Not that Antarctica was *all* fresh air and sledding," Santo said. "What with the giant mutant-killing robot and all."

"I just don't want to think any more about 'human-mutant relations'. Just for a few weeks. Just not think about it. I can't do that so long as I'm in Karma's class."

"You could drop," Santo pointed out.

And risk delaying moving up to the next level of classes. Risk delaying his graduation. The X-Men might even hold that against him if he applied to join. He ground his teeth. "Doesn't matter. I wouldn't be able to get away from it anyway. Not while there's bigots wandering the halls."

"Yeah, I heard there's a mutant who used to be with the Reavers here," Santo said. "What the hell's up with that?"

"I don't know what Headmaster Summers was thinking," Vic said. "None of us are safe with that bigot here. Every time I see him, I see one of the Purifiers." The Reavers and the Purifiers were different groups, with different kinds of fanatics, but they'd been united by hating mutants. Vic had to pause the game. He couldn't keep his focus steady. "I don't even care if he thinks he's 'reformed', or whatever. He should've lost any right to be here the moment he tried to harm a mutant for being a mutant."

"Want me to beat him up?" Santo asked.

Vic took a deep breath and let it back out before resuming the game. "No," he said, in a voice that meant *yes*. "That'd just make things worse right now. Besides... if I ever get the chance, I'll beat the hell out of him myself."

"I'll vouch for your good character in the discipline hearing," Santo said.

"If they did trials by peers here, no one would ever convict me," Vic said.

From across the couch, Cipher said, "I've been keeping an eye on him. If he steps out of line, I'll be there."

Even after all this time, Vic couldn't help a little jump at Cipher's voice. She was suddenly *there*, lounging on the cushion next to his like she'd always been there. Maybe she had. She did this kind of thing all the time, with the ease of someone who'd grown up with her mutant powers. Early on, Vic had wished she'd stop that. Now he understood that this was just part of who she was, and how she preferred to communicate with other people.

"You missed a drop in the last room," Cipher pointed out.

Describing her mutant power as "invisibility" didn't capture half of it. She had the power to make people not notice her. Whether in person, in pictures, or on camera, if she wanted someone to not see her… their eyes just slipped right over her. She'd spent most of her life not wanting to be noticed. Her name was Alisa Tager, but she vastly preferred "Cipher".

When she let people see her, she was a slight Black girl with long locs and a black-and-gold X-Men uniform. She'd been a student here longer than anyone in her class had realized. Hell, longer than most of the instructors. She'd sneaked into classes to take them.

Vic hadn't seen her since that moment after martial arts class, in the locker room, when he'd been about to pummel Josh Foley. He'd clenched his fist to strike and suddenly she'd been there – standing right behind Josh, and shaking her head with a warning in her eye. Josh had looked behind him, right at her, but he hadn't seen her at all.

Santo didn't jump, but he did stop playing long enough to get up and hug her like he had Vic. "I've been keeping it together," she said, when Santo asked how she was doing. "And keeping an eye on things here. Hey, we just need to round up Graymalkin and we'll have the whole team together again."

My first team. Those words still meant a lot to Vic, though Santo had been put on another force of X-Men in the meantime. Vic had only gotten through his war with the Purifiers because these three mutants had fought alongside him.

"I should've gone out in the field with you," Cipher told Santo. "Everybody's squeezed in here too tight. Even the X-Men are showing their tempers."

"Yeah?" Vic asked. This was the first he'd heard of it.

"Cyclops and Wolverine are squabbling on comms again," Cipher said. "Wolverine thinks the Institute is lying to students about what we do to get them to come here rather than the Jean Grey School. He thinks this place is stealing his students. I heard Headmaster Summers and Emma Frost talking about it during practice in the Danger Room."

Santo swore. "Those two let you practice with them?"

"Well," Cipher said, "they didn't exactly know about it."

"Summers and Frost train at maximum danger level," Vic snapped. "You shouldn't be there. You could get hurt."

"Yeah, but I didn't," she countered. Her voice was a firm warning to back off.

Vic sank farther back into the couch cushions. He hated the way he'd sounded just then. When Cipher said she'd sneaked into the Danger Room, a spark of fear had leapt up his back, ignited into a blaze. He'd been on edge for weeks, even when there was nothing to be on edge about. It had left him brittle. His nerves were dry kindling.

He wouldn't be any good to Santo playing like this. The tension still crept into his voice when he passed his controller to Cipher. "Give it a try. It's good when you play it with other people."

"You could've fooled me. You've been playing it alone for hours."

He glanced sharply at her, and she just looked back, eyebrow raised – like a challenge. She'd never said how long she'd been in here, checking up on him.

"I'm going to get something to eat," Vic said, pushing off the couch. His cheeks felt hot again. His body was going into fight-or-flight mode. The slightest trigger set him off these days. "I've been in here too long."

"I'll come with," Santo said, putting down his controller.

"*Don't.*" Vic headed for the door, not waiting. "You two catch up without me."

Vic didn't see either of them again that evening. He stayed out late in the library, studying to give himself an excuse to stay away. By the time he got back, Santo and Cipher were gone.

Well, Cipher might *not* have been gone, but he figured she was.

The next morning, his laptop's calendar alarm went off at six-thirty, two hours after he finally managed to fall asleep. He groaned. He'd forgotten that there was an early assembly scheduled.

He wasn't sure what the Institute's auditorium had been in

its past life. A command center, maybe, or a storage silo. The ceiling was high and vaulting. Any other trace of its original identity had been wiped away. The rounded ceiling and circular walls had been plastered with acoustic damping foam. A short, wooden stage ran flush against the rounded wall.

Graymalkin stood behind Emma Frost and Headmaster Summers. Vic sat alone and waited. Karma stepped up to join the other instructors. Vic got a sour feeling in his stomach the moment her gaze crossed his.

Headmaster Summers spoke first. "We've been encouraging all students to sign up for field training and excursions." He wasn't using a mic, but his voice projected seemingly effortlessly. The room quieted at once. "Especially for those of you who intend to apply to join the X-Men. But even those of you who intend to remain civilians can still benefit from field training. Out there, you'll learn things classroom instruction, labs, and even the Danger Room could never give you."

Stupefied silence from the audience. None of them knew what Headmaster Summers was driving at. Vic had an idea. He'd seen the sign-up sheets for the field expeditions, and all the blank spaces underneath them.

Karma spoke next. "Interest in these field excursions has been low to nonexistent. The volunteer rosters are lower than they've been in this school's history."

She and Headmaster Summers had to know exactly why interest was dropping. The satellite news channels were full of stories about anti-mutant militias like the Purifiers and Reavers. Things always seemed to be getting worse. Especially after what had happened to Vic and his friends, everyone wanted to hunker down.

"These expeditions will continue to accept volunteers," Karma said. "However... starting this week, students may also be compulsorily assigned to them. At the expedition leader's discretion."

That caused a stir. Karma let the students talk among themselves before continuing.

Vic folded his arms over his chest. Knots of students were already strategizing about which trips to volunteer for so that they wouldn't get stuck with one they didn't want.

He didn't have any illusions that he would have a choice. Karma was looking right at him. She'd been making plans for him. A day ago, he would have given most of what he had for a chance to get out of the Institute – hell, to get out of Alberta entirely. But not like this. This was having the choice ripped away from him.

A hundred objections built up under his throat. If it had been anyone but Karma up there, he would have voiced them. Their argument still burned in his memory. The more he thought about what he'd said, the less he liked how he'd sounded.

Vic tried to meet Karma's stare. He couldn't manage it very long. He dropped his gaze to the ground and held it there for the rest of the meeting.

CHAPTER THREE
Elixir

"They're sending me to some kind of underwater habitat," Josh said. It was a comparatively nice day for northern Alberta – clear skies, no wind, above freezing – so Josh could bear sitting outside in a light jacket. He pulled his knees to his chest. "The X-Men built it years and years ago, when they were working on improving mutant-Atlantean relations. They needed a neutral meeting ground."

"Sounds mighty miserable already," Outlaw said.

He snorted. Hearing that from just about anybody else would have made him feel worse. From Outlaw, it was so frank and thoughtlessly honest that he had to bite back a laugh.

The truth was that seeing her made him happier than he'd been in weeks. Not that he was *happy*, but with someone who didn't hate him around, he felt more like a person. The two of them sat outside, under the shade of the silvery Wakandan airship Outlaw had arrived in. Outlaw didn't want to go below, anyway. She was here to visit Josh, not to get any more wrapped up with the X-Men than she already had.

"That's not the worst of it," he said. "The place has been out of commission for decades. Mutants and the Atlanteans found better ways to communicate. The X-Men send teams to repair and maintain it every once in a while, but it's barely in operation."

"Now you get to be one of those repair teams," Outlaw said. "Lucky for you. Convenient for them, too, to have free labor."

"Damn. I thought *I* was cynical," Josh said.

Outlaw's teammate Atlas Bear paced gloomily under the airship's fuselage, checking the hull for wear and tear. Like the airship, she was Wakandan. She was the airship's owner and pilot. She tossed a few glances his way, but whenever Josh had returned them, she'd turned her back on him. She was impatient to leave.

Outlaw's real name was Inez, but it was easier for Josh to think of her as Outlaw. She dressed the part: big cowgirl Stetson, a tan leather vest, jeans, and two old-fashioned but vicious-looking revolvers at her hips. It didn't seem warm enough for the weather, but Outlaw said she wasn't cold. Josh didn't know if he believed that.

He knew better than to pry. One thing he'd learned fast about mutants here was that they all had their own style, and attached themselves to it. Josh felt out of place in his jacket, slacks, and gas-station Canadian maple leaf t-shirt.

Outlaw couldn't have been all that many years older than him, not in absolute terms. But a lifetime of experience divided them. She'd spent all her life working as a mercenary. He'd met her partner Domino briefly, not long after Outlaw had rescued him from Wolfram's gang, but had only learned that she was a legend in her field later. The next time he'd seen her, it had been on a news report – her face framed by an explosion.

"We're going to spend a full day crammed into a sub half the size of a school bus," he said. "Just to descend a mile underwater."

Outlaw shook her head. "Distances can trick you. At that depth, it's gonna be more like going to an alien planet."

"Exactly. I had no idea. It's going to take that long to descend because they're going to be hyperpressurizing our air. Pressurizing it so much that it would kill us if we did it any faster."

"*Pop*," Outlaw said helpfully.

"I think 'crumple like an aluminum can' is how Karma put it." Josh was astonished by how much he needed someone to complain to. His chest felt light, airy. He couldn't make himself stop talking. He'd kept words bottled inside him for too long. "But it's not just the pressure. They're going to be changing the air we breathe. Our air is going to be, like, one percent oxygen, the rest inert gasses. The air is so pressurized we'll be getting all the oxygen we need from that. Think about that."

"Sounds like fun," Outlaw said.

He gave her a look. "You really believe that?"

"Nah," she admitted. "I could make it fun, though, if I were going with my friends. But they're probably going to put you to work."

Before the briefing where Karma had gone over, in detail, everything that would be happening to them, Josh had worried about the pressure. But he'd thought the pressure would be locked outside. He imagined ceilings creaking, bulkheads bowing inward, and any water leaks spraying inside with the cutting power of a chainsaw.

Somehow, he would have been more comfortable with that than getting hyperpressurized himself. The station was actually open to the water. The lowest deck had a pool with a hatch that opened straight to the sea. They'd be able to swim right out into the ocean. They could perform repairs on the station's exterior. All for the "low" cost of breathing an air mixture that, if used at the pressures his body was meant to function at, would quickly kill him. Not even his healing abilities would save him. Once their bodies were adapted to the pressure, none of them would be able return to the surface without a lengthy, uncomfortable depressurization, just as long as the trip down.

He must have given away more in his expression than he wanted to. Outlaw said, "Well, now you've got your chance to get away from those classes you're always complaining about."

Josh snorted. He bit back a louder laugh.

"Unless your other teachers decide to give you homework." Outlaw's voice dropped an octave, a parody of seriousness. "They're not going to give you homework down there, are they? That's just the kind of low-down thing a teacher would do."

"Oh, God. I hadn't thought about that."

Outlaw reached into the satchel at her feet. "Granola bar?" she asked.

Josh immediately forgot what he'd been about to say next. "Hell yes."

The snack varieties at the Institute were wanting, and the supply runs that stocked them inconsistent. He didn't even open the package she offered, but tucked it into his jacket.

In another lifetime, he would have eaten it on the spot. He had a stash back in his room. His time with Wolfram's gang had left him with some food habits he hadn't shaken.

Outlaw raised an eyebrow. She dug into her satchel. After a moment, she produced an almost-full carton of wrapped granola bars. She slid the whole carton across to him before he could open his mouth.

He was ashamed of the way his heart dropped out of his chest. Someday, he'd become more like the person he'd been before Wolfram's gang had gotten ahold of him. But that day wasn't today.

"You doing all right in your classes?" she asked. "Grades good?"

"For what it matters. They're fine." Great, actually. He didn't have much else to do but study. "It's not like any college is going to accept transcripts from here."

"The point ain't the transcripts. The point is to *learn*."

"I guess." Josh had learned more about human anatomy from his healing classes than he'd ever expected. For what that was worth. He did not want to go on like this for the rest of his life, but that was what these people seemed to be preparing him for.

"It's either learn the easy way or the hard way," Outlaw told him. "This place is the easy way. I know what my limits are. Learned them through years of hard knocks. You've been through a lot yourself. You figured out yours?"

"I never want to find out," he said. But he didn't want to talk about that. Not with her. She was too important to him to bore like that. "What about you? You knew you were a mutant most of your life. Did you ever go to a school like this?"

Her laugh was sharp and sudden enough to make him flinch. "No. Never had the opportunity. I don't think I would've gone if I had. But that didn't mean I didn't have a lot to learn. Still do, to be honest. A place like this might've been good for me. Even if I went my own way in the end."

"Easy for you to say when it's not you staring down years of this."

She grinned. "Fair enough. But I think when you get a little older, you'll be surprised how nostalgic you feel when you look back on this part of your life."

"Is that your way of telling me it's going to get worse from here?"

Her smile softened. "I'm trying to tell you to look on the optimistic side of things."

It seemed to Josh that they were describing two edges of the same sword. "That's a teensy bit hard right now. Everybody here–" he'd been about to say *hates me* but stopped when he realized how that sounded "–can leave when they want. I'm a prisoner."

Now that smile vanished entirely. But the warmth remained in her eyes. "I'm not going to lie. It's a real rotten thing, what's been done to you."

Neither of them ever talked about the fact that she had helped put him here. Some words were better unspoken, including the thought dangling at the end of her sentence: *"But not as rotten as what the Reavers did to people like us"*.

She never would have said it to him. Not after all the things they'd been through together. They both would have died fighting Wolfram if it hadn't been for each other. But he knew she felt those words, and strongly. She'd marched for mutant rights even before she'd become a mercenary. If they hadn't had that history together, she probably would have hated him more than anybody here.

That was the reason she didn't just offer him a ride out of here. They'd only spent a brief time together, but it had been enough to learn that she hated seeing anyone imprisoned. She'd helped build the legal bars keeping him here... and she wasn't going to do anything about them.

She'd saved his life. He'd saved hers. And they hadn't let go of each other since. The classic start of a friendship, at least in the superpowered world he'd been tossed into.

And that meant that every way he disappointed her cut him to his core. Even when she never voiced that disappointment aloud. *Especially* then.

"You said you went your own path," Josh said. "How did you decide what it was?"

"I went out and I barreled into things," Outlaw said. "'Normal' work never really cut it for me. I don't *look* like a mutant to the naked eye, but I've never been one to hide who I am. I wasn't willing to go home for a variety of reasons, and my powers are suited for righteous violence." Outlaw was super strong, had super endurance, and healed far more quickly than an ordinary human. "Plus, I liked it. That's how I ended up a merc."

"I can't imagine doing that," he said. "I don't want to be a doctor. I just want to..." He frowned, struggling for words. "Want to get away from all of this. And rest."

Not that he had any idea where he wanted to get to. Home was thousands of miles away, and full of people who didn't want him anymore.

"You're on a long, hard road. You could have taken a much easier path."

"What, going to prison?"

"Breaking out from prison. You know bars can't hold you."

Josh chewed the inside of his lip. The last thing he wanted to do was talk about what his powers could do. It was the secret he'd kept ever since he'd gotten here, though Emma Frost seemed to have plucked it out of his mind.

Since he'd come to the Institute, he'd used his powers only for healing. Nothing else. It was all he wanted to do with them. Outlaw was one of the few people left alive who knew he could be more than that.

Wolfram had shown him. By breaking Josh's arm over and over again, and forcing him to heal himself, Josh had learned to anticipate Wolfram's blows. Instinctively, unconsciously, he'd reshaped his arm to avoid the worst of them. His elbow had softened, and bent but not broken with the blow.

That had been more than just healing. And if he could do that to himself, then, with other people... he could do the same. Or worse.

He shoved that thought away. He didn't deserve that kind of power. Didn't want anything to do with it.

Snapback to a packed gymnasium, cheering a hulking suit of armor clomping onstage. An evening Reavers rally at his high school, staged with the full cooperation of the principal, who Josh normally detested. But this had made her cool.

All of Josh's friends had gone, and he was there cheering right alongside them. Feeling a vicarious rush of power as the gym echoed with the powered armor's powerful, clanking footsteps. Feeling good, knowing that the mutants he'd seen on his parents' news shows would finally have some justice coming their way.

Josh said, "A year ago, I thought my life was going to be so much better than this."

"Isn't it?"

"What do you mean? A year ago, I had a home. I had friends. I wasn't hated by everyone I knew for what *actually* turns out to have been very good reasons."

"Hold up. I don't mean your circumstances."

He tilted his head and glanced at her.

"I mean you," she said. "As a person. Do you think you're a better person than you were a year ago?"

Josh needed some time to consider that. Then he said, "I honestly don't know."

"I think you're better," she said.

A year ago, Outlaw would have hardly noticed him except to hate him. To her, he would've been just another bigot. And now he wasn't.

The tricky thing was that she was right. He didn't think he would trade anything for who he had been.

That didn't make him any less miserable now.

Developing mutant powers had shocked him out of the undemanding intolerance the rest of his world – parents, teachers, everyone in town – had shared. He wished he could believe that he would've eventually come to the right answer on his own. But he didn't think he would have. Just because he'd come around, that didn't make him a good person.

Outlaw zipped her satchel up again. As much as he didn't want her to leave, he knew she was on a timetable. Josh glanced again at Atlas Bear. This time, she met his gaze for a second, but no longer. He knew Atlas Bear wasn't a mutant, but not much else. And that white-hot glare of hers was getting under his skin.

"What's her deal?" he asked Outlaw furtively.

"Precognition," Outlaw answered. "She sees–"

"The future," Josh finished. "Yeah, I know. I've met the type." Blindfold still unnerved him. But she stayed away from him so long as he kept himself at a distance from Laurie Collins.

"I've never met any precogs with a 'gift' like Atlas Bear's," Outlaw said. "Not much of a gift. She sees potential futures, all right. But only dark futures. Futures where the world ends. She sees how it could happen. It used to drive her out of her wits."

Outlaw stood, helped him to his feet, and started to sort out her satchel. She had to get ready to go. Outlaw and Atlas Bear were on their way to another job. Taking out the carton of granola bars had left a void that everything else had tumbled into.

The piece of Josh that remained an extrovert still came out. Every once in a while, he had to try to meet people. With a static frisson of anxiety still crackling across the back of his mind, he stepped toward Atlas Bear.

"Thanks for bringing Outlaw," he told her. It was an awkward conversation starter, but it was all he could come up with. "I hope it wasn't too far out of your way."

Atlas Bear just looked at him. "No," she said.

"So now you're off on a top-secret job?" he asked. "Can you tell me anything about it, or is it classified?"

"Extremely classified," she said impassively.

"Shoot, Shoon'kwa," Outlaw said, packed up and stepping past. "It's just a bounty hunt. You can tell him that much."

Atlas Bear waited until Outlaw had stepped up the airship's

boarding ramp and out of earshot. Then she turned to him. Apropos of nothing Josh could see, Atlas Bear said, "I've been having trouble sleeping lately."

"Sorry to hear that."

"Now I know why. I thought it was our bounty, but it's not. It's you."

Josh was starting to seriously regret trying to make conversation, with her or with anyone. It would've been a lot simpler to live here if he'd been an introvert. He opened his mouth, but Atlas Bear spoke first.

"It wasn't that long ago that, when I identified a threat to the world, I would take it out. Preemptively." Her gaze sharpened. She stepped around him, as if studying him. "It got me in a lot of trouble. Exiled from my country, even. Thank all your stars that I'm not like that anymore."

The air seemed much colder than it had a moment ago. Josh stood, frozen in place, as Atlas Bear circled. "Outlaw knows you're more than just a healer," she said, "but even she doesn't know a fraction of it. What about you, Joshua Foley? Do you know?"

He didn't answer. He had no idea if he did, or didn't.

She stopped in front of him again. "Do you know how terrible a villain you could be?"

"I know," he said, in a soft voice.

"No," she said, in a softer one. "You don't."

She left him like that, breathless and voiceless, as Outlaw came back to say her goodbyes and for an astonishingly warm hug. He gave as good a hug as he got, pretending nothing was wrong. It was cold enough out here that she didn't seem to think anything strange about his shivering. She tapped her hat's brim before she boarded the airship.

Atlas Bear followed Outlaw up the boarding ramp. She looked back at him only once the ramp began folding up. "I'm singularly impressed," she said obliquely, "with your ability to make the wrong decision at every opportunity."

Josh's blood felt like ice, and not from the cold. He waited for Atlas Bear to say anything else, but she didn't. She saw his expression shift. Her words must have had the effect on him that she'd meant them to have.

The boarding ramp folded into the airship's hull. Josh stepped back from the airship just as its thrusters began roaring, kicking clouds of ice and dirt into his stinging eyes.

The airship receded into the sky and darted into the clouds. Josh stared after it, still trying to think of everything he wanted to say.

CHAPTER FOUR
Elixir

When Josh stepped through the descent capsule's hatchway, he hesitated, staring, until Karma's firm hand on his shoulder moved him ahead.

And he'd thought the two-day boat ride out here had been cramped. This was not going to be fun.

The "half the size of a school bus" that he'd been told was technically accurate. It failed to account for the complex system of air pumps and gas tanks embedded in the ceiling and walls. What they were left with was a round cabin ringed by six thickly cushioned seats, and one closet-sized toilet stall.

They were to be here for a full twenty-four hours. What was worse, they couldn't even stand to stretch. Karma had told them that, unless they were using the bathroom, they were to stay seated with their safety harnesses on. The descent capsule would be moving slowly, but unexpected crosscurrents or ballast releases could bounce them into the bulkheads.

He paused again. It took his eyes a moment to adjust. There were overhead lights, and a single tiny porthole, through which the blue of a partly cloudy afternoon sky shone. Josh kept his eyes fixed on the porthole as he stepped inside. His pulse was racing. It took effort and concentration to keep that from showing.

Anole shoved him from behind. Josh stumbled forward but didn't dare look back. Karma must not have been watching.

The repair team had spent two days cruising the Atlantic aboard the *Xcaliber*, a claustrophobic speed yacht that suddenly seemed luxurious compared to this. The *Xcaliber*'s pilots had stayed low-profile, steering them away from major shipping lanes. The X-Men operated as unobtrusively as they could afford to. The *Xcaliber* belonged to the Jean Grey School. As part of an effort to thaw relations between the New Charles Xavier Institute and the Jean Grey School, this would be a joint operation. Station X-41 predated the schism between the institutions. Rather than squabble over its ownership (and the cost of its upkeep), for once they'd done the sensible thing and split the responsibility between them. A student from the Jean Grey School was joining them, too.

The descent capsule had spent the trip in the *Xcaliber's* hold. Now it had been lifted out and then lowered behind the *Xcaliber*, to which it was still loosely tethered.

Josh picked the seat farthest from the door and stowed his duffel bag in the slim space underneath. The trip prep handouts from Karma had advised them to pack light. Josh had only packed clothes to last for the twelve days of their assignment, and that was assuming he wore each outfit twice. He still had to cram the bag into the space allotted to him.

Nature Girl was the next aboard, after Josh and Anole. She had to tilt her antlers and slide through sideways to fit through the hatch, and she sucked air through her teeth as the tip of her antler caught on the hatch's frame. Josh winced in sympathy. Things were not likely to get any more spacious below.

Josh had never seen her before this trip. She was the student from the Jean Grey School. He had hardly seen her during their boat ride. She hadn't just been avoiding him, either. She'd stayed in their shared quarters when the others were out on deck, and went out on deck when the others went inside.

He couldn't say for sure who had volunteered for this mission and who had been conscripted. The volunteer sheet for this assignment had been empty before Headmaster Summers made his announcement. Afterward, though, there'd been a rush to volunteer for expeditions and missions as students scrambled to make sure that they wouldn't get forced onto one that they hated. Josh hadn't bothered. None of the expeditions sounded appealing. Now he wished he had. He would have rather been doing extreme environment survival training in Death Valley than this. At least Death Valley would have been under the open sky.

He'd hoped that the Jean Grey School wouldn't have needed to resort to conscripting volunteers. From what little he'd seen of Nature Girl, he doubted she would have rushed to sequester herself thousands of feet undersea. Hell, though – he could have been wrong. He didn't know any of these people, not really. Least of all her.

There were seats for all of them: five students and an instructor. But there would be six students total on this trip. The last, Karma had told them, was a special case. He wouldn't need transportation to the station, but would join them there... by swimming on his own.

Triage kicked his backpack, trying to force it under his seat. Graymalkin was the last inside. He stepped in front of Josh. "That's my seat."

In another lifetime, Josh would have answered that he didn't see anybody's name on it. He sighed, and moved one over.

"The X-Men have all kinds of fancy ships," Triage said to Karma. Josh was starting to get the idea that Triage was one of those people who talked a lot when they were nervous. "The *Xcaliber*, X-Planes, X-Copters, hell – even spacecraft. You can't tell me there's not an X-Sub."

"There's not an X-Sub," Karma said, and then: "that you're allowed to know about."

After her students had gotten their packs and suitcases stowed away, she added, "A submarine wouldn't cut it for this. The best modern nuclear subs have a crush depth of about nine hundred feet. We're going five times that deep. A sub's engines would be wasted. The descent capsule is everything we need. We're not going there fast. If we *did* go fast, we'd regret it in a hurry. But not for long, if you catch my drift."

Someone moaned quietly. Josh couldn't tell who. He felt so far away from his body that he wouldn't have been surprised to find out it was himself. Disappointed, but not surprised. The last thing he needed to do here was show anyone his weaknesses.

The descent capsule lurched. After a brief queasy moment, Josh wondered if the capsule had stopped. Then he caught water lapping against the porthole and realized they had been cut loose from the *Xcaliber*.

The water didn't splash against the porthole for long before the descent capsule sank below the waves.

The porthole showed them a shimmery, rippled-mirror view of the waves from their underside. That fell away into a placid blue, shot through with spears of sunlight shining through specks like dust motes swirling through the sea.

Josh swallowed. He had never gone a day without seeing the sky, he realized.

The surface vanished under a curtain of bubbles as the capsule loosed its first tank of ballast.

Karma was the only one of them who wasn't watching. Not only had she faced a thousand worse dangers in her career as an X-Man, but this was her third trip to the station. She settled into her seat and unfolded a slim silver laptop. The glow of the screen heightened the shadows around her eyes as the light from the porthole grew deeper.

Graymalkin would be her assistant on this trip. Belatedly, Josh saw that Graymalkin had not booted him out of his seat for no reason. That seat was different than the others. A monitor was mounted discreetly overhead, and a keypad was on its armrest. None of the other seats had the same, not even Karma's.

"Acoustic communications on," Karma told Graymalkin.

"I have been signaling," he said.

The station was so far underwater that radio messaging wouldn't work. Radio couldn't cut through the sheer mass of all the water squeezing on top of it. So the station communicated with the surface via acoustics. Simple sound, transmitted through the sea, pinging code. In another moment, Graymalkin reported that he was getting a ping back.

The station's automatics were too primitive and their acoustic transmission too limited to say much else. But the ping meant that the station's automated systems should have been starting to wake up after a long, lonely slumber. According to their briefing, it would take the station almost a full day to get its air warmed and recirculated.

The atmospherics machinery *clunked*. The overhead vents began to hiss. Nature Girl jumped, and so did Josh. It felt good, at least, to know he hadn't been the only one. The others all looked to Karma. Judging from the way she hadn't flinched, hadn't even taken her eyes off her laptop's screen, this was all expected.

Over the next hour, the columns of sunlight vanished. The blue got dimmer. It faded to twilight. Josh could no longer make out the underside of the waves through the cloudy waters.

The hissing noise persisted. His hands and feet felt loose, disconnected from the rest of his body. Not numb, exactly, but not entirely present. The feeling spread to his arms and legs, and then settled queasily in his stomach.

He and the others had gotten an extensive safety briefing, and been told what to expect to feel as their air changed. The air they were being introduced to had been specially formulated by Beast to avoid some of the worst effects of hyperpressurization, like terrible joint pain. Judging from the swimminess in his head and stomach, not all of the side effects were gone.

Like Triage, Josh used to deal with anxiety by chatting with other people. It helped get his mind off himself. Old habits clung hard. The most he felt up to right now was listening, but the others didn't give him much to listen to. Triage tried sustaining a conversation, but gave up after a while. Josh squirmed, anxious for *something* to happen.

Graymalkin frowned at his armrest's keypad, searching for something. "'Press key to continue?'" he muttered.

That counted as something. Josh blinked. "You're doing a bit, right? A *which key* gag?"

"Why would I do that?"

Not for the first time, Josh tried to place Graymalkin's accent. It was almost, but not quite, British, with a heavy country brogue, and something stranger that he couldn't place. "I forget you're not from around here."

"From the ocean? No, I'm not."

"Don't have much of a sense of humor, do–"

"*That* was a joke," Graymalkin said. Josh got the distinct feeling that Graymalkin had been running conversational circles around him, and he'd only just now figured it out.

Josh had worked hard at not judging mutants by their appearances. He had gotten better, but Graymalkin tested him. His skin was such a pale gray that he looked something between a statue and a muscular, bleached body. Up close, his skin looked too smooth and sleek – like he was always wet, though Josh faintly suspected, if he reached over to check, he'd find Graymalkin's skin was as dry as a reptile's scales. Graymalkin's pure white eyes didn't make him any easier to read.

"I may be over two hundred and fifty years old," Graymalkin said, "but I am also seventeen years old."

Triage's warning about prompting people for their traumas still rang in Josh's ears. He didn't say anything, just listened. Graymalkin was ready to talk about it on his own.

Graymalkin said, "When my father found me laying with a boy, he beat me halfway to death. When he thought I was dead, he buried me alive. But I wasn't dead."

Josh had heard that Graymalkin's mutant abilities, his strength and endurance, functioned best in darkness. "Your powers. They activated in the dark."

"My powers kept me alive and comatose for over two hundred years. In stasis, essentially. Until I was unearthed by accident."

Josh forgot all his discomfort. To have a chance to talk with someone from centuries ago, and who remembered it like it had just happened… it was like something out of a movie. "That's incredible. I'm sorry about making fun of the whole 'press key' thing. I can't imagine how much you've had to learn to get by. How long have you been here?"

"Josh," Anole said, from across the cabin. "Leave him alone."

Josh ground his teeth. There were plenty of people at the Institute that he never would have gotten along with, but, of all the students he could have ended up with, Anole had to have been one of the worst.

"I can manage for myself, Vic," Graymalkin said. He sounded bemused as he spoke again to Josh. "I am incredibly privileged to have ended up at the Institute. I don't enjoy talking about my past, however. I would not go back to it even if I could."

There was a little barb at the end of that line. Graymalkin was plainly implying that was one of the differences between them. Josh couldn't tell him otherwise right now, not without looking even smaller than he felt. "I appreciate you telling me as much as you did."

Graymalkin turned his attention back to the screen above. The frown returned. "So when the display asks me to press a key – it's not a test? I don't need some way of finding the *right* key?"

Josh grinned. Now he understood more of what the problem

was. "Not everything is school. You'll fail all your tests if you overthink them like that, anyway. It's just prompting you to tell it to continue."

"Why would a device need to do that? If it's ready, it should just continue."

Josh craned his neck to peer at the screen above Graymalkin. Fuzzy green text on a CRT monitor. He hadn't seen anything like that outside of decades-old movies.

The whole station was going to be like that. Karma's laptop was probably the most advanced electronics they'd have on this trip. Unless any of the others had brought their smartphones along. Josh had left his. No bars, no point.

Time ticked by. Josh swallowed and tried to focus on keeping his ears popped. His restless energy wouldn't go away.

Triage's pack was so big because he'd taken along books as well as clothes, including one of the medical textbooks Warren had given them. He tried to study, but his concentration visibly waned, and eventually he gave up. Karma *tap-tap-tapped* at her laptop while Graymalkin monitored the controls. Anole laid his oversized right arm across his lap and stared at the ceiling.

Nature Girl had picked the seat closest to the porthole. She twisted against her harness, peering outside. For a while, Josh couldn't figure out if she was interested in whatever was out there, or just didn't want to be paying attention to anyone inside.

Then a flash of movement caught Josh's eyes. A shimmery, silvery shape darted just past the window. Then two more. Nature Girl raised her hand as if to wave.

If there were others, Josh couldn't see them. When Nature Girl craned her neck, her antlers blocked his view.

Before long, there wasn't much to see anyway. The murky midnight blue outside faded to a deep and impenetrable black. The capsule passed through the last layer of the sea that sunlight could pierce.

From here on down, there was nothing but an open black expanse, deep as space. The porthole cast a cone of light into the empty dark. Other than a few flecks of particles rising past it, there was nothing out there.

And still Nature Girl peered out, trying to see.

Josh looked around the capsule. They made a strange bunch, and not just in the way that any group of mutants was a strange bunch. Their powers were a poor match for this mission in particular. Not one, but *two* healers. An animal empath. A mutant with some physical traits of lizards but who was decidedly not amphibious. Graymalkin. And Karma, whose telepathic powers conjured a person's fears in front of them. Josh was besieged by a number of anxieties already, and now he had a new one to add to the top of the list.

"None of us have powers suited for this," Josh said.

Karma looked up from her laptop. "You just noticed?"

From the way the others were staring at him, Josh guessed he must have missed something during their briefing. "That's the goal," Karma said. "When you're gifted with mutant powers, it's easy to lean on them. Sometimes to the point where you fall over. This trip is meant to take you students out of your comfort zones. None of your powers are a clean fit for life undersea."

"I get to be the exception," Graymalkin said. His abilities were powered by darkness. It was hard to get darker than a mile underwater.

"This is one of the Institute's educational goals," Karma

said, speaking now to all of them. "Teaching you how to be comfortable with your powers, but also how to be competent *outside* the sphere of your powers. If the only thing I ever learned was how to terrify people with telepathy, I would have been killed a long time ago. You've all been studying very hard in your respective fields. But there's more to being an X-Man than being good at one specific thing. Even for those of you who don't intend to try to become X-Men," she added, glancing again at Josh, "there's a lot more to surviving as a mutant than being good at one thing.

"When you lean too hard on a single talent," Karma continued, "even when you're the best at it – *especially* when you're the best at it – you end up isolated. On an expedition like this one, we all need to be working as a team. You're going to have to depend on each other to get things done. It was the same way when I took my first trip here, when I was a student."

Josh swallowed. He sure as hell couldn't rely on anybody here.

Maybe not even if his life was at stake.

"Crosta is going to be in his element," Anole said. "Literally. He's Atlantean."

Josh's attention perked. Anole meant the mysterious sixth student. Josh had *heard* of the Atlanteans, the water-dwellers led by Prince Namor. Namor was a mutant himself, and often allied with the X-Men. But Josh had never seen an Atlantean in person.

Karma held Anole's gaze for another moment. There was something going on between them that Josh didn't know about, and didn't *want* to know about.

"'Literally' speaking, water is a particle, not an element,"

Graymalkin said, under his breath. Josh was pretty sure that he was the only one who'd heard.

"Crosta," Karma said, "is going to be surrounded by strangers from a different culture. And he's had plenty else to get used to. He'll definitely be out of his element."

Anole blew air out his nose. "I've already proved I can work on a team. Graymalkin, Rockslide, Cipher, and I helped take down the Purifiers. I shouldn't have been picked for this."

"You did very well with a team of your friends." Josh got the impression that Karma was choosing her words carefully. But her voice was iron.

"You can't always work with friends," she continued, "and this is going to test you in different ways."

"You can't team up with somebody you can't trust," Anole said. He didn't look at Josh, but he wasn't hiding his meaning, either.

Beside Josh, Triage said, "In that blowup at the Chicago Natural History Museum, Tempus and I worked with Sabretooth. We sure as hell never trusted him."

Anole glared at Triage. Triage had hardly been Josh's advocate, but he met Anole's stare dead-on. Though Josh didn't miss Triage's implication that he didn't trust Josh, either.

"Sabretooth wouldn't turn you over to anti-mutant militias," Anole said.

"He could have eaten us," Triage said.

"That's enough," Karma interrupted, though with more impatience than anger. "Anole, you're in one of Magneto's classes. How do you think the rest of the X-Men felt when they started working with him?"

"Probably pretty bad," Anole said. "But it wasn't on them

to twist themselves in knots to accept him. *They* never forgot anything he'd done. He had to prove he'd changed."

Josh could no longer restrain himself. "You don't think I've changed?" he asked.

"I don't think you've changed in any of the ways that matter."

"You don't know me," Josh said.

"I think I know enough." After a pause, Anole added, "You've had some of the bigotry scared out of you. Sure. But take away your mutant powers, give you the chance to go back home, and you'd be right back to it. Same as you used to be. Going to the same old hate rallies."

This time, there was anger in Karma's voice. "I said, that's *enough*," she snapped.

"Tell me I'm wrong," Anole told Josh.

He wanted to. Sometimes the words even formed in his throat. They always had the cadence of a comforting lie.

Karma said, "The biggest reason you're all going to work together is because I'm telling you to. At the Institute and especially on this mission, you obey my orders. Those of you aiming to join the X-Men, think very carefully about what you say next." Before anybody could spoil things by pointing out how many times the X-Men had disobeyed orders whether they'd come from the authorities or Charles Xavier, she added, "The next person who speaks gets toilet cleaning duties when the capsule reaches the station."

The threat had its intended effect. The descent continued in silence. After a few minutes of it, Karma, satisfied, returned her attention to her laptop.

As Karma warned, the capsule rocked as it sank through the deep ocean's currents. Ordinarily, the motion wouldn't have bothered Josh. He did fine on planes. But whatever was happening to the air had already left his stomach reeling. More than once, he only just managed to restrain himself from unbuckling his safety harness and launching toward the toilet.

He would have had to get in line. Three times in two hours, Nature Girl bolted from her seat into the toilet stall. The thin walls did not cover the sound of her retching.

Josh tried to focus his healing talent inward. Whatever was happening with his stomach was too subtle for him to fix. Triage seemed to be having more success. After the second time Nature Girl ran to the toilet, Triage asked her, "Want me to take a look? See if there's anything I can do to help?"

She looked at him for a long moment before shaking her head. "I can manage." It was the first time Josh had heard her speak. Her voice was even-keeled, not the shy-girl stereotype he'd assembled in his head.

He tried once again to focus his powers. He could sense the trouble in his gut and throat: the twitching muscles, the building spasms... but he couldn't do anything about them. He wagered that the source of his problem was in his nerves, in his brain and his fears, which were too complicated for his powers to manipulate.

He lost track of the number of times his ears popped. Every time he swallowed, it seemed like. They had been warned to swallow often, or else risk ear damage. That was also why none of them were allowed to sleep, though their descent was twenty-three hours long. Sleeping people wouldn't swallow on time. It would have been a hell of a thing to wake up to a burst eardrum, even with two healers aboard.

The silence only broke every once in a while. When it

did, Josh wished it hadn't. "Every thirty feet puts another atmosphere of pressure atop us," Graymalkin said once, as if anybody needed to hear.

At the start of the trip, Josh had dreaded Karma devising some kind of communal activity to keep them all awake. Some kind of game or, God forbid, singing. But that didn't seem to be Karma's style. She kept an eye on them to make sure they stayed awake, but kept most of her attention on her laptop.

Once, when she stood to use the bathroom, she left her screen open. Josh caught plain white lines on a black screen, drawn into boxes with ASCII sprinkled all over them. A blur of dots, letters, and symbols. He smirked when he recognized it.

Graymalkin peered at it, too. When he realized Josh had caught him peeking, those pale cheeks reddened. "It looks complicated," he said. As if to try to justify his curiosity, he added, "I was hoping there was something we could do to help."

Josh's grin widened. "It's a video game."

"What?" Graymalkin looked closer. He didn't ask what a video game was. Josh figured other students would have introduced them to him long ago. "It looks like a spreadsheet."

"It's an old-fashioned kind of game. A roguelike. I had a buddy in high school who was obsessed with those. He'd play them in the school library because the PCs could run them and they just looked like CompSci homework to the librarian."

At least, that kid *had* been Josh's buddy. Before Josh's other friends had pushed him away from their group for being too weird… and Josh had gone along with them.

If Graymalkin noticed the shift in Josh's mood, he didn't show it. "Nonsense. I'm sure it's important."

Graymalkin could believe what he wanted. It felt good to see that Karma was a little more human than she wanted to show to her students.

Karma spent the next few hours lost in dungeon crawling, but eventually even she had to bow to the realities of her laptop's battery life. She snapped it closed.

Somewhere along the trip, the silence had become stifling. It was a heavy, physical thing – like a fire blanket tossed over them. Maybe it was a symptom of the hyperpressurization, and this was just how they would all feel from now on.

Josh's head felt like it had been wrapped in a wet towel. The feeling mostly faded, but the sense of weight remained. The air pumps above had never stopped hissing. He hoped some of the feeling was claustrophobia. He could get over claustrophobia. At least he hoped he would. But there was also a kind of social claustrophobia here that he'd never felt before.

Anole was seated directly across from him. And he would not stop staring. Josh could not meet his gaze for longer than a few seconds. He wondered how that kid who'd played roguelikes in the school library felt when he'd started to realize how his friends were talking about him.

Nature Girl was the first to break the silence, so suddenly that Josh wasn't sure if he'd fallen asleep and hallucinated it.

"Squid," Nature Girl said. After a moment, she added, "*Giant* squid."

Josh looked to the porthole. There was nothing but raw black. Anole sat on the other side of the porthole. From the way he peered back and forth, he couldn't see anything, either. "Where?"

Nature Girl gingerly raised a finger, pointing toward the far side of the capsule – and downward.

"She's heading away," Nature Girl said. Her voice sounded smaller than before. Lonelier. "We scared her."

Triage looked wide-eyed at the hull, though he couldn't have seen anything. "Do we need to brace for an attack, or something?"

"She would never hurt us," Nature Girl said accusingly.

"Sorry," Triage muttered.

Everyone's voices sounded strange to Josh's ears. Higher pitched, but not so high that they sounded like they'd been inhaling helium. (According to their pre-mission reading, some older sea habitats *had* used helium in their air mixtures, leaving the squeaky-voiced crews hardly able to understand one another.) There was a strange, sonorous quality, too, that could just as easily have been inside Josh's ears rather than the actual sound.

"How much longer is this night gonna go on?" Triage complained, a few minutes after the squid "sighting".

Graymalkin checked his watch. "It is half-past nine o'clock in the morning."

Josh's eyebrows lifted. It didn't feel like morning. The darkness pressed in on all of them. To his body, this was the longest all-nighter he'd ever pulled, a four am that wouldn't end. The time of day no longer seemed real.

After an eternity of this, a single ray of light shone past the porthole.

It was like a solar ray, but coming from below rather than above. It was the wan white of fluorescent lighting.

All of Karma's admonishments couldn't keep her students in their seats.

Everyone but Josh and Nature Girl clustered around

the porthole. Even Graymalkin gave into temptation and unbuckled his safety harness. Josh remained in his seat. As much as he wanted to see, he wanted to keep his distance from Anole even more. And he could still see a little from this angle.

The thin light from below, strangely enough, only made everything seem darker. The light shone through great, black, dusty clouds. For the first time, Josh saw how murky everything around them was.

"Did something kick up a lot of the sea floor?" Triage asked. He started to turn to Karma, but then darted his gaze to Nature Girl. He didn't have to say what they were all thinking. *Giant squid.*

"It's the smokers," Nature Girl said. Station X-41 was near Black Smokers' Trench, a canyon full of undersea geothermal vents. According to their briefing, it had been another reason why the X-Men had chosen this site for an undersea station, way back when. Beast had been interested in studying the trench. "They're pumping a lot of smoke and silt into the sea, and sometimes it drifts past the station." Her voice grew distant, as if a good part of her were elsewhere. "They host a really quite complex ecosystem."

"I didn't think there'd be so much smoke..." Triage said.

Triage trailed off as he spoke. All of the others' eyes were riveted to the porthole. They must have seen something. It was a while before Josh saw it too. By the time Josh did so, the descent capsule was drifting alongside it.

A big metal husk rose out of the gloom. Station X-41. Josh had seen pictures of it that made him think of a shuttered auto plant, an abandoned museum, a haunted library, and all at the same time. None of those seemed accurate now. The old photographs had been too grainy, and the light too blurry. The reality carved out in front of him by the station's thick floodlights was much more sharply defined.

The station stood off the seafloor on six legs. It was a huge, oval-shaped metal slab – and bigger than Josh had expected, about half the length of a football field. It was wider below than above. From what Josh remembered from their briefing, the station had three decks, and the third was the smallest. It also had most of the station's livable space. Much of the rest was utility cabins and machinery.

The more Josh saw of the station and its smooth curves, the more he realized what it really reminded him of. It looked like a crashed alien spacecraft, sunk to the bottom of the ocean. Its hull was stained an ugly black and gray from years of the geothermal vents' soot. But its exterior lights were clear. They shone fiercely into the gloom. They must have emerged from some kind of retractable cover when Graymalkin sent the station its wake-up call.

Graymalkin returned to his seat to guide the capsule through what seemed like a mostly automated docking process. He frowned at his display, and at several points seemed close to asking Karma for help, but always held off. Every time that happened, a pit in Josh's stomach opened a little wider.

Karma finally raised her voice loud enough to get the others to return to their seats. With their heads out of the way, Josh got a better view. The station's lights spiked into the drifting clouds. Particulates from the smoke drifted past them. Josh remembered standing in an empty mall parking lot after midnight, looking up into snowfall.

Graymalkin's watch said the night had been over hours ago, but morning never came down here. There was still an agonizing wait for docking and disembarkment.

Finally, at eleven o'clock in the morning of their endless midnight, the descent capsule clamped onto the station's waterlock.

CHAPTER FIVE
Anole

Vic couldn't explain why his nerves were so keyed up. Or, rather, which of the thousand reasons his nerves *had* to be keyed up was the most responsible. It could have been the sleep deprivation. The rolling deck. The caffeine and energy drinks he'd gulped down (bad idea, it turned out he hadn't needed help to stay awake). The heavy, coppery-tasting air. The muted pain in his joints. The nausea rolling in his stomach.

Or it could have been Josh Foley, sitting at the other side of the capsule, trying to look unobtrusive.

Vic hadn't planned on ever turning his back on Josh Foley. But the restlessness of twenty-three hours in the descent capsule stacked up more than he'd thought. His nerves itched to *do* something. When the capsule clanked onto the station's waterlock, he was first in line at the hatch.

He was premature. Karma and Graymalkin had yet to verify that the atmosphere on the other side was both breathable and warm. Their probes tested the air in the waterlock. Vic drummed his fingers on the hatch – first from his normal-sized hand, and then his big and gangly one.

Karma passed around palm-sized black devices on wristband straps. Vic's brain was so fried that he'd forgotten about them. Air quality sensors. "Wear them on your wrists, strap them to your belt, I don't care," Karma said. "Just keep them on you at all times. Don't underestimate how dangerous air trapped in confined spaces can be. The ventilation system could have had any number of problems. If you hear yours go off, don't look around for the cause, just run right back to the descent capsule. Got it? I don't want to see any of you so much as making a middle-of-the-night trip to the bathroom without these."

The next step was to crack the hatch open and let their air quality sensors get a good whiff of what was on the other side.

The air that rushed out was strangely warm and musty smelling. Someone behind Vic coughed loudly. Karma said, "Yes, the air mixture down here is a little different. It might take you a bit to get used to breathing it."

"You mean, adjust to the smell," Triage said.

"It'll happen faster than you think," Karma said. "Speaking from experience."

Despite the smell, none of their air quality sensors went off. This mix was breathable, at least. "Smells like fried gym sock," Josh noted. Vic bristled, like he bristled at everything Josh said.

"It reminds me of gunpowder," Graymalkin said.

The hatch rolled open into darkness.

Just when Vic was about to ask if it was supposed to be that way, Karma said, "Huh." The trepidation in her voice didn't soothe Vic's nerves. "Usually the interior lights turn on when the exterior ones do."

Gradually, his eyes adjusted. There *was* light on the other side. A thin, almost invisible bar of it flickered on the ceiling, accompanied by the buzz of a failing fluorescent.

"We know what our first repair job is going to be, then," Karma said. Any hint of nerves was either gone or hidden.

"De-creepifying the place," Triage said.

"I'll tell you the truth," she said. "It's always going to be a little bit creepy."

Even after the air pressures equalized and the wind stopped, Vic couldn't escape the impression that something was breathing on him. The surprising heat on the other side didn't help.

More light spilled from the crack of an almost-closed hatch just ahead.

"Don't worry," Graymalkin said. "There's no reason to be afraid of the dark while I'm around."

That was true, and yet Vic had trouble convincing his feet to step forward. He mentally kicked himself for being first at the door. It took Karma clearing her throat to get him to push into the dark.

"Hey, aren't lizards able to see in the dark better than people?" Josh asked.

"Actually, we have worse night vision than baseline humans," Vic said. If Josh Foley wanted to pretend to be less of a bigot, he could start with his language. "And I am 'people.'"

Josh didn't have anything to say to that. Vic had hoped he wouldn't. He didn't want to hear an apology.

He stumbled through the door. Things got better once he

stumbled as far as the next hatch. All of the station's hatches unlocked with the spin of a big, heavy wheel. The wheel stuck at first. Graymalkin stepped next to Vic. Together, they yanked it open. Light spilled into the corridor. Vic was finally able to orient himself.

The station map they reviewed in their briefing looked nothing like the real thing, of course – the real thing looked dirtier and dingier – but it was better than nothing.

This third, uppermost deck was the smallest on the station, but it was where Vic hoped to spend most of his off-time. It was where the best quarters were. Station X-41 had been built for diplomatic conferences between mutants and Atlanteans. That meant private cabins for VIPs. Since there were no diplomatic guests now, or ever again, there was no reason why the training team couldn't take those quarters for themselves.

Hatches all along the next corridor led to those cabins. Farther on, the corridor terminated in a passage to the conference room, and another hatch to the hydroacoustics communications cabin. Opposite the latter, a corrugated metal staircase and thin railing led down into shadow.

"Graymalkin, why don't you go to hydroacoustics and float our radio buoy?" Karma said. "The rest of you, let's survey the place. Take note of any damage."

The station had a radio buoy they'd send to the surface. The buoy would pick up the station's acoustic pings and then retransmit them as radio. That way, they could stay in touch with the *Xcaliber*. Vic didn't know why Karma was parking Graymalkin up here if the rest of the station was having more lighting problems. Maybe that was the point, though. Keep them all out of their comfort zones.

The deck underfoot was a soft, spongy substance. Some kind of nonslip surface. The corridors were wider than Vic expected. That was nice. Three of him could have walked side by side. That made sense, in retrospect. This station had been made by mutants, for mutants. They'd want to fit people up to Colossus-sized through here. That made things easier on Vic's overgrown right arm, too.

Vic spun the wheel on the hatch to the conference room and peeked inside. This was the only interior cabin he'd seen photographed. Karma had shown them all pictures of Charles Xavier, Headmaster Summers (not that Cyclops had been a headmaster back then), Jean Grey, Storm, Wolverine, and Iceman seated together with Prince Namor and other Atlantean nobility. They'd either smiled or glowered at the camera as their characters allowed. The conference room had the largest window on the station, framed behind all of them. Outside, the rays of the station's exterior lights beamed into the oceanic night.

The conference room had looked a lot brighter and cleaner back then. The big table was still there, scratched up but imposing. Twelve seats stacked atop it like closing time at a diner. The picture window was closed up under heavy steel shutters, big gray slats. Two of the seven overhead light panels were out.

There were more workstations and controls around the periphery than the photograph had captured. The conference room doubled as the station's command center. And no wonder – with one exception, the conference room was the largest cabin on the station. They couldn't waste all that space. There was a great deal to monitor and control: sensors, sonar, tectonics, atmospherics, and the station's electrical defense grid.

During their assignment briefing, Karma told them that

another repair team had upgraded some of the electronics "a while back". That, too, must have been years ago. Vic spotted a pair of CRT monitors wired into the corner of the ceiling. Not even flatscreens. No controls other than knobs for brightness and contrast.

The conference room's electronics had come from a different era. Among the simple switches, dials, and monochrome green screens, little receipt-sized matrix printers abounded. It had taken Vic a moment to grasp that some of the computers *printed* all of their output rather than displaying it on a monitor.

The place looked and felt like a museum of technology. Anole sniffed, expecting a burning dust scent from the station's heaters. Nothing. The smell of the air mixture was still too strong. It made the back of his tongue taste like cotton.

Vic only just stopped himself from jumping when something in the bulkheads *thumped*. Graymalkin must have released their radio buoy.

Vic didn't linger. While he'd been poking around, the others had gone right for the guest cabins. Despite how long he'd been up, he had no desire to sleep. He couldn't imagine the others felt much differently. He jogged to keep up with Karma.

Karma went right for the last hatch on the row. She opened the hatch, peered inside, and then hiked her thumb at the darkness. "This one's mine," she said.

"Dibs on that one," Triage said quickly, nodding to the next closest hatch.

The others were a little slower to catch on to the fact that there were only five of the private quarters to go around. It gave Anole time to peek inside one of the cabins, make sure he wasn't grabbing anything with a mold problem or worse, before calling dibs. Next was Nature Girl. And then, with a long pause for the sake of being polite, Graymalkin.

That left Josh without. He stood to the side, having never bothered to enter the race. Good. Josh could share the crew quarters below with the Atlantean.

Karma closed the door on hers without even dropping her bag. "Don't get too settled in," she said. "Lots of work to do before it's safe to rest." Either Josh or Triage must have muttered something snarky, because Karma said, "You really want to know how many times I've had to fight sleep deprivation on a mission? A day without sleep is kid stuff, especially at your age. Get to it. Check out the lower decks."

Vic had steadied his nerves enough to once again go ahead. The sooner he got this over with, the sooner he could stop feeling like something or someone was here waiting for them. He stepped to the corrugated staircase and started down.

He kept a tight grip on the railing as he descended. No footsteps followed him. He kept expecting the stairs and floors to be wet, but the station's interior was dry as Magneto's sense of humor.

The second level's main corridor was the same width and height as the one above, but somehow it seemed more confining. Vic needed a moment to pin down the difference. It was in the noise. The deck here was corrugated metal plates rather than the nonslip matting above. The plates rattled underfoot. Down here, he was also closer to the station's rumbling old generators, and to the complex chemical factory of its atmospherics system. The vents pinged and popped and hissed with sounds carried up from below. The lighting here was in worse shape, too. Half of the overheads were out.

More of what he'd learned in their briefing was breaking through his mental fog, though. Most cabins had lockers of emergency supplies. The nearest was at the base of the stairs. Its hinges screamed when he opened it. He pulled out a big, heavy flashlight only a little smaller than his forearm.

It wouldn't turn on. He opened the back, and found batteries so corroded they'd melted into the flashlight's frame. *Damn.* They'd been told that wouldn't happen.

He spun the nearest hatch's wheel, pushed it open, and peeked in. The station's little kitchenette was right where it should have been. Electric stove, grimy-looking countertop, metal cabinets and cupboards. When he turned back around, he nearly stepped into Nature Girl.

He tried and failed to not appear startled. "You're quiet," he said.

She tilted her head. "The rest of the world is loud."

He didn't know much about Nature Girl. According to their pre-mission briefing, her given name was Lin Li, but it didn't feel right to call her that yet. Not until he knew her better, or even knew if that was the name she preferred. Mutant names and callsigns could be a touchy subject at the Institute, and Vic didn't doubt it was the same at the Jean Grey School. It was better to play it safe with her callsign until she said otherwise.

They were alone for the moment. Triage and Graymalkin's voices echoed down the stairwell, but they weren't getting closer. Graymalkin must have pulled him aside to help with hydroacoustics. And Josh had wisely decided that he'd rather not be close to Vic without Karma interceding between them.

"Except down here…" Nature Girl added.

It seemed plenty loud enough to Vic. The more he paid

attention to the pops, pings, and cracking noises from the vents, the more they worried him. He wondered if the station's atmospherics system would always sound like that. He held his air quality monitor up to a vent. No alarm. The end of the hall had another emergency locker. The flashlight from *that* one worked. It flickered a few times when he switched it on, but then the beam held steady.

The next hatch groaned as he shoved it open. The lights on the other side were completely out. Vic's flashlight showed him a cramped workstation, with rows of metal dials, knobs, and more wall-mounted printers. Emergency control cabin. After a quick survey, he shut the hatch again.

Nature Girl stopped by two open passages. No hatches on these. They were at the center of the station, though. Only the rooms around the periphery, or that otherwise had an essential need to be secured, had hatches. Privacy was nonessential. Vic gave the two cabins a cursory look. Racks of hard cots lined the bulkheads, army-barracks style. At least Josh would be uncomfortable. Not that *any* of them would be comfortable, but he would be less so.

If the upper deck had been "cramped but livable", the middle deck was "cramped but survivable". It had everything people would need to survive, but not much more. In addition to the kitchenette, they also had a "dining room" that, according to the station plans, doubled as a break room. Vic couldn't imagine relaxing in there. It was smaller than his dorm room at the Institute. All it had was a bolted-down table and three chairs.

"Break-down room," Vic muttered. If Nature Girl appreciated it, she didn't say anything. If he'd had to choose a place to descend into madness, this would have been near the top of the list. It had all the charm of the cement-and-brick warren of freezers, refrigerators, and the tiny staff restroom in the back of the convenience store he'd used to work at back in Indiana. Some of the other staff would go there to cry after encounters with abusive customers. This place had the same mood: pervasive, stressful, industrialized depression.

There were no bathrooms up here. The kitchenette had no sink. The only running water on the station would be on the bottom deck, in the sealed-off section called the "wet cabins". That seemed like an excessive precaution to Vic until, during their briefing, Karma had explained why: it was as much to keep odors isolated from the station as the moisture and humidity. The dry parts of the station had one big, integrated air supply, and the filters had only been meant to scrub the most dangerous contaminants. Anything that smelled bad would linger for a long time. She hadn't just been talking about bathroom stink, though, but mold and rot. Hence, no running water up here. Station X-41 had been developed with the ethos that the best way to preserve it was to keep it as desiccated as a pharaonic mummy.

The other hatches on this deck led to a small workshop, meant for quick assembly and repair jobs. One of the station's drysuits had been laid out on a table, in pieces. Vic circled it.

They were called drysuits because that was exactly what they were designed to do: keep their wearers dry. Vic and the others could have swum as they were, but the water was too cold to support that for long. The suits were filled with air, but more for insulation than any other reason. They were more like spacesuits than diving suits: huge, hulking things with astronaut-like bowl helmets, and motors strapped to the back. Vic lifted one of their arms. It took real effort.

At least they wouldn't have to use them for a number of days. The suits required a day's training before use, and their schedules were currently too full to allow it. He expected that most of their first full day here would be spent rooting through storage and painstakingly checking every drill, every soldering iron, and especially every flashlight and battery.

Now that they were here, the enormity of what they'd been asked to do was finally dawning on him, heavy as the weight of all the ocean overhead.

While he'd been mentally preparing himself for this expedition, Vic hadn't quite understood how isolated they'd be. The surface was only a mile overhead, after all… but the lengthy descent had driven home that more than physical distance separated them from the open sky. If they swam straight up while their bodies were acclimated to this pressure and air mixture, they'd die. Radio signals wouldn't penetrate that far into water. Acoustic communications were much more tenuous. Earth might as well have been the moon.

He'd never felt a pit in his stomach quite like this one. He desperately hoped that was the sleep deprivation affecting him. He took a deep breath and, careful to keep his expression neutral, tried to focus on the job.

The deck had two more cabins: one for food and basic supplies (mostly empty now), and another that held the station's freshwater tanks and water filtration system. Other than looking both cabins over, Vic and Nature Girl didn't spend long in either of them. All the indicator lights on the filtration system were green – and good thing, too, that would have sent them back home right there. They couldn't go on without drinkable water.

Not, Vic thought, that going right back home would have been all that bad.

Nature Girl stuck close to Vic. He was glad for that. He didn't know if it was nerves or sleep deprivation, but he was getting increasingly apprehensive about going to the third and lowest deck alone. It was like descending into the cellar of a house that had been abandoned so long ago that it *had* to be haunted.

To keep his mind off it, he asked, "Did you sign up for this trip, or get drafted like me?" It was hard to keep the resentment out of his voice.

Nature Girl surprised him when she said, "I volunteered."

He glanced over. "For *here?*" he asked, as if that hadn't been exactly what she'd just said.

She didn't point that out beyond a quick roll of her eyes. "I told you the world was quieter down here. I was hoping it would be."

"Quieter than– ooh, you mean your powers. Your animal empathy."

"And plant empathy," she was quick to add. "There's still life down here. But it's not as busy as on the surface."

"And you, um, wanted that?"

"Are you having hearing problems? Ears not quite pop right?"

"No, it's just–" Vic wouldn't have thought it was possible for a gay guy to be so awkward around girls, but here he was. "Let me try again. I don't understand. I thought you loved all of that."

"I do," she said.

Vic stopped at another staircase, longer than the last, descending into darkness. Vic stood at the top of the stairs. His courage oscillated like a sine wave. He took a breath, and then took the first step.

"That's the problem," Nature Girl said, in a smaller voice, as she and Vic headed downward.

He didn't have a chance to answer. A muted clanking echoed from below. He stopped. It was louder than any of the noises they'd heard so far, but also muffled, like it had come from behind a closed hatch. The tempo of Vic's pulse kicked up a measure. Nature Girl halted too.

"I'm sure it's nothing," she said.

"Could you not tempt fate aloud?" Vic asked.

"This isn't a horror movie, Anole."

Clang. Slightly different, shorter and sharper this time. Vic's stomach lurched. He tried to convince himself he hadn't heard it, but he couldn't do it.

"You sure about that?" he asked.

He and Nature Girl stood at the edge of the next staircase, looking down. Neither of them moved. Nature Girl had a kind of nervous smile – the kind that said she didn't believe what they were both thinking, but still couldn't stop thinking it.

"Let's split up, gang," Nature Girl said. "What could possibly go wrong?"

CHAPTER SIX
Anole

One thing Vic had learned during his time at the Institute was that the quiet mutants tended to be the snarkiest. "I could let you go down first," he said. She didn't have anything to say after that.

One of his mutant powers was color-changing chromatophores in his skin. He could camouflage like a chameleon. That wouldn't be much good at the moment. He had specially made clothes with artificial chromatophores that would camouflage with them but, like an idiot, he'd worn ordinary jeans and a polo to try to stay comfortable during the descent.

He could have stripped them off to blend in, but he wasn't willing to say he was that anxious yet. Not in front of Nature Girl. She might take that entirely the wrong way. She didn't go to the Institute; she didn't know he wasn't interested in girls.

He glanced behind them. Still no sign that the others were finished with whatever had held them up. Swallowing, he started down again. Nature Girl kept a few steps behind him. Without her, he probably would have turned around.

These stairs were longer than the last. The station's third, bottom deck had higher ceilings than the others. The power generators and atmospherics plant took up most of that. The extra distance left Vic feeling like he was descending from a cellar into a tomb.

His flashlight was still all the light they had until they reached the hatch at the bottom. He spun the wheel open.

For once, none of the lights at the bottom were out. Vic was going to have to talk with Karma about that. Neither the lights nor the emergency flashlights were supposed to be in as bad a shape as they'd found them. That was another thing that would worry the hell out of him if he thought about it too much, so he made an effort not to.

There were more hatches down here than elsewhere. Two bisected the corridor. They were there for emergencies, if part of the station needed to be sealed off. This section, so close to the wet cabins and the diving pool, was more susceptible to flooding. If the station suffered a sudden air pressure drop anywhere, even in the upper decks, water wouldn't just come spilling through the leak – it would push up through the diving pool, too.

Vic traced the noise to a single hatch, to their left. In class, Karma had once said that the best way to confront fear was to march right up to its source. He made himself believe that. He grabbed the hatch, but it stuck on him after a quarter of a turn. He shook his head and repositioned. He gripped the wheel with his much-larger right hand, and this time the wheel gave way with a *crack*. Nature Girl flinched.

Noise spilled out of the crack in the hatch. Noise, and no light. A twisted jungle of shadows leapt out alongside the beam. The station's atmospherics system took up most of the space on the other side of the hatch. It looked like a factory, shrunk to room-scale. Big, silo-looking gas canisters, pipes everywhere, and rumbling metal boxes with vents lay everywhere. For a delirious moment, Vic imagined looking down and seeing a fleet of tiny tanker trucks lumbering between his legs.

The pings and pops were much louder here. A hiss briefly screeched from the valve of one of the gas cylinders. A hose connected to the wall gurgled three times. Something higher up in the ductwork *clinked* several times, coming closer to the floor each time, as if some piece of debris had shaken loose and was falling down it. When he pointed his flashlight upward, the beam got lost in a labyrinth of ventilation ducts so thick that he couldn't see the ceiling. The loudest and most persistent noise, though, was the rumbling of fans. The noise vibrated with a resonance that made Vic's teeth feel like they were grinding.

The cabin had too many shadows, corners, and nooks to check from the entranceway. With a sigh – a grim acceptance of the fact that *of course* he would have to go in, just like a horror movie – Vic stepped inside, and made a careful circuit of the cabin.

His flashlight cast so many moving shadows across the fringe of his vision that he felt surrounded by them. He had more than one reason to feel uneasy. Whenever he stepped on a certain part of the deck, the sound of one of the fans changed. It went lower, like it was starting to grind. He tested it until he saw duct walls bowing inward. It was causing a fan blade to clip its casing.

That couldn't have been intended. The system's structure must have settled over the years.

The atmospherics system had plenty of built-in alarms that should have sounded if anything had gone wrong, but, after seeing how many of the lights had failed, Vic didn't trust them. He held his air quality monitor at different heights, checking for any pockets of unbreathable air that might have settled.

Again, no alarms. Things seemed to be working fine. No one hid here, no matter how much Vic's imagination insisted they were just under the next shadow.

"You owe me for going first," he told Nature Girl.

"You've got that huge arm to defend yourself," she said. "Down here, I'm just a normal human. Aside from the antl–"

Clank.

Vic's muscles were keyed up. He couldn't keep himself from jumping. The noise was louder this time, but still muffled. It hadn't come from this cabin.

Vic and Nature Girl looked at each other.

"It really is probably nothing," Nature Girl said.

Vic stepped back out into the corridor. If he trusted his hearing – big *if* at this air pressure – the clank had come from behind one of two hatches at the far end of the corridor. His memory of the station map said the two power generators. The closest hatch would go to the main generator, and the farthest to the backup.

"Give me the flashlight," Nature Girl said. "I'll go first this time."

"Get your own flashlight," Vic told her. "I'm not actually scared." *Definitely not,* he told himself. It was just that he had an iron grip on his flashlight now, and the thought of going without it made something inside him crumple.

That was all. Not the same thing as fear.

He approached the closest of the hatches and spun it unlocked. As much as Vic tried to fake nonchalance, when he pulled the hatch the rest of the way open, the first thing he did was aim his flashlight inside like it was a loaded weapon.

He wasn't sure what he expected to find amiss. Every iota of his rational judgment said it couldn't have been an intruder, not unless that intruder had coincidentally arrived on the same day as their team. All he knew was that he was taut as a bowstring and that phantom heat was back in his cheeks. His body expected a fight.

The less rational side of him couldn't help thinking about the diving pool, and what might have slithered up. The pool was supposed to be secured from the outside, but he didn't know how reliably. Then he couldn't shake thinking about the lights, and the idea that the reason so many of them had burned out was they'd been *on* all this time, while someone lived here.

The main generator took up most of the space inside. It was an unassuming metal cylinder that stretched from the deck to the ceiling. The top of it was wreathed in a crown of wires. They unfurled darkly overhead. The lights were working, but shadows splattered over the deck. Stepping into the cabin was like stepping under the bough of a dead tree.

This cabin wasn't as filled with pipes and other machines as atmospherics, and the shadows didn't writhe as much, but there were still plenty of places where anything could have concealed itself. Vic walked the circumference of the generator. There was nothing hidden, but also nothing that seemed likely to have made the noise.

The power generator itself was silent. It was a microfusion power plant – new, experimental, and highly classified tech at the time the station had been built. By the X-Men's standards, it was a little past "old hat" now. These days, Beast was playing with string deconstructors, repulsor tech nodes, and quantum scraping when he wasn't just skimming energy off the top of energy-rich parallel universes.

All of the indicator lights on the generator's one control panel were a steady green. It only output a trickle of the power that a larger fusion cell might have provided, but it was enough for the station. The generator had been made to never need to be opened, never need maintenance. It was just sealed power in a can – sink and forget, good for a hundred years.

Then again, the lights were supposed to have lasted a few more decades, too.

The backup generator was in the next cabin over. Vic stepped back outside, and over to its hatch. Its cabin was smaller than the last, and so was the generator. Otherwise, the two looked very similar, except a few more of the ceiling lights were out.

A thin breeze brushed Vic's face. He halted underneath a ventilation duct. The cool air felt nicer than he thought it would. Like any cold-blooded creature, he was accustomed to paying close attention to his body heat, but he'd lost track of it over the past few minutes. He'd started to overheat. He looked up, angling his face into the draft.

Beside him, Nature Girl asked, "You watch many classic horror movies? Ever seen *Alien*? That scene in the warehouse-looking area, with all the chains and dripping water…"

Just like that, the peaceful moment was over. He was suddenly conscious of the bundles of wires overhead, dangling down almost to his scalp. "I hate you," Vic said. "You have no idea how much I hate you."

"'Here, Jonesy, Jonesy... here, kitty...'"

"I had no idea you knew this much about horror movies. From what I heard about you on the *Xcaliber*, I always thought you just, you know, hung around outside with animals."

"And plants," Nature Girl said. "But it's not like I didn't have a phone. Or other interests."

"That's fair," Vic admitted.

"Besides," she said, after a moment, "that movie had a very good cat."

Something shifted out of the corner of Vic's eye. He shone his flashlight toward the motion. The beam showed him a mesh ventilation grate he hadn't noticed before. It was about a foot off the ground, and two feet tall. There was nothing else there, and nothing moving.

The half-dead overhead lights left too many shadows. Vic would have shrugged the motion off as his imagination if Nature Girl hadn't gone very still. She'd seen something too. He froze. He was suddenly hyperaware of all of the cabin's noises, from the hissing of the ventilation to the electrical buzzing behind the walls.

Whatever the motion had been, it couldn't have been an animal. Rats couldn't have survived here so long. More to the point, though, Nature Girl would have been able to sense an animal.

He rounded the generator's corner, flashlight leveled. He swept the light across the deck. Gradually, he made a circuit of the cabin. Nature Girl followed silently.

He turned and saw her standing by the same mesh ventilation grate where they'd started – which was now open.

In the instant before he could say anything, the grate swung closed.

The slam was large enough to make them both jump – even Vic, who had seen it coming. Nature Girl leapt with astonishingly leonine reflexes and planted her back against the generator. Vic leaned forward, his hands on his knees, his heart slamming on his ribs.

If he'd had the breath, he might have laughed. A loose ventilation grate, clanging open and closed with the breath of the station's uneven drafts.

"Well," Nature Girl said, when she could speak again, "I was hoping there wouldn't be a jump scare."

"You *wanted* it to be an *Alien* alien?" Vic asked. Knowing that the Brood was somewhere out there, in real life, was bad enough.

"Something that would make me feel a little less stupid for being afraid of it, sure."

Vic cracked a grin while he caught his breath. Just about anyone else at the Institute would have been making fun of him for days, and he would have deserved it.

All they had left to explore was the diving pool and its adjoining compartments, the so-called wet cabins. Vic had no idea if that was their official name or not, but it stuck in his imagination. It was evocative and a little bit gross.

The wet cabins were separated from the main corridor by two hatches in a row. It was like an airlock. They closed the first hatch behind them. Humid air washed over Vic the second he swung the second hatch open.

The wet cabins' air supply was insulated from the rest of the station behind layers of filters and an inward-blowing pressure differential. The air on the other side *tasted* different. It had a metallic tang.

By the standards of the surface world, the cabin on the other side wasn't all that large. About the size of two of the Institute's classrooms shoved together. After a day in the descent capsule and a tour of this cramped station, though, Vic felt like he'd stepped into a cavern. This was the largest cabin on the station. The ceiling was just as high as it had been in atmospherics and the generator chambers, but nothing hung from the ceiling except a quartet of rotary ceiling fans.

This place had plenty more than just the diving pool. Three rows of cabinets and counters ran through the room, all covered with tarp to protect from dust and moisture. The lumpy shapes underneath were faucets, beakers and glassware, microscopes, and similar equipment. This had been a laboratory.

Though Station X-41's primary mission hadn't been scientific, when Beast had drawn up the plans for it, he hadn't been able to resist adding this. The tools were no doubt meager and primitive by his current standards. Vic would have bet reasonable money that, somewhere inside the cabinets, he'd find knives and dissection trays for examining deep sea fauna, and refrigerators to keep their parts preserved. Nature Girl might have been thinking the same. She stepped around the laboratory counters with a raised eyebrow and a markedly skeptical expression.

The diving pool was on the far side of the cabin. From this far away, he saw only a big, circular depression built right into the deck, ringed by railings. It reminded him a little of the entrance to the shallow side of a swimming pool. Nonslip stairs led down into it from all sides.

The stairs terminated in a solid titanium hatch. The pool was closed now. Good. Vic didn't want to know how quickly his claustrophobia would lurch into agoraphobia if he looked down and saw the deep ocean.

There were two other cabins in this sealed-off section of the station. Both their hatches were to Vic's left. The first led to their laundry and showers, and the second to the toilets. For the first time, it occurred to him to wonder exactly how cramped, smelly, and awful both would get. He shuddered. If anything, the humidity here made the station smell worse. He just hoped the last visitors cleaned out the bathrooms really well before they left.

The churning of the atmospherics plant was muted in here. It was almost quiet. The lights were all working fine. They reflected in a distorted sheen off the railing guarding the diving pool. Nature Girl frowned and rubbed along the rail with her finger.

"It's wet," she said.

Vic stopped beside her. It sometimes grossed the other Institute students out how often he used his tongue, even though they were mutants too. He never forgot the look that *Glob Herman*, of all people, gave him after he used his tongue to catch a falling smartphone. Glob could be astonishingly expressive for a mutant with lidless eyes floating around in the gelatinous mass of his head.

Funny how Vic could hesitate to be himself even around other mutants. But, what the hell. Nature Girl ought to understand. She knew how lizards smelled best. He flicked his tongue out over the railing. He didn't extend it far enough to touch it, but enough to sample the air, and drag some of it back toward his nose. He sniffed.

"Salt water," he said, with a growing sense of wrongness.

Nature Girl looked around. Vic spotted more flecks of water dotting the stairs and the deck. He stooped, and flicked his tongue out again. His sense of smell was sharp enough to distinguish between warm and cold water. This water hadn't been cold. If it had just seeped in, it should have been as cold as the ocean around them.

Any seawater previous crews had dragged in would have evaporated long ago. There would have just been rimes of salt left. And there was no dusting of salt to show that this was a leak or any other recurring issue.

He looked up at Nature Girl. She bit the bottom of her lip. All around them, silence.

Almost. Something was, very quietly, shuffling. It was like burlap rustling, or two pieces of cloth rubbing together.

Vic tilted his head, all of his focus on his hearing. Now that he was paying attention, he could tell it was close. Too close. Not just in the same room, but right there – beside them.

One of the plastic covers that had been thrown over a laboratory counter was twitching. As he and Nature Girl watched, it rustled again.

The flashlight's grip bit into Vic's palm before he realized he was holding it any tighter. It didn't feel like even the meager protection it had before. Rolling his feet to move quietly, he stepped around the side of the counter.

The deck below was empty. Whatever was moving the cover wasn't there. As Vic watched, though, the cover moved again.

It had to be on top of the counter. Whatever was moving couldn't have been larger than a housecat. Nothing bigger could have fit under the dust cover, not unless there was a gap or trashcan. He looked to Nature Girl. She raised her hands, plainly as confused as he was. Not an animal, then, whatever it was.

He grabbed the corner of the cover. Raised it slightly. At that motion, the lump stopped moving. Nature Girl stepped to Vic's side and grabbed the next corner.

Together, they yanked.

In a terrific clatter of crashing metal, breaking glassware, and smashing ceramics, half of the counter's contents tumbled to the deck. The chaos was so abrupt and noisy that it took Vic several seconds to find the source of the motion.

It wasn't a creature. An object. A big metal cylinder sitting on the countertop, arms extended outward and molding into two black discs.

As Vic watched, the arms raised. Then, as if after a moment of reflecting upon the rubble, lowered. It was some kind of agitator, sized for laboratory glassware. Probably something Beast had rigged up to keep solutions from settling. It must have been plugged in and left switched on. When the rest of the station had powered up, so had it.

Vic hadn't realized he'd been holding his breath until now. He took several steps backward, trying to breathe. Adrenaline pumped through him.

There was only so much anxiety and tension he could take while this sleep deprived.

He was so focused on soothing his nerves that the sound of the hatch behind him opening didn't register. By the time it did, it was too late. He'd already taken his next step back.

He bumped into something cold, wet, and ridged like bone. Something, someone, that was as tall as he was.

He leapt forward, scrambling for – he didn't know what for.

To reach cover behind the counters, maybe. He slipped off the still-wet deck, and he went crashing knees-first to the floor. The pain wasn't quite enough to keep him from whirling around, ready to use his flashlight as a club.

A blue-skinned Atlantean stood in the open hatchway. He had solid red eyes, glowing and unblinking, and a damp towel slung over his shoulders. A whorl of the towel was bundled around his finger and halfway into his aural canal, as if he'd just been in the middle of cleaning his ears.

"There you are," Crosta said. "Finally. I was wondering when you'd arrive. But *must* you have made that damn racket?"

CHAPTER SEVEN
Anole

By the next morning – or "morning" – Vic still hadn't pieced his nerves back together.

Fortunately, the biggest effect it had on his nerves was that it left him grumpier than normal, so he doubted anyone noticed. He was always going to be irritable around Josh. Only now he had a second person to hold responsible for it.

"There's a limit to the number of times I'll apologize," Crosta said. "Arriving early seemed like a reasonable thing to do. I still don't understand why it wasn't."

Karma had called them all to the conference room on the upper deck. It was the first time they'd all been in the same place together since everyone had rushed down to the diving pool yesterday. After that, Vic hadn't thought he'd sleep for another three days, but that had been before Karma had put them to work cleaning up the mess and then reviewing the rest of the station. They needed rest, she'd said, but they also didn't need to be jolted awake by a power failure, electrical short, or atmospherics alarm.

After hours spent crawling around the generators, spelunking through crawlspaces, and getting covered in dust and oil, exhaustion had settled over Vic's shoulders like a lead-lined cloak. He didn't remember collapsing into bed, just dragging himself up to his quarters. He'd woken face down on a bare mattress pad, the bedsheet he'd been told to bring still neatly folded in his pack.

He'd not woken happy. Vic's mouth tasted like week-old death. It hadn't gone away after guzzling and spitting water. And of course the water here tasted weird – metallic and fulsome, like the air. Vic hoped his body was getting used to it. And that his body *could* get used to it.

In the conference room, someone had opened the picture window's shutters. The steel slats had lifted like venetian blinds. The old photograph with the X-Men hadn't done the view justice. The station's exterior lamps streamed into the abyss, the beams bright as moonlight.

The clouds of soot from Black Smokers' Trench had vanished while they slept. The geothermal fissures didn't vent every hour of every day. Their activity came and went. Now the station's lights lit hundreds of feet around them. The seafloor, black and blue under the station's pale lights, stretched into a dusty eternity. The shadows carved cliffs and crevices underneath the lights. There was no life, nor sign of it, and no sky.

Nighttime over an alien planet. The station's clocks said it was 5:15 am, but as far as Vic's internal clock was concerned, he'd fallen asleep in the night, and woken in the night.

The station's old analog clock reading the time was all the morning they were going to get. According to that clock, Vic had slept for nine hours, but he still felt exhausted.

Karma looked the same as ever. Maybe the lines under her eyes were a little more severe, but her laptop screen's muted glow washed out the sharpness. Her hair wasn't even mussed. Vic supposed the X-Men were just used to this kind of thing. Nevertheless, she sounded nonplussed when she said, "You were supposed to arrive the day *after* we did."

"I wanted to make the journey early," Crosta said. "Your invitation included the codes to the door locks. Why else would you have given them to me?"

Vic had difficulty reading Atlantean body language. Crosta's flat red eyes and the bony, ichthyoid ridges along his face either didn't reveal his feelings at all or in a way that Vic recognized. Living at the Institute had accustomed him to social awkwardness, though. Crosta seemed twitchy. He kept folding and unfolding his arms and looking away from Karma when she spoke. He didn't not want to continue this conversation.

Karma dragged out the silence, forcing Crosta to add, "I wanted to get inside the station as soon as I could. I don't like swimming at this depth. The pressure is unbearable even given time to adapt, and the water is… poorly oxygenated. Your invitation said the diving pool entrance would be lit. It wasn't. I thought someone wanted to keep me out."

"We've had some trouble with the lights," Vic said drily.

"I've noticed," Crosta said, just as drily.

"You could have notified us to expect you," Karma said.

"How would I have done that?" Crosta asked.

"Left a sign or a note," Karma said. "My people thought you

were an intruder and reacted appropriately. We broke a lot of glass and lab equipment."

Vic still had deeply mixed feelings about Karma's classes, and school in general, but one thing that had boosted her as a person in his eyes was that she hadn't blamed him and Nature Girl for the damage to the laboratory.

When Crosta didn't reply, even after a long silence, Karma let out a deep breath. "All right. Water under the bridge, so to speak. We *are* glad to have you here. The X-Men are always eager to tighten ties with the Atlantean people."

"I'm not sure I am one of the Atlantean people," Crosta said.

"That's far from what Prince Namor told us," Karma said.

Their pre-mission briefing had included a segment on Crosta and the Atlanteans. Crosta's red eyes were not Atlantean-standard. Like Prince Namor himself, Crosta was a mutant. His eyes kept him from blending in among Atlanteans in the same way that Vic would never be able to fit in back home. Prince Namor had suggested that Crosta consider applying for training at the Institute. From the way Crosta was behaving, Vic guessed that the "suggestion" had been more of a "demand".

Crosta had the power to create massive, destructive shockwaves at will. They were apparently even deadlier underwater than in air. The shear could rip a person to shreds. Like the rest of the mutants here, his power wouldn't be directly applicable to repairing the station.

"I'm glad to be here," Crosta said, in a voice that made it evident that he was anything but. Vic watched Crosta and, after a moment, decided to believe that Crosta hadn't *meant* to sound angry. He just wasn't a very good actor.

"With that out of the way, let's get to what we came here

for," Karma said. "Hard work." The others were not yet awake enough to groan, but a collective breath sighed out of them.

"You could at least make it sound like you're not a prison guard," Josh said.

Karma just smiled.

Their mission brief had given them several areas of the station to repair, upgrade, or just maintain. The generators' coolant intakes needed to be scrubbed. Containments to be cleaned out of the airways. Atmospherics components to be replaced. The exterior hull needed to be scoured of soot buildup, and the station's defense grade repaired.

Karma's monitor showed the same deck schematics of Station X-41 she'd shown them in their briefing. Diagrams of decks one, two, and three were splayed out next to each other like the station had been dissected and pinned to her screen. At this distance, Vic couldn't read any of the text. Karma had used a drawing tool to mark red circles around some cabins.

"Of these, the defense grid is going to be the trickiest," Karma said. The station's primary mode of defending itself was a grid of conductive filaments wrapped around its hull. If the need arose, they could pump an incredible amount of wattage into the surrounding sea. "The last crew reported that it was starting to lose coverage in a few important areas, especially around the diving pool and the first deck's docking waterlock."

"Do you really think we'll need the defense grid?" Josh asked. "We've got a lot of other things on our plate."

"Always be thinking about self-defense," Karma told him. "That goes for all of you whether you're thinking about becoming an X-Man or not. Never take a trick out of your sleeve just because you think you won't need it. I don't need to tell most of you that just being a mutant will attract all kinds of hate, wherever you go."

Whether they'd consciously intended to or not, all of Karma's students had all sat so that they didn't have their backs to the hatch. But not Josh Foley. He didn't know what it was like being a mutant, and probably never would.

"We're going to have to adjust the scope of our work," Karma said. "There are a few other things we didn't plan on needing to do, but will need to."

"We were told none of the batteries here would erode," Vic said. "And that the lights wouldn't burn out."

"Not even Beast is perfect," Karma said.

"Beast designed all this?" Josh asked. He must have tuned out the part of the briefing that had gone over the station's history. "I thought he was supposed to be good."

If Anole had had hackles, they would have risen. Station X-41 had come out of an earlier stage in Beast's career, when the technology that had gone into it had been fantastic and experimental. Josh had no place criticizing a genius like Beast. Karma said, "The station's an engineering marvel when you look at all the challenges Beast and his crew surmounted. Back in the day, so much of the tech they'd used to build it had just been developed. They couldn't have done long-term testing." Karma paused. "At least not without time travel, and I'm sure *that* was a can of worms he didn't want to open right then. Not again."

The team lapsed into a sullen silence as Karma enumerated their tasks. It was more than just light bulbs. Their preliminary inspection had found dead and frayed wires, burned out old transistors, and, upstairs, readout tickers that refused to function. And that was without an exterior inspection. Vic would have bet most of his money that the defense grid was in worse shape now than when the last crew had left.

"So that's our list," Karma said, after she was finished overwhelming them. "Now. How would you all like to do this?"

They all stared at her.

"Well?" she prompted.

"Excuse me," Triage said. "Is telling us that *not* your job?"

"No, I'm your teacher. My job is to teach you. You're not going to have a teacher with you the rest of your lives. You're going to need to organize projects without guidance. And some of you," she said, her eyes flicking to Graymalkin and Triage, "have said you're interested in leadership."

Graymalkin shifted. This was probably far from what he'd had in mind. Nevertheless, he said, "We will try."

"You'll do it," Karma corrected. She looked around them. "I know how big this is. I've done it before. I'm going to place myself at your disposal to help with any tasks *other* than managing this project. Give me orders. Put me to work." She checked her watch. "After I finally catch some sleep."

Josh had been staring straight at the window, as if he hadn't been paying attention. Hearing that snapped him out of it. "You've been up this whole time? While we slept?"

"Someone had to be. On a mission, always sleep in shifts. Make sure somebody's watching your backs." Vic had no idea how the X-Men did it. If somebody had tried to make him stand a shift last night, he would have collapsed on the spot. He bet that he wasn't alone. Maybe that was why she'd never asked. "Mutants are an endangered species. It's not an accident that we're getting more endangered all the time."

With that cheering thought, she left them staring around the table at each other.

Vic looked across at Josh. This was the first time they'd been left in the same cabin together, without Karma, since this trip had started.

Graymalkin caught the look passing between Vic and Josh, sighed, and then slid Karma's laptop to his side of the table. "Well," he said, "this is going to be interesting."

The others were well aware of the tension between Vic and Josh. In the war of popular opinion, Vic knew he had the advantage. None of them seemed to like Josh. Not even Triage, the only one of them who would speak more than a few words to him.

But, annoyingly, none of them had overtly taken Vic's side yet. He didn't understand. They'd all had experiences that ought to have put them firmly against Josh. Any hope Vic had had that they were just holding back until Karma was out of earshot were dashed as soon as Karma left. They hardly looked at Josh. Josh stayed in the background, sullenly watching but not participating. There was going to be a reckoning sometime. Vic didn't know when, and he didn't even look forward to it, but it would happen.

Graymalkin stumbled along trying to use Karma's laptop until Triage sighed, pulled the laptop over to him, and asked Graymalkin to just tell him what he wanted to show. The meeting only got more awkward from there.

Vic's stomach roiled. Not quite hungry, not quite sick, but something that combined the worst of those. After the meeting, he stopped by the kitchenette, where someone – probably but not necessarily Karma – had brought their food from the descent capsule. He had his choice of an unappetizing mix of rice cakes, dry cereal, nutrition bars, jerky, and nuts. There were a few other things like oatmeal, but to get water to go with any of those, he'd have to trek down to the wet cabins, and eat there. He didn't have the energy right now.

To his dismay, he discovered that the last crews had left some food. There was a pile of dried black crud at the bottom of a cabinet that must have once been… Vic didn't even know what. And, strangely, five bottles of hot sauce. Four full, one half-empty. Their contents had settled into neat layers of peppers, red liquid chili, vinegar, and oils.

He couldn't tell any of the nutrition bars apart. Anything prepackaged had had to be unwrapped before coming down, lest the packaging implode. The bars had been wrapped in anonymizing cellophane. The most he could see of any of them was various shades of brown, with or without dark pieces.

He only ate until the pangs in his stomach stopped. Food tasted odd, dull and cheerless, like half of his taste buds had gone on strike. The station's smell had become a cloying feeling on the back of his tongue, and masked everything.

He'd been irritable and on edge ever since coming back from his trip home, and he was starting to think he'd never get back to normal again.

This was his "normal" now.

As Vic stepped out of the kitchenette, he passed Nature Girl and Josh on their way in. An angry heat rose to Vic's cheeks. But Graymalkin stood in a hatchway at the end of the corridor, chatting with Triage. Graymalkin gave Vic a warning look.

"What is with the antlers?" Josh asked.

Nature Girl tilted her head, and just looked at him. Her eyes were hard.

"Don't only male deer and elk have antlers?"

"Are all people in the non-mutant world that gender-essentialist?"

"Well," he said, caught off guard, "no, I mean, I think I was–"

"Josh," Vic said, a warning tone in his voice. He and Josh could spar freely. That was fine. But questioning who Nature Girl was was a step beyond. "Drop it."

Josh dropped it.

Though Graymalkin never said so aloud, he plainly put together the work crews in such a way as to keep Vic and Josh apart. Not a bad idea, though being treated like a potential problem still stung. No matter how many times their plans were revised, somehow they always ended up somewhere distant to each other. Vic ended up with Crosta in the wet cabins while Josh was somewhere up on deck two.

Vic and Crosta had been assigned to make that exterior inspection Vic had dreaded. At least in the station, he could avoid thinking about the icy water crushing in on them. Out there, it would be unavoidable. They hadn't gotten a good look at the station's defense grid during their descent. The filaments were hard to spot from a distance. On approach, Vic had only seen a few strands, reflecting light like dew on a spider's web.

Each strand of the defense grid was a silver filament about the width of Vic's fist. The station itself was shielded and well grounded, protected from its own discharges. The defense grid could discharge in all directions at once, or concentrate fire around a particular segment of the station. At least, that was the theory. The grid had corroded over the years. Parts of the mesh had lost connection. In a few places, filaments had cracked from the weight of soot from Black Smokers' Trench, like a house's roof caving in from too much snowfall. The last crew down had said some parts of the mesh were missing, but they hadn't had the parts to repair them.

While Crosta waited to dive, Vic stood at the hatch controls. The hatch was closed but he could still test the bar locks underneath it. "Testing" mainly meant opening and closing them a few times to make sure they didn't stick. The last thing they needed was for someone to get stuck out there because the mechanism had jammed over the years. He watched the indicator lights blink on and off.

Vic still struggled to read Crosta. He had no idea if Crosta's flatness, or at least what Vic was interpreting as flatness, was deliberate, or an artifact of the cultural and species barrier between them. To break the silence, Vic asked, "They didn't give you a choice about coming here either?"

For a long time, it seemed like the silence had neatly reassembled itself. Then Crosta said, "I chose to come here."

Vic had heard other students say the same words, with many different voices but always the same meaning, about the Institute. They'd "chosen" to go to the Institute. Like choosing between the rock and the hard place. The frying pan or the fire.

Unlike a lot of other mutants, Vic had a loving family. His parents were wonderful. But the last time he'd gone back home, to Indiana, the Purifiers had come looking for him. They'd taken his father hostage. Thinking of it made his vision flash white. Flashes of frozen images peppered his imagination. The bare metal skeleton of a bridge's underwork. A hulking, armored Purifier with a sword. His own blood, drizzled on metal.

His right arm, lying on the ground, far away from the rest of him.

Vic wouldn't have pried if they hadn't been alone. But he couldn't let that hesitation go unremarked upon, not if he and Crosta were going to spend the next ten days crammed in a steel can together. "You really don't sound like you did."

When Crosta said nothing, Vic said, "I get it."

"Do you?" Crosta asked. His affect was even flatter.

"You'd be surprised," Vic said. "You don't need to tell us your whole story. But some of us don't mind sharing ours. You might hear a few things that sound familiar."

"I don't know that I'll be here long enough to 'get to know' anyone. I've decided I'm not joining the Institute. This is only– I'm here for a few days, just to help."

Vic let that silence marinate while he finished testing the exterior locks. It was a long, tedious process, but they needed to go through it. They couldn't afford the hatch jamming while someone was out there.

"One would think," Crosta said, "that having Prince Namor, a mutant, as our monarch would change the way Atlanteans thought of other mutants."

"*One* would think a lot of things about people that turn out not to be true," Vic said. Wolverine had once been a member of the Avengers, but that hadn't changed the way humans thought about mutants, not in the long run.

Vic hit the toggle to open the big titanium hatch.

Until Vic and the others had a chance to train with the drysuits, no one but Crosta was allowed to dive, and Karma was still out like a sack of flour. Vic wasn't sure his lopsided regenerated arm would fit in the drysuits anyway.

The diving pool's hatch split in the middle, and ground slowly open. For the first time, Vic saw the open ocean with his bare eyes.

Now that he'd gotten more used to the station, he'd hoped the ocean wouldn't seem as intimidating. This morning, he'd looked out the conference room's picture window without getting dizzy.

But no, when the titanium hatch opened, a chill gripped his throat. He'd expected a black pool, a dead infinity. He'd forgotten how far off the seafloor the station was. The station's exterior lights shone straight down. All of Station X-41, including the docked descent capsule, could have fit into the water between this vantage and the seafloor and still leave space to spare. It made for a greater sense of vastness than a simple black abyss would have. Vic would have preferred the abyss.

There was a big difference between viewing the ocean through the window and seeing it directly. A big part of that difference was knowing he could fall in.

Crosta sat on the edge of the pool, swiveled his legs around, and slipped into the water. Vic winced. When Crosta's head bobbed above the surface, Vic asked, "You going to be able to handle the cold all right?"

"I wouldn't have been able to come here if I couldn't," Crosta snapped.

"Hey, I'm just checking on you. I don't want to assume anything. Even for Atlanteans, I'm guessing this is cold."

Crosta didn't say anything for a moment. He just looked at Vic. Gradually, his shoulders untensed. "I will be fine," he said, in a more even voice. Then he sank into the water.

After Crosta disappeared into the ocean, Vic headed upstairs to the conference room. Nature Girl was up there alone, silently working, running the radar and sonar tests Graymalkin had assigned her. The defense grid had its own workstation on the far side of the room. Vic sat, and tried to remember how he'd been told they worked. There was a big gulf between Karma's briefing and the reality in front of him. That reality included a lot of backlit white buttons with incomprehensible abbreviations. There were three different switches labeled "Start".

Crosta didn't have a radio. Radio signals wouldn't penetrate more than a few yards underwater, and he wouldn't have been intelligible speaking through one anyway. Every once in a while, he swam to the conference room's window and rapped on the acrylic glass. The first time, he'd made Vic and Nature Girl jump. Crosta pointed in the direction he'd made his most recent repairs. Vic ran a harmless test current through that section.

Nature Girl stood and stepped to a different console. Station intercom, Vic recalled. "Hey, Graymalkin?"

"Here," Graymalkin's static-scratchy voice answered, from wherever "here" was.

"I think something's wrong with the sonar. I keep getting weird signals."

"First of all, are you sure it *is* a glitch, and not something actually out there?"

"I'm not 'sure' of anything. Sometimes it's there, and sometimes it's not, and it's not showing up on radar. It would have to show up on radar, too, if it's real, right?"

"Maybe," Graymalkin said. He meant *he didn't know*, Vic thought. "It's not a school of fish, or something of that nature?"

"Fish don't travel in schools at this depth," Nature Girl said, like she was speaking to a child.

Graymalkin sighed. "Put it on the maintenance list."

Vic and Crosta made an efficient, if silent, team. Vic suspected Crosta preferred it this way. He certainly seemed more relaxed out there than he had inside. Nature Girl, too, remained silent. Every once in a while, her console *pinged*.

If the next ten days were going to be like this, Vic would go mad.

Crosta signaled to Vic that he was going back inside. Good enough time for a break. They'd been at it for hours. This station had been designed to accommodate many more guests and crew than just the seven of them, but Vic couldn't imagine this place at full occupancy. Even compared to the Institute, this was cramped. Despite Graymalkin's best efforts, Vic couldn't avoid Josh forever.

Vic was clomping down to the second deck when he looked up and saw Josh and Triage in the corridor. They were headed toward the same destination: the kitchenette. Vic swallowed hard, but didn't stop walking. Josh slowed. Vic hoped – expected – that Josh would find somewhere else to be. But Josh stepped into the kitchenette after Vic. Triage followed.

Vic grabbed a pair of nutrition bars without trying to guess what they were, and then a scoop of trail mix in a plastic cup. He still wasn't hungry. He just needed his stomach to not hurt. He was thirsty just looking at all the nuts and granola, but he wasn't about to trek down to the wet cabins just for a glass of water. That would have looked too much like he was retreating. Besides, something about the humidity down there made food taste even weirder. Everything still tasted bad, but at least up here it was a dull and tasteless weird.

He sat at the seat closest to the bulkhead, back to the wall. Josh carefully picked through the trail mix, depositing only the pretzels and chocolate on his paper plate.

"What the hell are you doing that for?" Vic asked.

Josh glanced sheepishly at him. "Something about this air makes everything taste awful. I used to like raisins. I can't stand them down here."

He was getting his grubby hands all over their food. "Did you wash up?"

"No," Josh said, and then with a bitterness he'd held back so far asked, "Have you?"

Well – no. And Josh had just seen him come down from the first deck, so there was no point in denying it.

Vic asked, "Can't you two just use your healing powers to make your sense of taste normal again?"

Josh and Triage looked at each other. "It doesn't work like that," Triage said.

"Yeah? Why not?"

Triage scooped up a bowl of dry honey-nut cereal. "There's nothing *wrong* with our taste buds. This is just... how they work in this air mixture, and at this pressure. There's nothing to heal."

Josh scowled as he sat at the other end of the table. He'd gone as far from Vic as he could get without scooting his chair away. He must have known that Vic was trying to drive a wedge between him and Triage, but he said nothing. "You two seem like you're getting along well," Vic noted, an edge in his voice.

Triage found a seat one removed from Josh, but still on Josh's side of the table. He shifted. "I wouldn't say that. We've got work to do. We have to do it as a team."

"Is he managing all right?"

"We're doing OK."

Vic looked to Josh. "Just one of the boys again, right?"

Josh's scowl deepened, but he still didn't do what Vic most wanted him to, which was to leave. Vic knew he shouldn't have kept going, but it was like picking at a scab. Once he started, he couldn't make himself stop. He couldn't be in the same room as Josh, but he damn well wasn't going to be the first to leave.

If this mission was going to work at all, Josh was going to have to stay out of *his* way. Not vice versa. Josh needed to understand that. Here and now.

"It must be just like being a soldier again," Vic said.

Josh pushed his food back. "It wasn't like that. I was never a soldier."

"Yeah? Was it more of an informal thing, then? Like going to a pep rally?"

"You all need to take a step back and thi–" Triage started.

Josh spoke over him. "The rallies were feeding us propaganda, all right? We were kids. It wasn't my fault."

"Every bully I've met has always had an excuse," Vic said.

Triage planted his hand forcefully on Josh's shoulder, and tried to pull him up and out of the room. Josh didn't budge.

Vic just kept picking at that scab. His blood was pounding in his temples now. "You said 'we'," Vic said. "Your friends in the Reavers ever get shocked out of that propaganda when they found out *you* were a mutant? Or did they just show you who they are?"

The implication, which Vic didn't need to say, was that if anyone but him had been shown to be a mutant, Josh would have been in the mob that attacked him.

Josh muttered something under his breath, a single word that Vic couldn't make out. Then Josh was out of his chair, lunging toward Vic.

Vic had been waiting for this. He hadn't realized how much he'd wanted it until, without his hardly having to tell his body to react, he'd shoved his chair aside.

Josh's first blow landed on Vic's right arm, his regenerated one. It made a good shield. He hardly felt Josh's fist land. Josh's second swing, though, came in impossibly fast. It slammed into the soft flesh underneath Vic's sternum. It hurt, but the surprise was worse, and it was what took his breath away. Vic *whoofed* and took an involuntary step back.

Josh had anticipated the first block. Vic had thought Josh was just another sheltered, over-privileged kid. He hadn't expected an experienced fighter. Josh hadn't been in his self-defense courses for longer than a few weeks. Vic remembered someone had said something about Josh being held captive by some kind of gang.

Vic had no time to think about it. He stepped back in with a more defensive stance. His arm blocked another fist. This time, when he saw Josh's shoulders square up to throw a harder punch, he sidestepped and whirled his smaller elbow into Josh's face.

Josh grunted but kept his silence, even when Vic forced him back against the bulkhead. Josh rolled his back when he struck the bulkhead, cushioning the impact and muting the noise. Vic stayed quiet, too, when Josh slipped another hard punch through his defenses.

"*Stop!*" Triage said, trying to force himself between them. "Neither of you can afford what'll happen if Karma–"

"Shut up," Vic and Josh hissed, in unison.

Triage's voice had been the loudest thing in the room so far. They had to keep quiet or they'd wake Karma. Or one of the others would get her. Vic badly wanted to keep going, finally express the rage that had been building in him all along. It felt strangely good to know that Josh felt the same.

When Triage tried to intervene again, Josh shouldered him aside. Vic didn't take advantage of the gap in Josh's defenses. He waited until Josh had recovered his stance before going in again. He wanted this to be a fair fight; he wanted to be *better*.

Josh focused on feinting and weaving, keeping Vic from landing a hit with his powerful – and cumbersome – right arm. Vic pretended to be overfocused on punching, and then stomped on Josh's foot. Josh couldn't keep quiet on that one. He yelped, and stumbled. Vic grabbed Josh's arm, yanked it behind him, and pinned him against the bulkhead. Vic twisted Josh's arm higher, and pushed his face into the metal.

Josh's hand turned strangely liquid in Vic's grip. Not sweaty – but like Josh's skin and muscles were flowing like melting wax. Painful-sounding cracks and pops resonated through Josh's arm and wrist. Vic *felt* them.

He was sure he hadn't twisted Josh's arm hard enough to break any bones. Josh's wrist gave way in a direction it shouldn't have. The shock of the feeling made Vic loosen his grip.

Then Josh's arm was suddenly oriented opposite the direction it should have been. It was like Josh had two left arms. Whatever had happened, it didn't slow him. He grabbed Vic's elbow from an angle that, a moment ago, would have been impossible. Then he yanked Vic off balance.

Vic stumbled face-first into a corner. He grappled the walls, struggling to stay upright. Josh struck him in the back of his head, twice. And he'd even tried to give Josh a fair fight, too. He'd have time to fume about that later, once he figured out what had just happened. He whirled around and raised his right hand in time to catch the next blow.

And in time to see Nature Girl standing in the open hatchway, fury etched into her expression.

Josh caught Vic's eyes focusing on someone else. By the same unspoken rule that had kept Vic from striking while Josh had pushed Triage away, he held his next punch.

The two of them froze mid-grapple. The seconds stretched on. On the other side of the cabin, Triage was leaning against the table and massaging his forehead.

"Are you two done?" Nature Girl demanded. "I said I need some help."

The noise of the fight hadn't drawn her down. She'd already been on her way. Vic and Josh followed her up to the conference room – not pretending that nothing had happened, but not acknowledging it, either. Triage's footsteps followed them.

Vic's breath came ragged. Josh had gotten some good hits in. Josh walked with a limp as he climbed the stairs, but it vanished by the time he reached the top. If he and Josh were going to pick up this fight later, Vic mused, he was going to have to find some way to circumvent that healing ability. Or be faster than it.

Not to mention figure out whatever dark magic had happened with his arm.

Nature Girl returned to the station she'd been at earlier. The sonar didn't show a blip so much as a patchy fog of green, some parts brighter than others. There was no data on distance, or direction, or anything else. Vic supposed that in the old days, operations would have had to be trained to read it without help.

"No idea what to do about all this," Nature Girl said. "Nothing's showing up on radar."

"Did you ask Graymalkin?" Triage asked.

"Of course," Nature Girl said irritably. "He's not answering intercom calls. I just need somebody to look at this with me, in case... well..."

In case it's not a malfunction, she didn't need to finish. Vic tried to push that thought away. He had enough to be anxious about already.

"What about Karma?" Josh asked.

"I'm not waking Karma and have it turn out to be a glitch."

Vic glanced to the corner of the room, to ceiling-mounted CRTs that only looked four decades old rather than six. "Can we get any camera views?" he asked.

Figuring out the cameras was an adventure by itself. The station's exterior cameras had been installed years after everything else on the station, and the controls were awkwardly placed next to the workstation that controlled the defense grid. Triage and Nature Girl bent over it, arguing over which of the buttons and joysticks did what. Vic stayed out of it.

One of the monitors snapped on with a loud, electric *pop* somewhere behind it. An image wavered: a grainy black-and-white of an infrared camera feed. Sharp, white light glared across the corner of the screen, beaming down onto the craggy seafloor. It was one of the station's exterior lights, heating the water.

In the margins, underneath the shadows, a thousand squirming shapes flowed through the darkness.

Vic hardly heard Josh swear. The shock of the sight, so soon after the brawl, made him dizzy.

"Somebody get Karma," Vic said. "Get her *now*."

Nobody moved. He didn't know that anybody was listening. Triage asked, "Where's Crosta? Is he still out there?"

"No, he shouldn't be–" Vic stopped. He realized that he'd never actually seen Crosta come inside.

Josh lurched toward the security station. He grabbed one of the two miniature joysticks that Triage and Nature Girl had argued over earlier, and jammed it downward.

The camera panned down. There'd been a white blotch at the bottom of the screen. As the camera reoriented, they could see it was shaped like a figure. It writhed and twisted, caught in a struggle with the shadows.

The glow meant the figure was hot-blooded. Crosta. And whatever he was fighting was cold as the sea.

A motion in the corner of Vic's eye drew his attention to the conference room's window.

Part of his view of the seafloor was occluded by an inky black shadow.

Whatever it was, it was shaped like a person. It floated in the darkness between the exterior lights' beams, so Vic could make out the murky silhouette but not much else. It hung in the water, so still that, for a moment, Vic wondered if he was looking at a floating corpse.

Then it surged forward and smacked into the acrylic glass.

Triage yelped. Vic flinched and backpedaled.

The reflection of the conference room's lights in the window had changed. It took Vic a second to figure out why. The pane had visibly *shifted* in its frame.

Whatever was out there, it had struck the window with more force than a person could. More force than Vic would have thought possible. Vic hadn't seen it grab anything for leverage.

A moment of absolute, surreal silence followed as Josh, Vic,

Nature Girl, and Triage watched the shape draw back. It held itself still, as if considering.

It rushed forward.

Vic never saw the impact. Only the blinding spray of salt water that came after.

CHAPTER EIGHT
Elixir

When the conference room's window caved in, Josh reflexively moved to shield his face. Wrong direction. Something cracked him painfully in the back of his head.

Reality blinked. His world fuzzed. Even the pain disappeared under a wash of sensory static.

It was not until afterward that he pieced together what happened in the next few seconds.

Wolfram had shown him what he could do with his power. He could stitch up skin, mend muscle bones, and change himself in other ways that he didn't want to think about. While fighting Vic, by instinct he'd broken his fingers, his wrist, and his elbow, and then remolded them into something more useful. He hadn't done that in a long time, but it had come right back to him. He didn't want to know what else he could do. He focused on his limitations.

He couldn't dampen pain. He couldn't fine-tune his brain or

nervous system. He couldn't heal himself if he was unconscious. Healing wasn't an automatic process. He had to focus.

The water had knocked Anole off his feet. The overhead lights died in a cascade of sparks and electrical shorts. Josh realized that he'd cracked his head on the conference table.

He pushed to his feet. The water had nearly swept Josh's feet out from under him. The flood still shoved against his legs. It was so cold that he didn't perceive the temperature at first – just the shock. It soaked through his socks, froze him down to his toes.

Josh only had time to briefly marvel at the strength of the flood. Less than a foot of water had crashed into his feet, and it had bowled him backward. Anole had been standing closer to the window, and the water had knocked him to the deck *behind* Josh. He'd lost track of Triage and Nature Girl, but if they were still by the workstations, the force of the water would have smashed them into the rear bulkheads.

The water was still coming, but not as fast as it could have. The station may have been primitive by present-day standards, but it was brilliantly designed. Some of its defenses were mechanical tricks, and they didn't need power. The weight of the in-rushing water caught the window's shutters. The force of the water slammed the metal slats shut. But the shutters' seal wasn't perfect. Water sprayed inside, cascading down the slats.

By some fluke or genius of electrical engineering, the workstations and monitors remained on even as the lights sparked out. Josh's gaze flashed by the overhead monitor in time to catch the bright infrared figure free its arms, and then bring its hands clapping together. In a brilliant flash of heat, a white sphere sprouted between its palms. Crosta's shockwave.

The image turned to static.

Half an instant later, the deck jolted, and then slipped from underneath Josh's feet. He sprawled on the deck, landing flat on his back. His vision went white and frothy.

Water rushed around him, harder than it had a moment ago. One of the shutter slats had been snapped in half by the shockwave that had just rocked the station. Alarms shrieked in his ear. At the same time, the rest of his body felt like it was somebody else's. Getting numb. The seawater here was not cold enough to be as dangerous as falling through a frozen pond in winter – but, for anyone who didn't have the Atlanteans' adaptations to the sea, it wouldn't make any difference after a few minutes of immersion.

The only part of his body that felt warm was his stomach. He held his hand there, and now that felt warm, too. Blood soaked through his torn shirt.

The shock settled in. He had a neat, thin, but deep cut across his abdomen. Most of his body had numbed, but a profoundly cold pain was just catching up with him.

Josh focused his healing powers. It took all his attention to seal his skin back together. By the time he finished, Anole was shaking his shoulder, trying to pull him up. He thought he saw blood on Anole's ridged green forehead, but the darkness made it hard to be sure.

On the other side of the cabin, Triage knelt over Nature Girl. From Triage's stance, and the hand he held over Nature Girl's shoulder, Josh figured she'd gotten hurt, too, and that Triage was healing her. A purple-red bruise stained Nature Girl's cheeks.

They couldn't stay here. Water surged out of the conference

room's hatch. It cascaded into the corridor, flowing heavier every second. Anole pointed. "Move it!"

Even with Anole yanking him, getting all the way to his feet was a struggle. Josh's head swam. From the angle he'd landed at, water shoved against his chest like a linebacker trying to pin him to the field. The brief moment of gratitude Josh had felt toward Anole died when Anole gave him a kick. Healing the gash took energy, and he wasn't even finished yet. Josh had closed the surface wound, but there were still deep tissue injuries, torn muscles, ruptured blood vessels... at least the cold numbed the kick.

Anole whirled, and it occurred to Josh that Anole's kick might not have been born just out of frustration.

A shadow lashed out of the darkness and into Anole's shoulder, knocking him aside.

The shadow would have landed atop Josh had Josh's reflexes not caught up and raised a foot. His heel landed in tough but supple flesh.

The shape recoiled. Definitely humanoid. Josh could see it hunch as it backed up. If it made any noise, it was lost under the shrieking of the alarms. Whatever had broken the window had made it inside before the shutters closed.

Something in the figure's hand caught in the lights from the corridor. It gleamed. He caught a wickedly sharp tip. Maybe the cut on his stomach hadn't come from glass. Nor had the impact he'd felt been just water. It could have attacked Nature Girl, too.

Adrenaline pounded through his heart and finally overcame the shock. He shoved himself to his feet. Anole was gasping, trying to get his breath back from the creature's body blow.

The creature came at them again. As it crossed the circle of light cast from the open hatch, Josh caught an instant's sight of it. His first, brief impression was that of an Atlantean.

The creature was back in the darkness before the rest of his wits had caught up to the things that *weren't* Atlantean. The ragged, sloughing skin. The bloodless flesh underneath, not bleeding where the broken window must have sliced it.

And the maw of icicle-spiked gray teeth. With teeth like that, it hardly needed another weapon. But it charged forward with its dagger swinging. Much too fast.

Josh raised his arm to shield his face. Pain slashed through him. A line of searing heat raced down his arm from wrist to elbow.

He couldn't spare the focus to heal. Nor could they stay to fight. Nature Girl and Triage were already up and almost through the hatch. Even though it made his arm tight with pain, Josh grabbed one of the conference table's chairs and hurled it at the intruder.

Josh staggered out into the corridor just a step ahead of Anole. As soon as Anole was out, Josh reached past him. He grabbed the hatch to swing it shut.

A shadow of pale skin and bony spite slammed into him. He crashed into the bulkhead. His vision blurred and doubled.

The creature was already past him and Anole, onto the others. Nature Girl yelled. She ducked a swipe from the creature's knife. Triage barely sidestepped another.

Anole raised his huge right arm, fist clenched, and smashed it into the small of the intruder's back. The intruder grunted, seemingly more from surprise than pain, but the momentum of Anole's blow was enough to force it against the bulkhead.

The creature made a sound that Josh didn't think any

living creature could reproduce: a deep, guttural growl. It was disturbingly fluid, like the creature's vocal cords were rotted through.

Josh's vision had shaken loose. He couldn't quite bring anything into focus. But there was no mistaking the flash of silver around the creature's mouth. It was baring its teeth, an inhuman number of them, and moving in on Anole.

"You have no idea what kind of mistake you made," Karma said.

Karma stood at the end of the corridor, just outside her quarters, ankle-deep in the water gushing around them. The intruder spun to face her.

She didn't sound fazed at all. Just angry.

"Let me show you," Karma told it.

As if an invisible tripwire had snapped under its feet, the intruder doubled over. At the other end of the corridor, Karma flinched, but otherwise held steady. The creature snapped its head back and forth, looking for things that weren't there – or at least that Josh couldn't see.

This time, Anole's punch landed in the back of its head with a meaty impact that Josh heard even over the sirens. The blow would have knocked out or killed a normal person. The creature staggered a step forward, but then whirled and snapped its maw at Anole. Anole drew his arm back just in time.

The creature didn't stay to fight. Instead, it *cowered* – flinching at something none of them could see. The past thirty seconds had given Josh a lot of candidates for the title of Worst Sound He'd Ever Heard, but the gurgling shriek the creature emitted leapt to the top of the list. The creature retreated toward the stairs to the second deck, and leapt down them.

Josh planted his back against the bulkhead, gasping for breath and for the energy to finish healing himself. Salt stung his eyes and nostrils. The taste of it filled his mouth, mingling with his spit. He coughed, and wiped his eyes and lips. The pain in his arm cooled to a dull throb as he stitched flesh and skin and muscle back together.

On the other side of the corridor, Nature Girl slid to sit on the floor. Blood had painted the shirt under her arm red. With Triage concentrating his healing power on her, though, the bleeding had already stopped. The bruise on her cheek had vanished, too.

Anole started after the creature as soon as he recovered his footing. Josh started after him, but Karma stepped ahead of them. "*Don't.*"

She pointed to the conference room's hatch. Water was still rushing into the corridor. For the first time, Josh realized that all the station's interior hatches had been built with the same plan as the shutters. They opened inward. If the water had surged inside any faster, the force would have slammed the hatch shut… and trapped them on the other side.

Better to lose a single cabin and its occupants than the entire station. Luck and the shutter design had saved him, Anole, Triage, and Nature Girl.

Josh scrambled for leverage. The water kept pressing against his ankles and made the deck slick. Even with Anole helping, it took more work than he thought to pull the hatch shut. Anole spun the wheel, locking it. The metal shook with the water still crashing against it on the other side.

The water around their feet dropped. Some of it cascaded down the stairs to the next level. Most was draining into grates placed for just this kind of emergency. Even still, the damage already done to the station must have been immense.

The conference room had held most of the station's controls. And if the cabin wasn't fully flooded now, it would be soon.

Now that he had more than two seconds to think, the terror of what had just happened caught up with the rest of his senses. And the cold. He did not know when he had started shivering. Only that he could not stop.

Anole turned back toward the stairs the creature had disappeared down. Once again, Karma stepped in his way. To Josh's surprise, Anole actually *snarled* at her. "We need to go after it before–"

Karma's voice was a striker held above flint. More dangerous than Josh had ever heard her. "It doesn't sound like it's alone, does it? How many of them are out there?"

Anole didn't have an answer.

Without the conference room's cameras, or its radar and sonar, they couldn't tell anything about what might have been happening out there. That sea of shadows had looked like an army. Nature Girl had enough of her voice back to answer: "I couldn't count."

"*Prioritize,*" Karma said. "We're not going to accomplish anything if we put all our time into chasing down one intruder while the rest of their friends tear us apart from the outside." Karma snapped her fingers at Triage and Nature Girl. "Emergency command center. Second deck. Get the defense grid online." She turned to Anole and Josh. "Find Graymalkin and Crosta. Get them to that command center. It's our most defensible place. I'll go after that – thing."

"Alone?" Anole asked, aghast.

"Yes," she snapped. No further explanation warranted.

The water level was down to the heels of her boots, and hardly splashed when she stepped. She turned toward the top of the stairs, about to charge down, and stopped. She held her hand to her temple as if dizzy.

"What the hell is it afraid of?" she asked. The question didn't seem to be aimed at anyone.

"What?" Triage asked her.

Karma shook her head. Josh couldn't tell if she'd even heard Triage. She clambered down the stairs, taking them three at a time.

Josh took the wet stairs carefully, a firm hand on the railing. He couldn't move as fast as Karma, who quickly got ahead of them. The grated steps were still dripping with water. He wasn't an X-Man. He didn't have Karma's balance or well-tested sense for tightrope walking over danger. If he took these stairs any faster, he was going to fall and break an ankle. Even Anole only took the steps two at a time.

When they reached the bottom, the corridor in both directions was empty. Slick-floored from water draining down, but empty. A tremendous clattering reverberated from the direction of the stairs that led to the next deck down.

Nature Girl and Triage were just behind Josh. Nature Girl said, "The last time I spoke with Graymalkin, he was in the cargo compartments on the third deck. He wasn't answering intercoms. That's why I came to find you."

That had only been a few minutes ago. It already felt like days. "Crosta is outside," Josh muttered. "And we can't go out there."

"We're going to have to if he can't get back in on his own,"

Anole said, voice tight. He didn't sound like he relished the idea.

Josh didn't know how much Anole had seen. The infrared figure struggling on the monitor, the shadows swarming him – the white sphere sprouting between its hands. Crosta's mutant power was the ability to create shockwaves like that. He must have used it to defend himself. They hadn't heard anything from him since.

Anole looked round every corner and into every open hatch they passed. He was plainly looking for a fight. He didn't find one. He stepped into the emergency command center and checked the shadows while Josh waited outside. Nature Girl and Triage stepped past him.

Josh had caught a glimpse of the emergency command cabin on his initial tour. There wasn't much to see. It was a closet-sized space with no chairs, bad lighting, simple grated floors, and a smell like iron filings that tickled his sinuses. The cramped workstation, with its single "new" CRT monitor, duplicated the most important functions from above.

If the creature was on this deck, it had hidden itself well. Nature Girl and Triage could shut the hatch to the emergency command cabin, so they'd at least have some warning if something tried to fight its way inside. The clattering noise from below had stopped. He couldn't hear anything else from the third deck, just the alarms.

"I can't use the defense grid," Nature Girl hissed, as she squeezed into the cabin's only seat. Triage peered over her shoulder at the workstation.

"Why the hell not?" Anole asked.

"The third deck will be flooded too," Triage said. A jolt of dismay squeezed Josh's stomach. He'd almost forgotten. With the loss of air pressure, water would have been sucked up from the open diving pool.

"If the diving pool's still open, I can't turn it on without shocking anyone who's down there, too," Nature Girl said.

"And Crosta is out there," Triage added.

"What's left of him," Nature Girl said.

"Don't talk like that," Triage told her.

There was worse. "Crosta and I were running tests on the defense grid," Anole said. "It was disconnected from main power."

Josh swore. He wished that had occurred to Anole *before* Karma had charged off.

"I think I know how to switch it back on," Triage said, and then, "At least I *did*, back up in the conference room." None of them had trained on these workstations. From the way Triage was looking at them, they might as well have been labeled in High Sh'iar rather than English.

The sirens only seemed to be getting louder. "Could you shut off that damn no–" Anole started. Nature Girl flipped a sequence of switches, and the alarms ceased. All that was left was the ringing in Josh's ears.

"Thank you," Anole muttered.

"They'll sound again if there's another breach," Nature Girl said, and then: "I think. I mean, they're *supposed* to."

Triage looked at her, eyebrows raised. She shrugged. It was the best she could offer. Triage looked nauseous to hear that. Josh figured he looked about the same.

Nature Girl and Triage were the best two people to handle this end of things, though. Josh and Anole wouldn't do much good crowding over their shoulders. Anole looked to Josh, his lips set in a tight line. Josh walked out, and Anole followed a step behind.

Together, they headed toward the staircase down to the third deck. Triage closed the hatch to the emergency command cabin after them. The lock clunked into place. Triage and Nature Girl would at least be safe while they worked.

Josh and Anole were alone. Without the sirens, everything was disturbingly quiet. If Karma had come this way, though, it couldn't have been that long ago. When sound finally came, it was loud enough to make him jump. A heavy clunking resounded through the station's hull, like an impact. It sounded like it was coming from above, from the first deck.

Anole took the lead down the stairs this time, though he stepped just as carefully as Josh had last time. He rolled his shoulders to loosen them up, ready for a fight.

Another noise gradually resolved over the ringing in his ears: lapping water. He looked over Anole's shoulder. Black, foam-whorled water sloshed against the bottom of the stairs.

Anole snapped a look back as if to make sure Josh was still following. His scowl only deepened when he saw him. Every few steps, Anole glanced back. It was as if, now that they were alone, he didn't trust Josh to be behind him. Josh grimaced. He'd thought he and Anole both had worse things to worry about than each other.

Then it struck Josh, with a force that hadn't landed before, that it wasn't a performance. It wasn't even hate. Neither of them had time for hate.

Anole was behaving rationally. He was treating Josh in the way that made the most sense to him: a threat. Josh's cheeks burned. He tried to put it out of his mind, focus on the danger most immediately in front of them, but had trouble managing.

The flooding was deeper than it looked. Anole tried and failed to stifle a gasp as he plunged knee-deep into the seawater. The cold bit into Josh, too.

The water had sluiced down from the upper decks and pooled here. The drainage system must have been working hard, but it had its limits. The station had lost too much air. The water was fighting to fill the void, and the drainage pumps couldn't keep up.

Water dripped from all over the ceiling. Little freezing droplets fell on the back of his neck and brow, and dripped salt into his stinging eyes. For far too long, it was silent.

Then a heavy impact reverberated through the bulkheads to their left. Something shrieked, and it didn't sound like any noise a person could make. Anole immediately started wading in that direction.

Josh reached out, but Anole was already too far ahead. "Wait!" Josh said. "She told us to find Crosta."

"Go find Crosta then!"

Josh was pretty sure that the last two things Karma would have wanted were for Josh and Anole to split up, and then for Anole to go charging toward a fight. But Josh knew nothing he could say would stop Anole.

Josh turned toward the wet cabins, glad to be rid of him. He didn't look back. The water didn't push against him here like it had above. Its level was dropping. A deep gurgling stirred it underfoot. A sharp, cold draft brushed his skin as he passed by a ventilation grate.

He got through the first hatch between him and the wet cabin without incident. When he opened the second, a wave sloshed over his legs. The water level inside was higher.

"Crosta?" he called, and was not surprised when he received no answer.

Turbulent, choppy water crashed against the laboratory counters. Most of the lab equipment had spilled off them. Josh had not gotten farther than three steps inside before he smashed his shin into something heavy and sharp-cornered. When he looked down, a toppled microscope and its stand peeked back at him through the foam and waves.

There had to be more dangerous laboratory equipment bobbing around, too. He waded carefully ahead. The water was so deep and murky that, for what felt like half a minute, he couldn't locate the diving pool. Finally, he found a patch of brighter water – the ocean reflecting the station's exterior lights.

He paused by the diving pool's edge and peered down. The water inside the station was filthy from all the dust and contaminants it had picked up, but outside the station was only a little clearer. The seafloor had vanished. Great mushrooms of dust billowed up, only just starting to settle. It must have been kicked up by the shockwave.

A rack of drysuits hung high enough off the deck that the water touched only their heels. Josh looked over them uneasily. He and the others still hadn't been trained on them. They hadn't even checked the suits' pressure seals since coming down. They looked too bulky to fight *or* flee in.

He turned away from them. He needed to get outside the station, yes – but all he needed to do was find Crosta, or verify that there wasn't much left of Crosta to be found.

The sound of metal shrieking against metal screamed

through the station. A heavy *clang* reverberated through the hull overhead, followed an instant later by more ear-splitting alarms. Another hull breach.

Josh heard the water a second before he felt it. The rush of an uncontrolled, frothing flood echoed down the stairwell. Then torrents of seawater burst from the ceiling.

He couldn't do anything about it down here. He had to trust the rest of his crew. He returned to the diving pool's side and sucked in a deep breath. The longer he hesitated, the more difficult it was going to be to do what he needed to.

So he didn't let himself stop to think about it any longer. There was no time for regrets like the present.

He had plenty of time to dwell on that thought in the subjective eternity after the jump, midair between the diving pool's edge, the deck, and the sea.

CHAPTER NINE

Elixir

Josh dived headfirst, arms steepled in a classic diver's pose, and cut through the water, hardly feeling the cold. He was already so frozen from the floodwaters that the ocean was less of a shock than he feared.

The salt water was a different matter. It had been irritating before. Now it felt like someone shoving needles behind his eyes.

He'd gone swimming in the ocean once, when he was six. His parents had taken him. He'd worn goggles. The experience of salt water leaking into them once, though, had put him off submerging his head for the rest of the trip.

The sudden sense-memory made him convulse. The last damned thing he needed to be thinking about was his parents. That was one of the functions of grief, though: to pop into his thoughts at the least appropriate time.

He forced himself to focus and prize his eyes open. For

a while, he couldn't see much more than a cloudy light. He blinked until the fog resolved into the blurry, unblinking beam of one of the station's exterior lights.

Somewhere after striking the water, though, he must have somersaulted. He was right-side up now. An open field of metal, beaded with lights, suspended above him. For as cramped as Station X-41 had felt inside, it looked a whole lot bigger out here. From underneath, it was a leviathan. It did not look like a ceiling as much as a horizon. It was almost as daunting as the open water below.

The sudden, acrophobic shock made his stomach churn. A vast, granular dust cloud stirred far underneath his kicking feet. The beams of the station's lights vanished into the plume of dust. He knew that, if he looked much longer, it would convince himself that he'd fallen out of the sea and into the sky.

Falling, falling, *falling* toward a thunderhead. Or down into a plume of volcanic soot.

He had to look away.

Far to his left, across the plane of the station's hull, a whorl of shadows twisted and writhed. He blinked and looked again, trying to fold the blurs into a coherent picture. The shadows became five or six silhouettes, chasing a green-skinned figure.

The salt in Josh's eyes wouldn't let him see much more than the shape and a hint of color, but that had to be Crosta.

Crosta's shockwave hadn't rid him of his attackers. At least not all of them. If Crosta *had* destroyed or scattered the first bunch, they'd gotten reinforcements very quickly.

Josh didn't see the flash of any knives. Crosta's assailants were using claws and bare hands. They didn't seem to be trying to kill Crosta, but herd him.

Josh looked up, and his heart leapt into his throat. He couldn't see the diving pool. He'd *just* gone through it, and it wasn't there. When Crosta had first arrived, he'd complained that the lights below the diving pool weren't working.

He'd taken a good, deep breath before diving, but it wouldn't last forever. He already felt the pressure mounting in his chest. A few seconds of increasingly frantic searching found the pool. He hadn't dived as straight as he'd thought. It had ended up more behind him than above him. It was still hardly visible – just a lighter blur against the murky canvas of the station's broad hull. The wet cabin's lights were muted down here.

Crosta was swimming away from the safety of the open diving pool. He might still have been able to find it – if he weren't fighting for his life at the same time. He was just barely staying out of reach of the shadows.

Crosta's assailants darted around him with the same impossible, torpedo-like speed as the one who'd broken through the conference room's window. They harried him like trained soldiers. Every time Crosta raised his arms to bring his hands together and create another shockwave, one of the shadows would dart at him, and force him to stop and swim away.

Josh had only an instant to think. Crosta wasn't going to see *him* against the station's dark hull any more than he could have seen the diving pool. His lungs were already squeezing, but he swanned open his arms and legs and swam down.

Down, and down – until he'd placed himself between Crosta and the beam of one of the station's exterior lights. The background glare would make Josh a nicely visible silhouette from Crosta's perspective.

Josh waved his arms frantically, trying to make as much motion as he could. Burning oxygen all the while.

Josh's chest ached. He couldn't keep this up for more than a few seconds. Just as he was about to give up and start back toward the diving pool, Crosta whirled. His gaze fixed on Josh even as he kept fighting.

Josh pointed vigorously toward the diving pool, and then swam toward it. He'd stayed under far too long. The pool's shimmering surface looked small from this depth – just a pale circle of wave-distorted light. His throat convulsed, and he only just managed to keep himself from opening his lips. Before long, he wasn't going to be able to resist the impulse to aspirate.

He could no longer think of anything else but getting back to the station. All he had to do was break the surface and the burning in his lungs would end.

A bloody red cloud burst from Josh's right shoulder, followed by a metal spearhead.

His whole body shuddered like he'd been shocked. A thick, crimson erupted from his shoulder. The spear's shining, polished tip jutted through scraps of his skin and a cloud of blood.

He did not feel the pain at first. Even when he did, it didn't seem as urgent as the jerking halt of his momentum. He was entirely focused on reaching air.

He tried to push upward, toward the too-distant diving pool, but the spear was an iron rod in his shoulder. He was being held down.

His vision fringed black at the edges. The rippling diving pool was at the center of a tunnel. It was getting no closer.

No. Worse. Someone was dragging him down.

The spear twisted sideways against him. It forced him to pivot face-to-face with the creature who'd held it. It was a crescent of teeth. Beaded red eyes with no pupils.

When he'd had fought Anole, Josh had remolded his arm to escape Anole's grip. He hadn't meant to do it. He knew he *could* – Wolfram had taught him that much – but he never wanted to do it again. Panic had seized him. He hadn't thought about what he was doing. He'd just acted.

The last thing he was capable of doing now was thinking.

He reached for the creature–

–and what had once been a blur of rippling shadows cracked into excruciating focus. Sharply defined webs of veins, folds of muscle, peeling skin, dead scales.

Every moment of Josh's life, every single second – even before his awakening as a mutant – he'd felt his body like this. He'd just pushed it below the level of conscious awareness. It was all too much. Only he wasn't conscious now, and he wasn't unconscious either, and this wasn't his body he was feeling.

It was all wrong. The webs of its veins were blackened and dry. The muscle tissue was dead. Somewhere digestive fluids still flowed and gurgled, even as the heart that should have powered it lay still and rotted. The creature was somehow more alive than the sum of its parts.

There had to be a way to fix it, to make it right–

–Josh's head breached the surface of the diving pool. He gulped down, stopping only to convulsively vomit water. His chest burned so badly that the fire radiated down his arms and legs. He would have slipped underwater again if he wasn't being held up.

Crosta was behind him. His firm grip kept Josh upright. Josh knew it was Crosta without even looking. He felt his identity under his scales and cuts and blood. That level of awareness faded as Josh returned to the waking world.

Crosta moved him toward the side of the pool. Crosta swam more powerfully than any human, but even he couldn't lift Josh up, not without leverage. Josh weakly grabbed onto the railing and pulled himself onto the first of the stairs. It felt like mountaineering. His head was swimming by the time he collapsed onto it.

Blood washed over the step. There was more of it with each wave. Josh hadn't hallucinated the bite of the spear. The spearhead had vanished. He had no idea what had happened to it. It hadn't breached the surface with him.

Inside, the water had drained below deck level. The ceiling still dripped, but the water in the diving pool was only a few inches higher than Josh remembered it. The second breach, the one that had happened just as he'd dived, must have been sealed.

Crosta sprang out of the pool. He was gasping for breath, or the Atlantean equivalent of it. His gills were dilated, though they wouldn't function outside of water. He was battered and bruised. "We have to close the–"

The hatch at the far end of the cabin clapped open. Josh was in no state for a fight, but it seemed like one was coming his way regardless.

The creature who'd burst through the conference room's window backed through the hatch. Karma was only steps behind it. She held her arm near her face, guarding herself while she marshalled a telepathic attack.

The creature flinched, but so did she. Her lips loosened. For a terrifying moment, it looked like she was losing the mental battle.

Then Anole was there. He darted past her, crashed bodily into the creature. It had been distracted by whatever battle it was having with Karma. It didn't see Anole coming, even when Anole was right in front of it.

Anole knocked the creature back as far as the diving pool. It was back in the physical world now. It jabbed an elbow under Anole's chin. Anole backpedaled, coughing.

The creature swiped at Anole. It was a feint. Josh saw it even as it was happening, but didn't have the breath to call out a warning. Anole was already off balance. By raising his hand to ward off the blow, he'd left a perfect opening for a knife thrust to his belly.

The instant before the inevitable happened, Crosta was there. He grabbed the creature by its free arm and twisted it around behind him. He raised his hands, energy crackling over his fingers like St. Elmo's fire, then brought his palms crashing together.

Josh had enough energy left to duck.

A flash of light and heat *whumphed* through the cabin. Crosta's shockwave was so intense that it was more of a feeling than a sound. The creature's bony limbs scraped Josh's back as it sailed overhead and crashed into the pool.

The next thing Josh was aware of was Crosta grabbing him by his arms and hauling him the rest of the way onto the deck. Anole had been knocked flat by the force of Crosta's shockwave. Karma was upright and trying to catch her breath from whatever had transpired between her and the creature.

Crosta turned to the diving pool's controls. "Seal the ha–" he started again.

The waters frothed as the creature reemerged and kicked

and swam toward Josh's side of the pool. The waters were so choppy that Josh could have been hallucinating it, but he saw other moving shadows down there too. More of the creatures, getting closer.

He didn't think he had the energy to fight, but apparently he had enough to raise his leg and kick the creature squarely in its forehead. It jerked backward, stunned enough to fall deeper into the water.

Crosta wasted no more breath on words. He found the correct switch. The pool's double-sided hatch started grinding shut.

The creature reached through the closing gap, scrabbling for purchase.

Josh had wondered if the station's hatches had any safety mechanisms to prevent people from getting caught inside. He'd never wanted to have to find out the answer. He got one. The door snapped shut with a squeal that didn't sound entirely mechanical. The creature's arm remained on their side of the door. The creature didn't.

Josh lay on the bottom step of the closed diving pool, heaving air. The shadows Josh had seen outside the station still danced behind his eyes. "There's an army out there," he said. "I saw it. It's all over us."

Karma backed toward the bulkhead and reached for the intercom switch there. "We're all in. Hit the defense grid–"

Triage's voice was barely recognizable as it grated through the speaker grille. "We haven't tested it! Nature Girl *just* sealed the second breach! If there's a gap in insulation–"

"Do it!" Karma told him.

Silence on the other end. Josh could only picture Triage in

that closet of electronics, biting his lip and debating whether to obey. Josh squeezed his eyes shut. He was lying in a pool of water, and there were still drips and trails leading to the upper decks. Even if he was just standing on the metal deck, and their protection from the defense grid had been damaged...

The lights dimmed. A horrendous, terribly organic screaming came from outside the station. It was all around them. It wasn't that different from the noise Josh had heard when the pool doors had pinched the creature's arm off. Only there was a lot more of it.

The lights returned to full strength.

"Again," Karma ordered.

The lights dimmed darker. The shrieking was weaker this time. There wasn't as much of it. It might have been Josh's imagination, but it seemed a little more distant.

"Again."

This time, when the lights dimmed, they didn't come back on. The intercom was still working. Josh heard the static crackle of Triage breathing into it.

There was no shrieking this time. Silence soaked the cabin. Aside from some clicking over the intercom, which might have been Triage clacking keys, they heard nothing.

Karma wouldn't take silence for an answer.

"Again."

CHAPTER TEN
Anole

"They are called Aqueos," Crosta said, with considerable reluctance.

Crosta's expressions were still too alien for Vic to read, but not the way that he didn't meet anyone's eyes.

There was not as much room in the second deck kitchenette as there had been in the conference room, but it was the only place left on the station, except the wet cabin, that had the space to hold all of them. It had a table, it had chairs, and that was all they could ask for at this point.

Vic squeezed his legs together. If he'd sat how he was comfortable, he would have knocked his knees on Nature Girl's. Nature Girl's antlers still invaded his airspace. Graymalkin sat on Vic's other side, squeezing his knees in too.

They'd found Graymalkin not long after chasing the invaders off the station. One of them had caught him in the cargo hold, underneath its bright lights, and trapped him under a pile of storage crates. The creatures had tried a divide-and-conquer strategy, and nearly succeeded.

As hard as it was to squeeze into the kitchenette, the whole team wasn't even here. Triage was just down the corridor, listening in, while watching the cameras from the emergency control cabin.

"They're related to the Atlanteans," Josh said. A statement, not a question.

Crosta's gaze flicked up to meet Josh's. "Yes," he said, eventually. "But they are animals."

"They use technology," Josh pointed out. "Knives. Spears. Refined metals."

"They are not civilized."

Josh didn't seem to know where to push next. But Nature Girl spoke up. "They're not alive," she said. "Are they?"

Somewhere, water was still dripping. It made a steady beat, a tick-tick-ticking of a clock, as they waited for the next answer. Crosta seemed to be considering his words.

"They *were* Atlanteans," Crosta said. "They were defiled. Simply killing them would have been far more merciful. They've been infected with… what I think you would call vampirism. The disease animated their corpses without bringing them back to life. They became the ghouls you saw today. Bestial. Murderous. Merciless."

The language didn't sit right with Vic. At the same time, he couldn't point out why. The creatures used tools, used intelligent tactics… but, in combat, they had been utterly maniacal. Incarnations of snarling rage.

People sometimes said the same thing about mutants, though.

"I know it's not that simple," Karma said.

Karma did not look like herself. None of them did, really, but Karma was almost a stranger. Her face was drawn tight. Shadows underlay her eyes.

"I never said it was simple," Crosta growled.

Karma bowled right over the warning in his voice. "They were organized," she said. "They attacked like an army. They came here with a purpose."

Crosta didn't seem to know what to do with someone like Karma, trampling his boundaries as he drew them. "They're opportunists."

"I *know* they had a reason," Karma said. "What was it?"

Crosta shifted in his seat again, like he'd been pinned there. "I don't know," he said, with an uncharacteristic stammer.

Vic chewed on the inside of his cheek. Crosta seemed to be doing his best to tell the truth while keeping his dignity intact, but Vic didn't trust himself to read Atlantean emotions yet.

After that answer had sat for a moment, Crosta asked, "How are you so certain they had something in mind?"

"You don't want to find that out."

Graymalkin gave Karma a strange look. He didn't press her on it.

The others looked as strung out as Vic felt, which was quite a bit. Their hair had dried out stringy, and their clothes had absorbed enough water to make them jump up a size or two. Nobody had had time to shower off afterward. The flood waters had been filthy, too, and not just with ordinary sea sediment. The station, and all of its nooks and crannies, was covered with grime and dust. The flood had dumped it atop them.

Not for the first time in his life, Vic was grateful he didn't have hair. He'd heard the superpowered life wasn't easy on hair. It was always getting filthy, burned up, torn out, electrified, mutated, turned radioactive, and worse.

Most of them had blood on their clothes. Vic, too. Having two healers on this assignment had turned out to be more useful than anyone could have guessed. Josh's shirt had a ragged hole in its shoulder where he said he'd been speared, but that and the stains were the only sign of it. The skin underneath was pristine.

Vic felt half-present. Part of him was here, around their little table, and the rest of him was still in battle, defending that station. The fight had ended hours ago, but his memories were so vivid it felt like it was still happening all around him. His heartbeat hadn't slowed since. That couldn't be healthy. Everything seemed dreamlike, unreal. Numbed. For minutes at a time, his emotions would hold themselves at a remove. It didn't last. At an unusual sound, or sometimes at no provocation at all, all the rage and terror would come flooding back, and he'd feel like he was in the fight again.

After leaving Josh, he'd gone chasing after Karma and the creature. He'd rounded a corner and nearly ran into it. He'd only discover later that it had found Graymalkin and trapped him under toppling crates in the cargo bay. It must have hidden from Karma as she'd gone by. Vic had probably surprised it as much as it had surprised him. But it had the sharper reflexes. It had pinned him against the bulkhead, choking him, until Karma had doubled back and intervened. A telepathic assault from her had set the creature running, swatting at invisible fears.

Karma had doubled over from the exertion of it. Which was odd. He'd never seen her power have that effect. They reached the wet cabin just in time to see Josh and Crosta emerge from the diving pool.

The horror of the fight hadn't ended after they'd secured the station. After the fight, he and the others had found miraculously dry towels in a cabinet in the bathroom. Vic carried his towel, red with his blood, slung over his shoulder. As Vic had trudged past the porthole, motion caught his eye. He'd stepped closer to take a look.

A torrent of debris, twisted metal scrap and bent bolts, drifted past the acrylic glass. And a trail of bubbles was streaming up.

He had to step to the edge of the window and look down to see the broken hulk of the descent capsule, resting on the seafloor.

He'd been so much in shock that he hardly registered his own horror.

The descent capsule's destruction was the reason those alarms had gone off that second time. The creatures had ripped it off its moorings. The stress had broken the waterlock, and flooded the corridor. Nature Girl had only just sealed the breach before Triage had fired the defense grid.

Vic wouldn't have felt safe leaving in the descent capsule, anyway – as the Aqueos had just proved, it was no match for a concerted attack. But the psychological pressure of existing here had gotten that much heavier.

Until someone came down to get them, they were trapped.

The worst thing was that it had not taken them long to find out that they couldn't contact the surface.

The station's hydroacoustic communications system was housed in one of the few cabins on the first deck that had escaped serious flooding. But their surface buoy, the one that was supposed pick up their acoustic pings and retransmit them as radio, wasn't answering.

Karma pressed Crosta about the Aqueos for several more minutes before she seemed to accept that he didn't have an answer. Or, at least, not one that he would give up. She massaged her forehead. "Can you tell us *anything* else about them?"

"Only that they only survive on an act of charity. Prince Namor was once offered the chance to exterminate them. He chose mercy, out of respect for the Atlanteans they used to be." He shook his head. "He thought he had them leashed and collared. Obviously, they've found some way to slip their bonds. Their mistake. Prince Namor does not offer second chances."

"When I went out there, it looked like they were focusing on you," Josh said.

Crosta's voice again lost its firmness. "It would seem so."

"Any idea why?" Karma asked.

"I am the only Atlantean here. It could be that they were trying to… infect me." He sounded far from certain.

"They used an awful lot of energy, and took a big risk, for coming for just one Atlantean. We killed more than one of them. There must be something they see as worth it."

"When the jellyfish stings, it doesn't put any thought behind it. It doesn't have thoughts. It stings because that is its nature."

"They're not animals," Nature Girl interrupted. "I'd know if they were."

Vic wasn't sure the English language had a word to describe what the Aqueos were. "Vampirism" and "ghouls" were approximations. Vic had read about vampires, from Morbius to Dracula and beyond. What he'd seen of the Aqueos didn't match.

The diving pool's closing hatch had caught one of the creature's arms and pinched it off. The arm had flopped and twitched on the deck for seconds afterward. But the horror show hadn't stopped when it finally ceased moving. Over the next several minutes, its corpse-gray skin turned the color of ash. Black, threadlike tendrils snaked across its skin, like its veins had become living worms. The arm was safely locked in one of the laboratory cabinets.

Vic felt sick whenever he thought about it. The last severed arm he'd seen had been his own. He was young, but he didn't feel like it. He'd seen so much violence.

Crosta said, "Their existence isn't a secret. People from the surface have had contact with them." He was subtly turning the tables on Karma, asking her why *she* didn't know more.

"I know a lot, sometimes a lot more than I'd like, but I'm not an encyclopedia," Karma said. "Although if we *could* get in contact with the surface, maybe we could find out more."

Nature Girl and Triage hadn't been able to determine where the communications problem was. It could have been with the station's acoustic transmitter, in which case someone would have to swim out and repair it. The buoy could have drifted. Or some noise in the ocean might be garbling their signal. There was even a chance, a slim chance, that the outage was temporary. The longer they went without getting any answer, though, the harder it was to pretend that the problem was natural.

The Aqueos had found the buoy and taken it out. Or they'd sabotaged the acoustics transmitters in a manner that hadn't given away the cause. Either of those options said a great deal about the Aqueos' sophistication and their understanding of the station's technology.

The station had a backup buoy. *One* backup. It wasn't camouflaged. When the station released one, it would shoot upward in a shower of bubbles, an easy and obvious target. If the Aqueos had destroyed the first buoy, they'd have no trouble figuring out what to do with this one. And the Aqueos were still out there.

The external cameras spotted them every few minutes: dark, flitting shapes, passing along the periphery of the station's lights like birds through a cloud. They surrounded the station on all sides, and above. The scales on Vic's back chilled whenever he thought about them.

Their second attack had come only twenty minutes after the first. A formation of Aqueos had slipped closer, spearpoints glimmering in the station's lights. Triage had watched them from the emergency control cabin, via the single CRT monitor in there. Two bolts from the station's defense grid scattered them.

The Aqueos kept coming back at irregular intervals. In the four hours since the first attack, they'd returned three times. Each time, the defense grid had cleared them away.

But they never stopped testing the station.

It didn't matter whether they were "civilized", or whatever standard Crosta was trying to hold them to. They were organized, clearly communicating with each other, showed understanding of the station's technology, and were laser-focused on whatever purpose had brought them here. Vic couldn't believe they were "bestial", like Crosta had said. But they were… alien. Very alien.

Karma sighed. "The good news *and* the bad news is that, if we're out of contact for another day, the Institute will know something's wrong. They'll send help."

Vic hadn't said much so far. But he had to ask, "How is that bad news?"

"Because if we can't tell them *why* we lost contact, they're not going to come prepared. They're going to send a rescue team when what they really need is mutants capable of smashing these monsters into the seafloor."

That seemed astonishingly bloodthirsty for Karma. Then again, Vic had never seen her in a crisis quite like this one, either. It felt so strange.

Karma continued: "If the Institute sends an unarmored descent capsule, it won't stand a chance. The Aqueos will tear right through it. Just like they did ours."

"Why didn't they attack when *we* came down?" Nature Girl asked. Everyone looked at her. She wilted a little under the attention, but had steeled herself enough to go on. "We were just as wide open. Why did they wait until we were in a more defensible place?"

It was a good question. Nobody had the answer.

"Why aren't we all in that descent capsule right now?" Nature Girl asked. "Wrecked at the bottom of the ocean?"

"Well," Karma said. "We wouldn't *all* be in it."

Crosta was the only one of them at this table who hadn't arrived in the capsule. He just stared straight down at the table. The same thought must have occurred to him, too.

Vic believed that Crosta had no idea why the Aqueos had attacked. Maybe he hadn't taken more affront to Karma because he couldn't argue with what she'd said, and it was bothering the hell out of him. He knew *he* was somehow the reason this attack had happened – or at least the reason it had happened like it did. But that was all he knew.

Karma ground her teeth, but didn't press him again. "All right. Graymalkin, tell us what our other problems are."

"We're well stocked on food," he said. "We brought more than we needed for our planned ten-day stay, and everything except what was in the kitchenette was sealed and protected from the flooding."

Vic's throat felt dry when he asked, "*But...?*"

"But air is a different story. When the creatures, the– ah, the Aqueos tore the descent capsule off its moorings, the damage breached the air vents. Water flooded into atmospherics and ruined the compressed gas tanks. If we'd been a fully trained crew, and a little more on top of things... well, that's not worth dwelling on. Triage and I got a backup in place, but the backup was only intended for emergencies. It would last a full crew a day or two so they could evacuate. For the seven of us... I'd say maybe four days. Maybe more. Maybe less."

"One way or another," Karma said. "I expect we're not going to be here in four days."

That was not very morale-boosting. Karma didn't sound like she meant it as a joke. Something was rattling the deck plating. Vic peeked underneath the table, and saw that it was Josh's leg, bouncing up and down. Irritation flashed through Vic's temples. He nearly snapped at Josh. He knew his reaction was out of proportion to the offense, but his nerves were taut as guitar strings. Every little pluck made him *twang*.

Graymalkin cleared his throat. "Every deck took damage, but the upper deck got the worst of it," he said. "The conference room is a total loss. There are some pockets of air in it trapped in its ceiling, but otherwise it's flooded out."

"The ocean lives there now," Josh said. Vic's mood was such

that it took him far too long to figure out Josh had tried to tell a joke.

They all dealt with anxiety and dread in different ways. Vic had lapsed into silence, while Josh fidgeted. Too much nervous energy. Josh was becoming a motormouth. His interjections were forced, and his humor mirthless.

"The ocean's always lived here," Nature Girl said. "We shouldn't have come."

"Didn't you volunteer for this mission?" Josh asked her.

"Obviously I shouldn't have," Nature Girl said.

"Both of you, *be quiet*," Karma said.

The sharpness in her voice brought a deep silence over the kitchenette. Karma nodded to Graymalkin to continue.

Graymalkin looked at her uneasily. "Most of the other cabins up there weren't fully flooded, but are still damaged beyond our ability to repair. Unfortunately, this includes all of our guest quarters." Vic's heart sank. His bag, with his phone and his clothes and everything else he'd brought with him, had been up there. "About the only cabin up there that wasn't badly affected is hydroacoustic communications. For all the good it's doing at the moment."

"We'll need to keep it crewed, just like the emergency control cabin," Karma said.

"Yes. There is, however, the security problem."

Karma raised her eyebrow, but nodded at him to go on.

"The first deck is the most dangerous part of the station. It's not just risk of more flooding. We lost full security camera coverage of the exterior. Some of the cameras were destroyed when the descent capsule was torn out. We can still see in *most* directions. But if the Aqueos work out where we have our blind spots…" He shook his head. No need to finish that sentence. "The damaged cabins are accessible from outside."

"So if another Aqueos got into the conference room, we'd never know they were there," Josh said.

"The corridor outside the damaged waterlock is also flooded. There are only regular hatches holding back the water there. If the Aqueos got in, they'd just have to spin the hatch wheel and push."

Wonderful. Vic let his head fall back and *clunk* against the bulkhead.

It got worse. "And power?" Karma asked.

"Triage, Nature Girl, and I mapped out our power consumption," Graymalkin said, with a glance at Nature Girl. From her grimace, she must have known what was coming. "In most circumstances, we wouldn't have any worries about power. The microfusion cells down there should last for years of ordinary use."

Josh's legs stopped bouncing. "I don't like the way you said 'ordinary'."

Graymalkin nodded. "The defense grid is an emergency system, not designed for repeated use. A handful of deterrent shocks at most." Vic remembered the way the lights in the wet cabin had dimmed when Karma had ordered the initial series of blasts. Several of them never came back on. "We've fired it too many times already. I'm afraid our power grid is going to burn out. It's like using a parachute over and over again without safety checking it. Sooner or later, it's going to fail."

"Any idea how long?" Karma asked.

"It could fail the next time the Aqueos attack. It could fail ten days from now. The only way to know for sure is when it happens. And all Triage, Nature Girl, and I can tell you is that it's getting worse. You've all seen lights go out and not come back on. Pieces of the electric grid have already burned out."

Karma stared ahead as if neither seeing nor hearing him. "All right," she said, after a moment. "Let's assume we're going to have help arriving in three days. All of our efforts should be geared toward surviving that long, or shortening the time we'll have to wait by getting in touch with the surface."

Vic thought three days was on the optimistic side, but didn't say so. He understood what she was doing. Giving her team a goal, whether invented or not, was straight out of the Institute's own leadership courses.

"Given the danger, we'll handle everything in teams unless absolutely necessary," Karma said. "Nature Girl. You and Triage have already made a good pair. Crosta, Graymalkin, and I are going to come up with our next steps. Anole, you and Elixir will–"

"I'd rather work with Graymalkin," Vic said. "Or you."

"I don't care," Karma said. Even with the way she'd already been acting, the coldness of her voice surprised him. "You and Elixir are going to take first shift in hydroacoustics."

Vic's gaze fixed on Josh. Josh kept his eyes on Karma, though he must have noticed. Among all the other horrors on Vic's mind, he hadn't forgotten about Josh, and the way Josh's arm had molded like clay in his grip. He couldn't prove to the others it had happened, but he knew it had.

Josh's power was supposed to be like Triage's – limited to healing. If there was more, Josh definitely knew about it. He was hiding it.

"Are we going to communicate with them?" Nature Girl asked abruptly.

Karma blinked. "With who?"

"The Aqueos. We know they're intelligent. They want something. Maybe we could... find out what."

Crosta was shaking his head before she finished the sentence. With a strange air of finality, Karma said, "They won't talk."

Nature Girl sank into her seat. Vic's frown deepened. "How do you know?" he asked.

Karma pretended she hadn't heard. She turned to talk privately with Graymalkin, a motion meant to break up the meeting and send everybody out on their tasks.

"Karma," Vic said, louder.

With an air of considerable reluctance and irritation, Karma took her attention off Graymalkin and back to Vic.

"What are the Aqueos afraid of?"

Everyone was looking at Vic now, but no one more intently than Karma. "How do you mean?" she asked.

"You attacked the Aqueos with your power. You showed it its fears. Doesn't your telepathy let you... see what those fears are, too?"

"It does," she said. "Usually."

"And this time?"

"It didn't."

For as readily as Vic had believed Crosta, he was just as sure now that Karma was lying. "It didn't," she repeated, "and it doesn't matter."

He wanted to ask again, to press her like she'd pressed Crosta. The question seized in his throat.

Their classroom relationship might have gotten rocky since he'd come back from New York... but she was still Karma. She wasn't a martinet, or a habitual liar, or a classroom despot. If she was hiding the truth, she had good reason.

Maybe. He wasn't sure of anything anymore.

At the start of this meeting, he thought he'd known who and where his enemies were. Josh Foley across the table. The monsters outside the station's hull. Everyone else, he may not have liked, but he at least trusted them, even Crosta. And he'd assumed they trusted him.

"Go," Karma said, looking straight at him. "Get to work."

CHAPTER ELEVEN
Anole

Vic and Josh did not say a word as they climbed the steps to the first deck. Even if they'd been friends, talking would have felt too much like tempting fate, like drawing attention to themselves. Vic couldn't forget Graymalkin's warning that one of the Aqueos could be in one of the flooded compartments right now, and they'd have no way of knowing.

The first deck was steeped in silence. Vic swallowed as they passed the closed hatch to the conference room. He kept his ears perked. If someone were to open that hatch while he and Josh were working, all that rushing water would be between them and the stairs.

Maybe Josh would survive, depending on how many abilities he'd hidden. Vic wouldn't. Anoles, the lizard from which Vic had gotten his callsign and powers, had some tricks to help them last underwater. Their hydrophobic skin would make a thin sheath of air around them. But they weren't true water-breathers, and neither was Vic.

Vic and Josh did not say anything as they worked. When they needed to, they communicated with looks and gestures. They sent some test signals up to the buoy, just in case it was still there. Vic didn't expect to receive a reply, but somehow reality didn't even meet *that* low expectation. The last workstation they needed, the one with a ticker-tape printer to spit out any signals they received, refused to start up.

The wiring behind it had burned out. It must have happened the last time the defensive grid had fired.

There was only space for one of them behind the console. Vic didn't trust Josh behind him, but he sure didn't trust him monkeying around with the station's comm equipment, either. Vic was small enough to be a better fit, anyway. He pushed himself in back-first, in a seated position so he could keep one eye his voltmeter and one on Josh.

Vic knew Josh was about to break the silence five seconds before he did. Josh steeled his shoulders. "Look–"

"I don't want to hear it," Vic interrupted.

The way Josh looked taken aback was a bit satisfying. But Josh didn't stop. "I just want to make sure we can work together until we can all get out of this."

"I've got no problem working together," Vic said, carefully neutral.

Not technically a lie. That didn't mean he trusted Josh. If Josh picked up on that, he didn't say so. "Good," Josh said.

The console plugged into a heavy, ancient-looking outlet. It just wasn't working. Vic pushed himself farther back, gripping the voltmeter with his teeth. There had to be another outlet back here, or something else they didn't need and could unplug. The last thing he wanted to do was run out an extension or anything else that could get in the way of the hatch closing in an emergency.

Josh's leg was bouncing on the deck again. "What if it's the acoustics equipment that caused this?" he asked. "Or the sonar?"

Vic spat out the voltmeter. "What the hell are you talking about?"

"What if the Aqueos are attacking because of all the noise the station is pumping into the ocean?"

"The Aqueos are intelligent enough to use weapons and to sign treaties," Vic said. "If they had a problem with this station that they didn't in all the years it was here before, they could have *said* so rather than try to murder us."

"I thought you said we should try to communicate with them, like Nature Girl suggested."

"No," Vic said. There was more of an edge to Vic's voice than he meant, but he didn't try to dull it. It felt good. "I've thought about it. Karma's right. I don't think there's anything out there that wants to, or could, communicate."

"I guess I don't have as much experience with these things as you do," Josh said, with a bitter edge to match Vic's.

"That's right, you *don't*. This is something you get pretty used to as a mutant. All kinds of people out there hating you, attacking you relentlessly, and damn sure never open to 'talking it through'. That's what life as a mutant is. Their reasons don't matter."

Damn it. None of the other outlets had power. They'd either have to waste time disassembling the bulkhead to replace the wiring, and likely lose the whole thing again the next time the defense grid fired, or risk running an extension after all.

"You think the whole world's out to get you, all the time?" Josh asked.

Vic grabbed the console's back corner and pulled himself out. "No. Not the whole world. Enough of it. It'd take a miracle to get through to some of the people attacking us, and miracles are in short supply." A miracle like Josh had had, waking up to find out he was a mutant after all. "I've learned that the best way to deal with a bully isn't to be the nice guy. It's to fight back."

"Good advice," Josh said, with a pointed stare. Vic picked up the intended message clearly.

Josh constantly amazed Vic. He actually thought *Vic* was the bully here.

The lights flickered. An instant later, the alarms went off, shrieking in their ears. Vic and Josh kept staring at each other as the lights went dimmer and darker.

Karma insisted that the alarms be sounded every time the Aqueos approached. She wanted to give everybody time to prepare for the worst.

By the time Vic and Josh got to the emergency command cabin, the excitement was over. The Aqueos had sent another raiding party, probing the station's defenses. Nature Girl had spotted the Aqueos raiding party coming as she'd flicked through the cameras. She still sat with her hand on something like an old-fashioned channel knob on a mid-twentieth-century television, flipping through camera angles.

"Can't you check those feeds any faster?" Karma asked.

"We only have the one monitor," Triage said balefully.

Karma held them at the ready for an interminably long time

after the attack. Vic understood why – they had to be together and on guard if anything had gotten through – but the wait was still agonizing. There wasn't enough room in the emergency command cabin for all of them, so Vic lingered in the hallway. The dimmed lights and close quarters reminded him of tornado drills in school. He felt like he should be squatting against the bulkhead, hands over his head.

"There's something interesting about these attacks," Nature Girl said suddenly.

"Really? I was bored up until now," Josh said.

"Shut up, Josh," Triage said, saving Vic the trouble. Crosta stood between Vic and Josh. With his stiff demeanor and fishy breath, he was like a wall.

Nature Girl went on as if they hadn't said anything: "They've come from different directions each time."

"So they're testing us," Karma said.

"I don't think they would know about the exterior cameras," Triage said. "On something as big as this station, they'd still be pretty hard to spot. If they don't see them, though, they can spot the portholes pretty easily."

"And they figure there's not enough of us to watch every angle all the time," Karma said. That cabin didn't give her much space to move. She folded her arms, and faced one of the other bulkheads. "They're going to slip through eventually."

Silence. They all knew it.

When she turned back, her voice sounded numb. It was unlike her. "When the alarms went off, it took you all ninety seconds to rally here. You need to be much faster. Thirty seconds, maximum."

And those alarms came at irregular intervals throughout the

rest of the day, like a thready heartbeat. It was just unpredictable enough to make Vic jump every time it went off, and keep his pulse racing through the long wait outside the emergency control cabin.

As bad as the day was, the night was worse. (To whatever extent there was such a thing as "night" here.) His sleep shift was scheduled from ten am to four pm, the same as Josh's. With the guest cabins still waterlogged, they were stuck together in the old crew bunks on the second deck. Though Vic didn't think he could sleep in the same room as Josh, he was dead asleep the moment he lay down.

The next alarm went off at ten fifteen.

Karma kept them at the emergency control cabin just as long as every other time. Vic hadn't slept for long, but his mind felt like it had been blasted apart. The drumbeat of his racing pulse, his adrenaline, and his lurching, sleep-distorted imagination turned the world into a lurid nightmare. He had to focus to remember where each hatch led. Every shadow hid an Aqueos.

He fell asleep again as soon as Karma released them, but the alarms went off again at eleven thirty. And one. And two fifteen. The last came so close to the end of their sleeping period that there was no point in trying to rest again.

By taking the risk of threading an extension up the stairs and through the hatches, Vic and Josh got all of the hydroacoustics consoles working again, but to no more avail than before. Their signals radiated into an empty ocean.

After two hours of radio silence and one alarm, Vic went to the kitchenette to try to find something to eat. None of them were supposed to travel alone, but Josh said he wasn't hungry. Vic didn't believe him for a moment, but didn't argue. He sent Josh to go check in with Karma, Graymalkin, and Crosta in the emergency control cabin just down the hall. So long as they were all on the same deck, Vic figured that would have to be close enough.

Afterward, he'd check with Graymalkin to make sure Josh had done as he'd been told, too.

Nature Girl and Triage were supposed to be on sleep shift. So he started when he entered the kitchenette and saw them at the table, wordlessly staring out the porthole.

"No point in trying to rest now," Triage said, by way of explanation. "It's been an hour and a half since the last alarm."

He was right. The Aqueos were due for another attack any minute.

Vic hadn't gotten used to the smell of the station's air, but it was worse now. The flooding had left a wave of humidity that, even with the air processors chugging as hard as they could, would take weeks to clear out. The humidity had deepened the smell, made it heavy enough to stick to the inside of Vic's nostrils. Vic could only imagine long-dormant, desiccated molds in the air vents coming back to life. In spite of how hungry he was, he couldn't imagine food tasting good.

He reached under the cupboard and pulled out one of the bottles of hot sauce. It still looked like something out of a geology class – a slice of earth divided into neat sedimentary layers. Rough, pebbly pepper. Smooth red magma. And clear vinegar and oils. He was starting to understand, now, why these had been left here.

"Hold up just a minute," Triage said. "You're not actually going to…?"

"It's *hot sauce*," Vic said. "Peppers and vinegar are preservatives."

Triage and Nature Girl looked at Vic doubtfully, but Vic was beyond caring. He just wanted to taste something. The station's last crew had known exactly what this air mixture and pressure would do to the next crew's sense of taste and smell, and what it would take to beat that.

It took quite a bit of shaking to merge the layers together. They still weren't quite blended by the time Vic lost patience and poured out it over a bowl of trail mix. On the surface, this much hot pepper would have knocked him writhing to the floor.

Here… the flavor exploded in his mouth. The taste of salt in particular came alive. Vic realized he hadn't tasted salt, even on salty foods, at all here. The heat was as muted as everything else, but, since it was so strong to begin with, it was strong enough to break through to him. It was maybe the first pleasant thing he'd felt since boarding the station.

Seeing him wolf down trail mix covered in hot sauce, Nature Girl and Triage set aside their skepticism long enough to try some. A minute later, they were all clustered around the bowl, pouring more hot sauce and dipping every food they could think of.

Vic was still groggy, but a flood of energy surged back into him. Until now, he'd eaten as poorly as he'd slept. This at least went partway toward making up some of his deficits.

"You don't suppose this is going to lead to any, um, digestive issues?" Triage asked.

"You're the healer," Vic said. "Can't you make it better?"

"An irritated bowel is not an injury. Everything's working as it should. There's nothing to heal. You probably don't want me experimenting in there unless it's an emergency."

"It could become an emergency," Vic said, though he

did not for a second cut down on the hot sauce. Vic chewed thoughtfully. He'd been trying to find an opportunity to do some prying. "What does it feel like when you heal people?" he asked Triage.

"It's a bit like... there's a heat in my hands, and I can seep it into other people when I touch them. I feel injuries and send the heat there."

"You're in the same medical courses as Josh," Vic said. "Does his healing ability work the same way?"

"Yeah. Why?"

"How do you know it does?" he asked.

"Because that's what he told us."

Vic could tell he was getting close to sated because the thought of a granola bar dipped in hot sauce was starting to seem weird again. He let that line of questioning die there. He'd gotten what he needed to know.

"It's not Josh I'm worried about," Triage said. "It's Karma."

Vic raised his brow. "Yeah?"

"I don't think she's taking this very well."

"Come on, Triage," Vic said. "She's an X-Man."

"Triage is being nice," Nature Girl said. "Karma seems like a different person."

Vic thought he'd had enough to worry about already. He wanted to call the way Karma had been acting "troubled", but maybe the better word was that it was *troubling*. Being snappish and irritable was understandable, given the stress. What was not understandable was that she hadn't even put herself on the sleep schedule. Vic didn't think he'd seen her eat, either. The lines under her eyes read like she hadn't slept in days.

"I don't get that," Vic said. "She's faced a lot of dangerous situations before this. Fought pretty vicious enemies. All the X-Men have. Why has this one got her so brittle?"

"Maybe this is how the X-Men all keep surviving," Triage said. "Heroics aren't all quips and puns and fast knockouts. There's terror and stress and trauma–"

"We know," Vic and Nature Girl said, in unison.

"Yeah. Sorry. I know we all know." Triage pursed his lips, as if frustrated by his inability to find the words. "I just think it's something we all ought to keep in mind. She's spending all of her energy looking after us. She has no one to look after her."

Vic didn't get the chance to answer. The station's alarms sounded, as loud as if the horns had gone off in his ear. Break time was over.

This time the Aqueos had tried to slide right up to the underside of the station. Graymalkin had been at the camera controls, and almost hadn't seen them until it was too late.

Karma kept them for even longer than previously. She scanned relentlessly back and forth through the camera feeds, as if sure she'd missed something.

She didn't seem to notice Vic watching her. He tried to count the seconds since he'd seen her blink, but gave up somewhere after seventy. Bright red veins crawled across her eyes. He debated saying that she needed rest, but lost his nerve.

After she released them, Vic caught up with Crosta in the stairwell, about to follow Graymalkin down. "Got a second?" Vic asked. "I need to ask you about that fight you got into outside the station."

"I appreciate your concern," Crosta said, with a voice that made it clear he didn't appreciate much of anything right now. "But, as I've explained five times, I am well. Elixir did an excellent job of healing me."

"No, no, that's not it. I want to know how the Aqueos fought. How did you... and Josh... fight them?"

"A good question. Not even your instructor asked me that." Coming so soon after the conversation about how Karma hadn't seemed like herself, hearing that was like an icicle in his stomach. She *should* have asked. Crosta continued: "There's not much point in denying it: they moved like they aimed to subdue me. There were at least three times when they could have killed me. They were trying to herd me. Maybe capture me." His expression remained opaque, but his body language made it clear how uncomfortable this made him.

"They speared Josh," Vic pointed out.

"That's true. They did go after him with intent to kill. I wonder if they knew how dangerous he was." For the first time since Vic had known him, he smiled. "I'm dangerous myself, and killed several of them with my shockwave, but they were able to harry me to the point where I couldn't create them. Josh, though... all he had to do was reach out and touch an Aqueos, and the creature fell apart."

The icicle in Vic's gut went deeper. "What does that mean?"

"I mean – just that. The Aqueos just... fell apart. No violence, no explosion. Just arms and leggings, drifting off." Crosta clapped Vic on the shoulder in a manner probably meant to be reassuring. "If the rest of you are a fraction as powerful, the Aqueos have made a terrible mistake coming here."

CHAPTER TWELVE
Elixir

Josh hadn't eaten since coming out of the ocean. Hunger he'd felt beforehand finally caught up with him. After the next alarm, he ducked into the kitchenette, and was surprised to see Nature Girl there.

"Aren't you supposed to be sleeping?" Josh asked.

"Aren't you supposed to be working with Anole?" she asked.

"He's gone to chat with Crosta." Josh hadn't asked why. The more time away from Anole, the better.

"There's only twenty-five minutes before Christopher and I have to get up anyway."

"Christopher? Oh- right." Triage's given name. Christopher Muse. Interesting to know who was on a first-name basis with who.

Anole called Josh "Josh", but not out of any sense of closeness. Where names weren't a sign of friendship, or of knowing someone outside of the bounds of their role, they seemed to be some kind of power play. If social rules at the Institute were this complicated, Josh could only imagine what it was like for the X-Men.

"In your head, do you think of me as Josh or Elixir?" Josh asked.

Nature Girl looked at him. "Which do you want to be?"

The first answer that came to mind was: "Neither."

For the first time since he'd met her, Nature Girl actually looked interested in something he'd said.

He found himself going on almost against his will. He wasn't made to stay trapped in himself. The more he talked, the less he needed to think about what he'd done to the Aqueos outside. Those few seconds had become a lifetime of blurred memories. "Josh Foley wasn't a good person," he said. "And Elixir is just a word."

She smiled, though there was no humor in it. "You don't know what you want to be when you grow up."

"In a few words? That's not a bad way of describing it. I was in high school when ... I found out I was a mutant."

"You're not as alone as you think. The Institute and the Jean Grey School are a crossroads for a lot of people."

"What about you?"

Nature Girl took a long time to answer. Josh was briefly transfixed by the sight of her dunking a granola bar into what, judging from the open bottle nearby, was hot sauce. Mutants could have some strange tastes.

Finally, she said, "The world up there is a big, heavy weight, and I don't have it in me to be a hero."

Nature Girl hadn't said much to him before now. Maybe she, too, couldn't stand keeping her thoughts sealed up inside her.

She'd hardly seemed extroverted, but everyone needed some sort of human connection. Josh didn't figure she was wholly self-sufficient, or she wouldn't have gone to the Jean Grey School.

She didn't like him, but the longer Josh spent inside his own head, the harder it was to blame anybody for that. At least she wasn't openly hostile.

"I think you're holding up pretty well now," he said. "You're not panicking, or tearing your hair out, or any of the other things I feel like doing."

This time, there *was* some humor in her smile. Not much, but some. Funny thing was, he'd meant his words *as* a joke, but they sure hadn't come out sounding like it. "The thing is, I'm used to the stress," she said. "That's the problem."

"Does this kind of nonsense happen to mutants all the time? I mean, I know it does to the X-Men, but to students?"

"Not all the time. Just a lot. That wasn't what I meant. Do they teach you much about the future at the Institute?" she asked.

"You mean about time travel? A little."

"What about how, of all the future timelines we've seen, so few of them end up well for mutants? Or how it's somewhere between hard and impossible to change that?"

"Honestly, the rules for time travel with the X-Men are so convoluted I had trouble following." After Blindfold and Atlas Bear had given him not-so-oblique hints about his future, he'd wanted to know as little about it as possible.

"It's hard for mutants to keep hope sometimes."

"Is that why you went to the Jean Grey School? To try to become a hero?"

"Kind of. I've worked with Rogue and some of the other X-Men in the past, but never really had a chance to train. I wanted to give the Jean Grey School a shot. One problem that places like the Charles Xavier Institute and the Jean Grey School have is that, if anything, they're *too* focused on mutants. My teachers have a hard time remembering mutants are a small part of a bigger world."

"You think the rest of the world is in for a bad time, too?"

"No, I think it's screwed." The sharpness of the words sounded odd in her voice. "I know it is. It's my powers. I hear every animal, every insect, every plant around me. I can't *stop* hearing them if I wanted to. All the consequences of over-development, climate change, mass extinctions, plastics everywhere... it's all around me. I can't stop paying attention. And I know it's not going to get any better."

Josh had had a lot of different people try to tell him what the future would be like over the past few days. He hadn't thought Nature Girl would be one of them. "I think there are always ways to change the world," he said.

"That was what I thought. Then I got involved in some of the fights the X-Men can't always protect us from. And I started to find out more about what everybody's limits were." Not just her limits, Josh noted. "You know, for a person who used to be a bigot, you're a pretty good listener."

Used to be. Josh wished he could convince himself that Anole hadn't been right – that he wasn't the same terrible person as before, just in different circumstances. "I'm trying. You know, every time I learn more about being a mutant, I find something new to be depressed and upset about. You've known you were a mutant a lot longer than I have. How do you stand it?"

Another thin smile. "I don't." When he tilted his head, she said, "That was why I came here. The voices of the wild and the pressure were piling up and up and… I thought it would stop if I went somewhere they couldn't reach me."

"I mean to say… you went under a mile of ocean water to *escape the pressure.*"

"Yeah. That part of it worked. I don't feel as much of the wild as I used to."

"Do you feel better, then?" he asked.

She shook her head, slowly but firmly.

Josh pressed his lips together as he tried and failed to think of a way to answer that. For a long while, he and Nature Girl sat and maintained uneasy eye contact. Josh couldn't tell whether the gulf between them was five or five hundred feet. Maybe both at the same time.

The lights winked out.

His nerves, already stretched to their breaking point, nearly snapped. He waited for the lights to flicker back on, as they had after the defense grid fired. He braced for sirens to start blaring in his ear. He counted the seconds under his breath.

A crawling sensation trilled down Josh's back. He'd gotten as far as *three* before he realized that this time was different. The air recirculators had stopped. The fan blades still swished through the air, but slower, gradually coming to rest.

Every other time one of the lights had gone out, it hadn't happened everywhere. His eyes had had time to start adjusting. The kitchenette's hatch had been open to the corridor outside. If there had been lights on anywhere, even as far back as the stairwells, he should have seen them.

There was no power. Anywhere. They were lost in an impenetrable dark.

He jolted upright. His knees banged against the underside of the table, but the adrenaline dampened the pain. Somewhere in the pitch dark, Nature Girl yelped as her plate knocked off the table and audibly shattered.

On his way to the hatch, Josh's foot tangled on the leg of a chair. He'd seen it on the way in, but there was not even a glimmer of light for him to tell where it was now. His mutant powers and sense of bodily awareness told him that his pupils were fully blown. If there had been any light, anywhere, he would have detected it.

The vibrations of unsteady footsteps told him Nature Girl was right behind him. He got outside the kitchenette and grappled along the corridor wall, trying to remember where the emergency kits with the flashlights were. He'd seen other people use them, and their training had *covered* where they were, but in the total dark and the fog of panic, his fingers couldn't find them.

A screech and a shocked, panicked yell echoed up from the deck below. Josh froze in place. The yell had sounded like Crosta's. But the screech was a voice he'd never heard before.

A burst of noise, of metal scraping and banging against metal, erupted somewhere ahead. Josh flinched back. He realized too late that the noise was deck plating bouncing as something heavy barreled down it.

Dry, scaly skin crashed into him.

He'd grabbed the creature by the arm and drawn back his fist to punch it before he realized he was holding Anole's arm.

Anole's fist swished through the air, glancing off Josh's cheek. "It's me, it's Josh!" Josh said, hoping that would get him to *stop* rather than swing again.

Anole grabbed Josh's arm, feeling it in several places as if to be absolutely sure. "What in the hell is going–" Anole started.

He couldn't finish. Another presence thudded toward them, slamming footsteps into deck grating. Razor-sharp pain ripped along Josh's shoulder. It knocked Anole into the bulkhead, and Josh back into Nature Girl.

Aqueos.

This Aqueos couldn't have climbed through the docking hatch and gotten all the way up here in the half minute since the power had gone out. It must have already been here, waiting. This attack had been coordinated.

There was more shouting, close to his ears. Nature Girl's voice, and then Anole. Josh was too jarred to make sense of it. His shirt was hot and sticky on his skin. His blood.

In the instant Josh had come into contact with the Aqueos, its body had flashed through his awareness – the same way that it did when he healed people.

Josh jabbed the heel of his palm into the darkness. It struck the Aqueos's arm and deflected it. Josh's fortune ended there. The Aqueos turned its full attention to Josh. Searing pain ripped down his arm.

A gnashing *snap* of jaws pierced the darkness, close to Josh's ear. The Aqueos shrieked in rage.

Graymalkin roared back.

At least, Josh thought it was Graymalkin. The voice had the right cadence, but it was louder and angrier than any other noise he'd heard Graymalkin make. It was a battle cry.

Then another weight, a fourth body, slammed into all of them. Josh was thrown into the bulkhead. The impact knocked the air from his lungs. He slid to his knees, breathless.

Josh had harbored a dread that someone on the station had betrayed them and let the Aqueos inside. This put that fear to rest. The Aqueos had pulled off this attack with ingenuity and a great deal of careful planning. One thing they didn't have was foreknowledge. They didn't know about the mutants' powers. Graymalkin was nigh-invincible in the dark.

Josh had fallen close enough to the Aqueos that his hand brushed its ankle. That strange awareness of its body returned. He sensed it regaining its balance and tensing to counterattack. Then it jolted. Graymalkin had struck faster.

Josh's awareness of the creature extended inside as well as out. A web of bruises and fractures splintered down the Aqueos's ribs. If the creature had had breath, it would have had its wind knocked from it. Even undead, it still staggered.

Josh could have killed it. So long as he was in contact with it, he could have done the same thing to it that he'd done to the Aqueos that had speared him.

Graymalkin grabbed the Aqueos and hurled it. Josh's sense of its body vanished. The Aqueos audibly crashed into the ceiling and fell some distance away.

Josh forced himself to his feet. Blood still soaked his shirt, but the bleeding had stopped. His healing instincts were starting to kick in, but he was stunned, and they'd been slow. Somewhere in the din, he heard another shout. Crosta. After a second, his voice dampened in timbre and volume, as though stifled.

Somewhere in the dark, a hatch slammed on a bulkhead. It took until he heard Karma's voice to realize that the noise had come from the emergency control cabin. "Get to the generators!" she barked.

She had the right idea. More Aqueos would be swarming toward the station right now. They needed power for the defense grid, or they were beyond dead.

A throaty hissing alerted him that the Aqueos had gotten back to its feet. He reflexively sidestepped, and felt the breeze of something swishing through the air beside him.

Everything was a jumble of chaos. More footsteps thudded to his left. A brush of elbow-to-elbow contact gave him a flashbulb image of Nature Girl charging past him, antlers lowered.

The Aqueos shrieked in pain and a deep, red rage. Then there was a heavy impact in the darkness, and Nature Girl grunted. Josh pressed himself against the bulkhead to let Graymalkin get past. The noise moved out of arm's reach.

Josh stumbled over something heavy beneath him. An instant's contact determined it was Nature Girl, crouched on the deck. He bent by her, his hand on her arm.

Something about the darkness made Josh's powers more vivid. He could sense everything about every body he touched. The medical training he'd gotten at the Institute helped him put words to her injuries. She had contused ribs, knee abrasions, and a spasming paralysis of the diaphragm – which was to say she'd gotten her wind knocked out of her.

Without hardly thinking about how, Josh eased her injuries, too. His energy segued into her. He coaxed air into her lungs. "Thanks," she breathed, when she could.

The creature had not stopped shrieking. It didn't need to breathe, but it *must* have drawn in a lot of air to make all that noise. Anole yelled too. But he was swiftly cut off.

Josh scrambled forward on hands and knees. He wanted to call out to ask where Graymalkin was, but didn't have the breath to do so. His hands found Anole on the deck. His injuries were more serious: deep lacerations, down to the bone, on his arm and shoulder. A sprained ankle and broken toes where the

Aqueos must have kicked and stomped Anole's foot out from under him.

"Don't you–" Anole started to say.

Too late. Josh had already unleashed his healing energies. By the time Anole had gathered enough of his wits to push Josh away, his flesh was mostly stitched closed.

Anole sputtered one of the most vicious curses Josh had ever heard.

Josh just pushed past him, toward the shrieking Aqueos. The last thing Josh wanted to do was get closer to it, but it was blocking the stairwell leading down to the generators. He and Anole would have time to argue medical ethics and the right to refuse treatment when they weren't about to get their heads sheared off.

A jarring impact briefly turned the pitch darkness an astonishing variety of colors.

The pain caught up with Josh a moment later – as well as a flashbulb memory of knuckles on his cheekbone. That hadn't been the Aqueos. Anole had punched him.

Long-concealed rage boiled over. Josh shoved Anole back into the bulkhead. This was absolutely not the time to address it, but he couldn't help that first, impulsive shove.

He left Anole, forcing his way forward. His thoughts raced along too many tracks. He had to get away from Anole. And orient himself (the first thing he did was crack his face into a bulkhead, so he wasn't doing great on that one). There was another part of him, though, piecing together a map of the station from all the sounds he'd heard.

Crosta's yell had come from below. The Aqueos up here had been on them soon after. *Too* soon after. The same creature couldn't have been responsible for both. Or for whatever had cut the station's power. There were multiple Aqueos aboard.

A flurry of activity ahead, just out of arm's reach, brought him to a stop. Graymalkin grunted and then gasped, like he'd been caught by surprise. If *Graymalkin*, fully immersed in darkness, could be bested by one of the Aqueos, that bode poorly for the rest of the team.

But Graymalkin wasn't down yet. Josh heard him suck his breath in. Then the deck grating jolted. An eardrum-piercing Aqueos shriek followed. That shriek was overlayered *atop* the first.

There were two of them ahead. That was where Graymalkin had been: fighting a second Aqueos.

Somewhere ahead, Graymalkin sucked in his breath. One of the Aqueos abruptly stopped shrieking. A second later, the deck reverberated with the impact of its body. It didn't stay down. The click-clack of scrabbling clawed feet broke off in two directions.

The Aqueos were splitting up. One of them was retreating down to the third deck. And the other was heading toward the stairwell up.

Fear squeezed Josh's heart. There wasn't much left up on the first deck. Just hydroacoustic communications... and all those hatches holding back the water in the flooded chambers.

All the Aqueos would have to do was spin one of those hatch wheels open and–

He didn't follow that thought to its conclusion. He reached out and found Graymalkin's shoulders. "Go up," Josh told him. As much as they needed power back, the upper deck was their most pressing emergency. They had to send their best fighter after it.

Graymalkin didn't need to be told again. His footsteps raced after the Aqueos heading upwards.

Josh's feet found the first step heading down. He took the steps by memory, as quickly as he could, hand tight on the rail. Someone thumped along behind him. He didn't know who until he heard Anole ask, "Where the hell is Karma?"

For all Josh knew, Karma had been telepathically attacking the Aqueos all along. But he'd heard no sign of her since that first barked order. She'd left everything else to her students.

Josh only knew he had reached the bottom when he extended his foot to take another step and met deck grating. He stumbled face-first into the opposite bulkhead. The second after he got his balance back, light flared in his eyes, bright and stinging.

Anole had found one of the emergency kits, and a flashlight. The beam danced as Anole spun to face down the corridor. It fell across the gray-green form of a skulking Aqueos.

Josh saw it only for an instant. The Aqueos crashed into Anole, and the flashlight went spinning. Josh reflexively caught it.

Each time he'd touched the Aqueos, he learned more about their bodies. Their basic features remained Atlantean. Their eyes weren't all that different. They had pupils that dilated open and closed.

Josh shone the flashlight in its eyes. The Aqueos was perched atop Anole. It halted, claws raised mid-swipe. It held in place for a quarter second too long.

Josh's stomach rebelled at the thought of using his powers against these things. Conventional violence, though – that was something else.

He slammed his flashlight into the creature's face. It fell off

Anole. Anole was up faster than Josh could get his foot back on the ground. Josh passed him the flashlight. Anole smashed his overgrown right fist into the Aqueos' head. Three hits, four hits, five – until it fell unmoving.

Corroded batteries aside, these flashlights really *had* been designed to last. The beam hadn't even flickered.

He and Anole were alone down here. Nature Girl must have gone with Graymalkin, or back to regroup with Karma and Triage.

Triage. Josh realized he hadn't heard a thing from Triage since the power had gone out.

Anole stood, gasping for breath. He glared at Josh as if to ask why he hadn't gone on ahead, then threw the flashlight back at him. Josh caught it, spun, and went down the corridor.

His cheek still smarted where Anole had punched him. It felt petty to dwell on it now, but it was better than thinking about the throngs of Aqueos that must have been swarming upon the station.

Somewhere behind him, Anole found another wall-mounted emergency kit, and cracked it open. He was still wrestling with its flashlight, trying to find the "on" switch, when Josh reached the hatch to the generator cabin.

The hatch wasn't sealed shut, like it should have been. It hung carelessly half-open.

The damage inside was obvious the minute Josh's flashlight fell across it. Torn metal plating on the deck. Wiring slashed and hanging loose from the ceiling. Something terribly strong had ripped half of the canister-shaped generator's side off like a cat clawing a curtain. It must have been an Aqueos. Josh *hoped* it was an Aqueos. The alternative was that they'd brought something even worse along with them. He couldn't have repaired this if he'd had full lighting, a technical manual, and a week to work.

They had minutes, at best. Josh's thoughts raced.

Backup generator. They still had the smaller backup generator. Josh turned shakily back to the corridor. His flashlight beam caught on the hatch leading to the backup generator's chamber. It was also open.

With the deck still slick with salt water, it was not safe to run. Josh ran.

He leveled his flashlight into the open hatchway. The backup generator was smaller, but all the same accoutrements were crammed onto it: wiring, monitors, piped-in water cooling, and more. It looked twice as complicated as the primary generator.

It took Josh a moment to comprehend what he was seeing, which was that nothing seemed wrong. It was too much to hope that the hatch had been left open for no reason. Josh stepped into the cabin, sweeping his flashlight across the corners.

Anole's flashlight beam joined Josh's. Josh only paused long enough to verify that it *was* Anole.

"Where the hell is Karma?" Anole asked. He must have seen the primary generator, too. "She's the one with the training and the experience for fixing these damn things."

"We're going to have to do without," Josh said tightly. He waved his flashlight around the back of the generator. All he saw were fragments of shadows, the shape and sharpness of broken glass, dancing everywhere he aimed the light. "Find Crosta. We both heard him fighting with an Aqueos down here."

Anole hesitated at the hatchway. "And leave you to work on this alone?" His tone didn't bother to hide the fact that he didn't trust Josh in here. He shone his flashlight at Josh's face. "You're not a microfusion scientist," Anole said. "You don't know anything about these power cells. What are you going to do? *Guess* at balancing thermonuclear reactions?"

Josh's flashlight fell across a six-inch throw switch with a rubber-coated handle. The color had faded with age, but it had originally been painted red. A large square around it had been marked off with tape that must originally have been the same color. Someone had wanted it to catch the eye. Josh grabbed the handle and yanked it down.

Immediately, something inside the generator snapped. Indicators lit across its side. The cabin remained dark, but the fans in the air vents started thrumming again.

"Well," Anole said. "Ah." Then: "That works too."

Josh glared at him. Anole's moment of sheepishness vanished quickly. He glared right back. They didn't watch each other for more than a second, but it was still a second Josh felt guilty about spending. Just *once*, it would be nice if Anole gave him the benefit of the doubt. At least while they were fighting for their lives.

His attention snagged on something red and glistening on the bulkhead. The color was much brighter than the faded paint on the throw switch.

It was blood. He knew before he finished aiming his flashlight at it. There was too much of it. It had been smeared around, too. Someone had been thrown against the bulkhead, and then – what? There was no bloody trail on the deck grating to show what might have happened.

Anole's breath caught as he saw what Josh had seen. Josh knew, from all the times he and his powers had touched the Aqueos, that they didn't have blood. At best, they had rot and ichor. The only person on the team – the only person with living, iron-red blood – who had been down here was Crosta.

Crosta, who they hadn't heard from in minutes.

A crashing noise drew both of their attention outside. Josh ran to the hatch, with Anole right behind him.

Without Anole's flashlight in his eyes, Josh could see pale, flickering lights all over the ceiling. They were just bright enough to see, not to see by. The station's lights were coming back on, but slowly.

Now that Josh knew to look for it, he spotted another streak of blood on the bulkhead, close to the deck. Something bloody had brushed through here. Or been dragged past. Then his flashlight beam fell on an Aqueos two dozen feet ahead, at the base of the stairwell.

Ichor ran in a stream down the side of its forehead, and its wrist was twisted at an odd angle. It must have been the source of the crash. It raised its good hand to shield its eyes from Josh's flashlight. Then it bolted down the corridor, toward the wet cabins.

A half second later, Graymalkin leapt from the stairwell, and right into the path of Josh's light. He cringed from it. Josh hastily lifted the beam, but too late. Graymalkin's pursuit had been disrupted. The wounded Aqueos reached the wet cabin.

Graymalkin barreled after it. In the dark, he was terrifyingly fast – a nightmare of a nocturnal predator. But the Aqueos knew exactly where it was going. Josh hadn't even reached the first of the wet cabin's double hatches before he heard the *plunk* of a diving body.

When Josh reached the other side of the last hatch, Graymalkin stood alone over the diving pool, peering down.

Before Josh could breathe a word of warning, Graymalkin jumped in, feet first.

Josh ran to the pool's edge, yelling his name. But Graymalkin had already vanished into the rippling water. Josh's flashlight didn't penetrate far into the inky depths. If the station's exterior lights had been on, he might have seen Graymalkin or the Aqueos in silhouette, but the power disruption had taken those out too. Now there was just infinite black, turned starry by the waves and the still-warming lights overhead.

An adrenaline-addled part of him wanted to dive in after Graymalkin, like he had after Crosta during the first attack. Without the exterior lights, though, the most he could have done was get lost and drown.

The diving pool's hatch should have been closed and locked. Josh could not help but notice there was no sign of forced entry. No bent or twisted metal, as there had been back at the primary generator.

At least he had an excuse to ditch Anole. "Stay here," he said. "Help Graymalkin when he comes back." He didn't give Anole a chance to answer, but just charged out of the cabin.

The only cabins on this deck that Josh hadn't already visited were the cargo holds. Their hatches were closed. He knew, deep in his gut, that he wouldn't find Crosta in any of them.

He bolted up the stairwell. By the time he reached the top, the overhead lights had *almost* brightened enough to see by. Karma's and Triage's muffled voices echoed along the bulkheads. A knot of worry inside Josh loosened. Triage was all right.

The knot didn't stay loose for long. Triage and Karma were arguing. "The warning light is showing that the diving pool hatch is open," Triage said, as forcefully as Josh had ever heard him. "We don't know if that makes it safe for any of us in *here*–"

"I don't care," Karma said. "Don't stop charging that capacitor."

There was only one system on the station demanding enough to need a large capacitor charge. Josh dashed toward the emergency control cabin. It was shut. He banged on it, spinning the wheel with his free hand as fast as he could. "Graymalkin and Crosta are out there!"

When he pulled the hatch open, he found Triage was seated at the workstation, eyes wide. Karma stood behind him, arms folded. The poor overhead lighting and pale glow from the monitor made them both look sickly. Karma stood stoic as statuary. She looked to him with exactly as much emotion *as* an ancient statue, eyes weathered blank by time.

Triage hunched over his console as if to shield it. "The capacitor's charged, but Josh is right. If they're out there, we can't–"

"How long have they been out there?" Karma asked Josh.

"I don't know," Josh said. "Forty, fifty seconds–"

That was all Karma needed to hear. "Long enough." She leaned over Triage's shoulder.

Josh felt like he'd plunged into zero gravity, like the station had entered freefall.

He couldn't move fast enough. Couldn't get between Karma and the controls in the fraction of a second he'd had after realizing what was about to happen.

She found the switch Triage had been protecting and slammed her palm into it – discharging the defense grid.

The lights popped, sparked, and flared out.

CHAPTER THIRTEEN
Anole

Most of the station's lights were out for good. That final, catastrophic discharge from the defense grid had spiked a fatal power surge through many of the station's systems.

Someone had set up three flashlights on the kitchenette's counters and cabinets, arranged in a ring. It was the best they could do to see by. Shadows erupted across every bulkhead, over every surface.

Vic's hands and knees were covered in ice-cold sludge. He'd just come from below decks, rooting around in the crawlspaces under the third deck, trying and failing to repair the power supply to that deck's heating system. It was one of the many casualties the defense grid's power surge had cost them. Vic's leg rattled the deck as he shivered.

The heat of his anger kept him from feeling it.

Vic was early for the meeting. He hadn't wanted to miss a minute of it. This was the first chance they'd had to all be together since the attack.

Graymalkin was the next to arrive. He moved unsteadily,

with a tremor in his step. He still had a towel draped over his shoulders, though he had long since dried out.

He had not been in the water when Karma had fired the defense grid, but he *had* been close enough to the open diving pool to become part of an arc as the electrical discharge found a path to more conductive hardware. Triage and Josh had taken turns healing him. They'd gotten the tissue damage and burns easily, but the nerve damage was more sensitive than either of them had wanted to address. He was likely to be jittery and halting for a while.

But he had made it. Not all of them had.

Crosta was missing. All their searching had found no sign of him anywhere inside the station, other than the blood smeared on the bulkheads. If he'd been in the water, close to the station – no one would ever find more of him than burnt meat on the seafloor.

Vic had nearly pushed Josh away from Graymalkin. His skin still crawled where Josh had touched him. By the time Vic had gotten over himself, it was too late. Josh had already laid hands on Graymalkin. Vic supposed he could trust Josh as far as working with them to fight the Aqueos. An hour ago, he hadn't even been sure of that.

Crosta had been the only other person who'd seen Josh do more than heal.

Vic hadn't had time to think about what to say to the others. Or even how to think about it himself.

One by one, the others filtered in. Karma was the last to arrive. She'd been in the emergency control cabin. The electronics had better surge protection than most of the rest of the stations. The lights were out but the workstation remained functional. Not all of their important equipment had been so fortunate. All but four of their exterior cameras had died. The exterior spotlights were still functioning, but they wouldn't do much good when nobody could see them.

Karma sat, stony-faced, between the shadows cast by two of the flashlights. "Let's hear it," she said. They all started talking at once. Vic was no quieter than the others. His voice was strained, and it took real effort to keep from shouting.

Of all of them, Triage spoke the softest, which somehow made his voice stand out more than the others. "Karma," he started, and then, summing up the bulk of everyone else's words, asked, "what the hell?"

"I had to do it to keep more Aqueos from getting aboard," Karma said. "Are there any other questions, or may we move on?"

Karma hadn't been the one to call this meeting. The story Triage told Vic was that while Vic had been crawling underneath the third deck, he and Graymalkin and Nature Girl had all threatened to stop working unless Karma addressed them as a group.

Graymalkin was the only one of them who hadn't added his voice to the chorus. He said, softly, "You endangered my life."

"You're close to invincible in darkness," Karma said, flatly – ignoring the fact that, with the station's exterior lights turning back on, it hadn't been completely dark out there. "And you had dived fifty seconds before the grid discharged. That was plenty of time to get out. And I'm still not clear on what you were doing out there."

"I was trying to save Crosta," Graymalkin said. "Of course."

Vic added, "Crosta is almost certainly dead if he got caught in that defense grid's blast." He'd meant to say it neutrally, like a statement of fact, but his voice faltered.

Karma set her hands on the table. Then, as if speaking to children, she asked, "Hasn't it occurred to you that Crosta probably allowed them in?"

Vic wasn't sure how to react to that. Part of him wanted to yell at her again. The rest wanted to pretend that she'd never said that.

"You can't mean that," Triage said. The poor lighting made it hard to tell, but Vic thought he looked a shade paler.

"Then you tell me how the Aqueos got in," Karma said.

Vic said, "I was with Crosta, by the stairwell, just a minute before everything happened."

Something about the intensity of Karma's stare made Vic's scales itch. "It would take less than a minute to open the diving pool's hatch."

"Crosta is a mutant," Nature Girl said. "He had no reason to do that to us."

Finally those eyes moved off him. Vic felt like he'd been holding his breath. He'd felt like that a lot lately. "How many mutants have betrayed other mutants?" Karma asked Nature Girl.

"He had no reason," Nature Girl repeated.

"The Aqueos hardly treated Crosta like an ally," Triage pointed out. "I had a look at that blood Josh found in a lab microscope. I've learned enough at the Institute to recognize Atlantean blood cells."

"The double-cross didn't go so well for him," Karma said, so calmly that Vic couldn't tell if she was trying to be funny or not.

No, *calm* wasn't the right word, Vic decided. Nor emotionless, or anything else Vic had been thinking a minute ago. She was displaying plenty of emotions: irritation, tension, impatience. But they were all buried under something bigger. Something so big that, at first glance, it looked like nothing at all.

The closest Vic came to putting his finger on it was thinking about the last time he'd sounded like she did. Back home, in Indiana. Seeing his father taken hostage by human supremacists. *Numb.* That was it. He'd been numb, terrified, in shock, and in a different mental state than he'd ever been in before.

He'd thought his *anxiety* had been bad. Karma was giving every impression not of someone who was affectless but of someone who was numb. She was not the same person who'd come here with them.

Josh sank into his chair. He was the only one of them who didn't look horrified by what Karma had said. The idea that *he* might agree with Karma's accusation just enraged Vic more.

"Anybody could have found a way to let them in," Triage said. "I mean- if we're going to start suspecting each other."

"The rest of us worked in pairs," Josh pointed out. "But Crosta spent most of his time with Karma and Graymalkin. Until right before the attack."

It was very hard for Vic not to think that Josh was deliberately getting on the wrong side of every issue. "Look, the Aqueos attacked us on the second deck very quickly after the power went out," Vic said. "They must have already gotten aboard before Crosta went down there."

"The Aqueos can move extremely fast," Josh said.

"Fast enough to climb inside the station, double-cross Crosta, disable the primary generator, and then launch themselves above deck to attack us?" Vic asked. "In about a minute?"

Josh shrugged. "I don't know how else to explain this."

The team had killed at least one of the Aqueos. Graymalkin had battered it to death during the fight. Without saying much, they'd all dragged its remains to the diving pool, and let it drop.

The Aqueos were already undead. No reason they couldn't eventually rise again. And no reason to take chances.

While they'd done that, Vic eyed the broken laboratory cabinets. It had been where he had deposited the severed Aqueos arm left over from the first attack.

The cabinet had tipped over, spilled its contents. No one had found the arm.

It was ridiculous to think that arm, even animated, could have found the latch controls, crawled up to them, and known how to use them. The thought was too silly to voice. It had to be the stress getting to him, firing his imagination into paranoia.

But Vic couldn't believe Crosta had done it, either. Or anyone else aboard.

"I'll tell you all what's been happening," Vic said. "This whole siege has been about Crosta. Their first attack came when he was outside. They didn't care about this station at all until Crosta got here. The first thing they did when they got inside was snatch him. And when the rest of us put up too much of a fight, they fall back."

The Aqueos were still out there. The functioning cameras caught movement in the fuzzy edges of the station's exterior lights. Every once in a while, a serpentine silhouette darted from shadow to shadow. But that last attack had been two and a half hours ago – longer than any span between raids since the attacks had begun. They had to know that the station was vulnerable.

Graymalkin voiced the thought that none of them wanted to say, for fear of jinxing it: "They haven't attacked since."

"Crosta traveled here by himself," Nature Girl said. "Why wouldn't the Aqueos have taken him then? Why wait until he'd reached a station with crew and defenses?"

"Crosta arrived early," Graymalkin said. Vic remembered all

too well how he'd found that out. "Maybe, without meaning to, he'd spoiled something they'd planned. Moved before they expected."

"But rather than wait for him to leave on his own," Vic said, "the Aqueos threw an incredible amount of resources into battering themselves against us." He had attained the peculiar level of stress at which he knew he was freaking out too much and *felt* like he was not freaking out enough. Putting all of this into words, trying to keep his voice steady all the while, only made it worse.

"If that's all true," Triage said, though he didn't sound convinced, "they must be on a very tight timetable."

"Coming up against a deadline," Graymalkin said.

Karma turned away from the table. She held her gaze on the porthole.

"Are you listening?" Vic asked her. "I'm not done yelling at you yet."

For far too long a time, she did not answer.

"Karma," Graymalkin prompted, his voice uncharacteristically firm.

"The Atlanteans know that there are darker things in the ocean than anyone from the surface has ever seen," Karma said, in a voice so bleak that, for a moment, it sounded like someone else was speaking. "The Aqueos used to be one of those things. They're not the worst that's out there."

"What the hell?" Josh asked. For once, he'd said something appropriate to the situation. For all Vic could tell, this speech had come apropos of nothing.

"Think about the reasons the Aqueos had to throw themselves against the station," Karma said. "The Aqueos couldn't have survived so long without *some* sense of self-preservation. But they threw themselves against us. No hesitation, no holding back. They're frightened of something worse than what we could do to them."

"That's quite a leap in logic," Graymalkin said gently.

"I know it's true." Her voice had lost that sense of despair and gone back to just numb.

It was hard to imagine Karma ever getting terrorized, not after all she'd been through. Vic wondered how long it had been since she'd gotten sleep. If she'd ever gotten sleep since that first attack had interrupted her rest. The weight behind his eyes was immense. For her, it must have been even worse.

"Whatever the reason they're staying away," Karma said, abruptly turning back to the table, "we have to take the chance that they also won't intercept our backup radio buoy if we release it." *Only there's already a problem,* Vic thought – because otherwise she would have already released it. Sure enough, she said, "The power surge fried the release mechanism. We're going to need to suit up and head out there."

Silence met her. She seemed to take it as a sign of assent. Or maybe she just didn't care. "We'll send out two people," she said. "No reason for us to expose more than we have to."

Vic's voice cracked when he asked the obvious: "How do we know you won't fry us like Crosta?"

"I will be one of the two heading out," she said. Vic noted that she didn't deny that she would ever do that. No denials. No counter-accusations. She knew she'd lost their trust.

But she was also signaling that she wasn't prepared to change how she was acting.

Graymalkin shook his head slowly.

"No," he said. "I think I'm speaking for all of us when I tell you you're in no condition to go on a dive."

"I need to do everything I can to get you all out of here," Karma said.

"I'm not sure *what* you need," Graymalkin answered, "but it starts with rest."

"There will be plenty of time for rest after you're clear of here." She pushed her chair back, about to get up. "Pick someone to come with me."

"Karma, do you mean to fight all of us?" Graymalkin asked.

The bluntness of Graymalkin's mutiny took Vic's breath away, but not Karma's. "*Yes,*" she said, instantly.

All the anger Vic had carried into this meeting was gone, replaced by a cold horror.

Graymalkin's jaw hung slack. Vic didn't see how any of the others were taking it. When Karma's glare fell on him, he couldn't focus on anything but her.

"I'm your teacher, but I'm also in charge of this station," she said. "My first responsibility is to get all of you out. I don't have to be agreeable while I do it."

With that, she stood, and left them alone.

Graymalkin followed her out of the kitchenette. Despite the drama, Karma was not as set as she'd seemed. Five minutes later, he returned to announce that Karma had agreed to rest so long as *someone* went out to release the radio buoy.

Graymalkin sat heavily. He had looked tired five minutes before he'd left, but not this tired. "That went better than I thought it might," he said. "And there's no sense discarding a good plan. We'll send two people out there."

"What do you think happened to her?" Nature Girl asked.

Graymalkin shook his head, staring into the table.

"You all know her better than I do," Nature Girl pressed. "Have you seen any hint of this before?"

"No," Vic said. "She's fought with the X-Men plenty of times, and I've never heard of anything like this happening to her."

Triage turned to Graymalkin. "You're her teaching assistant," he said. "You've got more fighting experience than most of us. I think that makes you in charge."

Graymalkin blinked, as if that hadn't occurred to him. "Yes ... I suppose it does."

"You're holding up better than the rest of us," Nature Girl said, with a small smile.

"I don't know about that," Graymalkin said. "But I am accustomed to insomnia." There were no lines under his red eyes, but, with his physiology, Vic didn't know if that would happen. "However, I... have been struggling with claustrophobia. I volunteer to be one of the divers."

"Are you sure about that?" Triage asked. "I had a look at those drysuits. They're not suits as much as they are closets you strap onto yourself."

"I'm sure," Graymalkin said. "I want to be somewhere where I feel like I can move around."

"Surrounded by Aqueos," Triage said. Graymalkin only nodded.

Silence. No one else was leaping to volunteer. Vic looked to his regenerated arm. It was big, hulking, cumbersome, and on some subliminal level he'd never get used to the weight. He wasn't sure it would even fit in one of the drysuits. Before he could offer to check, though, Josh said, "I'll go."

The scales on Vic's neck tingled in a way that someone with

hair might have called his hackles rising. He opened his mouth, his objection on the back of his tongue.

That moment by the auxiliary generator held him back. He'd just been standing there, yelling at Josh, while Josh had gotten the power back by himself. The last thing Vic was ever going to do was let himself be as useless as that again.

He still didn't trust Josh. He didn't think anyone else should, either. There had to be a better way to convince the others to see things his way.

"I'll help you get suited up," Vic said. "I need to check the suits to see if they can fit me, anyway. It could be important."

Triage gave Vic a warning look. "I'll come too," he said quickly.

Triage probably thought that Vic would be looking for some excuse to get Josh alone and settle their scores. He was right about that. But not about the method.

"Good," Vic said amiably. "It'll go faster."

Triage's eyebrows lifted. Graymalkin hesitated. He obviously knew some kind of power game was being played out here. He had to be questioning whether calling it out would make it worse. He chose not to question it.

For the scene Vic intended to cause, he wanted as many witnesses as possible. And not just to watch Josh.

Vic needed eyes on himself. He knew he was on the edge of losing it. It would keep *himself* honest.

Vic wasn't sure he could trust himself to do that anymore.

CHAPTER FOURTEEN
Elixir

Josh hadn't taken a close look at the drysuits before. They were like something between a spacesuit and a hazmat suit. They were a full head taller than he was. On the racks, the suits' arms folded criss-cross over each other. They were made of accordion-folded rubber and flexible plastic, and they still looked so heavy that they could double as clubs.

He'd just volunteered not only to wear one, but to take it into danger.

He was an idiot.

Graymalkin grunted as he unhooked his suit from the bulkhead. Josh did the same, except he didn't so much lift it as control its fall. The propulsion unit was like a backpack full of bricks.

None of them should have been doing this without training. And the suits were probably the least of the dangers they would be facing.

Even a trained drysuit user – drysuit pilot? – would have had trouble donning it. The wet cabin's lights remained out. No matter the angles Graymalkin positioned their flashlights, shadows leapt and boomed across the suits.

Triage walked to Josh, to help him with his suit. Anole stepped in front of him. Before either Josh or Triage could say anything, Anole was laying out Josh's suit and de-accordioning the arms. Josh exchanged a look with Triage, who pressed his lips into a white line.

Neither of them said anything. Josh didn't think Anole would go so far as to sabotage his drysuit. But it was hard not to be paranoid.

Anole helped Josh fit into his leggings and waist seal without incident. While Josh forced on his boots, Anole detached one of the suit's rubbery arms from its torso. Experimentally, he forced his regenerated arm through it. He managed to get his wrist through, barely. The suit scraped and squeaked on his scales. The sound was even worse when he pulled it out. He winced. Spots of blood welled up where his scales had scraped on the wrist rim.

"Want me to take a look at that?" Josh asked. He could not quite keep the mocking tone out of his voice.

Vic glared at him. Triage glared at *both* of them as he helped Graymalkin tighten his leggings.

While fitting Josh's chestpiece and tightening its straps, Anole kept his distance, as if afraid to touch Josh. Josh pretended not to notice. He pushed his feet into his boots.

"Do you want to be able to take your suit's gloves off when you're out there?" Anole asked.

"Huh? Why?"

"So you can heal by touch if you need to," Anole said. "Or attack."

Anole said that last bit casually, as though it didn't really mean anything. Josh's shoulders tensed involuntarily. He knew immediately what Anole was digging at. Just not how Anole had found him out.

"I'm being serious," Anole said. "I think these wrist clasps are adjustable. I can clamp them so that, if you take off the glove, the rest of your suit doesn't flood."

"Sure," Josh said, after a moment. "That'd be nice."

Josh didn't look at Graymalkin or Triage. He wondered how much they had picked up on, and if Anole really knew what he'd said.

For a while, Anole remained quiet. He helped Josh fasten his boots to his leggings.

Then Anole asked, "So when you attack someone, do your powers work like they do when you're healing? Just lay your hands on someone and–"

"*Anole*," Josh hissed.

"I think we deserve to know," Anole said. "It could be important."

Josh's hands slipped away from his boots. He could not look at Triage and Graymalkin, but the sound from their corner had ceased.

"I'm a healer," Josh said.

"Really? I doubt the Aqueos you dismembered outside would think so. And what about when you broke *your own damn arm* without touching it, just to–"

"I am a healer," Josh interrupted, voice strained.

"There's a pile of bones and scraps that used to be an Aqueos somewhere underneath the station that you could have fooled."

Josh knew that if he tried to say anything, he would be shouting. He couldn't have controlled his voice. So he didn't say anything at all. Hands shaking, he resumed fitting his boots.

Silence seemed to be the last thing Anole was expecting. The seconds ticked by. Still no noise from Graymalkin and Triage's corner.

"When were you going to tell the rest of us what you could do?" Anole pressed.

"Anole," Graymalkin said, "if Josh wanted to stand and clout you right now, he would be within his rights."

Anole took a staggered step back from Josh. He sounded like he'd just had his wind knocked out of him. "What?"

"I would not even report it to the Institute," Graymalkin said.

Josh stared at Graymalkin, slack-lipped. He had not expected help from any of the Institute's mutants, let alone something so strongly worded.

"You don't understand." The steel in Anole's voice hadn't left for long. It had come back knife-sharp. "Josh is dangerous. He shouldn't be going with you. He shouldn't be on this assignment. Shouldn't have even been allowed in the Institute."

"This is entirely the wrong time to bring this forward."

"Thank you–" Josh started to say.

"Be *quiet*, Josh," Graymalkin snapped. For the second time in ten seconds, shock coursed through Josh. He shut up. "If what Vic is saying is true, we're going to need to have a conversation. When the time *is* appropriate."

"Is what Vic said true?" Triage asked, sounding as hurt as he did angry.

"I *am* a healer," Josh repeated.

"You're a lot more than that, and a lot worse, and you've been hiding it all along," Anole said.

Josh picked up his suit helmet, but then set it back down. Its weight was too much. His heart wouldn't stop racing. Only half of him was present. The rest of him was lost to memory.

Those memories coursed through him with the pulse of the stress headache in his temples and the weight of his heart crashing into his ribs. Emma Frost saying *Omega-level.* The frenetic tremble in Blindfold's lower lip as she told him to stay away from Laurie Collins. The dark look Atlas Bear hadn't bothered to conceal, somewhere between restrained rage and dread.

He was back with his captor, Wolfram, who seized his arm and snapped it backward, over and over, until Josh "got it". Until he understood what he could do. His body, and anyone else's that he touched, was clay in his hands. Blood and bone and tissue became luminous, melted into energy under his fingers.

"All I want to do is heal," he said.

"Would *you* believe that, in our position?" Anole asked.

The answer was clear and easy to find. He wouldn't.

"Josh, you don't have to answer that," Graymalkin said. "And, Victor, help him get his drysuit on or get the hell out of here."

"You can't still mean to go out there with him?" Anole asked.

"I mean exactly what I say," Graymalkin said. "And until Karma is – until she's herself again, I would seem to be in charge."

Anole didn't have anything to say to that. This obviously wasn't what he'd expected to happen. Anole and Graymalkin had been teammates, Josh recalled, during the incident when Anole had lost his arm. For each of them, it had been their first team – a moment of real weight among the X-Men, their trainees, and other superpowered folk.

Anole's footsteps receded to the wet cabin's hatch. He didn't shut it behind him.

It took a few extra minutes for Triage, working solo, to help Josh and Graymalkin into their suits, but they managed. The last thing to seal was the helmet and visor. The world flexed and took on strange dimensions. When Josh looked to his feet, they seemed much farther than they had a moment ago. That, and the adrenaline still coursing through his veins, made him dizzy. He did not want to think about throwing up in a drysuit, but couldn't avoid it. The thought just made him sicker.

The suit's interior was cushioned and insulated, and already starting to get too warm. He clomped to the edge of the diving pool's stairs. He needed Triage's help to keep his balance. It was like walking under medieval plate mail. Outside of the water, he doubted he'd be able to move more than fifty steps without a rest.

A harsh pop and buzzing made him wince. An unintelligible electronic crackle boomed inside his helmet. Josh fumbled for the wrist controls, trying to remember where the radio's volume controls were.

"Say again?" Josh asked. No answer.

With the visor in place, he couldn't slap himself on the forehead, but he imagined doing it. Then he pressed the "transmit" switch on his arm, and asked again.

"I said 'radio check.'" Graymalkin's voice was so distorted that, if Josh hadn't known it was Graymalkin, he wouldn't have recognized it. "I suppose it's working."

"To an extent," Josh muttered.

As dangerous as it would have been to dive without support, he would almost rather the radios didn't work. He wouldn't be able to go anywhere to escape Graymalkin.

So long as Josh had avoided thinking about the unexplored depths of his powers, it had been like they didn't exist. He *had* been just a healer, even in his own mind. Now everything was laid out bare, and he couldn't avoid thinking about it.

Sallow light flickered across the ceiling. The exterior lights' reflections, filtering up through the diving pool, were brighter than any light left in the wet cabin.

The suits had flippers three times the size of their boots. Graymalkin's wobbled as he awkwardly climbed down the stairs. "Wait until I'm clear before following," he said, sparing Josh the trouble of pretending to want to volunteer to go first.

The oceanic expanse glimmered dimly below. Josh's chest seized up when he looked too long. He couldn't tell if it was trauma from the last time he'd dived and nearly drowned, or another symptom of the adrenaline. There was no real way to separate them. It had all fused together into a jumbled, melting nightmare. No single anxiety could be distilled from the other.

Making an uncharacteristic and unwelcome little joke, Graymalkin held his gloved hand to his visor, as if to pinch his nose before diving. He dropped into the rippling dark.

Josh watched him go. There was a flitting intersection of shadows, a silhouette of a flipper, and then nothing. Graymalkin was clear.

Josh's breath rattled inside his helmet, hot and ragged. He stepped forward.

The transition was not as much of a shock as he expected. It was like hopping into a billowy cushion. There was no temperature difference. No gush of water through a broken seal. Not even an especially loud splash.

The biggest difference was that the weight on his back and legs lessened as the water cushioned him. His breath fogged the visor, but only briefly. Fans behind his head whirred, and a sudden gust of dry air across his eyes made him blink.

A *click* resonated through his suit's frame. Then a gentle heat seeped into Josh's skin. Heating filaments ran through the suit's body, protecting him from the ambient cold. The suits were powered by microfusion cells that were only a little less – for the time – advanced than the station's generators.

All his visor showed him was darkness. For a moment it was as though the universe shrunk to him, his suit, and his shaky breath. He kicked, and the beams of the station's exterior lights rotated across his view.

Moving against the water was slow, but less clumsy than it had been in the air. His elbows and knees bent differently, and the weight, while still a factor, was less oppressive than it had been above.

He fumbled his glove over his wrist controls until he found the flashlight. Light sprang from above his left wrist. He swept the beam across the station's underside. A second later, Graymalkin's light joined his.

Their lights covered dismayingly little of the station's hull. They found no Aqueos, but didn't have the strength to peel back all the shadows, either.

Graymalkin was the first to click his off. "No light once we're clear of the underside," he radioed. "We don't want to draw attention."

"Like they won't see us no matter what," Josh muttered, but

without pressing the *transmit* button. He did as Graymalkin asked.

The suit's propulsion unit was like most of its other functions: awkwardly controlled by wrist pad. Josh flicked the right switch, and the propeller spun up. A deep-throated hum resonated through the suit. He struggled with the directional sticks, but figured them out before spinning himself upside-down.

Once set in a direction, the suit no longer needed a hand on the controls to keep going. Still, every time he wanted to change direction or modify his speed, he had to reach over to his other wrist. It was incredibly awkward. The drysuits' designer had intended their wearers to move slowly, and had plainly not planned on taking the suits into a fight.

The two of them motored in silence. As they approached the station's side, Josh rotated onto his back, facing upward.

Station X-41's exterior lights radiated over the lip of the station's hull, catching dust motes here and there before attenuating into the infinite black. If he ignored the thrum of his motor, he could pretend he was outside staring into the sky of a light-polluted city.

He started kicking his flippers, but Graymalkin stopped him with a hiss. "Propulsion units only. We don't want to make more visible motion than we have to."

Josh held back his first answer. He let his arms and legs hang limp while his propellers lifted him. They rose at a crawl. The Aqueos apparently had no trouble seeing in the dark, and Josh bet that their hearing was sharp too. The sound of their propellers carried a long way underwater. Acting stealthy was theater, performed for Graymalkin's sake. The Aqueos saw them. Whether the Aqueos did anything or not was up to them.

Josh clenched and unclenched his fists. His suit wasn't overly warm, but nervous sweat stung his eyes. He wished he could wipe his forehead.

He'd considered taking a weapon – a wrench, a knife, anything – but fitting on his suit's gloves had disabused him of that plan. If he didn't lose his grip on a bludgeon and drop it, it would just impede his mobility. A knife would have been more dangerous to him than the Aqueos.

"So what can you do besides heal?" Graymalkin asked, as they rose.

"I couldn't say," Josh said. "I don't experiment."

"Tell me what you *do* know," Graymalkin said curtly.

Josh had known even as he'd spoken that he wouldn't get away with evading the question, but some ridiculous part of him had insisted on trying anyway. "I can- I can, um, reshape myself. Parts of myself. Bones, muscles. I think I could do the same to people I touch, too." More weasel words. He didn't think that – he *knew* it.

"Victor said you killed an Aqueos."

"Then I must have."

"You don't remember?" Graymalkin's raised voice made the speakers buzz.

It was the truth. All Josh recalled about the moment was the Aqueos's cold skin, its dry black veins, the lance of pain in his own shoulder, and the unbearable fire in his chest. But he had already tried so many verbal dodges that he didn't blame Graymalkin for not believing him.

"You're set on not making this easy for yourself," Graymalkin said.

"Apparently so," Josh said.

They crested over the curve of the station's side. Graymalkin cut his propulsion, and so did Josh. They coasted to a gentle landing atop its hull. The surface was rough under Josh's heels, grimy with years of ashfall from Black Smokers' Trench.

Josh knew how badly this conversation had started, and found himself determined to make up for it. In halting sentences, he told Graymalkin what he knew: his capture and imprisonment, Wolfram torturing him into discovering the extent of his ability to control his body, and then the moment when he'd lashed out at the Aqueos.

There were some parts he still couldn't share. Repeating the things Emma Frost, Blindfold, and Atlas Bear had said would have just given those words more power.

"Does anyone else at the Institute know all this?"

"Emma Frost and Headmaster Summers know a little." Outlaw knew more, but Josh hadn't even told *her* the whole story.

"Why did you hide it?"

"I just want to be a healer." It must have been the fifteenth time he'd said those words, but they seemed to cross more of the gulf between them. Graymalkin was silent for a while.

Josh realized his own words had struck him differently, too. Now he could face up to the fact that they weren't true. At least not technically. He didn't want to be a healer so much as he wanted *not* to have his other powers.

He didn't deserve what he had. Anole was right. He couldn't be trusted with it.

"You have been a good healer," Graymalkin said, at last.

"I *am* a good healer." The tense was important to Josh.

Someone cleared their throat over the radio. Whoever had

made the noise was "politely" letting Josh and Graymalkin know they were there.

"How long have you been listening?" Josh asked, not even bothering to hide his irritation. It was hard to not resent the intrusion. He supposed it could have been worse. It could have been Anole listening in rather than Triage.

"Long enough to follow, not that it matters," Triage answered. His voice sounded even more distorted than Graymalkin's, but his tone was recognizable. The ocean was not kind to radio waves, even at short ranges. "Somebody needs to be here to watch you two."

The station's hull curved, cresting toward the third deck, a tremendous hump still above them. Shardlike shadows extruded from the hull where the descent capsule had been docked before the Aqueos had torn it from its moorings.

He and Graymalkin passed sunken portholes. Glimmers of light played across one of them, looking in at the second deck's main corridor. Light fell through the open hatch to the emergency command cabin, carving wicked shadows across the bulkheads.

Josh lifted his feet to step over a fist-thick metal rod – a filament of the station's defense grid. It was hard to forget that, at any moment, the grid could flood so much electricity into the ocean that he and Graymalkin would never feel themselves die. He looked about for Aqueos again. Then he wondered how well Karma was sleeping, and if anyone had thought to post a guard. Graymalkin's thoughts were apparently traveling along the same line.

"I wish we had the kind of healer who could cure whatever Karma's going through," Graymalkin said.

"What *really* happened after you went to talk to her?" Josh asked.

"Nothing much. She relented a minute after she left, and had had a chance to calm down."

Graymalkin had taken a slight lead. Josh searched for emotional cues in his gait.

"Something happened," Josh pressed.

"I offered her sleeping pills. She refused."

Josh blinked. "We have sleeping pills?"

"More like tranquilizers really. Standard medical kit for this station."

Graymalkin was being just terse enough to come across as dodging something. Josh realized he wasn't supposed to know about those. "They're in case someone gets out of control, aren't they? A way to subdue them."

"The deep ocean is an extreme environment. It's impossible to predict how people will react until they're taken into it."

"Do you think that's what's been happening with Karma? Too much of an 'extreme environment'?"

"She's been down here several times. She's never had this reaction before, not in any of the after-action mission reports I've read. I doubt she would have been placed in charge of this expedition if she had."

They threaded between the beams of the station's exterior lights. Josh was about to let the subject slide, but something about it was troubling Graymalkin, because Graymalkin didn't let it go. "'Refused' was not the right word to describe how she responded to my offer."

"She go off on you?" Josh asked.

"No," Graymalkin said, sounding like he wished she had.

"She told me that she'd taken some sleeping pills about a day ago. They hadn't helped."

Josh nearly tripped over another of the defense grid's filaments. "*What?*"

"I never thought I would say this, but I hope she was lying. It would be a very strange lie, though."

"What could she have gotten out of lying about that?" Josh asked.

"Nothing. There are two significant problems if she's telling the truth. The first is that she tried to put herself under without telling me or anyone else, and while the Aqueos were attacking. The second..."

"Hard to get worse than the first," Josh said. He needed a chance to come to terms with that before they moved onto anything else. His mind was still reeling.

"The second is that those tranquilizers definitely should have worked. They're strong enough to put down a Wolverine or Colossus."

"Karma doesn't have any mutant abilities that would make her resist tranquilizers?"

"Not that she's ever told me."

Graymalkin started to slow. Ahead, silhouetted against a ray of light, a squat chute like a chimney sprouted from the station's hull. Almost there. "She also told me," Graymalkin said, "that the rest of us should leave as soon as rescuers arrived. But that she was going to stay."

"You know, as nuts as that is, I'm not shocked at this point."

"I was," Graymalkin said softly.

"Did she say *why?*"

"There's something down here she thinks she needs to

destroy. I have no idea what, or where. She wouldn't say."

"She's completely lost it." From the way Graymalkin's face-plate swiveled to face him, Josh guessed he'd said something *verboten*. He hadn't known Karma as long as the others. He hadn't heard all the stories of her exploits.

Maybe that gave him license to say what no one else would. Graymalkin, notably, didn't argue with him.

The chute was topped by a metal hatch with a bar latched tight across it. The hatch was cracked open, and jammed against the bar as though something had shoved up against it. The hatch itself was fine. According to the instruments in the emergency command cabin, it was the locking bar that had failed.

Graymalkin and Josh's boots clunked on the hull as they circled the chute. Josh wondered what they sounded like from inside. He remembered the muted thumping he'd heard during the first Aqueos attack. He wondered if Karma could hear them.

An awful thought started to take form.

"I don't know much about vampirism other than what they taught us at the Institute, but it can be spread by bite, right?" he asked. "That's how it works in the movies, too. Does it work the same way with the Aqueos?"

Graymalkin's helmet shifted up, a gesture that might have been a nod. "I think that, if Crosta somehow survived the defense grid's blast, he's been turned into one of them. They used to be Atlanteans."

"Do you know how vampirism affects its victims' minds?" Josh asked. "You've been studying at the Institute a lot longer than I have." Come to think of it, he was pretty sure he remembered Outlaw saying she'd met Morbius once. He wished he'd asked her more about it.

"I know it's best to think of it as a disease, whatever its supernatural elements."

"Yes, but… if it *turns* Atlanteans, if it could make Crosta act like one of them, it's more than an ordinary disease. I've never heard of a virus that could change somebody's behavior in such specific ways. There's got to be a mental component to it. Something supernatural."

Graymalkin didn't answer. Josh could almost *hear* Graymalkin's frown of concentration as he circled the hatch.

The locking bar had two manual catches on opposite sides of the chute. Graymalkin stood by one, and pointed Josh to the other. "Keep your head back when we open this," Graymalkin said.

Josh wrapped his gloves around the catch release. He tried to break his train of thought. He couldn't quite manage it. Graymalkin couldn't hold down his transmit button and keep his hands on his release, so he counted down from ten to five, and then each of them finished it silently. At zero, Josh yanked back his release.

The locking bar snapped loose, and the hatch instantly flipped back. It cracked into the hull as hard as if the Hulk himself had thrown it.

A gray blur shot past Josh's visor. The beacon wasn't as buoyant as it could be. It still carried ballast it would drop as it rose. And it had still fired like a cannonball. Josh craned his neck back and watched it rise. If the Aqueos were watching, they'd see it. Once it reached the surface, it would be a sitting target.

They just had to hope that the Aqueos wouldn't be interested in this one, for the same reason they'd stopped attacking the station.

For the first time, Josh caught sight of a moving shadow, a serpentine figure slipping across a spotlight. It was astonishingly close – no farther than a hundred feet, if he could trust his curved visor's distorted view. Close enough to see the trident it carried. It was heading away, and vanished quickly.

Graymalkin had seen it, too. He stood paralyzed after it disappeared. "Let's head back in." After a pause, he added, "Try not to look scared when you swim."

Josh had no idea how to do that. He certainly couldn't keep from looking up as he and Graymalkin walked.

The truth was that the Aqueos hadn't frightened him any more than the conversation they'd just been having. He said, "So vampirism is a contagion, but not, like… a bacterial or viral contagion, right? It changes the way someone thinks through some kind of process we don't understand yet."

"Yes…" Graymalkin said uneasily. He kept his eyes above them, too.

"So there had to be a mental component to that contagion. How could that spread?"

"Through the bite, like the rest of the disease."

"Yes, but could there be any *other* ways that the mental symptoms could be spread? Just the mental symptoms?"

"I don't know… I suppose…"

Graymalkin's gait slowed. Gradually, he came to a stop. The currents swayed him back and forth.

"Who do we know who's had telepathic contact with the Aqueos?" Josh asked.

During that first attack, Karma had tried to use her fear powers to fend off the Aqueos. She'd never said what the Aqueos feared, either. Not unless Josh counted that moment in the kitchenette, when she'd almost broken down.

Graymalkin was still a second longer. Then his hand darted to his wrist controls. "Triage? Are you still getting this?"

They waited.

"Triage?" Graymalkin asked.

Josh spun slowly, checking once for Aqueos. Something else caught his eye. They'd paused near the porthole they'd passed earlier, the one looking in on the second deck. As dim as it had been, there'd been *some* light.

Now there was nothing. Just a sheet of black. The flashlights inside the emergency command cabin were gone, or out.

Josh put his hand on Graymalkin's shoulder. After Graymalkin ponderously turned to face him, Josh pointed toward the darkened porthole. They shone their flashlights in. The emergency command cabin's hatch was still open. But all the lights had gone out.

No one was listening to their signal. At least nobody they wanted to.

Josh's blood ran like ice. He'd felt bad enough when he'd realized Triage had been listening to them. If Karma had heard anything he'd said…

They couldn't run in these suits, not against the ocean's sludgy resistance. Josh hopped along with an occasional assist from his propulsion pack. He and Graymalkin launched themselves over the station's curved edge, and let gravity take over from there.

Josh no longer bothered to check for Aqueos. If the Aqueos wanted to attack, they were doomed anyway. Graymalkin intermittently radioed Triage, to no avail. Once Josh was past the station's lower corner, he turned on his pack and started kicking.

Graymalkin's hand landed on Josh's shoulder. They motored forward for a second longer, Graymalkin dragging from Josh. Graymalkin pointed straight ahead.

Josh fumbled for his wrist controls, and killed the motor.

Darkness stirred underneath the station, right around the entrance to the diving pool.

Josh leveled his wrist at the shadows and – ignoring Graymalkin's hasty grab to stop him – switched on his suit's flashlight.

The beam fell across a single figure floating underneath the diving pool, arms spread, sinking gradually. Josh's light dissipated too much over the distance to resolve color or detail, but a reflection glinted dully off the figure's head. A helmet, with a visor.

Whoever it was had turned directly toward Josh and Graymalkin, as if expecting them.

The spotlights on the far side of the station snapped off. Then the next closest ones.

The blackout rolled across its underside in steady beats. The lights died two or three at a time, in even rows, advancing toward Josh and Graymalkin.

When the blackout reached the figure, it vanished. Josh's wristlight beam attenuated into nothing, though it had touched the figure just a moment before. He waved his flashlight about, but found nothing more than dust motes drifting in the current.

His fear had escalated so far beyond ordinary terror that he almost laughed. He'd never had that kind of reaction before. He'd read war stories about people becoming manic in battle, but couldn't imagine what that had felt like. Until now.

Of *course* the worst, most frightening possible thing he could think of would happen. It only made sense. This was all logical, that manic part of his mind said.

It got worse still. The last of the station's exterior lights snapped off. The darkness crested over him and Graymalkin.

For a moment, Josh treaded water, scanning his wristlight back and forth into a gray obscurity.

Then that light died, too.

CHAPTER FIFTEEN
Anole

Vic knew he should have stayed to help Graymalkin and Josh suit up, but the voice saying so was a small one.

He didn't care if Graymalkin reported this. He didn't even care if the incident snowballed, cost him a chance at joining the X-Men, or his berth at the Institute. After he closed the second hatch out of the wet cabin, he sat against the bulkhead, resting his forehead on his bunched-up knees.

Breathing took deliberate effort. His regenerated arm was heavier than it had ever been. It felt half again his own size. It was a tumorous growth he couldn't escape. Somebody else's body, displaced onto his own.

After a while, his breathing calmed enough that he could stand.

Maybe he was wrong and all of the reasons he hated Josh were not good enough to keep treating him as an enemy. Vic had made his best case against Josh, and Graymalkin was still taking him on a vital assignment. And, after all that had been said, Vic couldn't convince himself that Graymalkin was wrong.

Somehow, he couldn't convince himself that Graymalkin was *right*, either.

Josh was an ass. A barely reformed bigot. He was definitely hiding something about the scope and nature of his powers. Vic figured that there were better odds than not that Josh would someday be an enemy of the X-Men, and would use their own training against them.

There was a chance, though, that he was just a bad person, but trying to get better.

And maybe Vic ought to have been acting a lot differently toward him than he had.

But doing that was hard. And the memories hurt so much.

The feeling was such a buried, deep-down pain. So buried and so deep that it had taken him too long to recognize it *as* pain. Like the shock that had followed his arm falling from his shoulder, it hadn't even hurt at first.

After about two minutes, he climbed the stairs to the second deck.

Vic passed the emergency command cabin. Its hatch was open. Inside, Triage was muttering to himself over the crackle of a radio handset. Vic assumed this meant Josh and Graymalkin were outside the station now.

Vic stepped into the kitchenette. Occasional crackles of radio chatter resonated from the corridor. Hollow footsteps clanked along the deck grating.

In the lighter dark of the corridor, Nature Girl's silhouette stepped through the kitchenette's hatchway. Then she paused, suddenly uncertain.

"It's just me in here," Vic said, from the deeper dark.

"I nearly jumped into the ceiling," she said.

"Don't you have one of the flashlights to carry around?"

"What, and give my position away to attackers?" He suspected she was only half-kidding. "Anyway, where's yours?"

"Must've forgot it," Vic said. He realized he had no idea where. Probably the wet cabins.

He couldn't keep quiet about what had just happened. Another sullen silence would just spiral inward on itself. Besides, she deserved to know just who and what Josh really was, too. When he started talking, the words kept spilling out.

Nature Girl just listened while Vic told her everything he suspected. "He kept describing himself as a 'healer' even after he admitted he was hiding more from us," Vic finished. "He's a lot more, and a lot worse."

"But he *is* a healer, right?"

In the dark, Vic couldn't see how she was reacting. "I just told you. He's more."

"People can be more than one thing," she said. "Mutants especially."

"I *know* that," Vic said. "But he's been lying to us."

"Why not let him define himself?"

Vic blinked. "Excuse me?"

"The older mutants are trying to teach us 'restraint and responsibility' with our powers. At least that's how it is at the Jean Grey School. The Institute came up with this assignment, where our powers wouldn't be as useful, and your teachers must be thinking along the same lines. Maybe this has been Elixir's way of being 'restrained and responsible.'"

"He hasn't earned the right to hide things about himself," Vic said.

"That's something he has to earn?" When Vic didn't answer,

Nature Girl said, "Cyclops keeps himself restrained. Even when he fires his eye-beam, it's rarely at full power."

Vic pulled a face. "Headmaster Summers never lied about who he was, or what he's done."

"You really don't think he's done terrible things over his career? Things he'd never tell you about?"

Vic's answer – that of course he knew that was true – caught in his throat.

"Over at the Jean Grey School, Wolverine isn't shy about telling us the kinds of things Cyclops did to–"

"I don't want to know," Vic said, quickly.

"You'd think of him differently if you did."

"That's what I don't want."

"Well, then."

There was a hollow *pop* of a bottle cap. Then Vic caught scent of hot sauce.

"Why are you so much on Josh's side?" Vic asked. "Do you like him?"

"Josh? No." Vic couldn't see the face she'd pulled when she'd said his name, but he heard it in her voice. "But what you're talking about is important to me."

"Yeah?"

Her gray silhouette shifted in the reflection of Triage's distant flashlights. She waved her hand to tap her antlers, and then waved across the rest of her body. "If I couldn't define who I was, I'd be alien to myself."

Vic pursed his lips. If this conversation had been in full light, he would have felt like he had to nod, or shake his head, or anything else that would show a reaction.

Here, he could just sit in the dark and consider. He'd been

tired for hours upon hours. He felt a year older than he had before Nature Girl came to talk with him.

Too many things were falling loose in his head for him to sort through. His eyes were leaden weights. He propped the smaller of his two elbows on the table and rested his forehead in the crook of his arm. All he wanted was a moment when he didn't have to think about all this.

When he lifted his head, Nature Girl had left. Or at least gone somewhere he couldn't see.

A shadow hovered in front of the emergency command cabin's hatch. It didn't have Nature Girl's antlers. Vic watched muzzily as the shape stepped through the hatch.

In a single instant, all of the flashlights Triage had set up there went out.

Vic was on his feet before he heard Triage's yelp. With no more light from the emergency command cabin, he couldn't see even the little that he had before. He smashed his toes against the edge of the kitchenette's hatch. The pain didn't stop him from running.

As he reached the emergency control cabin's hatch, he couldn't see anyone step out in front of him. But he could *sense* them. The deck grating shifted underfoot, moving with someone else's weight. The air stirred.

He pulled his regenerated arm back, fist clenched.

Colors exploded across the right side of his vision, jarringly bright against the darkness around him. His head cracked against the bulkhead before he realized he'd been struck.

The station spun about him, and he slumped to the deck.

By the time he found himself again, someone was shaking his shoulder. The beam of a flashlight pried painfully between his eyelids. He tried raising his arm to shield his eyes, but both his arms were strangely clumsy and distant, like he'd fallen asleep lying on them. The person shaking him was saying something urgent, but he couldn't focus past the roar in his ears or the spinning in his head.

The voice was feminine, but not Nature Girl or Karma's. But Vic knew it. He would have recognized it instantly if it hadn't been so out of place here.

He had enough feeling in his regenerated arm now to grab the flashlight, and force it away from his eyes. A terrible, icy horror was squeezing his heart.

"Cipher?" he croaked.

"Get *up*," Cipher hissed. As the rest of his memories caught up with him, he realized she'd been telling him that, increasingly angrily, for the past half minute. She snatched her flashlight back. He never saw her arm move.

But she was good at slipping past his range of perception.

"I can't carry you," she said.

"How- how are you-?"

"How do you think, cackhead? It's what I do. It's who I am. You don't see me unless I want you to." Cipher said this as though it were all terribly obvious, and that Vic was trying her patience by even asking. "The same way I got into Headmaster Summers and Ms Frost's training sessions in the Danger Room."

No, please. Not another person down here.

"Did you wonder why the descent capsule had seven seats for the six of you?" Cipher asked.

No, it hadn't. He was pretty sure it hadn't. His memories were drowning in a sea of adrenaline and panic. He couldn't quite get enough air to speak, let alone move.

Cipher drew back her foot and slammed it into his gut.

The kick had been hard, but it was more the shock than the pain that made him double over. Cipher drew her foot back again. She didn't follow through with the kick only because he planted his hand on the bulkhead and levered himself to a seat.

"Get the hell *up* before they find you," she snarled.

It took an incredible effort to stand, but the snarl in her voice helped him find it. As if he didn't have enough to be terrified of. Cipher not only wasn't supposed to be here – she was supposed to be his friend.

Cipher clicked off her flashlight. Apparently, she'd had it on just to shine in his eyes. Absolute black washed over them. "The first time I came by, I thought you were dead, too," she said. "So did the Aqueos, I guess."

"'Too?'" he asked, voice small.

"They murdered Triage."

Vic forgot how to breathe.

"I was below deck, waiting for Graymalkin and Elixir to surface, see if I could help," Cipher said. Her voice was choked somewhere between rage and despair. "They never showed. By the time I got back up, the Aqueos had slashed his throat. There was nothing I could do."

Vic had *just* heard Triage's voice. He took a halting step toward the emergency command cabin. Cipher stopped him with a firm hand on his chest. He was in no shape to push past her.

He must have been out more than a few minutes. That wasn't good, he thought dully. The kind of head injury that led to more than a few seconds of unconsciousness more often led to coma, or death. He could have been bleeding out inside his brain right then–

A kick to his shin disrupted his chain of thought.

Bile rose in his throat on a tide of anger. Cipher didn't have the excuse of trying to get him up this time. "Why are you–"

She answered by grabbing his other shoulder and spinning him around. A blow that was half-punch, half-shove landed on his shoulder, and forced him to stagger forward. He was too dizzy to resist. "I saw everything you did," she said.

Assuming he could trust his sense of direction, she was pushing him toward the stairs up to the first deck. He opened his mouth to ask, but Cipher interrupted: "Quiet. The Aqueos are still aboard."

There was too much churning inside him for the fear of that to reach him. But it made sense. The Aqueos that attacked Triage wouldn't have fled after winning.

Attacked. Murdered. Grief had not yet had a chance to catch up with him, but it was on its way.

He resisted Cipher's next push. He had to see Triage for himself. Maybe he looked dead, but was still breathing. Maybe Josh could–

Cipher shoved him back harder than he thought she was capable.

"You should have stopped this," she said. "You should have been there."

"I *was!*" He'd been right here.

"If you hadn't run away from suiting up Elixir and Graymalkin, I wouldn't have had to go down to make sure they got back safely. Triage was alone in the command cabin. I could have been there to help him!" Heat welled in Vic's throat. This was a nightmare. Like a nightmare he knew, nearly word for word, what she was going to say next: "What were you doing, Vic? Sitting in the kitchen. Being as much of a sulking, useless turd as you've been this whole time."

"But Josh was– I couldn't–"

His toes smashed into the bottom step of the stairs. "Up there," she said brusquely. "It's the last place the Aqueos are likely to look."

"But the first deck is mostly flooded."

"I know! I didn't just get here, damn it. The Aqueos know that too." The pressure of her hand briefly lifted, like she'd twisted around to listen to something. "Get into hydroacoustic communications. Get behind one of the consoles. Stay there."

Reluctantly, he headed up. Cipher was always at his back. She gripped his non-regenerated arm so firmly that it hurt, and held it behind him.

"I can't find Karma or Nature Girl," she said. "And Elixir and Graymalkin are gone. I waited for them. They never surfaced. The Aqueos must have gotten them. You finally got what you wanted, Vic. Elixir is dead."

Vic's arms and legs felt sluggish, like they weren't his anymore. His skin had gone so cold that Cipher's fingers felt like a corpse's against his scales. He could never move fast enough to satisfy Cipher's shoving.

"I should have shown myself sooner," Cipher said. "I saw everything you did to Elixir. All the ways you tried to hurt him. Well, good work. He's dead. If you live long enough to get back to the Institute, I'll make sure you won't be able to hide *anything* from the X-Men. You did everything but murder him yourself."

The mention of the Institute cooled some of the burning

in his throat. One of the Institute's most important classes for prospective X-Men had a month-long section devoted to keeping cool in pressure situations. The lessons seemed hollow, but repeating them under his breath still helped. "Think about where your fears are coming from and what they're trying to tell you," Headmaster Summers had said. "Don't ignore fear. Work with it. Analyze it."

The things Cipher was saying felt like knives under his scales, but weren't actually important right now. He had to control the situation first. "How did the Aqueos get in?"

"Excuse me?" Cipher sounded like she'd expected argument.

"I *said*, how did they–"

"I heard you!" she snapped. "It must have been through the diving pool."

"But you were watching the diving pool."

He raised his foot, expecting another stair step. His foot plunged through air instead. He nearly tripped. He stumbled onto the first deck.

"I don't know, then," she said.

"If it wasn't the diving pool, then it must have been..."

The next likely alternative was this deck. The old conference room was still open to the water. The broken waterlock that had once led to the descent capsule could also have been an entry point. The instant after the thought occurred to him, though, he knew that couldn't have been the case. Opening any of those hatches would have sent a torrent of floodwater through the rest of the station.

Cipher shoved into him, but for once he had the strength and leverage to resist.

She grunted and said, "The Aqueos were already on the

second deck by the time I saw them." So they *must* have gone past her if she'd been at the diving pool.

Or maybe they hadn't. The person he'd heard and felt step out of the emergency command cabin hadn't moved like an invader. They hadn't been rushed. Nor had they hesitated. They'd stepped like they'd known exactly where they were going.

None of this was right. He spun. The pressure of Cipher's grip on his arm was gone.

He felt his way along. He found no one. Cipher was gone. Of course, one of Cipher's favorite things to do was disappear, but he doubted she'd done that this time.

The more he thought about it, the more he was sure that the person he'd run into outside the emergency command cabin had been Karma.

Karma, whose telepathic gifts could make a person's worst fears seem real. And who had come across Vic right after he was wondering how catastrophically he'd misread Josh.

Cipher had never been here. Karma had forced him to hallucinate her. Vic felt like throwing up.

Somewhere in the dark, a hatch wheel groaned.

A spray of cold seawater made him flinch, and then the corridor was filled with the thunder of rushing water. If Cipher was there, if she made any noise as she was swept away, it was lost to the throbbing roar.

Vic couldn't have outrun the water, but he could have darted away from the most violent of the flood surges, and merely been swept off his feet rather than battered to death.

But that would have been surrendering to this. Giving it power. He held his ground. An icicle-sharp wall of water smashed into him.

Everything shifted.

The dry bulkhead against Vic's back would have been a shock if he wasn't dimly aware that he'd felt it there for a long time. His stomach lurched, though he hadn't moved.

He still couldn't see anything, but recognized the position he'd slumped into. It was how he'd fallen after being struck, just outside the emergency control cabin.

There was no barrage of rushing water. Part of him still expected to be drowning. He fought to control his breath. His chest convulsed and his hands shook – but he was all right.

Cipher had never been here. Wherever she was, she was safe from this.

A minute ago, he would have given everything he had to know she was safe. Now he just felt sick. Violated.

Vic had no idea how long he'd been trapped inside himself. A nightmare that felt like it had lasted hours could have come and gone in minutes. He couldn't avoid gasping as he crawled to his knees and got his bearings. But Karma didn't sweep out of the dark to imprison him in his nightmares again.

A thin, very pale light hazed the corridor. It was a sliver of a sliver of moonlight, but, against the absolute dark of the rest of the station, it was just enough to help Vic find the hatch to the emergency control cabin. He stumbled through.

The wan light came from the cabin's one monitor. Vic couldn't see the display, only the granite-gray light it cast. The cabin seemed empty.

But he still heard breathing.

Vic stubbed his toe on a hard, heavy cylinder. One of Triage's flashlights, rolling on the floor. Vic snapped it up and flicked it on.

Triage lay curled in the corner, his face hidden under his arms. He didn't react to the flashlight. He shook silently. If the nightmare he'd been trapped in was anything like Vic's, Vic doubted he even perceived the light.

Vic shook Triage's shoulder. Triage flinched away and lashed out with his foot. His kick went wide. He hadn't really seen Vic. Vic peeled Triage's arm away from his eyes. Triage looked past Vic, right through the bulkheads, at something far beyond them.

Vic shook his head. He could see the monitor from this angle. Movement caught his eye.

Triage had been watching the feed from underneath the station. The exterior lights streamed into the ocean, turned into staticky and funereal gray pillars by the infrared color-washing. Two figures sank toward the bottom edge of the screen. Even in the grainy image, he saw that their heads weren't the right shape to be Aqueos. They were too bulbous, too perfectly rounded. They were helmets, not heads.

The figures themselves were limp. Their arms and legs floated loosely at their sides, swaying in the currents.

As Vic watched, Graymalkin's and Josh's limp bodies fell below the edge of the display, and were swallowed by the black ocean.

CHAPTER SIXTEEN
Anole

Vic didn't remember charging downstairs. He had a vague sensory impression of taking stairs two at a time, his flashlight held steady in his prehensile tongue, but his mind had been elsewhere. Like on how tight he thought he could fit a drysuit's shoulder seal over his regenerated arm. And the physics of levering limp bodies in heavy drysuits out of the water.

And the whereabouts of Nature Girl. And Karma.

He couldn't do anything for Triage. Triage would have to bring himself out of his nightmare. He found no sign of Nature Girl, but it was a good bet that Karma had done the same to her. And Karma herself was nowhere to be found.

If Vic ran into her, he didn't know that he could defend himself.

Anole burst inside the wet cabins. A quick scan found no one inside, at least not in any of the obvious places. Josh's and Graymalkin's flashlights sat where they'd left them before they'd suited up. Anole ran to the drysuit racks. There were not as many of them as there should have been. Three of the racks were empty.

Their pre-assignment training had emphasized that no one was to don a drysuit without assistance. Vic didn't have the time. He lifted the suit's torso over his head, snapped the fitting straps into place, and then jammed his regenerated arm into the flexible, accordion-folded sleeve. On anyone else, the sleeve would have been too big. His arm barely fit. His scales still scraped on it, but not as painfully as last time.

If he hadn't started helping Josh into his drysuit earlier, he would have had no idea what to do next. Boots. Helmet seal. Air hoses and seals.

One glove fit on easily. The other… there was no chance. His regenerated hand was twice its size. Vic threw the extra glove back onto the rack. He cinched the seal over his wrist tight enough to bite. Like he'd told Josh, he was pretty sure he could keep it watertight, albeit at risk to his circulation.

He lumbered to the diving pool. The drysuit and all its accoutrements were incredibly heavy, but Vic's adrenaline-suffused muscles managed. For now.

He plunged into the ocean.

Turbulent, white-clouded water splashed over his visor. A cold shock rippled up his right arm. Streams of bubbles cascaded over him.

The exterior lights stung his eyes. The outside of the station was more brightly lit than the interior. Despite the black all around, the sea was strangely luminous and intense, like he'd left a space station in close orbit of the sun.

His suit's heating elements clicked on and warmed quickly –

everywhere, of course, except his ungloved hand. The cold there felt like ice squeezing his fingers.

There was no trace of either Josh or Graymalkin. Just cloudy dark below. Vic somersaulted, and swam downward.

The ocean floor resolved gradually, in rolling waves of ash dunes and spurs of ancient, coarse, black rock. For several awful minutes, Vic found no one. It was not until his fingers had gone numb that his wristlight found two drysuits slumped together beside one of the station's support struts, shrouded in multi-faceted shadow.

Vic swam hard, his pulse pounding in his ears. He set his hands on the shoulders of the closest drysuit and shook it. Whoever was inside didn't move. Vic shone his wristlight into their visor, but all he saw was the glare of his own light shining back at him.

He hooked his arms under one of the figures' shoulders and switched on his propulsion pack. Together, they rose into the station's brilliant, too-sunny underside.

It was not until they'd gotten far enough between the exterior lights' rays for their glow to diffuse that Vic saw who he was carrying. The glare hid most of Josh's face, but his eyes were open. His head lolled.

The two of them breached the diving pool. That was as far as Vic could bring them. His propulsion pack kept them afloat, but there was no chance Vic could heave Josh any higher. With the drysuit's weight, he wasn't sure that he could lever *himself* out of the pool.

"Josh. *Josh*. You gotta come back." Vic wasn't sure how to work his radio. He thought he remembered he had to press something to transmit. He grasped for his wristpad controls, but couldn't reach them and keep a grip on Josh at the same time.

Vic touched his helmet visor to Josh's, so the sound would at least carry through the glass. "Josh!"

Instantly, Josh startled and stirred. He pushed against Vic's grasp. And he looked at Vic with the most forlorn, terrified expression Vic had ever seen on him.

Vic had no idea what Karma had inflicted on him, and never wanted to find out. He lifted Josh's arms over the diving pool's edge. With Josh pulling, and Vic's own feet pressed on the hull for leverage, Vic pushed him up like a flopping fish. As soon as Vic was confident Josh would stay there, he dove back down.

By the time he returned with Graymalkin in tow, Nature Girl had found her way to the wet cabin. Vic didn't know where she'd been hiding until now, but she looked paler than he'd ever seen her. She was helping Josh remove his helmet. Josh's eyes were deeply shadowed, to the point of looking recessed.

She helped him lift Graymalkin onto the stairs, and then Vic himself. "Triage is coming out of it," she said. "He's in the command cabin. He says there's something happening at the workstation." Without pausing, she stepped to the diving pool's hatch controls.

"Wait." Vic nodded to the drysuit racks. They were still missing one too many. "Karma is out there."

"Let her stay there," Nature Girl said bitterly.

Nature Girl stayed at the console even after the hatch had shut. Vic didn't need to look over her shoulder to know that she was locking the hatch's exterior keypads – the only way to enter the diving pool from the outside.

Whatever Karma had done to her, whatever nightmare she'd brought to life in front of her, it must have been awful.

Triage wasn't in the emergency command center when Vic returned. Vic's stomach nearly fell through the deck until he saw the probable cause of his absence. A winking green indicator, calling for attention.

A message from hydroacoustic communications.

The emergency control cabin didn't have a full suite of systems to interface with hydroacoustic communications. Just the indicator light to announce when something up there needed attention.

Vic found Triage coming down the stairs from the first deck. Triage's face was flushed, and his eyes were red and wide. Vic couldn't tell which parts had stemmed from his nightmare, and which had come from whatever had happened up there. "Tell you when we're all together," Triage said, before Vic could ask.

The news had to wait until after a thorough search of the station for Aqueos and for Karma, and then a check for any serious damage or Aqueos activity outside the station. Triage called them into the kitchenette.

The rest of them looked just as jittery as Vic felt. Graymalkin seemed more affected than anyone else. The only person who said anything about this was Josh, who'd asked him if he was cold. Graymalkin hadn't answered. He'd stared right past Josh.

The flashlights ringed around the kitchenette provided no better lighting than before, but this time Vic didn't feel tired. Not after what Karma had done to him.

That had to be a bad sign. It had been too long since he'd slept for this energy to be real. Either he was due for a crash soon, or, he shivered to think, whatever had happened to Karma was starting to happen to him. Maybe to all of them.

He tried to swallow that thought, but that didn't help. It sat in his gut, a heavy lump.

"Rescue is on the way," Triage announced. "Our backup buoy made contact. The *Xcaliber* is still in the area. They knew something was wrong when we didn't make our radio check-ins. They've been over our position for half a day, prepping another descent capsule. There's a pair of students from the Jean Grey School, Armor and Shark Girl, that can travel underwater and acclimatize to the pressure faster. They're on their way."

Triage looked around, waiting for a response. Even when he didn't get one, a desperate mania remained in his voice. "We're going to get out of here."

Vic looked to the other side of the cabin. The spots where Crosta and Karma had sat were empty. The remainder of their sorry crew could even fit comfortably into the cramped kitchenette now. This didn't feel like much of a victory.

The Aqueos could have finished them off if they wanted to. They hadn't held off because of the bravery, tenacity, or fighting prowess of the station's defenders. They'd held off because they wanted to. They'd won. They didn't care what happened here next.

After several moments' silence, Josh outlined the theory he and Graymalkin had developed during their dive: that Karma had, by telepathically attacking the Aqueos, exposed herself to a form of their vampirism. Vic's gut tightened.

Nature Girl's lips hung slack. Vic couldn't forget what she'd said about wanting to leave Karma outside, but he couldn't blame her for it, either.

After Nature Girl had left the wet cabin, Vic had re-enabled the keypads that allowed someone outside the diving pool's hatch to unlock it. He'd set an alarm to trip if anyone used it. So far, no one had.

"The drysuits have acoustic beacons," Nature Girl said, after a moment. The suit radios wouldn't penetrate the water for more than a few dozen meters. They'd been meant to stick close to home. As a backup, they had the same communications systems the station used to reach the surface: sound. "We can track where she is."

"Yeah, but that's all," Triage said. "We can't defend ourselves against her."

"Hold up," Vic said. "If vampirism, or whatever sickness the Aqueos have, can spread by telepathic contact… you all know that she attacked us using her telepathy."

If they'd all been affected by a telepathic virus, they would have a hard time distinguishing its symptoms – at least the initial ones – from stress and sleeplessness. The lump in his gut got heavier. Ever since Karma had trapped him in that nightmare, he'd felt on the edge of being sick, and none of this was helping.

Triage paced in what little space the kitchenette allowed, kneading his fingers. He hadn't been quite so fidgety before. Not that Vic could recall. Now he wasn't sure.

Vic still wasn't tired. For days, he'd felt exhaustion as a deep weight behind his eyes. Now there was nothing. If he tried to lay down, he figured he'd just stare at the ceiling.

"Karma hasn't slept since her infection," Vic muttered.

Nature Girl heard him, but interpreted him a different way than he'd intended. "That means she probably won't be able to get far."

Graymalkin had remained conspicuously quiet. Now he said, "You won't find her close."

Vic and the others turned to Graymalkin. He stared straight into the table. "She took extra air canisters with her," he said. "Before she left, she kept talking about some kind of threat, something the Aqueos were afraid of, that they were doing all of this for."

"So they're terrified of… whatever she meant, but they're also working for it?" Nature Girl asked.

Graymalkin nodded miserably. "'Working for' doesn't seem like what Karma meant. It was more like they were worshiping it."

Vic glanced around the table. He briefly met Josh's eyes. Josh's eyebrows were raised almost to the fringe of his bangs.

"She was difficult to make sense of near the end," Graymalkin admitted.

Josh cleared his threat. "Do you think she might be right?"

"It doesn't matter," Graymalkin said. "She's sick. She's gone out and put herself in incredible danger because she believes it. I think that, in her own mind, she imagined she was protecting us when she attacked."

"*Protecting?*" Vic asked, so surprised that anger never had a chance to enter his voice. "How?"

"By discouraging us from following her," Graymalkin said.

She hadn't done that well enough. Vic was already taking mental tally of their remaining drysuits and air supplies.

Nature Girl pulled her chair closer to Graymalkin. "Are you doing all right?" she asked him quietly.

He shook his head. "The nightmare she gave me was… personal. Closed in. Constricting." Vic knew, without having to ask, that Karma had forced him to relive being buried alive. Amazing that he could be as forgiving to her as he was.

Of all of them, Graymalkin had spent the most time around Karma. He knew, better than the rest of them, what she'd been like before. "I noticed her behaving differently ever since the first Aqueos attack," Graymalkin told them. "I wish I'd said something. She got worse after Crosta was taken. I think *she* thinks that Crosta is important to… whatever the Aqueos are trying to do. And that, by taking him, they were one step closer to unleashing some kind of calamity."

"She doesn't know that she's sick," Nature Girl said. "It's scared her too much to think straight and given her some kind of monomania. This must all seem justified to her."

"She might know part of the truth." Graymalkin's jaw tensed. "The Aqueos haven't attacked us since taking Crosta. They never even moved to stop us from launching our own radio buoy. They've just kept an eye on us."

"After all," Vic said, "why should they keep attacking us when they've already got what they want, and we're not doing anything to do them?"

"Except Karma," Josh said. "Karma's trying to do something to stop them."

Vic's and Josh's eyes met again. Vic could follow the idea sizzling through Josh's mind as easily as he could trace it burning across his own.

It would have been much easier to do as Karma so plainly wanted: let her charge off on her own. Vic supposed he should have been proud of himself for never considering that. A sign that he'd done the right thing in joining the Institute and training for the X-Men. Mutants didn't leave mutants to suffer alone.

Until that moment, he hadn't thought Josh would think the same way. Hell, maybe Josh *hadn't* thought the same way, but something in him was changing. The lump in Vic's gut hardened into resolve.

Vic and Josh stood at the same moment. Josh was closer to the kitchenette's hatch, and made it out first. Vic was right behind, scooping up a flashlight on the way out. He still wished anyone but Josh had come on this expedition with them, but it felt good to be in accord with *someone* else. At least on this one issue.

The others' footsteps followed. Triage said, "Please tell me you're not about to do what I think you're going to do."

"Nature Girl, you mentioned the suits have acoustic beacons," Vic said. "Can you get a good idea of what direction she's moving?"

He glanced back. Nature Girl and Triage were looking at each other, conferring just as silently as Vic and Josh had a moment ago. Nature Girl nodded, but it was Triage who answered: "Yes, assuming she doesn't rip her beacon out of her suit. It is an *acoustic* beacon. She'll hear when we ping it."

"She believes she's given us good reason not to follow her," Vic said. "I don't think she'll risk damaging her suit's integrity over that." Not that it was possible for him to predict how or what Karma was thinking.

They stepped through the double hatches to the wet cabin. Vic's flashlight sweep found nothing amiss, at least not newly so. Tipped cabinets, destroyed equipment – and Josh, going straight for the drysuits.

Triage lightly touched Vic's shoulder, and pulled him aside. "Look," he said. "I'm not a coward." After a moment's consideration, he added, "I don't think so, anyway. But we're not equipped for this. We don't have a plan. We don't have any defenses against Karma's attacks. If the Aqueos come at you while you're wearing those suits, you'll be too clumsy to fight back. We need to wait for reinforcements. Someone from the surface who can fight telepathic attacks."

"Do you think Karma's air supply is going to last that long?" Vic asked.

Triage fidgeted with his hands. There was only one answer, and he couldn't say it. They were all trying to solve an arithmetic of lives. "We've lost Crosta already. Think this through."

Graymalkin added, quietly, "I do not know what the point of risking more lives is until we have a means of accomplishing something out there."

"Are you telling me not to go?" Vic asked Graymalkin. "You're in charge here. If you tell me not to go, I'll listen."

Vic had been about to say *If you tell me to not to go, I* won't *go* but something had stopped him just short of making that promise.

"It's quite possible we're not in our right minds," Graymalkin said. "I'm not sure any of us are in a state to make command decisions."

Not a *no*, Vic noted. Neither of them was willing to draw their lines in the sand. "Crosta is out there, too," Vic said. "I haven't given up on him. The Aqueos could have pulled him far enough from the station to survive the defense grid. Now that we've figured out more about what's happening, maybe we can come up with a way to help."

Vic had no idea how. But they weren't going to find the answers sitting in the station. "There are only three working suits," he said. "Not all of us can go. We'll need people to stay, let Armor and Shark Girl know what's going on when they get here, and tell the X-Men what happened if we don't make it."

Graymalkin hesitated a moment. He'd sealed himself into one of those person-shaped metal-and-plastic coffins before, but, from the way he looked at the suit, Vic knew at once that something had changed. Karma's nightmare had rattled him badly.

After a moment, Triage suggested, "We should probably keep one of the working drysuits here, in case we need to go outside to make emergency repairs."

Slowly, Graymalkin nodded.

Josh sat in a mess of disassembled drysuit parts. He, Vic, and Graymalkin had stripped their suits off in pieces when they'd come back in the station. Nature Girl had joined him, helping him sort out suit components.

Vic stepped over to them. "You've made up your mind to go, too?"

He'd asked both of them, but Josh answered: "Try to stop me."

Josh couldn't quite meet Vic's eyes, even as he tried to sound obstinate. Not for the first time, Vic wondered what he'd experienced in his nightmare. It had clearly shaken him. He was trying to hide it, but he wasn't very good at it.

Vic turned back to Triage. "I don't know about not being able to fight in drysuits," Vic said. He flexed his right fingers. "I'll have my regenerated arm. It won't fit the glove, anyway."

"At these water temperatures?" Triage asked. "Your fingers will freeze off."

"Not if there's a healer along with me."

Josh looked up sharply. This time, Vic couldn't meet *his* eyes. As an excuse not to have to, he bent and plucked his drysuit's helmet off the deck.

"We have two healers," Vic said. "One of you should stay here, in case there's another attack and people are hurt."

Triage shook his head. "Nature Girl and I know the emergency control cabin better than anyone else. We should stay to monitor the station and coordinate with rescuers."

"I agree," Nature Girl said, reluctantly. "Triage will need my help."

As an afterthought, Triage added, "And I still think this is a terrible idea."

"Josh?" Vic asked. There had been more to the question, but the rest stuck in his throat.

"You really want me along?" Josh asked.

"*Want,*" Vic said, "is a very strong word." But, for now, it was the one he was stuck with.

CHAPTER SEVENTEEN

Elixir

Black Smokers' Trench was active again. When Josh shone his wristlight upward, the beam attenuated into a particulate-filled nothing. When he waved the light around, he got a brief impression of a dark, tumultuous overcast. Clouds of ash.

He hoped it would hide them from the Aqueos, too.

The seafloor had gotten rougher since they'd left the station. The gentle dunes had given way to a cragged, rocky wasteland. The rock underneath them had sharp, crystalline shapes. Some of it curved and flowed like a dry riverbed. This was relatively "new" ground, just a few thousand years old – formed from magma from Black Smokers' Trench.

He and Vic couldn't afford to travel stealthily, in the dark. They needed their wristlights to follow the ocean floor, or, often, to keep from crashing into it. As they swam, they flicked their lights on and off briefly, trying to keep their exposure to a minimum.

It was astonishingly easy to get disoriented. More than once, Josh flicked his light on expecting to be facing the seafloor horizon, but had found himself canted downward – or, worse, away from Anole. The ocean hid worse dangers than a crash. The Aqueos could have been right ahead of them. Outside of the moments when Josh had his wristlight on to get his bearings, he never would have seen them.

"Swimming" in the drysuit felt like a mix between piloting and working out in a gym. The drysuit was already slick with the feel and smell of his sweat. The weight of the suit and the resistance of the water made his whole body feel sluggish. The propulsion packs could only help so much. To try to keep pace with Karma, they had to add their muscle power.

When Triage had told them Karma's beacon said she was two miles away from the station, Josh thought that a little slow, considering her lead time. Now she seemed impossibly fast. Triage had come down from the emergency command cabin to announce that he was receiving pingbacks from the acoustic beacon in Karma's suit, but that they were fainter. "She hasn't hung around."

"How far?"

"Two miles east of the station. The suit beacons aren't made for that kind of range, especially around sea floor geography. She's been staying low. If she goes much farther, we'll lose her."

"East?" Nature Girl said, frowning. "That's where Black Smokers' Trench is." The source of the soot and ash that had blanketed the station the day they'd arrived.

Now it was active again. Josh ground his teeth, and swam through his exhaustion.

He and Anole were alone. Josh wished Graymalkin had

come, but Graymalkin would have been miserable out here. The station's lights had reduced to a pallid haze behind them. Most of the time, Josh couldn't see them. He was alone inside his helmet, in a suit just a size too large to fit him comfortably... and that was it. Outside of those few seconds when he flicked his wristlight on, his universe consisted of nothing but his drysuit and the sound of his own labored breathing. The unbroken black and the effort it took to move his limbs made him feel like the whole ocean was squeezing him.

Graymalkin's powers would have been less useful than they seemed, anyway. The drysuit would have muted his strength. He was nigh-invincible in darkness... technically. In the ocean, that didn't mean as much as it seemed. He'd survive exposure to the water, but, without oxygen, would quickly lapse into the same coma state he'd been in when his father had buried him alive. If a current carried his somnolent body away, it would have taken a miracle to find him again.

The drysuit's heating filaments were a little too good. The exertion of swimming turned Josh's suit into a boiler. His eyes stung with sweat, and he couldn't rub them. The best he could do was dab the beads of sweat on his visor, leaving a smudge. He had no temperature controls. Or, if he did, they were impossible to find. Josh grasped all over the wristpad but didn't find a single knob or switch whose function he didn't already know.

Every two minutes, the quiet was broken by a distant, muffled chime, like the electric bell that used to sound at Josh's old school at the start of class periods. A ping from the station. The sound had gotten a lot weaker than the last time he'd heard it.

Anole's voice crackled in Josh's ear. "Faster... getting farther..."

Josh flicked his wristlight on long enough to find Anole disconcertingly far away. He pushed back in his direction. Anole's voice faded back in. "…if she goes much farther, she's not going be able to get back." Anole's voice was still muffled by radio distortion, bad speakers, old mics, and the acoustics of two closed-in helmets. Like everything else out here, conversation took more effort than it seemed it should.

"How do you mean?" Josh asked.

"I mean oxygen. She must be close to staying out here past the halfway mark on her air supply. She's been traveling in a straight line, no breaks. If she keeps it up, she's not going to have enough air to return."

Josh had been sure the drysuits had been intended for longer dives than this. But that wouldn't have taken into account the exertion of marathon swimming. A quick flick of his wristlight confirmed that the air gauge on his wrist pad was lower than he'd expected: around the two-thirds mark.

"If *we* go much farther, we won't be able to get back," Josh said.

Anole didn't answer. There didn't seem to be much to say about that. Nothing that would make it better, anyway.

Josh had to say something to keep his mind off the dread and feeling of pressure enveloping them. "How's your hand?"

"Arm's cold," Anole said tightly. "Can't feel my hand."

"Let me see." Josh was close enough to Anole to feel, from the push and pull of displaced water, where his arms and legs were.

"Don't–" Anole started to say, but cut himself off. Josh found his arm in the dark.

The two of them stopped swimming. Their propulsion packs held them aloft. Anole didn't resist when Josh felt his gloved hand down Anole's arm until he found Anole's palm and fingers. Anole's fingers were curled slightly, and didn't shift when Josh prodded them.

"Can you move them?" Josh asked.

Anole was close enough that he didn't need to transmit. His voice carried through the water. "I can't tell in the dark," he said bitterly.

"Try." Josh held Anole's fingers in his gloved hand, and waited. No movement.

Josh released Anole's hand. They had put this off for too long.

The darkness not only made it easy to get disoriented, but to see flashes of things that he shouldn't. Swimming lights, motion, and, worse, flicker-flashes of memory from Karma's telepathic attack. Those hadn't faded like images from a dream.

Fear settled into a cold, iron-hard lump in the back of his head. That fear wouldn't distinguish between those memories and his real ones. If Josh lived for a thousand years, he would never be able to forget that moment, bobbing in the diving pool, when Anole had shaken him out of his nightmare, and those two universes had crashed together.

In one, Anole was swimming beside him, suited up. In the other, Anole was twisted and bloated and blackened by age. Weeks of decay racked him in the space of seconds. Josh's bubbling hand gripped his shoulder. Josh's skin boiled and seeped over his bones, burning incandescent with his rage. Anole's flesh withered to leathery scraps. The ligaments holding his joints together rotted away, and his bones crumbled to milky-gray shards in Josh's grip.

He meant to do this to Anole, he *enjoyed* doing it, and he didn't know how he could make himself stop. And, just for a moment, when Anole had shaken him out of that other universe and back into this one, Josh hadn't been able to tell the difference.

Josh desperately wanted to think that, even if he hadn't had interceding layers of gloves and suit fabric between them, he wouldn't have killed Anole. But he could never be sure. So the question would never leave him.

In the dream, he'd been his own nightmare. The kind of hero that, when he'd joined the Reavers, he'd believed the world needed.

Anole shifted uncomfortably. He'd never know that, however little he wanted to do this, Josh wanted to do it even less. "Do I have your permission?" Josh asked quietly.

"Yeah," Anole said. "Whatever."

Anole hadn't thought the mechanics of this through. Josh needed to touch Anole with his own bare skin. When Josh moved to unfasten his own glove, Anole pulled back. "You take that off, you'll never get it back out. You'll never be warm or dry again until this is over."

"I've got no other way to do this," Josh said. To keep Anole from finding that an excuse to delay it, Josh loosened his glove's seals and yanked it off.

The cold was sharper than he'd braced for. It was like an icicle had jammed under his skin. But his wrist seal held, and the rest of his suit remained dry. He could withstand it. With his healing power, he could repair his freezing extremities as they went along.

He reached over and grabbed Anole's scaly, bare hand. The damage was worse than Anole had let on. Most of his hand was bloodless. His veins and capillaries had constricted to nearly nothing.

Josh found himself at an unexpected loss. He had never had to heat a cold-blooded being before. He had a lot of energy he needed to generate, and there were only so many places to draw it from. He started by burning some of Anole's loose fat cells. Then he coaxed some of his own energy over. Once Anole's blood started to warm, Josh prized open the capillaries, and flooded his muscles with energy.

Anole gasped. The pain from so many nerves coming back to life would be intense. Josh couldn't do much for that. He still didn't feel confident enough to fine-tune nerves. He kept a tight grip on Anole's wrist to keep him from pulling back prematurely.

It would have taken some work to fix this problem permanently. Reshape Anole's heart into a heat engine, give him more efficient fat-cell-to-energy-conversion, altered blood chemistry...

The moment he thought of it, he was back in that other universe, holding Anole's disintegrating body.

It was Josh, not Anole, who yanked his hand back first. Anole flexed his fingers.

"Thanks," he radioed, after the pain faded. He sounded reluctant.

Josh didn't trust himself to speak. By the time he did, he and Anole were underway again, and he needed all his breath to keep up.

There wasn't much point in putting the glove back on, not now that it was already filled with water. He'd never be able to manage the wrist seal with his other, clumsy fingers, either. He watched it drift to the seafloor.

Another ping washed across them. Their suits answered back.

Pings and pulses were the only message that would reliably carry this far underwater. They didn't have the bandwidth to send voice signals. Words would have arrived too garbled and broken by currents, distance, and interfering noises. Anole and Triage had taken survival courses together and knew the rudiments of long-distance signaling. They'd worked out a simple code. The first set of pings gave them their distance to Karma in intervals of a thousand feet. A pause followed, and then the next set of pings gave them her approximate bearing.

The acoustic pulses from the station usually came in five-minute intervals. These next pings arrived early. Josh stopped swimming. "What's going on?"

"Shut up," Anole snapped. "Let me listen."

Josh impatiently treaded water, staying close to the pulsing water of Anole's propulsion pack, just to make sure they hadn't separated in the dark. "It's a set of three signals meaning 'no,'" Anole said. "And then a bearing for turning around. I think Triage is saying that he's lost track of Karma and that we should turn around."

Josh swallowed. "She's out of range?" This set of pulses had sounded even weaker than the last.

"I can only guess that's what he means."

Josh's oxygen gauge had to be lower than the two-thirds mark now. If Karma was still out there, and moving at the same pace she'd maintained, she'd have been past the point of safe return.

"Do you want to head back?" Anole asked.

"No. Do you?"

In answer, the water over Josh's shoulders stirred as Anole kicked his flippers and swam on.

•••

By the time Josh and Anole should have gotten their next signal from the station, a different set of chimes rolled through the water. From the fact that it repeated, and that the pattern was similar to the last message, Josh guessed it was more noes.

They had to use their wristlights full-time now. Without Station X-41 to provide distance and bearing, it would be too easy to lose their course.

Pressing on was an act of desperation and bitter hope. If Karma had changed direction, he and Anole would never find her. Coming out here had every chance of making their situation worse, but it wouldn't have been desperation without stupidity mixed in.

"Why are you doing this?" Anole radioed.

"That hand of yours is going to keep needing healing." Josh was still trying to figure out how to draw the energy for that without burning too much fat.

"You absolutely didn't have to come out after Karma or Crosta. You barely knew Karma before you came on this trip."

"Are you saying it's not the right thing to do?"

"I'm asking you why you're doing it."

It was hard not to bristle at that. He forced himself to remember that Anole had plenty of reasons to feel that way. "I don't need to know somebody to care if they live or die," Josh said.

"You didn't need to know them well to hate them, either," Anole said.

Even on his guard, Josh was still caught by surprise. Anole's words bit him as sharply as the Aqueos's spear, running through his shoulder. "I never wanted to kill mutants," he said. After the nightmare Karma had given him, he desperately needed to believe that about himself.

"You just wanted us to stop existing."

The problem with arguing all this was that it was an entirely fair assessment. The thought of that nightmare had knocked his wind from him.

"Yeah," was all Josh could say.

He said it so softly he wasn't sure the radio had picked it up. But Anole said, "You know, that's the first time I've heard you say that."

Josh just looked at him. The fact that he had to move his hand to hit the "transmit" button again kept him from feeling like he had to make some noise of acknowledgment.

"Before, you were always ducking talking about what you did," Anole said. "Always trying to hide it."

"I can't do anything to change what I did," Josh said. "I'm trying to be better."

"I know you are," Anole said.

Josh was caught just as much by surprise by that as anything before. He reached for the "transmit" button, but fumbled and couldn't find it. What he'd come close to saying was that he didn't deserve the chance Anole seemed to be giving him. The others had come out of their fugues describing being terrified. The scariest thing about Josh's nightmare was that he *hadn't* been terrified, not while he was in it.

Anole raised his wristlight abruptly. Josh's gaze jerked up.

The horizon was closer than it should have been. It had never been especially clear, even under their wristlights: just a hazy boundary between the dark rock and the dark ocean. Where it had fuzzed away into obscurity before, though, now it was in sharp, razor-edged relief: a jagged line cutting across the sea.

They were coming up on a steep fall off. "Propulsion off,"

Anole said, and Josh did as he asked. They coasted to a stop at the edge of the cliff. Josh's flippers gently touched rock.

Vertigo nearly made him fall back.

A vast gulf of water opened underneath him, most of it the same impenetrable black as the ocean above. It was like standing at the edge of the sky, or a fragment of a shattered world as it spun off into nothing. But only part of the gulf was like that.

Past a steep angle, the water became unaccountably clearer. Red lights glowed down there – far enough below to prompt another wave of vertigo. They weren't bright, and the waters between them and Josh weren't *entirely* clear, which left them as more of a suggestion of red than light. Every once in a while, the intervening fog shifted just enough for one of the lights to shine through clearly. Ruby studs on a black velvet tapestry. Their distance was impossible to judge. They may as well have been stars shining on the other side of the world.

"Black Smokers' Trench," Anole radioed.

"Is that light lava?" Josh asked.

"Maybe some of it. Not all of it."

When one of the glowing specks shifted into clarity again, Josh watched it long enough to see it slide minutely to his left. It wobbled as it shifted, swaying like it was being carried.

Aqueos. It made sense that they'd have come from Black Smokers' Trench. They were undead, and had no blood to warm their veins, but that didn't mean they couldn't get cold. The trench provided them heat. They'd never find better in the deep ocean. Like lizards sunning themselves on rocks, they would congregate here.

The thought reminded Josh to ask, "How's your hand?"

"Fine," Anole answered. Josh couldn't feel his own fingers, but when he looked at them and tried to move them, they wiggled as they should have.

"The water's gotten hotter," Josh said. "I really don't like that. If it's warm all the way up here, we could get flash-fried in a second down there."

"Another reason I'm glad to be traveling with a healer," Anole told him.

Not a satisfying answer. There were limits to how fast Josh could heal Anole – and himself, if it came down to that. All his healing power couldn't glue their bones and ashes back together if they fell into the heart of an active undersea volcano. He didn't know the limit of his powers, not really, but he was certain he couldn't bring the dead back to life.

Motion ahead, at their height, made Josh start. It was so far away that his wristlight faded to nothing before the beam ever touched it. The crimson light from below shone off its underside.

Voluminous, inky black smoke poured from the trench. The cloud was the size of a mountain, and rose high into the nautical sky. It spread out above them, blanketing the ocean. This was the source of the gray-black haze that perpetually shrouded Station X-41, and the ash that covered its hull.

It was why the water underneath them was comparatively clear. The smoke came from the vent, yes, but not from directly underneath this cliff. There was still surface below them. The water was not clouded by the particulates that choked everything else. The currents carried the smoke away before it cooled and snowed ash.

A strong current pushed at his ankles. It was a heat exchange:

cold ocean rushing in to replace rising warm water. If he wasn't careful, it would make him slip in.

"Lights off," Anole said. He had already extinguished his wristlight. Josh did the same.

"You think Karma went down there?"

Anole looked at him. From his stance alone, he managed to say that was the most obvious thing he'd ever been asked. "The trench would definitely block her acoustic beacon. If Triage and Nature Girl lost contact with her, this is probably why."

Anole lifted his boot, and stepped over the edge. Josh's cry of warning caught in his throat. But Anole didn't plunge. He gently drifted downward. Josh's head spun. His vertigo had been so great that he'd expected anyone who fell to be swallowed by the abyss – maybe with a circle of Wile E Coyote smoke to mark their plunge into lava.

Anole pirouetted to face him. "Get off the cliff," he radioed. "If the Aqueos can see in the dark as well as I think, our suits will stand out like ducks on a target range. Not to mention, if the station tries to ping us, and your suit answers–"

"I get it," Josh interrupted. He tried not to think too much about what he was doing, and followed Anole over the edge.

They sank. Before long, Josh could no longer see the top of the cliff they'd dropped from. Black swallowed everything but the distant impression of the mountain-sized plume of smoke, and the red shadows underneath them.

He and Anole built momentum as they fell, and had to arrest it with kicks of their flippers. When they needed to leave the trench, they'd have a hard time struggling against the current pushing them down. Finding a hot rising current would make it easier, but it had a better chance of cooking them in their suits.

Rather than think about what they might find below, Josh distracted himself by thinking of the dangers that could catch them right now. He'd never been precisely sure how good the Aqueos's night vision was, but he doubted there was any light at all down here most of the time. They had to be sensing heat. There was simply not enough light around for even the most sensitive retinas. Anole had been right: they'd stuck out on that cliff, their heated suits highlighted against a backdrop of cold ocean.

That was the key word, though. *Interest.* Ever since the Aqueos had taken Crosta, they'd focused on something else. He wondered if they'd stopped caring about even their own security and welfare.

Not that the Aqueos had ever been big on those. They'd attacked the station with the ferocity of cornered animals. He had never seen one of them stop to help another. They may have been shaped like humans – with two arms, two legs, and a head – but their single-mindedness was utterly alien.

They were definitely capable of working together, though.

As Josh and Anole descended, some of the shadows resolved themselves into huge, dark silhouettes: square-shouldered blocks, domes, and strangely angled buildings.

Josh forgot all about the numbing pain in his hand, and the way his stomach churned with vertigo. He couldn't think of anything except trying to understand what he was seeing, and failing. The vista underneath him unraveled, dreamlike, into unmistakably artificial right angles, and then into blocks and streets.

Josh's pulse pounded in his ears. Neither he nor Anole said anything. The only other sound in his helmet was his increasingly ragged breath.

The shapes were buildings.

Josh and Anole descended into a dead undersea city.

Neither Josh nor Anole spoke as they fell. Josh knew he should have kept his eyes open for attackers, but he couldn't keep his eyes off the city.

The ruby lights took on additional definition. Some of them moved and bobbed like they were being held. Others, brighter, were stationary, and much larger. To Josh's relief, the nearest ones seemed too uniform and well-spaced to be magma, but he couldn't tell anything else about them. He could not help but worry that they'd been spotted. Neither he nor Anole saw anyone or anything moving among the buildings, though. The whole place seemed to be deserted.

The Aqueos weren't here in great numbers. At least not in this part of the city. This was where Karma had come, though. Josh didn't doubt there were Aqueos here, somewhere.

The minutes blended together until, with a rapidity that made Josh wonder if they'd started to plummet at aerial speeds, time suddenly took hold again. The buildings' shadows rose around them. Josh set down on a soft, spongy surface. He promptly sank into it.

The only light was a backlit haze. Embers of red light pollution simmered in the ocean overhead. All he saw of Anole was an impression of a silhouette so vague that it was hard to distinguish from the blobby afterimages the city's lights had left in his eyes.

Above, Josh had been afraid that the water would get too hot for them to survive. If anything, the water here was colder. He and Anole had sunk on a cascade of cooling seawater, an undersea waterfall. Josh's hand was numb again, and a dull, icy ache soaked up his arm, into his bones. The red light limning the buildings like distant fires grew brighter now that his eyes had readjusted. It was so strange, freezing in a place that looked like a furnace.

This was the first time Josh felt capable of speaking. "Your hand OK?" he radioed.

"Your night vision's better than mine," Anole said. "Could you tell how big this place was from the air?"

"Not *that* much better." If this city extended as far as the smattering of red lights they'd seen above, then it was too big for them to explore. "How are we going to find Karma in all this?"

"Think. What do we have that won't make much noise but still get Karma's attention?"

"The suit radios." Their signals would carry a few dozen feet at most. But it was better than anything else they had. Certainly better than searching by sight.

The glowing haze shifted. Josh caught the shadow flitting across them a moment before he saw the figure rising over the streets. It was swimming away and didn't seem to notice or care about Josh or Anole, but it was dangerously close. It could have launched from much farther than the next block over. Its silhouette looked like an Aqueos.

It was the first one they'd seen. Josh waited until the figure was long disappeared into the darkness before moving or speaking again. "If Crosta's still alive, he won't have a radio."

Anole's silhouette turned to look at him. "If Crosta is out there, I'm not sure we'll want to find him."

"I thought you said you weren't giving up on him."

"I'm not giving up on anybody or I wouldn't be here," Anole hissed bitterly. "And keep your voice down. The noise doesn't just stay in your helmet, and sound transmits a lot farther in water than you'd think."

Josh knew that. A week ago, he would have snapped back to say so. If this trip had taught him anything, though, it was that he couldn't cover his mistakes with insecurity. Making more noise to argue would have made its own case against him.

So he set off. He kicked free of the ash, pumping his flippers to ascend. Without his propulsion pack, swimming was heavy work, but not as heavy as trudging through layers of sedimentary ash would have been.

Josh stepped closer to the nearest structure. The ashfall wasn't as tall in its shadow. Josh could see a hint of how they'd been built. They were made of bricks of rough, knobbly stone, as rough as pumice. The poor light robbed it of every color except black, but Josh expected that any decorative flourishes had faded long ago.

Above, Josh had assumed the Aqueos built this city. Looking around more, he started to doubt. These buildings had been worn down by time. Most were missing roofs. Walls had crumbled. Anything that might have been decorative or retained cultural significance was buried or disintegrated.

There were very few Aqueos about. This place was too large to hold them, which spoke of being built by another people, for another purpose. All lost and meaningless now.

The only things left were questions without answers. The buildings' foundations had been dug *into* the magmatic rock, so this place must have been built after the vent had become active. Why, then, had the whole place not been buried under ash? Even with most of the smoke escaping the vent, this city should have been buried past its rooftops in compressed ash.

Unless some inhabitants had been keeping it clean for a very, very long time. An extremely devoted people. So single-minded that they either hadn't noticed the rest of the disrepair, or it just didn't matter to them.

Why build so close to an active volcanic vent to begin with?

The more he saw, the less he understood.

He and Anole didn't have many directions to go but toward the street they'd seen the Aqueos swim up from. They swam along one of the few buildings with an intact roof. Josh landed crouched, staying low, but shuffling to the edge for a better vantage.

Anole hunched beside him, and for a while they didn't speak.

The furnace-ember light showed them many and variegated shadows: squat and crumbling wrecks, mausoleums the size of office blocks, open squares, and, in the distance, towers like steeples and minarets. Not that different from what Josh might have expected of a mid-sized Midwestern town… had it been dragged to Hell and buried under ash and fire a thousand years ago.

He could not have seen so much from above. Here, the water was clearer, and his mind more prepared to accept what his eyes were seeing.

Thundercloud-sized smoke rose over the city, an inward-leaning cliff, overshadowing everything. Josh couldn't see the top of it. A feeble but steady orange light burned underneath it. The steepness of the light's angle cast strange shadows across the smoke, oily worms crawling up its undulating blisters and crevices.

The orange blaze smoldered and throbbed. It faded out and then rose back, like a fire under the billows. If the crimson lights they'd seen earlier hadn't been magma, this definitely was.

When Josh had agreed to go to the Institute, Outlaw had told him – threatened him, even – that he would have "adventures", see things he'd never forget. He hadn't really believed her. Certainly, he hadn't wanted to.

He mostly still didn't. But there was a small part of him, a very small part, that was more open to it now.

He waded through the roof's ashfall to the other side and, after checking that Anole was still with him, hopped off the edge. Onto the next street. Deeper and deeper into what he was sure was the most alien place on Earth.

CHAPTER EIGHTEEN

Anole

Vic didn't want to stop to ask for help, but finally he had no choice. The pain in his arm throbbed up his shoulder. He knew he ought to have called Josh over sooner. It still took a great deal of willpower to let Josh touch him. It was easier now to recognize that fear as unthinking.

He couldn't rationalize it to himself as he had before, under a layer of suspicion about Josh's motives. That had just been words he'd papered over a feeling that had preceded them.

It had come from memories of screaming men about to execute his father. Of the phantom pains of his missing arm lasting even after the new one had started to grow.

They paused close to a standing corner that was all that remained of a building. Vic held his hand out. His paranoia about Josh had always made a certain amount of sense, but never in the contexts that he'd felt it. Even if Josh had wanted to betray them, he wouldn't have done it down here, where he was dependent on outside help to escape alive.

Vic's fear wouldn't go away, and so he had to come up with words to justify it. The truth was that he didn't need the words. He was perfectly justified in hating Josh for the things he'd done, and not wanting anything to do with him.

But not to the point where he placed his life or any of the others' in danger. If the best way forward was to work with Josh, then he would have to do it. The X-Men did it all the time. They didn't deny their trauma, but worked with it.

When Josh held his bare hand, Vic tried not to think of all the things Josh was capable of doing to his body. It was bad enough thinking of the things that he *was* doing.

Vic's hand returned to life with a shock of pain like broken glass was crawling under his skin. He sucked air through his teeth. He hadn't transmitted his hissing, but Josh must have heard it through their helmets or just felt Vic squirm. "If you don't want it to hurt so much, don't put it off for so long."

Once Vic got enough feeling back in his hand to wriggle his fingers, he pulled away.

As they got farther into that leviathan city, Vic could make out more and more of their surroundings. At first, he thought his eyesight might have been getting better. The ambient light, what little there was, was growing subtly brighter. So subtly that it had taken him minutes to notice.

When he and Josh reached the city, he hadn't been able to see more than a dull red-orange haze across the water. When he'd been five years old, he and his parents had once visited an aunt in rural California and, in the middle of the night, had to evacuate ahead of a flash wildfire. He'd been half-asleep, and convinced he was having a nightmare. Only the nightmare never ended.

It was an increasingly familiar feeling.

The light had risen to the level of a darkened theater before the film started. Vic saw obstacles in the street before he stubbed his flippers into them. Josh's drysuit was no longer just a silhouette, and even had shades of texture.

They spotted a few more Aqueos as they went along, but none that were close, and none that seemed to see them in return. Every half-block or so, they radioed for Karma without really expecting an answer. This city was too large. If they wanted to get to her before their oxygen ran so low that they couldn't return to the station, they needed something else to go on.

He swam over a crumbled line of brick that might have once been a wall. On the next street over, he and Josh had another good view of the volcanic plume towering over the city, and of the strange light underneath it. Vic halted, sinking back into the ash.

Josh had noticed the brightening too. "This must be a regular event," Josh said. "This city's been here a long time. It'd be an awfully big coincidence if it erupted at exactly the same moment we're here."

The orange glow had been pulsing since the first time they'd seen it, but the light must have been steadily building along with it, like waves in a rising tide.

"Maybe not a coincidence," Vic said. "We wouldn't be here if the Aqueos hadn't attacked first. And they attacked after decades of leaving Station X-41 and its crews alone."

Josh shifted as he looked at the eruption. "What, you don't think they brought Crosta here to sacrifice to their volcano, do you?"

"Don't be stupid." Josh must have been reading too many comic books.

"It's a serious question–"

A flare of light from the volcano revealed a lanky, angular silhouette, astonishingly close. It glided toward them out of the dark, directly behind Josh.

Vic yelled, loud enough that he hoped he didn't need to be transmitting for Josh to hear him, and shoved Josh's shoulder to knock him aside. Water resistance made everything so slow. Vic's hand connected with only half the force he'd intended. It was just enough to make Josh stumble out of the way. Vic drew his arm back, bunching his hand into a fist. If one of them was going to get impaled, Vic would rather it be him than the person who could heal him afterward.

Vic took a defensive stance. The Institute's martial arts training was hardly going to be of use underwater, but he had no other resources to draw from. The attack he'd braced for never came. The Aqueos flitted back, hissing all the while.

It had been *going* to attack them. Vic was sure of that. It had crept up on them, a predator in ambush mode, gliding rather than swimming so that it wouldn't stir the water. If it was a predator, it was thinking twice now that its quarry had its guard up.

Vic's heart pounded. His breath rasped in his helmet. He wasn't willing to go after the Aqueos any more than the Aqueos was willing to go after them. He held his ground as the Aqueos circled them, keeping its distance.

Then the Aqueos turned and slipped into the shadows. When Vic aimed his wristlight after it, it was gone.

It had made a very different calculation than the Aqueos who'd attacked the station. Every Aqueos he'd seen, every single one, had thrown themselves into attacking him and his team with wild ferocity. Vic didn't know if it was showing a desire for self-preservation or making a simple tactical judgment. From everything he'd seen of the Aqueos so far, he would have put his bet on the latter.

That had been an attempt at an opportunistic ambush. At the moment, he and Josh hadn't been worth sacrificing a pawn. That was all.

Vic stared after the vanished Aqueos, willing himself to see some trace of it. It had disappeared in the direction of the boiling volcanic plume.

"What the hell do we do now?" Josh asked.

"It's got somewhere it needs to be," Vic said. "We follow it."

"*Toward* the erupting thermal vent?" Josh asked, but Vic had already pushed away from the street and started swimming.

Vic's muscles radiated exhaustion. Even if the Aqueos hadn't gotten a head start, he and Josh never would have caught up with it. He just had to hope this was the right way.

"You hear that?" Josh asked.

Vic strained his ears. At first, he didn't – but only because it was more a feeling than a sound. A subsonic rumbling, shivering the water. Vic craned forward, touching his forehead to his visor, and felt the vibration more clearly that way. It made his teeth itch.

Best not to think too much about what that meant. He reached to his wristpad and switched on his propulsion pack. They no longer needed to worry about the noise of their rotors. With the propulsion packs, they covered much more ground. Vic never caught sight of the retreating Aqueos, although that was quickly no longer a problem.

More Aqueos swarmed the sunset sky. Some swam, making

sleek silhouettes against the bleak orange horizon. Others moved closer to ground level, carrying crimson lights with them.

They all headed in the same direction. None of them seemed to be in a hurry. They moved without urgency but with a unified purpose. Vic had no idea why some swam while others plodded along the ground. Only the Aqueos on the ground carried lights.

There were more lights in the city than the vent and the Aqueos's staffs. Blotches of crimson glowed along some of the streets and walls. It had been spread like jelly across brick and rock. It was the same crimson color as the staffs the Aqueos carried. Though it was dimmer, there was more of it. If they exuded any heat, Vic couldn't feel it. He resisted the impulse to swim closer to check.

The next time he looked behind him, he saw even more of the glowing patches. It took Vic a moment to figure out how so many had seemed to appear. The glowing patches on buildings had all been spread on the east-facing side: facing the volcanic vent. He hadn't seen them from the angle he'd entered.

He and Josh crossed half of the city before the Aqueos roused a serious effort to stop them.

A line of five Aqueos emerged from the ember-red shadows. They made no attempt to hide themselves. They approached from directly ahead, placing themselves between the two mutants and the volcanic plume. Their silhouettes were sharp as knives against the terrible fire behind them. They could not have made themselves more visible if they'd carried the light-staffs.

Though they weren't carrying staffs, they all gripped

weapons: shapes like spears, harpoons, and even an Atlantean-style trident.

Vic and Josh exchanged a glance, or as much of one as they could through the visors. "Dive," Vic radioed.

They couldn't fight that many Aqueos in the open water, without cover or leverage. Vic somersaulted upside-down and swam as hard as he could. He felt rather than saw Josh do the same behind him. He hadn't started far from the street – maybe twenty-five, thirty feet – but the Aqueos closed fast. With the same devilish speed that their very first attacker had used to break through the conference room window, the Aqueos were on them.

Vic curled to his side just as a spear thrust through the water where his stomach had been. He lashed out with his foot, but without anything to hold onto, his kick didn't have the power to do anything but glance off the Aqueos's chest. He had no idea how that Aqueos moved so quickly and forcefully in open water. The laws of physics didn't work the same way for him.

He turned his fumble into a roll and a feint. He darted to his left, and then dove closer to the street. The Aqueos followed him down.

Grateful that he could still feel his fingers, Vic grabbed the corner of free-standing ruins that were all that remained of a wall, and pulled himself around it. The Aqueos may have been preternatural swimmers, but in close combat, their limbs were just as slow and clumsy underwater as Vic's. An Aqueos rounded the corner. Vic seized the haft of its spear in his regenerated hand, and smashed it back into the Aqueos's head. A satisfying *crack* reverberated through Vic's palm.

Josh had nearly reached the other edge of the wall. Two

Aqueos dogged him. One of the Aqueos grabbed his ankle and wrenched him back, dragging him into killing range of its trident.

Josh reached out and, for a delirious moment, Vic watched Josh's ungloved hand elongate – wrist and finger bones snapped and distending, becoming nearly as long as his forearm. He snagged the edge of the wall and pulled himself in. The Aqueos, not anticipating the sudden resistance, lost its grip. Josh's free foot snapped out and caught the Aqueos under its chin.

The second Aqueos was coming up on Josh fast from his side, a wickedly barbed harpoon held high. Vic wasn't sure Josh had seen it.

Vic seized the spear from his own assailant's limp fingers, drew his arm back, and hurled the spear as hard as he could. Even with his enhanced strength, his swing still felt too slow. When he loosed the spear, though, it sliced through the darkness too fast to follow.

It wasn't a perfect throw. The speartip didn't embed in the Aqueos, but ricocheted off its elbow, and then ripped across its flesh up to the shoulder. The Aqueos had no blood to spill, but the blow halted it all the same. It released its grip on the harpoon, kicking away.

The last two Aqueos had remained above the street, cruising about twenty feet up and twenty yards to their left. They coiled up, ready to hurl their spears. Josh took cover behind the wall. Vic did the same, and just in time. A spear cracked into the street just behind him, the force of the impact splitting its shaft.

Vic and Josh did not need to radio each other to know what to do next. They drew their legs up against the wall and kicked off it like Olympic swimmers from a pool, staying low and heading toward the nearest cluster of buildings. Better cover was available there.

It would also bring them toward the volcanic plume. Vic had no idea why the Aqueos were suddenly focusing more energy on them but, if he had to guess, it was because he and Josh were getting closer to that plume. All the other Aqueos were headed in that direction.

Vic and Josh couldn't stop to fight, not for long. Their odds of finding Karma were low enough, and would become zero if they halted. If they were going to fight, they'd have to make it a running battle.

The nearest building only had half its roof, but it was better cover than anywhere else. Vic glanced behind them. The two Aqueos were now approaching at astonishing speed. Another Aqueos, one of those Vic and Josh had brawled with, had gotten its balance back.

The Aqueos were always going to be faster, but the propulsion packs gave Vic and Josh a fighting chance to reach the building first. The front wall was riddled with holes that, had they been more regularly spaced and sized, Vic would have called windows. The cavities permeated the building. The more Vic saw of them, they more they triggered an instinctive, unreasoning fear deep in his bones. Most of them were tiny. The smallest was no larger than his fist. Only two or three were large enough to fit a drysuit. All of the holes were covered in shadow. They reminded him of a beehive, or insectile compound eyes. He couldn't imagine why any intelligent being would design a wall like that.

He didn't have more than half a second to think about it. He grabbed the side of a hole large enough to fit his drysuit, and heaved himself through, headfirst.

In the same instant, a slash of pain seared across his ankle.

He yelped. As he finished pulling himself to the other side, he caught sight of a stream of bubbles, mingling with a dark red cloud, coming from the side of his boot.

The Aqueos had given up their weapons and come at him with claws. The one right behind Vic had cut through his drysuit and into his ankle.

Bitter cold sloshed over Vic's foot. His drysuit had torn.

He almost wished the cold numbed faster. The salt water pouring over the gash stung more than Vic had believed anything could, and he would have believed a lot.

Vic ground his teeth. The pain was still fresh enough that he could channel it into rage. His pursuer slithered through the gap. He whirled around, letting the propulsion pack boost his momentum, and crashed his fist into the Aqueos's side.

As soon as he could, Vic righted himself. The fountain of bubbles from his foot stopped. The water level in his boot had already risen to the level of the gash. *It could have been worse,* he tried to tell himself as the pain clawed at his mind. The cursed thing could have bitten him, and then he'd have to worry about vampiric infection, too.

Movement from the corner of his eye drew his attention. Josh had wormed through another of the spongy holes, an Aqueos's claws swiping behind him.

The Aqueos who'd attacked Vic swam toward the ceiling. It curled its legs against the stone, kicked off, and vaulted ahead of Vic.

Vic could barely see it. His night vision had been spoiled by the growing light outside. In here, it was all back to shadows. He stepped back fast enough to avoid the claw swipe at his stomach, but not enough to avoid the one that *whanged* off his visor.

The Aqueos's claw snapped off a chip of glass the size of Vic's thumb, leaving a white mark permanently at the bottom of his vision. Vic crouched, ready to bowl into his attacker, fists swinging. But the Aqueos stepped back into the shadows.

Vic barely restrained himself from launching after it. That was what it wanted. He took a probing step forward, his regenerated arm ready to block. Deeper in the dark, the creature stepped back again. Vic realized, half a heartbeat before it would have been too late, that the creature was trying to distract him.

He half-turned. A second Aqueos was nearing him. This one must have just come through the same hole in the wall he had. It had nearly reached him, but froze when Vic saw it.

Sensing Vic's indecision and swaying balance, the first Aqueos moved in to attack. Vic couldn't cover both sides at once.

Somewhere, Josh had found the presence of mind to switch on his radio: "Covering your left."

Vic moved instantly. He turned fully around to the first Aqueos, exposing his back to the other. The first Aqueos tried to step back, but its momentum had already carried it too close to Vic. Vic cracked his regenerated fist under its chin. The Aqueos tried to turn the force of the blow into a somersault and a kick, but Vic, still animated by rage, was too fast. He hooked his boot against a divot in the floor, and used that leverage and a push from his propulsion pack to drive into the Aqueos.

Vic landed atop it, pinning it to the obsidian ground. Before he could think, Vic drew his regenerated arm back, and drove his fist into the Aqueos's chest.

Vic was still not sure how much punishment the Aqueos

could withstand before dying. If anything would stop them, though, he was sure that this blow would do it. He was sure that, if he survived, he was never going to forget the feeling of the Aqueos's ribs folding inward.

The Aqueos did not move again, not that he ever saw.

Vic turned and found Josh locked in a struggle with the Aqueos that would have ambushed him.

Vic had acted the instant he'd heard Josh's voice. No hesitation – just turning and trusting Josh to do what he'd said. As recently as an hour ago, Vic didn't know if he could have brought himself to do that. If he'd had the time to think about that, it would have stunned him, but one of the virtues of combat was that it didn't leave space in his head for more than the immediate.

Josh had somehow grabbed his own pursuer's harpoon. The Aqueos grabbed his arm and tried to force the weapon out of Josh's grip. Josh's arm didn't lock up like the Aqueos expected. His elbow bent *backward*. His shoulder did the same, visibly dislocating. The Aqueos stumbled.

Vic fought a wave of nausea. He'd seen other mutants do "worse" things to their bodies, but something about what Josh was doing looked like it *hurt*. Josh's arm worked just as well bending backward as forward. He shifted his grip, and thrust it into the Aqueos's thigh. The tip pierced through its leg, and drove into the rock.

The Aqueos scrabbled at the harpoon, trying to pull it loose, but the tip had rooted deep. Josh stepped back.

It wasn't the only Aqueos he'd trapped. Vic finally saw what had happened to the Aqueos chasing Josh. The cavity Josh had come through had collapsed. The Aqueos who'd pursued Josh was trapped in the rubble, hissing and snarling but unable to escape. Vic didn't want to think too much about how Josh must have contorted his body to get the leverage to do that.

"Damn," was all Vic managed to radio. He didn't have the breath for anything else.

"Yeah," Josh answered.

They wordlessly agreed where to go next: to their left, toward the next nearest outside wall. More unnatural cavities lined it. Vic and Josh dived through the first one large enough to fit their drysuits. They reemerged onto the ocher-shaded streets.

The spaces between buildings weren't really "streets" as Vic normally thought of them. They varied dramatically in width, going from as wide as a two-lane boulevard to barely large enough to fit him and Josh shoulder-to-shoulder. The only reason he thought of them as streets was that, so far as he could see, they continued unbroken in one direction: toward the vent.

The street narrowed just ahead, and sloped downward. This whole city seemed to be oriented around the vent. Or leading into it. The nausea that had been burbling in Vic's stomach since he'd seen Josh's shoulder dislocate turned to vertigo. Vic needed to concentrate to keep swimming straight.

Vic was reminded uncomfortably of a funnel. The city was pouring down the neck of the volcano. The streets' downward slope steepened. Fewer buildings obstructed their view. They had a much clearer view of the vent from here. The monstrous plume of smoke had become their horizon.

The angle Vic swam at sent more salt water sloshing up his ankle. The pain hammered into his cut. The last thing he needed was a stream of air bubbles revealing their location. He paused long enough to cinch his ankle straps as tight as they would go.

The pressure bit into his skin, but that was nothing next to the pain of the salt water in his cut.

"Let me take a look at that foot," Josh said.

"I'd have to take off the boot," Vic said. "I'm not going to risk losing that flipper."

When Vic rounded the corner of the next building, he got his clearest view yet of what waited ahead of them. Some kind of congregation was taking place at the far end of the city.

There were so many black specks in the water that, for too long a moment, Vic thought they were debris, ash particles swept up in a vortex of currents whirling around the vent. They were Aqueos. More Aqueos lined up outside the city, along the seafloor, in the canyon of shadows between it and the raised ridge of the vent. The only reason Vic saw them at all was that they held more light-staffs. They'd formed up into a line with a very shallow curve, like a formation of nineteenth-century infantry.

There was some kind of fracas in the middle of the swimming Aqueos. A dozen of them were converging on a single point.

As Vic watched, half of them abruptly fell away. The others closed in – and then the same happened to them, while the first six seemed to get their wits back together and formed up again. They were converging around a silver-orange silhouette, glinting reflected light.

Vic realized who that must have been at the same time that Josh radioed, "Karma!"

Though they could see her, she was well outside the range of their suit radios. Vic couldn't help himself. He swam upward, leaving the little cover the street offered them, and headed toward Karma. He prayed under his breath that Josh would be smarter than him and stay back. A quick backward glance confirmed that they were both idiots.

When he looked ahead again, a blast of white light instantly destroyed his night vision. It was so sudden that he didn't see where exactly it had come from, other than ahead. A moment later, a shockwave rippled over him, knocking him aside. His cheek smashed into his visor.

He'd seen and felt shockwaves like that before. From Crosta.

Vic's propulsion pack kept him on course through the wave. When his eyes readjusted, he couldn't see any sign of Crosta, but Crosta would've blended in with the Aqueos. Half of the Aqueos had scattered. The other half had stopped moving under their own power, and drifted to the seafloor like dandelion seeds.

Karma fell, her suit streaming a scintillating trail of bubbles.

Vic's breath seized in his throat. The pain in his ankle vanished. He swam harder than he thought he ever could have, but he still approached her at what felt like a snail's pace.

She was still moving. She thrashed, grabbing at her air supply. The shockwave had ripped one of her air hoses out of the back of her suit. She was trying to fit it back in, but the firehose pressure of the escaping air made it like handling a live snake.

Vic had been moving faster than he realized. It seemed like he was always half the ocean away from her until, abruptly, he wasn't. He had too much momentum to stop. Technically, he could have still dodged around her, and then come back for her, but time was holding them in a vise. Every second they stayed exposed held a dozen new ways to die.

He really didn't want to give her a chance to use those telepathic powers against him before they found some cover.

He reached her just as she finally snapped the air hose back into place. He hurtled into her side. The impact cracked his nose against his visor, but he held onto her arms. The force of the collision pivoted them toward the seafloor. Vic's propulsion pack shoved them along in a downward arc.

To his surprise, Karma didn't resist. She hadn't gone limp, but twisted around and bent her legs to brace for landing. She seemed to know what was happening. Vic cut his propulsion pack a few seconds before striking the ground, and the two of them coasted to a jarring but manageable crash.

They rolled onto a sheet of rock crumbled with ash and debris. Vic glanced behind them. Josh was coming to join them. Far behind and above him, the Aqueos were still regrouping.

Karma's visor had cracked. A spider web of thick, white-gray lines forked across the glass. Vic couldn't breathe until he verified that her helmet hadn't sprung a leak. His relief only lasted until he saw her expression.

He had never seen anyone so pale. The steep shadows from his wristlight only made it worse. One of her irises was solid red from a broken blood vessel.

Though she'd reacted to him crashing into her, she didn't seem to perceive him now. She stared right over his shoulder, at nothing.

She could have deployed her telepathic powers against him at any time. He just had to hope she wouldn't. "Karma." He was close enough for his voice to carry through the water as well as over the radio. Still no response. "It's Vic. We have to leave, now," he told her, though not with an expectation of being heard. He needed to say *something*.

He reached over to try to turn her around, face her toward

the edge of the city. For the first time, she seemed to see him. She grabbed his arm. Without him noticing, she'd hooked into a cleft on the ground and gotten leverage. He had none, and so her grip was like an iron bar. She lifted him so that he couldn't do anything to change this.

Her free hand fumbled for her wrist controls. She was already speaking by the time she found her transmit button. "... hopeless, but have to try." Her voice was as weathered as the city, and did not sound much like her.

"There's nothing we can do here," Vic said. "If there was, we're in no shape to do it."

"It was Crosta," Karma rasped.

Vic tried to free himself, but her arm was immovable. "I *know* it was," he said. He was up there. Nobody else could have made a shockwave like that. Vic didn't know if Crosta had been trying to attack the Aqueos, or if he'd meant to hurt Karma and simply hadn't cared if the Aqueos had gotten hit, too. If he had to bet, it would have been on the latter. "I don't want to leave anybody either – it's why we came for you. But if he's one of them, we can't do anything for him now. We have to come back."

An abrupt anger blazed in her eyes. Her grip tightened, and she held him just far enough off the seafloor that he couldn't reach it. "I came here to kill him," she said.

"Why?" Josh asked, before Vic could.

Josh had approached from the side, so as to not startle Karma. "He was going to release it," she said. "That's why they got him. His shockwaves – there was something special about them, something they needed to shatter the lock ..."

Vic and Josh exchanged a glance, or as much of one as they could through their visors. Josh placed his hands between them and tried to pry them apart. Nothing would shake Karma loose. Their suits were too slippery.

Vic didn't know if keeping her talking would get her to recognize that he and Josh weren't her enemies, or if it would just sink her deeper into her nightmare. "There's just you, me, and Josh here," he said. "We can't fight all those Aqueos."

"Anole–" Josh started to say.

"It's too late," Karma interrupted, with a bitterness that surprised him. "Just tried to get revenge. Couldn't even manage that."

Her grip was finally loosening. Rather than struggle and risk her tightening it again, Vic kept her going. "Nobody's killing Crosta," he said. "You understand. He's one of us."

"He's one of *them*," Karma spat. She spoke again a second later, but her voice was quieter, as if all that anger had fled her in an instant. "Doesn't matter. We're too late. All of us."

"Anole!" Josh said again, looking up. Vic followed his gaze.

The plume had darkened, though the magmatic light underneath had not. The smoke and ash boiled and seethed as though the *cloud*, rather than the vent, was about to erupt. The Aqueos above them had recovered from the fight, but they'd lost all interest in Vic, Josh, and Karma. They dived away from the churning smoke, heading deeper into the city.

The cloud hadn't gotten darker. Something was occluding the light from below before it refracted through the cloud. Vic's subconscious realized it was there before the knowledge percolated through the rest of him. The smoke wasn't churning because the eruption had gotten more violent. It was churning because something *within* was pushing out.

The Aqueos swam in advance of something enormous. He

couldn't see anything of it other than the effect it had on the volcanic plume.

Whatever it was, it was so big that he didn't want to believe what he was plainly seeing. It tossed pyroclastic spears toward the city, etching contrails of smoke across the midnight sky. He fought a strong temptation to look away, to make it not exist by closing his eyes.

He could not even see its shape, and he had seen too much.

Karma finally loosened her grip. Vic slipped free. She made no attempt to establish it again.

"There was never any hope," Karma said. "We were too slow. Crosta broke the seal before I ever got here."

CHAPTER NINETEEN
Elixir

Josh had experienced enormity before. He'd visited the Grand Canyon, hiked Glacier National Park on a school trip, and stared down Sentinels in the Danger Room. He'd felt tiny, insignificant, and like an insect in different measures. But he always understood what he was looking at.

This was beyond what he was prepared to perceive.

A chitinous, curling claw swept out of the smoke, trailing magma and ash.

The scale of the thing was meteorological. Only what was emerging from the vent was not as insubstantial as a cloud. It was very, very solid. Magma twirled in its wake, spinning into luminous dancing twisters.

The claw moved deceptively ponderously. From this distance, anything that big would seem slow. It must have been displacing enormous amounts of water as it moved. It plunged, tip-first, toward the city's outskirts.

Before it even landed, the buildings underneath it fell apart, flattened by the advance shockwave. Just before the tip of the claw crashed into the seafloor, the ground around it *shivered*. Dust and debris flew up around it in an expanding sphere of destruction. Another shockwave.

Clouds of dust flew up in front of it, heading their way. The shock traveled faster through the seafloor than the water.

"Jump!" Anole radioed.

Josh shoved away from the seafloor. Then the seafloor shoved *him*. It never actually touched him – at least he didn't think so – but a wall of water slammed into him from below. Then the backdraft yanked him back down just as quickly.

Debris and sand and rock had been thrown up in huge clouds around them. He couldn't see the expanding bubble of the next shockwave. He pulled his arms to his helmet to protect his visor.

The shock sucked his breath from him. He felt the shove like a brick to his stomach, but he was not aware how fast he was moving until he scraped across the ground and slammed into the side of a building. He braced himself for a rush of cold water, but his suit held.

The debris that had kicked up around them had turned into a choking fog, but it was already settling. The volcanic glow had gotten much brighter since the creature – the beast, the god, whatever it was – had begun emerging. It filtered through the dust in livid, ever shifting, crepuscular rays, shading everything the color of inferno.

Anole and Karma weren't far. Anole had grabbed onto jutting stonework and held on. Karma had skidded across the rock and edged up about twenty feet in front of Josh. So far as Josh could tell, neither of their suits had been punctured.

They could still flee. Although Josh had no idea where they would run, anywhere seemed better than here. He started toward the others.

Without a word, Karma picked herself off the seafloor and swam toward the eruption.

Josh swore like he never had before.

This all could have been a nightmare, a phantasm created by Karma's telepathy. He didn't think it was. Everything he knew about Karma's telepathic abilities said that her nightmares manifested from things they'd already been dreading. Josh certainly knew where the vision she'd sent him last time had come from.

This… he wouldn't have imagined any of this.

The thought of being trapped in a nightmare until he asphyxiated in his drysuit was less horrific than what he had just seen. Even if none of this was real, he still had an obligation to act as though it was. He switched on his propulsion pack and took off after Karma.

For whatever reason, Karma's propulsion pack didn't seem to be working. She swam with flippers alone, and Josh caught up with her quickly. He collided with her as planned, intending to steer her back towards the surface, but she grabbed his arm and wrenched him forward.

The move denied him the angle he needed to aim his rotors downward. Now his propulsion pack was carrying them both upward. Too late, he realized the arm she'd grabbed was the one with the wristpad. She'd planned for this, and effectively hijacked his suit.

Instinctively, he got ready to turn bones to jelly and slide loose. She pulled him closer. Their visors clinked together. She wasn't transmitting, but Josh heard her voice clearly through the glass: every note of desperation and despair, all the strain from days of staying awake. "We can't kill it," she said. "But we *have* to kill it. Have to try."

"Just how the hell do you think we're going to do that?" he asked.

"We have to kill it," she repeated.

She was looking in his direction, but not quite at him. "It won't even notice us," he told her.

"Have to," she said.

She didn't have any idea what to do next, he realized. Raw fright animated her. Only, unlike Josh's, her fear was urging her toward the beast rather than away. She'd been terrified past the point of caring about herself.

A deep, too-loud rumbling grated Josh's bones. The noise had started before the claw had descended, but had gotten louder since. Now it was a roar.

"Don't you get it?" she asked. When he didn't answer, she thrust a hand toward the beast-god direction. Josh was afraid to look, to see the source of the building roar. "It's a world-devourer! If it gets out there, it's going to raze whole continents!"

"How do you know that?" Josh asked, shouting to be heard.

Karma tossed her hand downward. "Because *they* know!"

The two of them had risen far enough above the settling dust clouds to see most of the city. Josh found the courage to follow her gesture this time. Karma was pointing at the formation of Aqueos on the seafloor, still carrying their light-staffs.

Incredibly, the line had held against the blast. He looked again, and reconsidered. Mostly held. A handful had been tossed back. Their light-staffs lay unmoving, out of position.

The rest of the formation was shifting to close the gaps.

Against his will, Josh saw more of the beast-god.

Another of its appendages had pushed through the cloud. This one was nothing as recognizable as a claw. It was sheet-black, even the parts of it nearest the volcanic glow. It was too stiff to be a tentacle, and bent in too many places to be a finger or limb. It had seven arched segments. Like the claw, it spun twisters of magma behind it.

It descended toward the line of Aqueos.

Josh held his breath, bracing for another impact. It didn't come. The appendage slowed. As it came above the Aqueos, it stopped.

The line of staff-bearers held steady, facing it down. The slight curve of their formation arched toward the thing.

Gradually, the appendage lifted, sliding away from them.

It was if the staff-bearers had arranged themselves to control it. *No*, Josh thought a second later – nothing that large could be controlled. They were trying to ward it away. That was what their staffs and the luminescent paste smeared around the city had been for. To make this thing pass them by. Maybe they even thought they could control it.

So far it seemed to be working. Josh wouldn't hazard a guess as to how long. Neither gods nor monsters were known for being governable.

"Where's Crosta?" Josh shouted.

"Why?" Karma asked.

"If anybody is going to know more about this thing, it's him!"

For a moment, Karma's cynicism made her sound almost like herself: "If you're still a step or two behind the rest of the class, he's been turned into one of them."

"What do you think sounds more likely?" he asked. "Getting help from Crosta, or charging off into that *thing* with just our bare hands?"

This time, she looked right at him, wild-eyed. Despite whatever her mental contact with the Aqueos had done to her, he knew a part of her remained coldly rational. *Too* cold. She'd been prepared to charge to her demise rather than live in the world this beast was about to create. If he could give her some other kind of hope, no matter how slim, she would have to take it.

Or so he hoped. He desperately wished he'd read her correctly.

She lifted her hand skyward. "The last time I saw Crosta was when we fought, up there. After he freed the- the-" There was no word she could use to finish that sentence. He didn't want to think that Crosta had released the thing of his own free will – but he didn't know *what* to think. "He wouldn't still be there."

The patch of ocean she'd waved at was empty, at least so far as Josh could see. It was about where he'd seen that first shockwave, the bright white one that had swatted Karma down. Some of the other Aqueos had fallen, too, stunned or killed by the blast, but Crosta wouldn't have been among them. He was unaffected by his own shockwaves.

Josh bet that Crosta wasn't immune to the shockwaves the beast made, though. If it had knocked his senses out of him and left him drifting, he would have fallen in... what direction?

Josh made his best guess, and scanned the ruined cityscape. Movement flickered in the shadows down there. More Aqueos. A few minutes ago, he would have thought that diving toward so many Aqueos would have been the riskiest, least sane thing he could have done. Now any direction that took him away from the beast seemed a sane one.

He tugged out of Karma's grip. He was prepared to use all of his slippery, bone-breaking powers to fight free, but she let him go, and then followed.

He didn't look behind him as he swam. He didn't want to know how close it was, how much of itself it had pulled out of the volcanic fissure, or how much was yet to come. He had the unaccountable feeling that he would die if he looked.

Anole had taken longer to recover from the blast, but was on his way up. Josh glanced back to verify that Karma was still coming, and then radioed Anole to tell them where they were going. Anole didn't answer.

More red-orange light pulsed over them. The inferno was shifting, casting new shadows. Josh resisted every urge he had to imagine what was happening.

The light showed him more of the city. The ruins had been In a wretched state before, but now it was worse. Even fewer buildings stood than before. Some collapsed even as he watched. Their rubble cascaded, fluidlike, across the streets. It was hard to tell where there *had* been streets. It reminded Josh of pictures he'd seen of the 1906 San Francisco earthquake, or cities post-carpet-bombing in World War II. What had once been a variegated and haunting alien city had been reduced to a field of broken rocks and loose brick, stretching across the seafloor.

The Aqueos were easy to spot against that backdrop. If any of them had been in the buildings when the first quake had arrived, they were buried now. These ones had been in the throng attacking Karma, and so had fallen atop the rubble.

Some of them looked just as battered as the city. He saw one that looked to have been bisected. Both pieces still stirred.

A glint of color caught Josh's eye. The Aqueos had a uniformly stony-gray pallor. Someone down there was more of a greenish gray. Even that little splash of color stood out among the others.

Josh no longer cared about stealth. He switched his wristlight on. A moment later, Anole did the same behind him. Their two lights played around Crosta.

Crosta lay atop a pile of collapsed brick as though reclining. His eyes glowed dimly. His gills were dilated all the way open – the Atlantean equivalent of gasping.

Crosta had more color than the other Aqueos but, by Atlantean standards, he was as gray as a week-old corpse. A deep, mottled, black-purple contusion ran along his chest. If not for the very slight motion of his eyes following Josh's descent, Josh *would* have believed he was dead.

Josh drifted to a landing a dozen feet away. As he got closer, he saw more of what had been done to Crosta. A line of unhealed puncture wounds ran along Crosta's neck. More lined his wrists, following the radial arteries. Vampire bites. There were far more than the archetypical two red punctures on the neck. In their rush to convert him, the Aqueos must have swarmed over him in a feeding frenzy.

When Josh came within two paces, Crosta bared his teeth. They were *not* the teeth he'd had before. They were long and sharpened, like daggers. It seemed impossible that they should have grown so long in the days since he'd been missing, until Josh realized it was his gums and other teeth that had receded.

Crosta lurched, and snapped at Josh's ankles. Crosta's legs and waist remained still. Josh jerked his boot back, and the bite fell short. Crosta didn't seem to have his full mobility. He rocked his upper body back and forth, trying to move far enough to swipe his claws at Josh's ankles.

Josh desperately did not want to use his powers to fight. *He was a healer.* Sometimes his instincts kicked in before he had the opportunity to think about it, like they had during the fistfight with Anole. He hadn't meant to break and re-form his bones. He'd just done it. That was the worst part of this. He was getting *used* to abusing his powers.

There were times when he couldn't refuse his instincts, and times when he didn't want to.

Leverage was the key to fighting underwater. Without the use of his legs, Crosta wouldn't have much of it. Josh levered his boot into a crevice, snapping and compressing his heel to force it to fit. He used the crevice like a fulcrum, swung forward, and slammed bodily into Crosta. He pinned Crosta's arms against the fallen bricks.

A moment later, Anole was at his side, helping him hold down one of Crosta's wrists. Crosta fought, but didn't have the strength to break free. He seemed to know it, too. His struggle was desultory. After a few seconds of it, he lay still, apparently giving up the fight. He acted every bit like someone who didn't want to fight, but who'd been compelled into one.

Josh's bare hand rested near Crosta's wide-open gills. He felt no movement in the water there. Nothing was going in or out. Crosta was not actually breathing. The open gills were a reflex. A remnant of him that remembered being alive.

Crosta was trying to say something, but it was lost against the roar of the earth. Josh craned closer, just outside of biting range, but still had to wait for the thunder to diminish before he could hear Crosta's voice.

"I'm so tired," Crosta said. "I can't sleep." His throat didn't sound rotted through, like the other Aqueos's. Crosta's voice was muffled by Josh's helmet, but Josh heard him well enough. The Atlanteans had developed deep, sonorous voices that carried well underwater.

"You're not going to sleep," Josh said. "We need you here."

Crosta seemed to be having trouble hearing him. He was shaking his head before Josh finished speaking. "It's so heavy," Crosta said. Josh didn't think that Crosta meant his weight. "Please."

The other Aqueos had seen them. Josh was sure of that. The nearest sent some bared-teeth snarls their way, but didn't move closer. Josh wondered if they could feel terror. Karma's powers had worked on them, so they must have. He wondered if this was the nightmare she'd shown them. He had a hard time imagining worse than this.

If Karma was right, they'd abducted and turned Crosta to break some kind of seal. They'd worked to bring their own nightmare to life. They were *still* trying to work with it, warding it off or bargaining with it.

Maybe they'd had no choice. They'd been forced or controlled to do this, knowing what would happen. And maybe that was the horror that Karma had touched and that had driven her out of her mind. Josh did not think he'd ever know, and did not want to.

Josh nodded in the direction he still couldn't bring himself to look, toward the beast. "Did the Aqueos use you to bring *that* here?"

"It was locked away," Crosta said. "Sealed behind a slab of- of something not quite physical. It felt like marble one moment, steel the next. It was so, so fragile compared to what was locked away... but *it* still couldn't get through, and neither could we. Could they." Crosta briefly closed his eyes, and tried again. "Neither could the Aqueos."

There was some part of the original Crosta left. The Aqueos had not fully turned him. Crosta said, "They needed a mutant to break through. The final ingredient in their rituals, a water-breathing mutant with destructive powers, combined with all their other powers."

Anole's muffled voice filtered through Josh's helmet. He was trying to say something without radio. With a start, Josh realized Anole's wristpad had been destroyed. The casing had shattered. The interior wiring lay exposed and torn.

He must have smashed it on something when the wave had dragged him across the seafloor. He wasn't radioing them because he *couldn't*.

The roar was rising again. Anole raised his voice to try again. Josh barely heard him ask, "Why would they free it?"

"Devotion. Worship." The rising swell of the earth nearly stole his next word: "Terror."

In her unannounced speech back in the station's kitchenette, Karma had told them all that the Aqueos feared this creature, whatever it was. Josh hadn't believed her at the time. She'd been into their heads, though, and had plucked the truth right out of them. No matter what other disease her telepathic contact with the Aqueos had inflicted on her, she'd been lucid about that.

The Aqueos *worshiping* this thing was an angle Josh hadn't

considered before. Fanaticism was a kind of holy terror. The pious called themselves "God-fearing" for a reason.

When the roar oscillated lower, Anole asked, "How can we fight it?"

"Fight?" Crosta looked at Anole as though he hadn't understood the word.

The hellish light abruptly faded, as though a cloud had scudded across the sun. The hair on the back of Josh's neck prickled. Crosta could see whatever was happening behind them, and his lips hung loose.

"You don't fight," Crosta said. "You serve."

Josh could finally no longer resist looking behind him.

More of the beast-god had emerged from the vent, although not, so far as Josh could tell, its main body. If it had such a thing. More bleached-white claws and multi-segment appendages ringed the vent... braced as if about to heave something even heavier up from below.

Some of the claws were cracked and weathered, but others had a pearly sheen. He wondered if he hadn't miscategorized what they were. Not claws, but teeth. None of them had landed with the same shock as the first, but the seafloor around them had started to fracture and split, crumbling into the vent – like it was chewing through the earth from the inside out.

If the Aqueos had ever thought they could control this thing... no, that seemed less and less likely every time Josh considered it. They'd been terrified of it long before it had breached the surface. It must have had power over them even then. Something to make them do as it bid. He wondered if he'd ever know what, then realized he was glad he didn't.

The source of the shadow was the largest appendage Josh had

yet seen. It was a shapeless, shifting mass, like a pseudopod. It stretched toward the line of staff-wielding Aqueos. Like the last limb, it halted above them.

The appendage rippled, undulating reflected inferno-light across its sheening skin. It shifted, stretching and widening. For a moment, Josh wondered if it was going to extend a touch like the Sistine Chapel's God to Adam, or blossom open to bring the Aqueos into itself.

It swayed to the left. It moved ponderously at first, but picked up speed as it went. It elongated and flattened, becoming thicker on one side than the other – like the blade of a fan. By the time it started swinging back around, it pulled a riptide behind it, generating an enormous undersea wave heading toward the formation of staff-bearers. The sea shimmered like a heat distortion where the wave passed.

"And even when you serve them–" Crosta choked.

The Aqueos shifted their line as if to brace for impact, but nothing they could do would save them. The wave crashed into them with terrible force. Some of them went flying back, losing their staffs. Other staffs snapped in half. More than half the lights just extinguished, and Josh could not see what had done it.

With the warding glow gone, the pseudopod plunged back down. It landed directly atop the formation of Aqueos. It withdrew, dragging across the seafloor, kicking up whirlwinds of dust as it ground the Aqueos into the obsidian.

When the pseudopod rolled back, there was no sign of the Aqueos that had been there. Not a single glowing light.

Anything else Crosta had to say was lost when the wave reached them. It had greatly attenuated by the time it arrived, but the blow still staggered Josh, and swept him back.

Dust billowed around his visor. By the time it drew back, he didn't know where he was. His head hurt like it had been rattling around inside a tin can. The sea around him was a tempest of dust.

He rolled to his feet. He couldn't have lost himself for long. The clouds had just started to settle. He'd been pushed back about a dozen and a half feet. Karma and Anole were picking themselves up not far away.

Anole glanced at Josh and froze. His mouth moved, but Josh couldn't hear him.

Josh caught on just an instant before it would have been too late. He hunched and braced himself just before Crosta collided with him from behind.

Crosta's claws clanged off the back of Josh's helmet. If Josh had moved any slower, Crosta would have ripped through his air hose. Josh dipped, using Crosta's momentum and unstable balance to flip him over his shoulder and into the ground.

In the chaos, Josh's bare hand came into contact with Crosta's skin.

He had tried his best to avoid that. He didn't want to know how Crosta had changed. He didn't want to feel the withered black veins and rotted stomach he had in the other Aqueos. But in that flash of contact, he could not stop himself from instinctively stretching out his powers.

Crosta wasn't like the other Aqueos. Just as Crosta retained more color than them, there was a memory of life left in him. His veins weren't dry. He still had blood in him – his heart just wasn't pumping it anymore. It had congealed in his lower extremities. His stomach was empty and dormant, but not rotted.

There were maybe things he could do about it.

Josh clamped down on his thoughts before his instincts could carry them away. Whenever he found a use for his powers that went beyond healing, he lost control.

All he wanted to be was a healer. All he trusted himself to be was a healer. This awful potency bubbling up inside him was too much to control.

Healers didn't have anything to do with the dead. Corpses had nothing left to heal.

Josh made his decision in half a heartbeat.

Crosta's blood could be reoxygenated. His heart restored. His tissues purged of decomposition toxins and his cells restored. The biggest reason that even the recently dead couldn't be revivified by most healers, brain damage from oxygen deprivation, wasn't operative in Crosta's case. His brain was fine. Vampirism had kept his brain active and intact.

"Have you been taught what the words 'Omega-level' mean?" Emma Frost had asked him. She'd gone on to tell him, but the way Atlas Bear had sized him up, reading his future with burning contempt, had told him more about it than he'd ever wanted to know.

Crosta jerked away, convulsing.

Josh crashed to the seafloor in waterborne slow motion, his hand still on Crosta's skin. He felt Anole's hand grab his suit's shoulder before he realized Anole was there. He clinked his visor against Josh's. "What did you do?" he demanded.

Josh didn't know how to answer. Crosta was spasming beside him. Even as the seizure racked Crosta's body, more of his color returned.

Rather than waste time searching for the words, Josh looked about, hunting for a flat stone or something like it. "Help me find something to keep him from swallowing his tongue."

Josh couldn't search far. He had to keep his bare hand on Crosta. If he let go, Crosta would die for good. He still needed Josh to stitch together his cells, to rejuvenate necrotic muscles, and draw oxygen into his blood and brain.

Karma hovered over Josh's shoulder. If she'd done as she'd promised, and tried to kill Crosta right there, Josh couldn't have stopped her.

She started searching with Anole. She was the first to find something: a splinter of broken brick, about half again as long as it was wide. Josh jammed it in Crosta's jaw, and angled the stone to pin Crosta's tongue to the bottom of his mouth.

Crosta's convulsions eased as more water filtered through his gills. There was so much more to fix – Crosta's liver and kidneys and spleen had started to rot, his muscles had lost their tension, his skin had loosened and torn – but those were problems he could handle. That fell back into the boundaries of conventional healing.

A flare of light from behind him made him turn. More fire and pyroclastics were bursting from the vent, as if something underneath was surging up. A spray of magma had erupted toward the city. As Josh watched, fiery globules passed directly overhead, mid-arc.

Others aimed lower. If Josh trusted his sense of their trajectory, they would strike very near him. Or directly atop.

"We need to get Crosta out of here," Josh said, loud enough for the others to hear. "We all need to get out of here."

Karma shook her head. She held up her wristpad. In the gloom, it took Josh a moment to see what she was showing him.

Her oxygen gauge was only a hair above empty. In all the fighting and turmoil, Josh had completely forgotten about oxygen. Her air supply must have been low even before the hose had gotten knocked out of her suit.

She'd come out here intending to never return. She'd probably figured that, if she couldn't stop the Aqueos, there wouldn't be a world to return to.

He checked his own gauge. A little over a third. Anole's meter had broken with the rest of his wristpad, but he probably had just as much left. *Maybe* if they swam fast, practiced their breathing exercises, and somebody from the station met them halfway with a spare tank, they could make it back. But Karma never would.

It was too late, anyway.

Josh looked back at the way they'd come, and the cliff they'd descended. He was just in time to see an enormous black shape heave across the ridge. The magma's light didn't reveal much except its shape, and a brief, glimmering reflection like oil separating in water. It moved like a tongue, slippery and sliding. The pseudopod-appendage draped across the cliff, blocking the route he and Josh had taken. The rock cracked and crumbled from its weight.

Anole shouted something. Karma yelled "Behind–!"

Josh spun. Two of them moved in on him, teeth and claws bared. Josh's incredulity nearly kept him from reacting in time. His indignation was nearly as paralyzing. These Aqueos must have seen what had happened to the staff-bearers. They were *still* attacking, while the ocean above turned molten gold and the earth shivered underneath them, doing their god's work as though it still mattered. As though the beast wouldn't crush them, too.

The others had their own assailants. Anole backpedaled from

another attacker, while Karma was facing down two of her own. Karma's first attacker recoiled, though she'd never touched it. She was using her powers. They were afraid of something *worse* than what was happening, and Karma was showing it to them. Maybe that was why they fought.

Josh let Crosta gently fall to the seafloor, freeing up his arms. He took a defensive stance. He and Vic only had to hold off their attackers until Karma could deploy her powers against them, too. The second circled him, and then darted in Josh's side. Josh broke his ankle, twisting it out of joint to whirl to his left. The spin gave his elbow enough momentum to knock that Aqueos off its feet.

He could not turn back fast enough to defend himself against the first Aqueos as it rushed him. Searing heat lashed across his gut.

He staggered away. A cloud of blood drifted where he'd been standing. Its tendrils snaked back to the Aqueos's claws.

Karma drove off Josh's attackers before they came back at him. Josh didn't see which shadow they fled into. An eruption of air bubbles washed over his visor, blinding him. He held his hand over his gut, trying to staunch the flow of air. The air felt oily slipping through his fingers.

The gashes had gone deep. His powers could address that, though. He couldn't repair his suit. The burning of the cuts vanished as he sealed his skin... but the relief was lost underneath the cold salt water filling his suit.

Fire blossomed to his left. A chunk of magma splashed across the cityscape, hardly more than a hundred yards away. It illuminated another stream of air bubbles. Anole had been hit, too. Air boiled out of a rent in his suit's shoulder.

If Josh remained upright, his suit would "only" fill above his waist. Anole's suit had been torn well above the level at which his air intake snaked into his back. In probably less than half a minute, the rising water would cut off his air.

If Josh could have traded drysuits with Anole, he would have. He was astonished to think that. Somewhere along the line, he'd missed how much Anole had started to feel like a teammate, and a more important one than him.

The ground shook, bouncing violently up and down, and spilling more plumes of dirt. Josh's knees gave way. He shoved himself back, trying to swim upward. The mounting weight of the water in his suit made that a struggle.

A meteor splashed into fiery shards to his right. This one had landed farther away, but it was much larger, and set a wider swath of their horizon alight. It also cut off their last avenue of escape, other than straight up – into a sky covered in boiling smoke.

A shadow rolled across the far horizon. Where he'd seen the cliffside earlier, there was now just inky, roiling blackness. The rock was covered up. The beast's pseudopod had slipped down the ridge, and was lolling lazily their way… crushing the city as it went. From this distance, it seemed to move slowly, but in fact it must have been rolling faster than a freight train. The quake got worse as it came closer.

A pyroclastic projectile burst against the appendage's side, detonating in a scintillating spray of molten rock. If the beast noticed, Josh saw no sign of it. The light show revealed no additional detail, no texture, on the appendage's skin. It remained solid, slick black.

The others swam up from the seafloor, too. The ground was

shaking so hard that they would have broken their legs if they'd stayed. Karma held Crosta slumped across her shoulder, kicking mightily with her flippers. He doubted she'd have the strength to keep it up for long.

Josh, Anole, and Karma pressed closer together as the world shook apart and rained fire around them. Josh's shoulders bumped into Anole's back. The back of Karma's dead propulsion pack brushed Josh's bare hand.

Josh couldn't tell if the salt he tasted was sweat or seawater. It stung his eyes fiercely. He squeezed them shut. Behind his eyelids, on the other side of the livid afterimages, he still saw Atlas Bear.

He still didn't understand her. She – and Blindfold – were precogs. Atlas Bear's precognition in particular was supposed to focus on disasters and world-ending crises. They should have seen this coming.

"*I'm singularly impressed,*" Atlas Bear had said, "*with your ability to make the wrong decision at every opportunity.*"

Maybe that was the problem. Maybe she *had* seen this coming.

She hadn't said that he would *act* the wrong way at every opportunity. She'd said he'd make decisions.

All he wanted to be was a healer. If he could have locked the rest of his powers away, and never thought about them again, he would have. But that, too, was a choice. A decision to not act was still a decision.

The water level in his suit rose past his thigh. Cold pulsed through his bones. He already couldn't feel his feet. He was having trouble staying afloat. Before long, he'd start sinking no matter how hard he swam.

Realizing that made things a lot simpler.

He reached to his helmet's seals.

Anole only figured out what Josh was doing when Josh unlatched his helmet and started twisting it off. Anole yelled, and reached out to stop Josh, but he was too late.

Salt water flooded in through Josh's broken neck seals.

Josh instantly choked. Even fighting against that and the spray blinding him, he found the next catches on his chestplate and under his arms, and released them. His suit's torso fell off, dragging his leggings with it. The rest of his suit came apart in pieces.

Then there was no more flooding, no more spray. Just him, floating in the ocean.

He had already begun to change. He tasted the water not only on his tongue and up his sinuses, but through his skin.

Josh remembered Crosta had once complained about the poor oxygenation of the water at this depth. He'd been right. There was not much energy to be found here. The eruption and the quakes had spilled all kinds of toxins into the water.

His vision narrowed to a tunnel, dancing with stars. His chest burned.

His contact with Crosta had refreshed his understanding of how Atlantean gills functioned. It was nothing he could have explained in words, or written in chemical formulae, or drawn on a biological diagram. His understanding went as deep as his blood and bones, and deep as the instincts that controlled his powers.

Disassembling his lungs, swapping the tissue for gill filaments along his neck, took all the energy he had left. That energy crashed right back through him, though, with the first rush of oxygenated blood pouring into his brain and muscles.

Gradually, the black at the fringes of his vision began to clear.

The salt water stung like needles driving into his eyes. He couldn't see. Before he realized what he was doing, he blinked a second eyelid into place. Another trick he'd learned from Crosta: Atlanteans protected their eyes with a clear, vertically slit, nictitating membrane. His eyes still burned, but now he could hold them open.

Without his suit, he was a nimble swimmer, and slipped loose from Anole's clumsy glove and numb fingers. Karma grabbed for Josh's ankle, but he was well out of her reach.

Emma Frost had never used the word "healer" with him. *Biokinesis*, she'd said. She was the type who always chose her words with care. She meant exactly what she said, and no less.

He hated, hated, *hated* what he'd done to himself. He only avoided throwing up because it had been too long since he'd eaten.

He could not remotely justify what he had done to himself as "healing", except to the extent that it was helping him stay alive. He'd broken the only vow he'd ever made to himself, the only promise he'd ever taken seriously.

He didn't have the time to dwell. He swam toward the pseudopod. He moved a lot faster than he'd thought he could. At first, he'd thought his flippers had miraculously stayed on. Then he looked back and saw that his feet had elongated. His bones had stretched out and spread taut webs of skin between them.

He hadn't meant to do that. His instincts had taken over.

He looked down at himself. With the drysuit off, he saw more of what was happening to him. Light rippled underneath his skin. His body was phosphorescent, changing color. There was too much energy inside him. His skin was no longer tan-pink but yellow-gold.

Whatever he'd unleashed in himself, it was like setting a wildcat loose from a cage. It would not go back in. What did it matter if he had good intentions?

The thing Blindfold and Atlas Bear had been afraid of seemed to be happening now. He was losing control. His body moved several seconds ahead of his mind.

At first, he thought he'd swum away from Anole and Karma to protect them from himself. Now that he was away, though, he kept swimming. He swam with purpose. He was heading *to* somewhere, and he could not even tell himself what it was.

He'd messed up. He'd messed up bad. Until now, the one thing that even his instincts had avoided doing was to mess with brains and nervous systems. Even his subconscious knew he couldn't handle it. By altering his body chemistry so radically, though, that was exactly what he *had* done. He couldn't have avoided it. His nervous system was as much chemical as electrical.

His thoughts flew in so many directions that he couldn't trace their paths, let alone anticipate where they were going. He wasn't even sure that the "him" he thought of as *him* was the only one there anymore. His mind had fractured into multiple threads of consciousness, multiple purposes, none of which quite squared with each other.

"It will not happen this time," Blindfold had told him, when he'd approached Laurie Collins. *There was tangible fear in her voice, underneath the anger she used to disguise it. She hadn't thought she or anyone else could protect Laurie from him.*

His skin glowed. It wasn't uniform. Strange, inky black

blotches bubbled across his arms. They didn't last. Every other part of him was golden as a trophy.

He lost track of time.

The beast's appendage ground through the city ahead. The shape was so dark that judging distance was impossible. Not until its gullet-black silhouette consumed half the sky did Josh realize that it was moving as fast as a runaway tractor trailer, and that he was nearly on it.

He drove into the appendage with such tremendous force that, if his mind hadn't already been in pieces, the crash would have split him apart. The beast's flesh was soft and rubbery, almost elastic. He sank several yards into it.

He must have passed out for a moment. When he returned to himself, the world had pivoted on its axis. The ruined city had become a flat plane in front of him. The appendage continued to roll, bringing him with it.

"I know what my limits are," Outlaw had told him. *"Learned them through years of hard knocks. You've been through a lot yourself. You figured out yours?"*

"I never want to find out," he'd said.

The only way he could have answered Outlaw's question was to be pushed to those limits in the same way he knew she'd been.

He needed to touch the beast. To feel it more fully. He drew his hand back, and plunged it through the pseudopod's skin.

Its skin should not have broken – and had not broken when his whole body had plunged into it – but it split easily when he exerted his powers, like skin on lukewarm gravy. Josh's arm plunged through layers of dermis, up to his elbow, before contacting softer tissue.

Josh had never felt flesh like the beast-god's before. But it *was* flesh – distressingly organic, bundled with more ropey nerve fibers in a square inch than Josh had in most of his body. His awareness of the beast radiated downward, through the rest of the tendril.

The nerves he'd touched were not exceptional. There were just as many, bundled together just as tightly, through every tissue he sensed. Josh didn't want to think about the scope of this creature's intelligence if it had a brain just as complex. Maybe this network *was* the creature's brain, distributed through its whole body. Josh's mind was insect-sized by comparison.

The sheer vertiginous scale of it almost made him black out again. Only by deliberately avoiding thinking about it could he keep himself from swaying over the edge.

More of the creature existed underground than above. Far more. What he had seen so far were just shreds of the beast-god's whole self. His awareness kept pushing down, deeper and deeper. There was no end to the beast. Not to the beast, nor his own sense of it. He expected any moment to find it tapering off, to at last perceive its outer extremities, but the creature just kept going down and down, down and down and down, dizzyingly deep.

It felt larger than the Earth itself. Josh did not think the whole of it rested in this dimension. He did not see any way it could have. He raced farther along its nerves, thousands and thousands of miles of them. Still there was no end to it.

"When we say 'Omega-level'," Emma Frost had told him, *"it sounds too much like it's been mapped out and categorized, scientifically analyzed. What 'Omega-level' really means is 'uncharted'. That no limit to that mutant's power has yet been*

discovered. Or, possibly, exists. It means a power that has an upper boundary we haven't found yet."

The beast-god might have stretched on into infinity, but Josh had infinity to throw right back at it. Death coiled in his muscles.

Limitless death, ready to snap loose and fly farther than he would or could imagine.

The beast-god's flesh was alien, but the energy plying through its veins was the same kind found in living creatures everywhere: organic chemistry, burning calories, multiplying cells. The same kinds of energy that he'd turned against the Aqueos to murder them.

It should not have been him with this power. It should have been anyone but him. But that no longer mattered.

Already his body had gotten ahead of him.

Here he went after it.

CHAPTER TWENTY
Elixir

Josh did not know for sure when he came back to himself. A constant, dull buzzing noise grated on his nerves. When he'd put enough of his mind back together to ask the question, he'd been listening to the buzzing for a long time.

He knew right away that someone had tampered with his memory. He was sitting on something hard, and in a very small place. Like a cell. His head was slumped. He looked up, and the world went blurry – but not before he saw a radiant vision, a goddess in white.

The world unblurred gradually. A single dark window, hardly larger than a basketball, hung over Ms Frost's head. The walls were close and claustrophobic, yes, but this wasn't a cell. This was a descent capsule, similar but not identical to the one he and the rest of Karma's team had come down in. His ears hurt. He recognized the buzzing noise now. Air circulation. Depressurization was underway.

Emma Frost sat directly opposite him, her hands steepled.

Josh groaned. At least he did not have to wonder long about who had tampered with his memory. And those memories were starting to trickle back in.

Anole. Karma. Crosta. The last he remembered of them, he'd been swimming away from them, and into the tongue of a world-devouring god.

He jerked out of his seat, or tried to. A seatbelt held him back. Nauseating dizziness rolled through him. If he'd gotten up, he would have immediately toppled over.

The seats beside Ms Frost were occupied. The green blur to Ms Frost's other side resolved into Anole. Josh's relief was a physical thing, a rush of icy water into his head, just as dizzying as the nausea.

"Well," Ms Frost said. "I had hoped that would resolve some of my questions." Underneath her customary aloofness, she sounded disappointed... or possibly concerned. She was hard to read in the best of circumstances.

Josh closed his eyes. She *had* rooted through his memories, but it hadn't been an interrogation. His memories had been scattered around him like shards of a shattered mirror. She'd looked into each one as she'd picked them up, but she hadn't been the one who'd broken them. She'd been putting him back together.

This was maybe the first time he'd been himself, in one mind, since he'd transformed in the alien city.

To her left was a gray, slick-skinned mutant Josh had never seen before. It had to be Shark Girl, one of the rescuers from the Jean Grey School that Triage had mentioned. The teeth and fins didn't leave much room for doubt. He didn't remember seeing her, but he *did* remember the woman seated next to her. Armor. She and Armor had been the only mutants close at hand who could dive faster than the capsules could take them. Shark Girl's body was resilient to the pressure changes, like Crosta's. Armor had the ability to surround herself with an impenetrable field of energy that could withstand even the pressure of the deep ocean.

It was Armor who had saved Josh and the others. One of the broken mirror shards showed him a flare of golden light rising over the wrecked Aqueos city. Armor's protective field, crackling with energy, descending from the smoke like a phoenix.

Josh had hardly noticed her. He'd been too busy keeping Anole alive. Anole's torn suit had finished flooding. The water had risen past his neck, cutting him off from his air supply. Josh had transferred oxygen from his own gills, through his boiling and malleable flesh, and into Anole's blood and brain. He had become Anole's lungs. But they hadn't been able to move. It took all the energy Josh could draw from the poorly oxygenated water to keep the two of them alive. Karma was close to running out of air, but she tended to Crosta, her breath ragged.

Armor had arrived at just the right time. She found the four of them alone, in the rubble of a smashed city, with no sign of what had happened to them.

There was no sign of the beast. No teeth, no many-segmented limbs, no coal-black tendrils. No Aqueos. The eruption had calmed – leaving only an orange glow, copious smoke, and growing shadows.

When Josh opened his eyes, Emma Frost was still looking at him.

Ms Frost looked more disheveled than usual, which was to

say that Josh saw all of two hairs out of place and a hint of lines under her steel-razor gaze. She couldn't have been accustomed to traveling like this. Usually she teleported as she liked. The tremendous pressures put a hitch in that. She could teleport as she wanted, but to *survive* a trip to Station X-41, she had to go through the same lengthy pressurization and depressurization process as everyone else.

She'd come because she was needed. Memories, sharp as glass, cut Josh's hand. The shattered mirror was reassembling.

He hastily looked down at his body. It was his own again... or at least what he used to think of as *his own*. No gills. No elongated limbs or membranous flaps of skin. Just "human".

Only with golden skin.

Karma and Crosta had returned to the station still infected with the Aqueos's vampirism, if only in mind and not body. Josh and Triage could keep their bodies alive, but their minds were several levels beyond either of their expertise, even with Josh's biokinesis off its leash. They couldn't have been sure that the rest of the team wasn't in the beginning stages of infection, either, not after the nightmares Karma had unleashed on them.

Josh had certainly not been in his right mind. Now he remembered his bones breaking without his prompting, his golden skin rippling, even once he was safely back in the station. They'd need an expert. The best telepath mutantkind had to offer. Emma Frost had rushed down on the next descent capsule, as fast as she could. She placed mental blocks on his powers, and on his memories. Now, carefully, she was starting to lift them.

Nature Girl sat in another seat, her eyes half-lidded. She looked like she could sleep for two days. The other seats in the capsule were empty, though. Triage, Graymalkin, and Karma weren't here. A pallid light shone across their tiny porthole. Somewhere much farther away, another porthole shone through the gloom. A second descent capsule.

"It was my working theory," she said, "that, when you and Victor went to find Karma, Karma trapped you in a complex nightmare in her usual style. Tailored to your fears."

No. Josh's heart pounded against his ribs. He couldn't have gone through that for no reason. "We weren't hallucinating—" Josh started to say.

"Imagine my surprise," she interrupted, "when I find that you and Victor share many of the same memories." Josh opened his mouth to speak, but Ms Frost wasn't done. "Many," she said, "but not all."

Josh looked to Anole. Anole met his gaze briefly, but turned back to Ms Frost, his brow furrowed.

"Victor also remembers seeing a ludicrously large creature emerge from the thermal vent," Ms Frost said. "But where you saw teeth and nails ... he saw beaks, and tentacles with suckers."

"It was dark," Josh said. Given the same poor information, his and Anole's imaginations could have filled out the details in different ways.

"He also recalls that drysuits were damaged by a volcanic projectile and not, as you remember, by an Aqueos attack. In fact, he remembers that the Aqueos *tried* attacking, but that Karma drove them off before they caused any harm."

"That's not how it happened," Josh said.

"I know that you believe that," Ms Frost said.

Josh looked around. "Where's Karma?" he asked. She must have been on the other capsule. "She'll confirm—"

"I had to quarantine and remove all of Karma's memories after her vampirism infection," Ms Frost said, with some hesitation. A rare admission of befuddlement from her. The Aqueos's infection must have taken deep roots. Usually Ms Frost's methods were not so blunt force. "She doesn't remember anything since the first Aqueos attack. Nor does Crosta remember anything since he was abducted."

That left Josh and Anole as the only two people who remembered what had happened at Black Smokers' Trench.

Josh fit the rest of the mirror together. Ms Frost had gone into Josh's memories with the idea that they had both been victims of a telepathic nightmare… and had been nonplussed to discover he'd seen the same beast. But she'd found small inconsistencies. Things they'd both remembered that couldn't both be true.

Josh slumped his head into his seat. In the thick of all that horror, he would have been relieved to discover that the beast-god had been conjured by Karma.

It was the other way around now. He felt like the world had been ripped away from him.

He couldn't convince himself that he hadn't experienced what he had. The scenes had been too vivid, too prolonged and full of suffering, and too alien to be the work of his imagination or anyone else's. It didn't matter if he and Anole had interpreted their experience in different ways. They'd both had the same one.

Josh had never seen Ms Frost confused or troubled before. She was good at cloaking it, but he still caught glimmers here and there. She must not have found anything else that indicated their memories were false, or she would have said so. It would have taken a lot of skill and care for a telepath to manufacture memories that *Emma Frost* would not immediately have flagged as false.

And there was something else.

Josh stared at the ceiling. Gradually, the tension seeped out of his shoulders.

He was confident that he could not have imagined the feeling of his awareness rippling down the limitless corridors of the beast's flesh, weaving in and out of dimensions far removed from his own. Or the supertemporal implosion that followed as he turned all that infinite energy against itself.

He could not have imagined what he had done, or who he'd become.

Josh looked at his hand. His skin was golden. The same shade of effervescent he'd been since he'd stopped lying to himself about who he was.

He'd started his life here wishing that his powers would go away. That he could ignore them, suppress them, and otherwise keep the truth from himself.

He'd never be able to do that again. Not even if he wanted to.

He wondered how many other mutants did not trust themselves to handle their powers. And then how many of those had the words "Omega-level" rattling around in their brains. The former category had to be pretty large. But the latter – there could only have been a few.

Josh never imagined he would be so relieved to see the snow-drenched Albertan horizon, the recessed steps that led into the converted missile silo, or the stuffy concrete walls of his dorm room. It was a relief so intense that he wanted to call it joy, though it came with no elation.

The exhaustion of the siege bore down on him. All he wanted to do was bundle under his covers and sleep for a week.

That was what he did.

Or so it felt like. It *could* have been a week, for all he knew. When he roused himself long enough to look at his phone, the date on the lockscreen shocked him. Ten days since he'd left. He didn't know the date he'd come back, or even how long the station had endured the siege. His constantly disrupted sleep left him feeling like he'd lived in a different world – a secret world buried under this one, where time worked differently.

He felt like he'd just broken a fever and come tumbling out of its dreams. No – that wasn't quite right. Maybe he'd returned to the fever dream after a brief sojourn in the real world.

A pile of phone notifications told him he'd received dozens of emails. They were all from his instructors. Each message had lecture notes and assignments attached. The timestamp on the first assignment email he'd received was dated less than an hour after his training team had departed for the Atlantic Ocean.

At first, he was incredulous that the Institute expected him to keep up with the classes he'd missed while enduring field training. Then incredulity turned to indignation. He tossed his phone on top of his laptop.

He remembered Outlaw telling him that sending him homework while he was out in the field was exactly the kind of low-down, dirty thing a teacher would do.

He couldn't sustain his snit for long. He had no one else to complain to.

He was, as he had always been here, alone.

Every time he saw his hands, his bare feet, or his face in the mirror, he had to remind himself they were still his. They looked half alien. His skin remained golden, the color of a wheatfield in summer. The same color as his hair.

He could have changed his skin back: turned it from golden back to its usual tan-pink. It would have only been a *little* more complicated than the healing he'd done before all this.

But that would have meant altering his body in a way that he couldn't stomach right now.

The truth was that gold had *become* his natural skin color. The pigment that made it gold was still being manufactured underneath his skin cells. He couldn't have reversed the change without the same kind of broad scale… *biokinesis* that had accidentally caused it to begin with. So he left it.

Over the course of a few days, it dawned on him that his old body didn't represent who he was anymore. Or even who he wanted to be.

His muscles ached from inactivity. Every half hour, he paced his room. He could have made the stiffness go away. He sensed the fatigue toxins percolating through his limbs, and the inflammations in his muscles. It would have been trivial to fix. It would even have been healing – limited in scope, like he used to do.

He couldn't. Not yet. The pain was, in its own way, more comforting than the thought of his powers.

He ventured into fragments of his old life a little at a time. First, out to the dining hall to collect food. Then, eventually, to return to classes. None of his instructors needled him about his attendance for that first week after he returned (though they continued sending him assignments). He supposed he should have been grateful for the consideration, but it was difficult to feel anything at all.

The other students kept a wide berth of him, but no wider than usual. The fact that he'd turned a new color made no difference. Students and faculty were accustomed to mutants' bodies changing. Compared to Pixie's dragonfly wings or Glob Herman's whole... deal, color-changing skin was nothing, even if it was a sign that his powers went beyond simple healing. It wasn't as though any of them could trust him any less.

If anything, they treated him better. They stepped out of his way in the halls, and didn't put up a fuss about sitting next to him in class. He even got a lab partner with no complaints.

He couldn't figure out what the difference was. Not until he caught sight of Triage on the other side of the cafeteria during a lunch period, pointing Josh out.

One of the students next to Triage was Laurie Collins, and the other was Wind Dancer. Their lips curled back when they saw Josh watching. They turned back to Triage, who kept talking. He lifted his hand once to wave toward Josh. When the other two looked back at Josh, the sneers were gone.

Josh blinked. He looked down at his rectangular pizza, not really seeing it. It was hard to fight the feeling that he didn't deserve Triage trying to smooth things over for him.

So subtly that he hardly noticed it, he was fitting in here.

Josh saw Triage in class frequently enough, but the other members of the Station X41 team hadn't had much to do with each other since getting back. Josh had heard that other mutant teams tended to bond under pressure. If that's what his team was doing, no one invited him.

Karma was well enough to return to teaching. Josh had signed up for one of her classes next quarter, one he'd turned his nose up at earlier. "Mutant Art and Literature Through the 20th Century".

Nature Girl had gone back to the Jean Grey School. When the 'copter from the school had come to pick her up, she'd embarked with a wave and a shadowed look in her eyes. Crosta had stayed with the team long enough to verify that he was healthy, and then returned to the Atlanteans. During one of Josh's many debriefings, Magik said that they'd extended Crosta an offer to enroll in the Institute.

Graymalkin remained at the Institute too, but Josh had heard from Magik that he'd reverted to a nocturnal schedule. Even buried far underground, it was a comfort for dealing with stress. It kept him mostly away from the other students. Josh included.

Josh figured that was a feature of Graymalkin's new schedule, not a flaw.

Anole seemed to be missing. Even among the diverse throng of the Institute's mutants, Anole should have been easy to spot. Anole had a chameleon-like camouflage that he'd hardly had a chance to use at the station, but, if he was hiding, Josh had the unaccountable feeling that he wasn't hiding from Josh alone.

Blindfold passed Josh by in the halls without remark. She couldn't see, but she would have known he was there.

Josh wondered if her vision of the future had changed, or the tragedy she'd warned him about was still yet to happen.

He wanted to believe the former. He was afraid to ask, and she said nothing.

Josh went through three separate debriefings: one with Headmaster Summers, one with Magik, and another with Emma Frost. All Ms Frost had done was stare at him – telepathically verifying no more hidden memories had shaken loose (or been implanted, or falsified) since the last time she'd studied them.

They always interviewed Josh alone. Josh gathered that his and his teammates' testimony still didn't add up and their interrogators didn't want them to cross-contaminate each other. Magik and Ms Frost were both hard to read. Josh got the discomforting impression that, though they didn't believe his story, they didn't exactly *dis*believe it either. Unlike the other two, Headmaster Summers wore his concern on his sleeve. He listened to all of Josh's answers with an air of utmost gravity.

More than anything else, that steeled Josh's nerves to keep telling the story exactly as he remembered it. He hadn't expected any support from Headmaster Summers, and was surprised not only to receive it – but also by how affirming it felt. He'd started to doubt himself.

The only new information Josh learned came at the end of his interview with Magik. She folded her arms and leaned back in her chair, considering him. "I don't expect you'll ever want to go back to Station X-41 again," she said, "but it would be helpful if you were to write a detailed report of the damages. The next repair team will reach it in a week."

Josh needed a moment to process that. He was surprised by the cold spike in his chest, and the surge of adrenaline. "You're going *back* to the station?"

"The damage wasn't fatal. Two flooded cabins, a damaged generator, and lots of waterlogging. Nothing that can't be repaired."

"Whoever goes down there will be vulnerable to the Aqueos." And worse.

"They'll be forewarned," Magik said. With a small, strange

smile, she added, "I understand Beast is anxious to return to the station after so many years away. Your story caught his attention."

So they were taking his and Anole's reports seriously enough to investigate. And to put significant time and resources into it. Josh wasn't sure which would be worse: if they didn't find any evidence to corroborate their stories, or if they did.

He chewed the bottom of his lip, and then shook his head at himself. No, actually – after half a second's thought, he *did* know which one would be worse.

Josh had picked up some nervous habits on the station, and hadn't been able to shake them. He bounced his legs when he sat, and drummed his fingers rhythmically under his desk. He'd liberated a basketball from one of the gymnasiums, and caromed it off the too-high, too-loud cement walls of his room.

He lay on his bed as he threw. It had become a nightly ritual. Sleep didn't come easily these days. Keeping his body busy helped him focus his thoughts.

Maybe he should have picked up some tics sooner. He didn't have anything else to do with all the energy he used to spend on socializing. The thunder of the basketball filled in some of the silence.

The knock caught him completely by surprise. The basketball slipped from his palm and bounced off the corner of his dresser and onto his desk. A stack of loose lecture notes scattered on the floor. His open bottle of Diet Sweet Drop spilled fizz and foam down the front of his desk, and all over his notes.

The basketball rolled innocently back over to him. He kicked it away. At least that gave Josh something to blame for his heart pounding so fast. "Yeah?"

Anole peeked inside. He looked at the mess of Josh's desk, and then back to Josh.

Josh cleared his threat. "Just about to clean up," he said.

"It sounded like there was a cannon firing in here."

Josh shrugged, sheepish. "You know how echoes get in this place."

He swallowed the instinct to apologize. His room was far enough from any of the others that there was no chance the thunder had bothered anyone. Anole would only have come this way to find Josh.

Anole stepped inside. Josh straightened, and gestured to the desk chair.

A month ago, Anole charging into his room like this would have terrified Josh. It still did, honestly – only in a different way. Josh wasn't afraid of what Anole might to do him. Josh was afraid of himself, and what he might say without thinking.

Anole sat. "Look," he said, "I just need to know how much of what happened to us actually... happened."

"I think all of it did," Josh said.

"But you and I have different stories. We saw different things."

"We saw the... what the Aqueos were worshiping," Josh said. He still didn't know what to call the thing. *Creature* wasn't grandiose enough. But he couldn't force the words *beast* or *god* out of his throat. They sat heavy enough in his thoughts.

"I saw octopus tentacles and some kind of bird's beak, you saw–"

"I've been wondering if both ways of seeing it might have been right." Josh would never forget the vertigo of his awareness careening through the creature's flesh, the way it had seemed to segue into other dimensions. Like reality itself had twisted in the beast's presence.

Anole just gave him a skeptical look. He, of course, hadn't felt what Josh had. There would have been no use explaining.

"Look at it this way," Josh said. "If anyone showed you solid evidence that you'd hallucinated what happened, would you believe them?"

Anole frowned as he pondered that. "No," he said. "I know what I experienced."

"So do I."

In that same stranscge, unshakable way, Josh knew he'd killed the beast. He'd turned all of its flesh against itself, everywhere. *Omega-level powers*, like Ms Frost had said. *No limit to that mutant's power has yet been discovered.*

It was easier and easier to think about that now, and Josh wasn't sure he liked it. Keeping the truth from himself had been comforting. Like calling in sick the day of a difficult exam.

With all his powers out in the open, he felt exposed. Like someone had ripped the blanket off his bed.

Anole folded his arms. He leaned back into Josh's chair, his eyes unfocused. Josh let him stay like that for a bit, but eventually Anole's presence started making Josh itchy. "Can I do something for you?" Josh asked.

"Are you doing all right?" Anole asked.

Josh was instantly, instinctively, on his guard. He couldn't help it. "Why do you ask?"

"Because I'm not," Anole said. "I'll be walking down the hall and think I see a spear thrust out from around a corner. Or just about to fall asleep and see an Aqueos in the dark."

Josh massaged his forehead while he thought of an answer.

His first impulse was to lie. Too big a part of him thought of Anole as an enemy and that showing vulnerability would just be giving Anole a weapon to attack him with later.

No. That wasn't the way to go here. "Haven't really been the same since we got back. It's been tough focusing, sleeping… that kind of thing. You know, this is the kind of trauma the X-Men have to deal with all the time."

"I suppose you understand a little more about trauma than you did before, huh?"

There was a barb in that question, but not a cruel one. Anole hadn't mentioned it, but it wasn't just nightmares of Station X-41 that kept him awake. He'd been dealing with a lot more, for a long time.

Anole and the other mutants here blamed him for what they'd gone through, and they weren't wrong. Whether Josh had personally harmed them when he'd been with the Reavers or not, he'd been part of the same system.

Now he understood the weight of what they were dealing with. And how much it must have taken for Anole to come here and talk about it.

"Triage didn't see everything we did, but he's been having trouble, too," Anole said. "We've been talking. We've gotten in touch with Nature Girl at her school, and talked about setting up some kind of conference call. We'll try to do it when Graymalkin's awake so he can drop in."

Josh's heart had been racing ever since Anole stepped in. Now his pulse roared in his ears. He folded his hands in front of his face, and breathed into them.

"That sounds great," he said, when he could.

"We've got a few other students interested, too. Laurie

Collins wants to get her dad involved. He's some kind of bigshot therapist. Hell, maybe see if Karma's interested, too. She's survived so much. She could teach us a bit about how to talk this out. Are you interested in joining?"

The sound of Laurie's name turned to ice in Josh's veins.

He forced himself to speak past the cold lump in his throat. "Yeah. Sure."

One way or another, he was going to have to address the future that had been foretold for him. Trying to hide from it was just as much a choice as charging headlong into it. And maybe the wrong one.

He had to make himself believe he could handle his power. That he was the right person for it.

Nothing else would save him.

Anole watched him for another few moments. Josh could see, etched in the lines on Anole's face, how much this was taking out of him, too.

Anole broke the awkward pause by standing to leave. Josh couldn't let the conversation end in silence, with him breathing into his sweaty palms. "Thanks, Anole."

"Josh," Anole said, as the door swung wide behind him. "The name's Vic."

ACKNOWLEDGMENTS

There are more people I can thank for the construction of this book than I can name, but I'm going to give it an attempt.

The Siege of X-41 wouldn't exist without my editor, Lottie Llewelyn-Wells, who has been with me for most of my journey as an author at Aconyte Books and elsewhere. She has an incredible stamina for putting up with me and my shenaniganry.

I also owe a great deal to *School of X's* general editor, Gwendolyn Nix, as well as the other authors who've worked in this series, in particular Carrie Harris and Robbie MacNiven, whose novels *Liberty and Justice for All* and *First Team* were referenced heavily throughout this novel. None of our work would have been possible without the writers and artists at Marvel comics, and especially the New Mutants / New X-Men series that started in 2003. If you have not read these books, I highly recommend them.

The gorgeous, film-poster art on the cover of this novel was composed by Christina Myrvold. You can find more of her art at *artstation.com/christinapm*.

Aconyte publisher Marc Gascoigne's continued faith in me has been astounding. Thank you to him and to everybody on the Aconyte Books team, including Anjuli Smith, Nick Tyler, Vanessa Jack, Joe Riley, Amanda Treseler, and Jack Doddy.

Finally, an incredibly special thank you to my perpetual beta reader (and life partner!), the brilliant Dr Teresa Milbrodt.

ABOUT THE AUTHOR

TRISTAN PALMGREN is the author of the critically acclaimed genre-warping blend of historical fiction and space opera novel *Quietus*, and its sequel *Terminus*. They live with their partner in Columbia, Missouri.

tristanpalmgren.com
twitter.com/TristanPalmgren

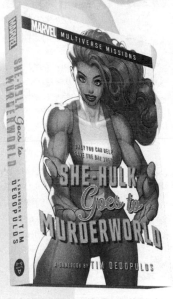

WORLD EXPANDING FICTION

Do you have them all?

MARVEL CRISIS PROTOCOL
- ☐ *Target: Kree* by Stuart Moore
- ☐ *Shadow Avengers* by Carrie Harris

MARVEL HEROINES
- ☐ *Domino: Strays* by Tristan Palmgren
- ☐ *Rogue: Untouched* by Alisa Kwitney
- ☐ *Elsa Bloodstone: Bequest* by Cath Lauria
- ☐ *Outlaw: Relentless* by Tristan Palmgren
- ☐ *Black Cat: Discord* by Cath Lauria
- ☐ *Squirrel Girl: Universe* by Tristan Palmgren
  (coming soon)

LEGENDS OF ASGARD

- ☐ *The Head of Mimir* by Richard Lee Byers
- ☐ *The Sword of Surtur* by C L Werner
- ☐ *The Serpent and the Dead* by Anna Stephens
- ☐ *The Rebels of Vanaheim* by Richard Lee Byers
- ☐ *Three Swords* by C L Werner
- ☐ *The Prisoner of Tartarus* by Richard Lee Byers
  (coming soon)

MARVEL UNTOLD

- ☐ *The Harrowing of Doom* by David Annandale
- ☐ *Dark Avengers: The Patriot List* by David Guymer
- ☐ *Witches Unleashed* by Carrie Harris
- ☐ *Reign of the Devourer* by David Annandale
- ☐ *Sisters of Sorcery* by Marsheila Rockwell
  (coming soon)

SCHOOL OF X

- ☑ *The Siege of X-41* by Tristan Palmgren
- ☐ *Sound of Light* by Amanda Bridgeman
  (coming soon)

XAVIER'S INSTITUTE

- ☐ *Liberty & Justice for All* by Carrie Harris
- ☐ *First Team* by Robbie MacNiven
- ☐ *Triptych* by Jaleigh Johnson
- ☐ *School of X* edited by Gwendolyn Nix